# Reviving the Rhythm

*Blind Rebels book 3*

amy kaybach

*Content and trigger warnings: This book is not recommended for those sensitive to discussions/depictions of anxiety/panic attacks, parent/child violence, non-consensual sex acts (not by main characters), and other adult themes.*

**Reviving the Rhythm - Blind Rebels book 3**

*Edited by:* Editing Fox

*Edited by:* Nice Girl Naughty Edits

*Cover:* Emily Wittig Designs

**ℝ**

*This book is for everyone who walks to the beat of their own drummer.*

*Don't let them steal your rhythm.*

*Just play on.*

# Note to Readers

Everything about Sammy has always been a little different. His character is fairly upbeat in comparison to his Rebel band-mates, but his book deals with some serious issues.

Sammy's book probably came to me the fastest of the four Rebel books. And it was towards the end of Sammy's book that I decided (with a little guidance and gentle pushing) that these stories were something I needed to publish. So it was around the time I was tying up the rough draft of Sammy's book that I started looking for an editor.

That experience was a scary one. Giving my babies to a stranger to tell me what was wrong with them- the idea was terrifying. I'd heard horror stories of authors working with editors that had basically taken their money. The whole idea was stressful for me. I eventually ended up with a short list of five. I contacted them and submitted a sample of 1500 words (the same 1500 to each editor). My list of five was quickly narrowed to two. It was a hard choice but I ended up trusting my gut. Once I started working with Hayleigh on the developmental edit for Bridging the Silence I knew I made the right choice.

The majority of this book was written during NANOW-RIMO (National Novel Writing Month - November) as a challenge to prove to myself that I could write 50,000 words in a month. And while I did hit that word goal (it nearly killed me) at the end of November, it was clear to me that Sammy's story wasn't finished and by the time I was "done" it was about 72,000 words give or take. But Sammy's story still wasn't finished.

After some major edits (first self-edits and then developmental with Hayleigh) his book ended up being over 100,000 words. It was during Sammy's edits that I learned a lot about characterization and how to flesh out my characters just a little bit better I think. As a result you get to know both Sammy and Melody better, especially compared to the original 72,000 original version of this story.

I hope you enjoy Sammy and Mel's journey.

—Amy

# Chapter 1

## *Melody*

I don't usually jog this early in the morning, but I woke up abruptly with my heart pounding when the stupid fire alarm in my apartment decided to go off. I was in the middle of one of those vivid dreams, the kind that seems so real that you wake up wondering if you were dreaming or remembering. All I remember now is that I was wandering around the dorms at my old college, looking for my roommate, but I couldn't find her. It's a recurring nightmare that I hate because it brings up feelings I don't like dealing with.

There was no smoke, no fire. Nothing. Just an annoying and tremendously loud beeping that bordered on the edge of a screech. What's worse is that it's one of those types of alarms that doesn't have a replaceable battery. When the battery's done, you have to replace the whole detector. I'll have my landlord check it. He assured me when I moved in that it was brand new, so it should still have the better of 8 years left on it. I can't help asking these things; it's the curse of being a fire department paramedic. You see the devastation that could be prevented with something as simple as a smoke alarm or a battery.

Days like today make running easy. There's a storm brewing offshore but right now it's warm enough that I can wear my favorite running shorts and tank, but crisp enough that running isn't a miserable chore. I don't love running, but I need to stay in tip-top shape as an EMT. I pull my mousy brown shoulder length hair into a ponytail and thread it through the back of my FD baseball cap, then head out of my downtown apartment to start my run.

By the time I hit the beach, I'm fully into my groove. I turn left once I hit the sand to head south toward Venice beach. There aren't many people on the shoreline this early, just a few brave diehard surfers here and there, taking advantage of the higher-than-normal surf thanks to the storm offshore. There are a few other runners and a couple of people walking dogs. Up ahead, a small group of people bend and flex in some sort of early morning yoga on the beach type of class. I change my path towards the water, giving them a wide berth.

*Right, left. Right, left. Breathe in. Right, left. Right, left. Breathe out.* It's all about the rhythm of the run. Concentrating on my cadence in the soft sand, I look out at the surf to the right as I jog down the beach. A pair of surfers bob in the ocean. The darker-haired one decides to make a run on the next swell. He paddles hard ahead of the wave, catching it right in the middle. He easily pops to a stand in his all-black wetsuit, knees bent with his body slightly pitched forward. He straightens and rides it most of the way in and then paddles back towards the longer-haired surfer who stayed behind.

A lady running with a Dalmatian jogs towards me from the opposite direction. I veer towards the ocean again to stay well out of their way. I might work in a fire station, but I'm not a big fan of dogs, especially bigger ones. I was bitten about a year ago by an overprotective German Shepherd protecting his owner during a call. He got me right on the ass cheek. Not only did it hurt like a mother, but I was the laughingstock of the house for a good week.

I nod at the dog lady as we pass. The song in my playlist turns to one of my favorite ones, a peppy tune from the eighties that has me pushing just a little harder, breaths coming just a little harsher. This is the burn I strive for.

Glancing back to the surfers, the one with the lighter, longer hair had decided to jump on a wave, but even from here I can see that he's not as stable on his board. His wetsuit is black with a blue trim and reminds me of a boy I knew. The wave isn't ideal, barreling over earlier than the others. I haven't surfed in a while, but even I know he probably should've waited for one from the next set. He hops up and maintains his crouched stance longer than his friend did.

He gets out of shape and the nose of the board pulls up on him. He gets thrown off the board backwards, and hits the water flat on his back, arms flailing out on the sides. Then he's gone from my sight. Half of his board pops up, broken, then the other half floats up a few feet away.

My run instinctively slows to a slow jog. I can't seem to find the guy who fell off the board. I don't want to go into the storm swell without a swimming aid, but I will if I have to. His friend paddles in the direction where I last saw his buddy, his paddles getting increasingly frantic. My heartbeat speeds up as I come to a stop.

"Dolphins?" Another jogger stops and searches the tumultuous sea to see what I'm watching.

I shake my head. "Surfer. Think he might be in trouble." I watch as the shorter-haired guy hauls his limp friend onto his board and starts paddling towards the shore.

"Nah, he's just riding his friend in because he broke his board. See the pieces?" The other jogger assesses the situation. Did he not see that he had to haul him onto the board or notice he's limp like a rag doll? His friend's strokes as he works them towards the shore on his board are quick and sloppy. Harried even.

I grew up surfing these beaches and sometimes still do, but I don't dare jump in. The storm surge has made the rip currents unpredictable. Instead, I start jogging towards the area of shore where the surfers will hit the beach. His friend doesn't move as he lies across the board like a noodle.

*Please be breathing. Please just be knocked out.*

But I know better. He was likely out before he hit the water. I couldn't tell for sure, but it looked like the edge of the board clipped him in the head. When someone goes into the water unconscious, they don't know to hold their breath. As the surfers get closer to the shore, I can sense the panic from the one paddling. He's hollering at his friend and his paddle is big and erratic. It sounds something like, "Come on, man. Wake up."

When he gets far enough in that he can touch the bottom, he abandons his board and hauls his friend over his shoulder and starts wading as fast as he can towards the shore; no easy task in currents like these.

I turn to the other jogger. "Call 911."

"I'm not from here. How do I tell them where we are?" He pulls out his phone but doesn't dial.

"Venice beach. Adjacent to the skate park. CALL NOW!" I toe off my running shoes and quickly slide my phone off my cuff and into my shoe. I jog into the surf towards the surfers.

"I gotcha, man. I gotcha." The surfer in the solid black wetsuit is huffing and muttering at his friend. His eyes are large as he wildly sloshes through the surf towards the beach. He's so panicked he doesn't realize I'm running next to him in the surf. His friend's lips are blue as he hangs over his shoulder like a wet dishrag. I try to assess him the best I can as he hangs over his friend's shoulder, and that's when it hits me. The surfer that reminded me of a boy I knew, *is* the boy I knew. Sampson

4

Denton, now the drummer for the Blind Rebels. My former high school sweetheart.

Our feet splash in about a foot of water. The ebbing water pulling the sand from under our feet, making it difficult to stand.

"I'm Mel. I'm an off-duty paramedic. Set him down in the dry sand." He's not hearing me and keeps jogging. I grab his arm. "Set your buddy down. Now." He finally looks over at me. "I'm a paramedic. Let me help. Set him down." I point to the dry sand.

He drops to his knees and gently rolls his friend off his shoulder and onto his back. "Sammy!" he sobs and lays over his friend.

I push him out of the way. My quick assessment tells me Sampson's not breathing and his heart isn't beating either. With two fingers under his chin, I tip his head back and seal my mouth over his and blow in two strong, long breaths.

"One. Two. Three. Four." I start counting off the chest compressions to thirty and then give him two more rescue breaths. Back to chest compressions, I press even harder than normal, willing him to live. His ribs give way under my hands when I start my second round of chest compressions as tears come to my eyes. I've given CPR countless times, but the feel of someone's ribs breaking under my hands is something I'll never get accustomed to. But make it someone you know, someone you used to love, that you still love in a way, and it's torturous.

"Come on, Sampson. Breathe. Breathe," I huff quietly as I continue compressions.

His friend sits on his knees at Sampson's head and brushes some of the wet hairs plastered to his friend's head away.

"Sam." His name is a gravelly gasp of despair. "Come on, man. Come on." He bends and touches foreheads with his friend, releasing a feral cry. Fuck, where is the damn rescue? I don't have time to react to his emotional friend, working hard to keep up the right rhythm to the chest compressions that I pray are helping keep Sampson's blood oxygenated.

Another round of breaths. My arms stiff, I start another round of compressions. More breaths. Yet another set of chest compressions. Two breaths. And then another. It's all more taxing than the run I was on and I'm starting to fatigue. At work, we have a partner and switch out to keep from becoming too tired. The murmurs around us signal a crowd has started to gather. No one offers to relieve me. They're all too busy filming Sampson's possible last moments. Sick fuckers. I may not be in his life anymore, but no one deserves this in such a dire moment. A life-or-death moment. I can't dwell on it, though, I've got to keep Sampson going until rescue gets here.

His friend returns to his head, resuming the forehead-to-forehead position as he speaks lowly. "Please. Stay with us. Fucking stay with us. I can't lose you, too."

I push his friend away yet again so I can give more breaths. I give one, and just as I go to blow in the next breath, water comes into my mouth as Sampson sputters a wet cough out. Rolling him onto his side, I administer some firm back blows between his shoulder blades to encourage the expulsion of the frothy liquid coming up.

"Cough it up. That's it." His cough turns into more of a vomit as first responders arrive, dropping to their knees beside me to take over. I scurry out of the way. They get oxygen on him as soon as possible and I move back as they roll him onto a board to move him up to the gurney waiting just beyond the sand. His friend holds his hand as he trots alongside him as he's hauled off.

"Good work, Tanner." The fire battalion commander gives me a firm grip on the shoulder. "I'll send a commendation to your captain."

I know Jules. He works at a neighboring house. We've

worked scenes together, usually vehicle accidents on the freeway between our districts. But I'm not listening to him. I am watching as they take Sampson away on a gurney. I pray that he's going to beat the odds and make it.

"Don't. I just did what anyone would do. It's my job, I just reacted. I think his friend might be in shock." I shrug it off. I don't want anyone to realize I know exactly who that is on the gurney being taken up on shore.

"Even right place, right time situations deserve a commendation." He turns and heads back up to his fire paramedic rig.

And just like that, the gathered mob's dispersed, and the beach is a little more crowded than when I started my run, but everyone's going about their business as if Sampson's life isn't hanging on the edge as he's being transported to a local hospital.

I return to my shoes and sit on the sand as I slip them back on, securing my phone back into my armband with my earbuds placed back in my ears. But instead of restarting my run, I wrap my arms around my legs and gaze out across the ocean. Watching the impressive twenty-five-foot waves that the storm is stirring up, I take in some of her peace and beauty, despite the ugly that just happened a few yards away.

Damned by my training, I know Sampson's not out of the woods. His lungs could still have too much liquid in them. Just because he got out a few gasps doesn't mean he didn't aspirate again. His blood gasses could be too far off. His brain could be damaged from lack of oxygen. Being a paramedic, I knew exactly what to do. But sadly, because of my training, I also know there's more at play against him than for him right now.

My stomach drops as I recall his friend's feral cry while I was doing compressions. The anguish in that cry is something I'll wake to, probably tonight. Some calls stick with me more than others. I can already tell this is one of those, even though it wasn't technically a call. Why wouldn't it? It's Sampson and Sampson's always had my attention.

Thank God I turned left and not right when I got to the beach this morning. I have to believe that I was put in Sampson's path again for a reason, just like I was back in high school.

I'll never know the outcome. It's almost better that way. I'd rather put my positivity behind each patient, each call. Knowing I did the best I could to give them their best chance during their brief time in my care is enough for me.

When I finally get up from the beach, I decide to ditch the rest of my run and walk back to my studio apartment in a mixed-use building in downtown Santa Monica. By the time I hit my stairs, I'm bone tired between my early morning wake-up call and the exhaustion that comes with several rounds of unassisted cardiopulmonary resuscitation. I head straight to the fridge and grab a sports drink. I pull out my phone and send my captain an e-mail, so he knows what happened just in case Jules sends in that commendation. I don't want him to be caught off guard.

# Chapter 2

## *Sammy*

"Sampson, you shouldn't be here." Sev stands, her arms folded, right hip jutting out in typical Sev fashion. Her blonde hair hangs just past her shoulders, stick-straight, unlike my unruly curly mop, and is tucked behind an ear on the right side. "It's not your time. You need to go back. Open your eyes Sam."

Fuck, Sevenya looks good. So much better than when she died. *Wait, she died.* How is she here? Although, I'm not sure where *here* is. It's just a white room. No furniture. No windows. Everything is just white. I'm not sure where Killian is, but he needs to be here. He loved Sev so much, more than she loved herself. He can help me talk her into going back to rehab one last time.

"Sev. You look good. I don't want to go. I just found you again." She starts to fade into the background as I approach her. "Have you seen Kill?"

"Killian's not here. It's not his time either. You have to go back. You both have to go back now." She holds out her hand as I begin to approach her again, slowly this time.

I don't know what she's on right now, but I can make her

better if I can just get her back home with me. The guys will help. I can afford a good rehab now. Kill and I can talk her into going one more time.

"Sev, come back with me. Killian will want to see you, talk to you. He understands, Sev. He does. We all do." I reach out to her, willing her to take my hand. "We can get you the help you need, I promise. We love you."

"I can't, Sam, you know that. You know why I can't come with you. Think." She's trying to tell me something.

"You have to go back, Sam. It's time to wake up." Her voice turns icy and then male. What the fuck?

"Sev!" I run towards where she was, but she's just gone. There are no doors in here. I can't get out of the room, so how did she? "Sev, come back. Sev? Sevenya!"

"You have to wake up, Sammy," she says sternly, despite being nowhere around. She never calls me Sammy. I can't see her anymore, but I can hear her.

"Sev?"

"Sam! Can you hear me? Come on, Sammy, open your eyes." Mav? What's he doing here? Did he see where Sevenya went?

"Just open your eyes, Sammy," they whisper together.

"Come on, open your eyes, buddy." Mav's voice is louder and Sev's is barely a whisper.

I don't want to leave the white room. I want to wait to see if Sev comes back, but I'm floating farther and farther away from the white room. It's darker here. And there are beeps. And it smells like a swimming pool. Or a doctor's office.

"Open your damn eyes, Sam." Mav's voice is rough and sounds far away and tired. And the beeping is growing louder. It's an unforgiving but familiar beat I can't place.

Someone squeezes my hand.

There's a heavy sigh, tired and resigned. "Please, Sammy, fuck. Just wake up." Mav never begs. Why's he begging me?

I try hard to open my eyes for him, but they're being stubborn. Like my eyelids are stubborn drunk, and not listening. All I can do is flutter them. Little flashes of another unfamiliar room break through the darkness.

"That's it, bud. Come back to us." The excitement in Mav's voice overtakes the tired, and I work harder to get my ornery lids to stay apart.

At first, everything is blurry, but then slowly slides into focus. I'm in a small, darkened room, too small to be a hotel room. The beeping is still there, like it's part of me. Mav leans over me, his brow deeply creased. He's unshaven, his shoulder length dark hair a wild mess, sticking up like he doesn't give a shit. He looks wholly unkempt, which is so not a Mav thing. And he's right in my damn face. When was the last time he brushed his teeth? Ugh.

He blinks his eyes as they connect with mine, and his whole body relaxes in a downward wave, his eyes fluttering shut for a second before coming right back to mine, like he had to prove to himself I'm really here, really awake.

"Oh, thank fuck. Sammy!" His voice is even rougher than normal as his eyes well with tears and he quickly scrubs his hand over his face, trying to keep me from seeing the moisture on his cheeks, but I see everything. I don't understand what's going on, but I am seeing it all. He bends further at the waist and leans his head onto my chest, pulling an arm around and underneath me, which causes a sharp, deep pain in my chest that almost steals my breath away. I sputter a cough. What the fuck was that?

"Dammit. You scared the absolute fuck out of us." His words are a harsh, jagged sob as he squeezes me tighter.

There's a weird little sink on the wall behind Mav. It seems strange that there'd be a sink in the same room as the bed and a plain analog clock. To the right is a tiny excuse for a TV and several flower arrangements sit on the windowsill.

*A hospital! I'm in a fucking hospital and I have no idea how I got here. Or why.*

As Mav continues to sob into my chest, I try to assess myself. What hurts? My throat feels like I swallowed broken glass or some shit. My chest is sore as fuck. Maybe I got hit by a tour bus or something. Mav's not helping as he squeezes the stuffing out of me. But I don't dare disrupt him. His sobbing gets stronger. I don't know what the fuck happened, but he's coming undone right here on top of me, which scares me even more than the fact that I'm sore and foggy and in a hospital. I try to pat his back to reassure him, but that seems to only make the crying worse.

My nose is itchy as sin, but I can't quite reach it to give it the satisfying rub I want. I try wiggling my nose to relieve the itch a little and that's when I feel the tubes move in my nostrils, blowing a steady stream. Oxygen.

The door to my left opens, and Cal walks in, turning his back to us as he shuts it quietly. Based on the quick glimpse I just got of him, he looks more haggard than Mav does.

His voice is subdued and gravelly. "Sorry. They're sedating Kill for another scan. I had to get out of there for a few." He turns slowly towards us as Mav lets out another ragged, hitched sob.

Cal's eyes grow wide as they lock onto mine, and then takes in Mav coming undone on me. His mouth gapes slightly and then he rushes towards the other side of my bed.

"He's awake." He puts a hand on Mav's still shuddering back. "You're awake. Oh, thank fuck! You're finally awake." Cal releases a long breath, and his body visibly relaxes in much the same manner as Mav's did a few minutes ago. I try to catch his attention, have him help Mav or at least get him off of me. But instead, Cal starts shedding tears too. Why the fuck is everyone crying?

Cal's long dark brown hair is pulled back into the sloppiest of ponytails. And he looks like he's been sleeping in his clothes for a month, much like Mav does. He's got scruff and dark marks on the bags under his deep blue eyes.

A nurse comes in and takes in the scene before heading right to some monitor things next to the bed. He stands, watching Mav come unglued and then looks to Cal.

"Can you, um, remove your friend so I can get some vitals on Mr. Denton."

Cal hustles over and grips Mav by the shoulders. Cal's voice grumbles as he says something I can't exactly hear. Mav nods and loosens his grip on me, allowing Cal to pull him away.

"Glad to see you back with us." The nurse shines a damn light in my eyes, and I can't help the squint.

"Can you tell me your name?" The nurse encourages me with a smile. In the background, the door opens and shuts.

"Uh. Sammy. Sampson Denton." My voice cracks as if it hasn't been used in a while. It burns like fire to talk, and I just realized my lips are chapped to fuck.

"Good. Do you remember what happened?"

I shake my head. I don't. I'm not sure what caused me to end up in the hospital.

"That's okay. And understandable. Do you know who he is?" The nurse points to Cal. Mav must have left. I don't see him anymore.

"Cal. My brother." He's not my brother by birth. Not many understand how close I am to my bandmates, but they are the only family I have left. The nurse just nods his head and smiles at me.

"And the other guy? The one who left. Who was he?" The nurse nods and jots something down on his clipboard.

"Mavrick. Other brother." He seems pleased with my answers.

"Are you in pain?" he asks.

"My throat and chest hurt."

"On a scale of one to ten, with one being not very bad at all, and ten being the worst pain you've ever felt, how do you rate the pain in your chest?"

"Seven?" He nods and scribbles on his clipboard.

"Using the same scale on your throat?"

"Same. Seven. Can I have a drink? Please." The nurse nods and writes some more.

"You have to wait for the doctor before we can give you any water. He'll be in really soon, okay Mr. Denton?"

"Sammy," I squawk out, then wince again.

"Sammy," the nurse says. "Your vitals are looking excellent now. I'm sure your friends can fill you in on what's been going on. But if you have any questions, don't hesitate to ask us." He smiles at me again and then up at Cal and leaves.

As soon as the door's shut, Cal sits on the edge of my bed and leans in to brush the hair off my forehead. It's something I've seen him do to his son when he's sick.

"What?" My throat burns again, and I wince. "Happened? Where'd Mav go?"

"You nearly drowned while surfing out by Venice Beach." His words are rough, like he's trying to remain calm, when underneath, he's a fucking mess, waiting to go off just like Mav did. He's holding on to a fine edge right now. "I don't know all the details. We can get you those soon, hopefully."

I remember surfing. Kill and I went together. A storm in the Pacific was pushing some awesome waves towards us. We went out early. The swells were amazing, fifteen-to-twenty-foot rollers. We'd been riding them in for a good hour, but decided it was time to pack it in. I was hungry and wanted to hit the diner.

"Mav'll be back in a few, Sam. I promise." He gives me a sad smile. "It's been a rough four days. He needed a minute. Plus, he probably wants to let Kady know you're awake."

I nod, my eyes heavy. Cal squeezes my hand and I go back to sleep. Just for a little nap.

# ℞

"MR. DENTON, can you open your eyes for me?" Who the fuck is this guy and why does he want me to open my eyes? Being awake is overrated. I'm trying to find Sev and the white room again. I want to talk to her. Apologize for not doing better as her brother to protect her.

"Come on, Sam, wake up for the doctor." Mav's voice is gritty and sharp. Like he's annoyed at me.

I open my eyes. Mav's standing next to another man, this one in a long white coat. Both are staring at me. Mav looks both worried and pissed, his arms crossed, and his lips pulled into a tight frown. The other guy just looks curious as he stands over me. It looks like he has one of those damn flashlights people keep sticking in my eyes.

"Mr. Denton, I'm Dr. Monroe. I've been taking care of you." He nods at Mav after his introduction.

"I'm going to sit you up a little to take a listen to your lungs." The doctor positions me more upright using the controller for the bed and then tips me forward with his arms. He instructs me to take deep breaths as he moves his cool stethoscope around my back. As he does this, Cal comes strolling into the room, tucking his phone in his back pocket. He perches himself on the windowsill and quietly watches the doctor do his thing. Mav's doing the same thing from the chair in the corner.

Cal's eyes are red-rimmed, and I don't know how it's possible, but he looks even more exhausted now. The dark spots under his eyes are even more pronounced and it looks like he's been crying.

"Lay back please." The doctor pulls my gown down my chest

amy kaybach

slightly to listen to my heart and when he does, Callum grimaces and turns his head. I look down and my chest is various shades of purple and blue. No wonder my fucking chest hurts.

Dr. Monroe notices me checking out my bruises. "You've got two broken ribs." He points to where they are broken. "It's not an uncommon injury from CPR. Nor are the bruises. It's why your chest hurts."

The doctor pulls his stethoscope back down to his neck. "The CPR likely saved your life. You're very lucky in that regard, despite what it might look and feel like." I just look at him. CPR? That's serious shit.

"The scratchy throat is from when you were intubated in the ambulance. It'll heal up in a couple of days." He looks me in the eye.

"Your recovery is not typical, Mr. Denton. You're lucky that your friend was able to find you and get you to shore quickly. And it was a miracle that someone at the beach knew CPR. You couldn't have picked a better person to go down in front of than an off-duty paramedic. And lastly, you got to the right trauma center quickly. Your guardian angels were all watching out for you. They lined everything up in just the right order." *Sevenya.* The doctor stares at me for a minute.

"I'll have a respiratory therapist come by and evaluate you fully, probably tomorrow morning. Depending on their recommendations, we'll start talking about when we can discharge you. Oh, and you're fine to have water and ice chips. Go slow at first. Any questions, just ring for a nurse, okay?"

I nod at the doctor, and he turns and leaves. Mav moves to the other side of the room and brings me a cup of water. I take a few sips, and it does soothe my throat, but I have to know.

"Was I dead?" I don't recognize the wavering in my own voice.

When I look over at Mav, he's lost all the coloring in his face. Cal's eyes are pinched closed. No one is answering me.

"When I saw Sevenya, was I dead?" I plead.

Cal's eyes snap to mine. "You saw Sev?"

I nod slowly as I watch the blood drain from his already pale face. It sounds crazy, even to me. But she was there. She was real. It was her, right down to the way she stood with her hitched hip and cocked head.

"I was with her. We were in a completely white room with no doors or windows. Sev was there. She kept telling me I wasn't supposed to be there, that I needed to open my eyes. It's all she'd say. I tried to hug her, and she disappeared. But even then, I could hear her voice. She kept telling me to open my eyes. Then her voice turned into Mav's, and I opened my eyes."

Cal and Mav exchange looks. Mav's is a dubious one. But Cal's isn't. He's got that twin connection shit with his brother Killian, so he probably believes me. Sev and I weren't twins, but we were all each other had. Which reminds me, I haven't seen Killian.

"Where's Killian?" I look between Mav and Cal. They both shift uncomfortably, but neither says a word. I know Kill would be here for me. He's my best friend. We were surfing together. Shit, maybe he got hurt too.

"Where is he? Did he get hurt?" My heart starts to race, and they can hear it as my monitor starts to beep even faster. Cal frowns at the monitor and steps forward so he can sit on the very edge of my bed. He pats my hand.

"He's upstairs on the fifth floor." Cal speaks slowly, as if he's choosing his words carefully, and glances towards my monitors and then over at Mav before looking back at me.

"But the doctor said he found me. Did he drown too?" Nothing's making any sense.

"No. The doctor was right. Kill was right there when you went off your board. He paddled you in. He was with you the whole time, even in the ambulance. I've never felt him so upset."

My thoughts turn to Sev and Killian. When Sev died, we were all upset. But Killian and Sev had a special connection, one that only I know some of the depth of. If Cal only knew how devastated Kill was when Sev died. But there are secrets kept, even from the closest family. And I'd never betray Kill like that.

"Because he was so upset, an ER doctor finally gave him a shot of valium to try to calm him down. But Kill had some side effects from the medication and ended up being admitted upstairs." The lines around Cal's eyes, the dark bruises under his eyes, tell me he's been doubly worried. Mav too.

"Side effects?" I hear the stress in my own voice. I don't need the monitors to tell me I'm getting worked up.

Cal sighs. "I need you to calm down a little, Sam." He looks to Mav again and then sighs. "Kill had what they're classifying as a 'cardiac event.' Then what they believe was a panic attack." He squeezes my hand, which tells me that this is fucking serious. More than they're letting on. They're breaking it to me slowly.

"His cardiologist believes both issues were related to the medication given to him in the ER. Apparently, they're both known as rare side effects. But there's a chance the heart issue could also be related to stress exacerbating an unknown existing heart problem. So they are testing the fuck out of him trying to disprove that."

Kill's seeing a cardiologist? That's real fucking serious.

"He was sedated after the panic attack but didn't do well coming out of it. He went all rage-a-saurus and tore out his IV and tried to fight an orderly. One of his nurses got knocked down in the process. She didn't get hurt, though. By the time I got back up there, he'd been restrained to the bed and doped back up."

Fuck. Cal should be up with Kill. I'm okay, I can already tell. Just a little tired and sore. He needs to stay with Kill.

"Anyway, they're doing another scan of his heart right now and sedated him again for that. I'm going to head back upstairs in a few. Maybe having me there when he comes out of it this time will keep him from getting too ornery. He doesn't need to be tied to the fucking bed again."

Callum's face tenses. "Our mom did that shit to him when we were kids because he wet the bed. Being tied to a bed is not a good memory for either of us."

Cal looks down at where his hand rests on my arm. He squeezes again and looks at me. Another sad smile, this one laced with the protectiveness that only Cal brings to this band. To his brother. To any of us that need it.

"I want to be there when the doctor tells him what's going on with his heart." The worry I hear in his voice deepens with the creases around his eyes and mouth.

He stands and I reach my arms out to him for a hug, which he obliges me with. I pull my non-biological brother to me and hit his back three times; our code for *it's going to be okay.*

"Tell Killian he needs to get better so he can get down here and help me scam on some of these nurses, okay? I think between the two of us we can convince them to give us each some sexual healing, if you know what I mean." I release Cal and his lips pull up a little bit. The worry lines are still there, but the little half-grin makes me feel a little better.

"I will. I'll probably stop back by later this evening to check on you." He starts towards the door.

"Either stay with Kill, or go home and sleep, Cal. I'm okay. Okay?" He turns to me and nods, but I'm not convinced he's listening.

"I mean it, Cal. I'll tell the nurses I don't want you in my room." He flips me off because he knows damn well I'd never actually ban him from my room.

"You should rest if you're tired, Sam." Mav settles into his chair and kicks his feet up onto the end of my bed.

19

I wait a few minutes in the sudden quietness of my room. Cal needs someone too. Mav needs to go with him. So Cal has someone to lean on if Kill's heart test results are bad.

*Oh, please, God. Don't let the results be bad. Please.*

"You," I start in on Mav, my throat still raw. "You need to go up there and be with him. He's holding it together by a fuckin' shoestring. Even I can see that. Then you need a nap too. And a shower." I sniff at the air, pretending to smell something terrible. "You both smell bad." I lie. I love knowing they're here for me. But Killian needs Cal, and Cal needs Mav.

"We're all fuckin' stressed, Sammy. No one's leaving you alone. The girls will be here later to visit with you. Then I'll go up and check in with Cal and Kill."

I don't need to be babysat.

"Just go back to sleep, asshole," Mav tells me. "I'm not going anywhere." He glares at me for a few minutes and then pulls out his phone and starts scrolling. Shutting me out. End of discussion.

When I wake up, Mav's still here or here again, maybe? I'm not sure. He's moved the chair, so he's closer to the side of the bed and he's changed out his phone for a magazine on dirt bikes.

"Hey, can I read that when you're done?" My throat still hurts a little but is way better than what it was.

"Actually, it's yours. Jax brought it for when you woke up. He brought some other ones too." He nods to a small bedside table on wheels that has a stack of magazines on it.

"I wish I'd woken up to tell him thank you." I sigh. Jax may work for us, but he's a friend, a part of our Blind Rebels family.

"I wouldn't let him wake you. Sorry, bud, you needed the rest. The doctor said it's what's best." He looks up and gazes out the window of my room. A window I can't even see out of because my bed's too close to it.

"I know. I just thought it'd be nice to have a visitor other than you or Cal."

"The girls will be up here in about twenty minutes. They've been dying to come back up to see you. They've been worried too."

Mav suddenly leaps up out of the plastic chair, causing me to jump. The chair skitters across the linoleum and hits the side of the bed. He paces the room a few times.

"You almost died, Sammy. Fuck it, you *did* die. Technically. On that beach, you were dead. Okay?" He walks through the room like a caged panther and tugs his hair. He's overwhelmed, overtired, and over-emotional. Mav likes control and everything in its place, and when he loses that, he gets all prowly, unsettled, and wild.

His voice softens a little and takes on a tinny quality as he turns towards me. Like he might start crying again. "They wanted me to be prepared to make decisions for you if you didn't have brain function, man." He takes in a ragged breath.

"I know we signed that power of attorney shit, but I never thought I'd ever come close to having to fucking use it. I mean, fuck, man. Not this soon." His voice scrapes roughly over the last word as he kicks the plastic chair again, causing it to turn over. Head tilted towards the ceiling, he squeezes his eyes shut tight, his hands fisted at his sides.

"You know Ari and Kady would kick your ass hearing you refer to them as 'the girls,' right?" I try to lighten the mood. I don't need Mav having a 'cardiac event' on me too. Whatever the fuck that is. I've never seen Mav this stressed or emotional. Not even when his ex-fiancée Becka was pregnant with Callum's baby.

The situation with Killian isn't helping matters. Fuckin' Kill. I wonder if they'll let me go upstairs and visit him if I promise to stay in a wheelchair or something. I have to thank him for saving me. I have to see him. Tell him about Sev.

Now my eyes well with tears. Fuck. Between Mav's stress-fueled tantrum and Kill being upstairs in a fucking cardiac unit. I don't know if I can take it. And I'm the easygoing one. So they say anyway. So how's this affecting everyone else?

Mav rights the chair, setting it next to my bed, then flops in next to me and squeezes my arm.

"Sorry. I guess I'm still dealing with all this shit. I'm so fuckin' glad you're awake though, man, I was getting bored." He picks at the spot on his shoe where the tread meets the side, then messes around with the flowers on the windowsill behind him. He's fidgeting like I do when I'm nervous.

"Who're the flowers from?" I lift my chin towards the beautiful, bright bouquet filled with yellow, orange, and white flowers. There's even a mini drumstick tied to the front of the vase with a bright green ribbon. That's kind of cool.

He smiles at me wistfully. "Your fans. They've sent so many." He shakes his head. "We finally told the nurses to distribute them to other patients, ones who don't have any. We kept all the cards from them for you. We knew you'd want to see them all." Mav holds up a stack from next to the bouquet.

I do. I want to read them all. But not now. Right now, I need to know more about Kill.

"So, tell me what happened with Kill. Cal was scant in the details department."

Mav looks at me. "You noticed that, did ya?" I nod. It was fucking obvious he was holding shit back. "He didn't want to stress you out. He's worried about both of you. We all are."

"Not knowing is stressing me out more." I shift on the bed. My ass is starting to get sore from all this lying around. I'm ready to be on the move, sore chest or not.

"You want the whole story?"

I nod. Mav will shoot me straight. That's one thing about him. He won't gloss over the gritty. It's not in his DNA. Mav

22

turns to face me completely and leans his elbows on his thighs, letting out a long sigh.

"So, Cal and I got here probably within 10 minutes of each other. Kill was a freaking mess. He was soaking wet in his wetsuit, but someone had given him one of those silver emergency blankets. You know, like the ones in a car's first aid kit." I nod, knowing exactly what he's talking about.

"He was babbling and not making any fucking sense. Just trying to get out of him what happened was a chore. But we could finally piece together that you guys were surfing and somehow, you'd gotten knocked out and fell into the water and drowned. Then he kind of just went silent like he does sometimes. I didn't think anything of it. You know Kill, he's quiet while he's processing shit. Cal got him to change out of his wetsuit and into dry clothes, at least."

Mav runs a hand through his hair and looks out the window.

"The doctor came out and told us that you were still critical. There were issues with your oxygen levels and since they intubated you in the ambulance, they still weren't sure if you were breathing on your own. There was a lot of waiting while they ran tests on you. They said they needed to test your brain function and some other shit about your lungs. But they wouldn't let us see you since we weren't 'family.' Can you believe that shit? Not family." He rolls his eyes.

"We had to get the lawyer to bring your power of attorney papers over. I invoked that so at least I could see you for twenty minutes at a time. That's right around the time Kill just kinda wigged out. He was pacing and crying and mumbling shit about you dying alone. Ari tried to get him to calm down, and he went off on her. That, of course, pissed off Cal, who turned around and went off on him." He shakes his head and runs a hand through his hair.

"It's a damn miracle we're even still allowed in here, man.

The twins started pushing and shoving. Security got called in and hauled them off somewhere. I involved Jax, who was stationed at the waiting room door, because I was too worried about you to deal with their shit. Jax somehow made it so that they could stay as long as they didn't cause anymore issues. Anyway, at some point a doctor said you'd stabilized, and they'd allow you two visitors at a time for fifteen minutes, but you were still in the critical care unit because you weren't awake yet. Kill insisted he stay with you the whole time. But he cried incessantly. Wouldn't eat. Wouldn't rest. He was just wound up far too tight." He crunches his fingers down in front of him to show how tight he was. "Even the damn nurses taking care of you were concerned for him. That pissed me off because they needed to focus on you, not him. Eventually, a doctor ordered him an injection of valium to calm his ass down, maybe make him sleep or something." He takes a deep breath.

"We finally talked him out of your room so that Ari and Kady could sit with you because they hadn't seen you yet. We thought the valium was working. He seemed calmer in the waiting room with us, but then it all went to shit. It started with Kill not being able to hold still. He'd tug the collar of his shirt and shift around like he was uncomfortable. Then Cal started tugging on his collar." He has a sadness in his eyes and a deep frown on his forehead.

"I'll never forget it as long as I live, Sam. Cal looked up at me, rubbing his chest hard and then gasped out, 'Oh God, we're having a fuckin' heart attack.' He bent over and moaned, holding his chest." Mav looks over at me, wincing at the memory. His eyes well with tears.

"I thought Cal meant *he* was having a heart attack. You know how the two of them use the royal *we* when referring to themselves sometimes. But then I saw Kill. He was so fuckin' pasty and clammy. I didn't know what the fuck to do. So I picked him up and carried him down the hall and around the

24

corner, back into the ER. They had me set him on a gurney and started cutting his clothes off and sticking those monitoring things on him and shit."

His tears start to fall again, silently this time. I pat the bed and encourage him to sit where I can at least touch him. He swipes at his face, frustrated with his show of emotion.

"Anyway, um..." He takes a breath as he sits gently on the edge of my bed. "Cal stayed with Kill and I stayed with you. The doctors admitted Kill to the cardiac unit upstairs. He was doing a little better up there, then had the panic attack Cal mentioned. Was having trouble breathing and shit. Anyway, you know the rest." He rubs a hand over his face and then into his hair again.

No wonder he had a breakdown when I first woke up. Fuck, how is any of this real? I nearly drowned. Kill's having heart issues. Mav and Cal look like they've both been rode hard and put away wet.

When Kady and Ari arrive twenty minutes later, they immediately start fussing over me and I have to admit, it feels pretty damn good. Kady fluffs my pillows. Ari sits on the edge of my bed, lightly rubbing my leg. Both chatter about this and that and nothing about cardiac units or drowning or power of attorneys.

With them comes a brightness my stressed-out brothers don't have in them right now. There was too much worry, too much stress overload. Cal and Mav are seriously harshing my vibe. As soon as he sees I'm in the most excellent hands of his wife, Mav takes off to go upstairs to check-in with Cal and Kill.

"How do you feel? Really?" Ari asks, settling on the edge of my bed.

"Physically? I'm a little tired. And a lot sore. Why'd they have to go break my other ribs. What is it with you resuscitators and breaking my bones?" I grin up at her, so she knows I'm joking. I need the comedy right now because the seriousness is too heavy.

I pull my gown up to my neck, making sure the blanket covers my junk because I don't need Cal and Mav getting wind of me flashing their wives. Nearly drowned or not, they'd kick my ass into next year.

She cringes at my bruises. "Ugh, Sammy, that must hurt."

"Fuck yeah, it does. Like I got hit by a bus. But the doctor said it's what saved me, so I can't even be mad about it." She and Kady nod at me tearfully. Fuck, the heavy shit's back.

"Mostly I'm worried about Kill. And Cal and Mav too. Everyone's stressed out, which is stressing me out." I shrug. Kady squeezes my arm while Ari squeezes my leg on the other side.

"Tell me some stuff about Gibson and Brio. I need some happy, no-stress shit." I feel the shake in my own deep breath and hope they can't hear it.

Ari starts with a story about how Cal thinks Gibson needs a dog, but she thinks it's not a good time. When I ask her why it's not a good time, she doesn't answer. Dogs are cool. They should totally get Gibson one. He'd love that. He has a stuffed one he carries around with him everywhere.

Kady shows us some videos of Brio crawling and toddling around the house. And one of Mav and Brio sleeping and snoring together.

"Like father, like son, I guess." She smiles. "You look tired, Sammy. Just ignore us. You should sleep if you need to."

I'm just starting to drift off when Mav pops his head in. "Kill came out of sedation a lot easier this time. Guess they changed up the meds or something." Fuck, that's good to know at least. A little good news for now.

"The doc will be there in a few hours to go over the results, but I've hit the fucking wall. I nearly fell asleep on the elevator ride up. I don't know how Cal's not dead on his feet up there, but he refuses to leave Kill right now. Jax is going to take me home. Aiden's still stationed at the elevators if you need anything. I'm going home to hang with the kids for a bit. I'll be back later."

I throw my extra pillow at his head, but it doesn't make it all the way to the door. "You better sleep, fucker, or I don't want to see your face. And take a damn shower."

He gives me the finger again and leaves, but not until Jax also pops his head in and gives me a wave. I guess it takes dying to realize how much you have.

# Chapter 3

## *Melody*

Twenty-five, twenty-six, twenty-seven, twenty-eight, twenty-nine, thirty.

*Switch to the head for two rescue breaths.*

*But he's looking at me. His bright blue eyes blink at me in slow motion and his lips turn up slightly. But it's not Sammy, the rock star, looking back at me. It's Sampson, the boy in high school, the one who broke my heart. "I want to kiss you, Mel. For reals this time."*

I wake up from yet another dream about Sampson and watch the fan above my bed spin, casting its shadows against my ceiling. I'm not surprised about the dreams. Sampson Denton broke me when he took off on the last day of school and never came back. He just proved what I already knew, even back then, that everyone leaves. It's just a matter of when.

*"I want to kiss you, Mel. For reals this time."*

Caffeine. What I need is caffeine. I swing my legs off the platform and quickly make up my bed. Then I make my way to the fridge to grab a Coke. My caffeine of choice is soda, but I'll drink coffee when I'm cold or if it's the only thing available. I know soda isn't the healthiest, but it's better than other vices.

I sit at my breakfast bar and swill my cola.

There's a sharp, but familiar knock on my door and a deep baritone calls out, "Donut delivery."

There is a God, his name is Clancy, and he comes bearing donuts.

I fling the door open and take the pink bakery box from him before he even sets a foot in my place. Setting the box on my small breakfast island, I rifle through it until I find my favorite, the pink-iced strawberry with sprinkles. By the time Clance has closed my door and joined me, the donut is half gone.

"Hungry much, Mel?" His brown eyes twinkle as he watches me devour my first donut. Trust me, there will be more than one. I mean, he brought the whole dozen with him.

"Sorry," I mumble, trying not to choke on the last vestiges of donut still in my mouth.

Clance hops up on the other stool. He's already in his workout gear. The dark blue t-shirt says Santa Monica Fire in white across the back with the fireman's ax over a crest on the front left. His dark hair is peppered with a little bit of gray, but the kind that makes him look distinguished instead of old.

"Jules from the Venice station came over during shift yesterday. Says you rescued some surfer three or four days ago, on your own time?"

I nod at Clance but don't look at him. I'm already choosing my next donut. "I was running down the beach. I usually run north from the pier, but this time something told me to run south towards Venice. I saw these two guys surfing the storm surge. One didn't get a good stance on his board and the wave went rogue and shot the board up and knocked him out."

Clance cringes. "I was surfing those waves later that day. Every fourth wave of the set would do that shit. Total board eaters."

I nod and take an old-fashioned this time. "From what I could see from shore, the board clipped him on the temple, and he went down backwards. I didn't see him again until his buddy started paddling him in. By the time he got him close enough to shore where I could see him, he was blue. Not breathing, no pulse, fully arrested. I did CPR. As the Venice rescue showed up, he coughed some of it up. Vomited up more water. They took over." I don't mention that it was Sampson Denton.

He nods. "Jules said you did a hell of a job with him. Talked to Cap about a commendation."

I shrug. "It's automatic. You know how it is. Training just kicks in and you go. It's not a big deal."

Clance shakes his head and gives me a look like I'm being ridiculous. "You saved the guy. It's probably a big deal to him, to his family and friends."

"How do you know he's okay?"

"Jules checked up on him. Sounds like he'll probably leave the hospital tomorrow." I look at Clance, trying to see if he knows exactly whom I saved. You'd think he'd recognize the name of the drummer of one of the biggest rock bands.

I'm glad to know Sampson made it. I wondered if I'd been too late. Most of the time, CPR is a last-ditch effort that fails. But it's worth it for the times it does work. I never would have checked up on him on my own, though. But considering who Sampson is, I am sure his death would have been all over the tabloids and regular news.

I used to check up on patients early in my career, but it affected me too much when the result wasn't good. It made me question why I was a paramedic in the first place, if I was doing the work that would make Dee proud.

"Good. I'm glad." I eye the box, trying to decide which donut to pick next.

"You going to eat the whole box before we hit the gym?" he razzes me. Only Clance can get away with that shit. He's super fit. Most of the guys at the station are. I take the sugar-raised donut and wrap it in a napkin, setting it aside for later.

"No, I'm going to run the rest across the hall to Mrs. Chamske. Otherwise, I may as well not even bother with the gym." I shut the box.

"Be right back." I go behind the dressing screen that separates my bed from the rest of the studio apartment and throw on my workout gear. "Okay, ready."

I give the box of donuts to my neighbor before Clance and I jog to the gym a few blocks away. A lot of the fire and police personnel patronize this particular gym as it's blue and red friendly. It's a no-frills kind of gym, in an industrial building, all equipment and low overhead. It's owned by a former policeman and his wife. We do circuit training today that has both cardio and weights together. I finish up my circuit a little after Clance and take a few minutes to rehydrate and catch my breath.

Clance pats the bench press. "I'll spot you, kid." He helps me get the bar set up as I lay on the bench. "Easy, Mel. You got this. Do it!" He makes sure that I don't get out of shape during my lift or in trouble. I can feel my muscles shake with strain, but I am able to do the press.

"Great job, five pounds more than last week. Slow and steady gains, Mel." He offers a hand to help me sit back up. I want to keep up enough strength that my job is easy. I won't be the weakest paramedic on the crew because I'm a female.

Clance was my first partner when I was hired on at the Santa Monica Fire Department as a paramedic. I was fresh-faced and naïve, and he could see that coming a mile away. Clance was the one who suggested I stop checking up on patients after calls. He could see it was bringing me down when the end result wasn't positive. I run my own ambulance now. Usually I'm paired with Daniella, but she's out on maternity leave due to a high-risk pregnancy thanks to some precursors to preeclampsia. Since she's been on leave, I've been paired with a floater, Stephen.

He's a good guy. Former military medic, so he's seen some shit.

We stop near Clance's truck across the street when we get back to my apartment.

"Why don't you come to dinner tonight, kiddo? Sofie's been on my case to get you over to the house." I love Clance's wife. Just like Clance is my big brother at the firehouse, Sofie's a pseudo big sister to me. They're the only family I have that matters. A chosen family is a big deal to someone like me, a kid whose own mother wrote her off years ago.

"Is she making lasagna?" Sof's lasagna is to die for. All that warm gooey cheese mixed with the homemade meat sauce that has the spicy sausage in it, not the regular. She even puts spinach in it. I dream of Sof's lasagna. I rub my stomach just thinking of it.

Clance chuckles. "I'm not sure what she has planned, but I bet if I tell her you're coming, she'll make lasagna."

"Don't do that. I don't want her to go out of her way. I'll come no matter what she makes." I love her and it has been a while since we've gotten together.

"Too late. I've been wanting the lasagna myself, but she never makes it just for me." He smirks as he shows me the text he just sent her, and I shake my head. He makes me sound so ungrateful by telling Sophie that I'd only come if she made her lasagna. I'd probably come anyway.

"Clance, not cool." I scowl at him, but he just laughs.

"Well, it worked. Look."

He shows me a text from his wife stating that she's at the grocery store, so she'll pick up the stuff for lasagna, but only if I come. If he comes home and tells her I've changed my mind, she'll freeze it.

"I'll bring some wine?" I offer.

"Make it a case of beer and you have a deal." He shoots me a wink before climbing into his old red pickup. "Be there at 6:30."

# R

I CHECK out the driveway as I jog up the stairs to Clance and Sof's cute little house, with a case of Heineken under my arm. I hope it's just the three of us tonight. I really want to just relax before my shift tomorrow.

As much as I love Sofie, it's not uncommon for her to try and set me up with a guy. She found her happily-ever-after with Clance and thinks everyone should be out there actively searching for theirs, especially me. I'm just off guys right now. I don't want their bullshit, don't need their hassle. Not to mention the hours of a fire EMT aren't always the most conducive to a healthy relationship. I don't see any unexpected cars in the driveway or even parked out front, so I might be safe from an awkward set-up tonight.

"Knock, knock," I announce as I let myself in because that's the kind of friends they are. I just walk into their house, expected or not. They'll always greet me with open arms.

"Mel-lah-dee!" She sing-songs my name as the smell of tomato sauce, cheese and garlic waft in from the kitchen on the right.

"It's been too long, you crazy girl. Come here!" Sof squeezes me tight and rocks me, despite the case of beer that Clance is actively trying to free from under my arm.

She holds me away from her and looks me up and down. "Shit, look how toned you are." She gives my arms a squeeze. "You're even more amazing. How that's possible, I don't know. Clance, you didn't tell me she looked this good." She brings me back to her for another squeeze.

God, I love this woman. She's the sister I never had. She's short, but slightly taller than me, and perfectly curvy in all the right places, unlike me with my short but athletic build and small breasts. I'm toned from hours of surfing and working out with Clance. Her hair is to die for. She has long, shiny brown hair that has that perfect wave to it, while mine is brown and mousy and mostly straight. And she always looks incredibly put together, whereas I'm a jeans and t-shirt girl when I'm not wearing my firehouse uniform.

Clance shoots me a wink. "She looks like the same ol' Mel to me."

"It almost makes me think I should work out." She's all smiles. God, I've missed her. Why'd I stop coming again? Oh yeah, all the awkward set-ups.

"You can come to the gym with me any time I'm off duty," I tell her. "I'll go easy on you and build you up like Clance has done with me. It's not a glitzy place, everyone's there for improvement. And my favorite part is that there aren't even that many mirrors."

"Hold your horses, I said almost, Mel. Almost." She laughs and starts back towards the kitchen. I follow along with Clance, who gets right to work putting all but one of the beers in the fridge.

"Besides, Clance loves me just the way I am. Right, babe?" She leans back from the sink for a kiss with her all too eager husband. These two. They've been married for eight years, and they are still just as in love as when I met them.

"Hmm, you know it." He gives her tush a little squeeze. "I'm going to let you two catch up while I check the score." He heads out to the living room.

"How can I help?" I stand in the middle of their spacious kitchen that has all the appliances and space one would dream about. Maybe one day, I could have something like this.

"Make the garlic butter for the bread." She puts me right to work, which I am happy to do. I love to cook, but when it's just me and my teeny kitchen, sometimes take out is just easier. It's why I don't mind cooking at the firehouse when it's my turn and I usually get no complaints about my dishes. It's because Sofie's taught me almost everything I know in the kitchen.

"Any interesting things going on with you, Mel? Any guys catch your eye lately?" I knew she'd start trying to meddle in my business.

"No. I'm not in the market right now. It's just too much work with the crazy twenty-four-hour shifts and honestly, I'm tired of the whole dating scene. Tired of trying to mold myself into someone else's life." I sigh.

"They aren't all like Grady, you know." She squeezes my shoulder and I hate the pity in her voice. I shrug from her grip to turn towards her.

"I know. I just can't right now. Who knows, maybe I'm just not cut out for a relationship anyway. I need someone who supports me as I am, not someone trying to fit me into their idea of a perfect person. I need to carve out my own space in the world." I shrug and peel the garlic.

"Just as long as you aren't holed up in that apartment of yours. I just want you happy, Mel. That's all." She cuts a tomato into the most perfect little squares. I still don't know how she does it.

"So um, how is Grady?" I shouldn't ask. I don't want to know. I don't want to care.

She turns to face me, setting down her knife and leaning against the counter. "Do you really want to know?" She eyes me.

"Yes. No. Yes. I dunno," I sputter with a half laugh, trying to cover the tears welling up in my eyes.

"Well, first off, Clance and I don't hang out with him anymore, not since you guys split. Clance made it very clear to Grady that we were Team Mel all the way." I smile through my impending tears because that is one of the reasons I love Clance. He and Sof don't even know the half of why we aren't together anymore. But they defend me anyway.

"But you know Clance, he knows everyone in this town."

I nod, because Sof's right. You can't go anywhere in Santa Monica or Venice and not find someone who knows Clancy.

"He ran into a friend of a friend a couple of weeks ago. Grady transferred out and took a lead investigator position somewhere up in the bay area in one of the little cities near San Francisco. I don't remember which one Clance said. Grady's been gone a solid four months now." Her eyes are watching me the whole time she's talking. "We debated telling you. And finally decided not to bring it up unless you did."

I swallow hard and nod. Somehow, knowing Grady is out of the area is exactly what I needed to hear. A weight has been lifted off my shoulders, one I didn't know I was carrying. It's satisfying, like taking a deep breath for the first time in a while when you didn't realize you weren't breathing deep enough to begin with.

Sof embraces me again, this time with a soft hug of support. "I know that shit went south between the two of you, and you know I'd never pry. But judging by your reaction to that news, I assume that you are good with Grady being gone."

I nod and look around to see where Clance is. He's still around the corner in his living room watching the game.

"Promise you won't tell Clance what I'm about to tell you? No matter what." I look in Sof's eyes to make sure that she knows this goes no further.

She nods. "Of course, Mel." She gives my arm a squeeze. "I promise."

"You know how Grady was with me, always cutting me down. It got to the point where I started believing the shit he spewed." I look down and she nods and reaches over to squeeze my arm.

"But what caused the big fight is, I caught him being unfaithful. In our apartment, in our bed. In my bed, Sof. *My bed*. And then they both turned it around on me. Blamed me." I shake my head.

Sofia hugs me. "That shithead. No wonder you broke it off so abruptly. Can't say I was sad to see him out of your life, though."

I shake my head. "It gets worse."

She raises an eyebrow at me and waits for me to finish. I glance back at the living room to make sure that Clance is still engrossed in his baseball game.

"It was with Derek." Her eyes widen as I nod, so she knows she understood me correctly.

"Wait. Grady was with Derek? Cynthia's Derek? That Derek?"

"That'd be the one. When I walked in on them." I try to shake the image out of my head. "Afterwards, they both threatened me. Said I couldn't tell anyone. Especially not Cynthia. They explained it away, telling me it was just a one-time thing. I don't think it really was. It was bad. I just couldn't."

She hugs me tight again. "Those cheating assholes. And you won't have to see either one of them again. I feel bad for Cynthia, though. She has kids with that cheater."

I know. Those kids are the only reason I didn't say anything. Cynthia was so happy when Derek finally agreed to move to Georgia last month. She missed her family so much. After that, I just had to worry about bumping into Grady, so I stayed out of Malibu as much as I could to avoid any chance of running into him.

"Hey, when's dinner? I'm starting to get hungry, you two Chatty Cathys," Clance calls from the living room.

"You'll eat when it's ready," she yells to him with a smile.

After eating my weight in lasagna and garlic bread, we each devour a still-warm brownie with melting ice cream, and after lots of laughs, I push my chair away and stand.

"I better go. I'm on shift tomorrow." I make my way to the

front door, but not before Sofia puts a foil-wrapped package in my hands.

"Put it in the freezer. Pull it out the day before you want it so it can defrost. It'll heat better that way. Oh, and here." She adds another smaller foil pack to the top. "Dessert. Or breakfast tomorrow." She winks and gives me a hug.

"Let me get my jacket, I'll take you home." Clance walks over to the closet near the door. "I don't like you ridesharing at night."

I'd protest, but I know it'll fall on deaf ears. Besides, it'll save me a few bucks.

"I can take care of myself, you know." Clance just glares at me. Like I said, deaf ears. I have a niggling feeling that he wants to talk to me about something. I hope he didn't overhear Sof and I talking before dinner.

I get in his old truck, and we start towards my place in the center of town. I quietly hum along with the radio, wondering if I read him wrong, and he didn't want to talk about anything. We're three blocks from my building when he starts.

"I know being the center of attention isn't your thing, Mel. But I have it on good authority Cap agrees with you getting a commendation for the surfer thing. And honestly, you should be proud."

"I just—"

"I know. But you did that. You saved that man by yourself. No partner. No state-of-the-art equipped ambulance. You did that, Mel, alone on that beach. I'm so fucking proud of you. I'll be sitting in that audience, with a huge smile on my face because I am just so damn proud of you, kid. If I have to work every holiday until next year, I'll make sure I have that day off so Sof and I can be there to celebrate with you. You've come such a long way, kiddo. A long way." His eyes shine as he smiles at me and squeezes my shoulder as he double parks in front of the residential door to the mixed use building my apartment is in.

"Okay. I'll let you know if I hear anything." I slip off my seat belt and open my door.

"You will. Trust me."

"See ya, Clance." He waits until I get in the door and then pulls away.

# Chapter 4

## *Sammy*

I'm supposed to be released sometime this afternoon. That's what the doctor and respiratory therapist told me yesterday anyway. I'm so antsy to get the hell out of here. I'd already be dressed, but I have no clothes since I came in wearing a wetsuit that they ended up cutting off me. I even ate my nasty breakfast like a good boy, and the nurse seemed pleased. I just want someone to let me the fuck out of this hospital.

*Mav: I'm bringing you clothes. Any preference?*

*Cal: Mav and I talked. You're staying with one of us when you're released. No bitching. You can choose who.*

I'd been staying with Killian, but with him upstairs, it would be better to stay with Mav or Cal anyway. I don't mind staying with either of them, not because I don't feel well enough to handle myself—I feel fine for the most part—but because I hate being alone. I don't even know why I keep my condo. I should sell it and just move in permanently with one of the guys.

I let Mav know that it doesn't matter what he picks as long

40

as it's not my suit because he'd do that shit just for the laugh of me walking out of the hospital in it.

I love both Mav and Cal and their wives and kids. But I'd like to stay with Cal for now. I want to keep my ears open for news about Killian. Cal said he's doing okay, more than okay, and that the doctors are just being extra cautious. But my gut tells me Cal's been sugarcoating things because he doesn't want to stress me out. So, I won't believe it until I see Killian with my own eyes.

Mav lets me know he'll be by in about an hour with something to wear. So now I wait on the doctor. I use the button to call up my nurse of the day, Seth.

"Hey, Sammy, what's going on?" He comes in and glances at the monitors, then back at me.

"I want to go up to the heart unit and see Killian. Do I have to wait until I'm discharged for that? Can't I just go up there if you know where I am?"

"Well, no, you're still hooked up to all the things right now." He motions to the monitor and IV. "We'll get your last readings soon and once the doctor signs off on the release, we'll untether you so you can go upstairs with your friend while you wait for your release to process."

"Hmph." I'm not usually a grumpy person. But this shit is pissing me off. "I'm not good at waiting for things."

"I get that vibe from you. But honestly, you've been one of the best patients to work with." Seth records some stuff on his iPad as he chats me up. "You need anything?"

"Maybe a couple more Jell-Os? The green ones or the orange?"

He chuckles. "You've eaten more Jell-O during your stint here than the entire peds floor does in two weeks. I'll be right back with those."

I make a reminder in my phone to talk to my accountant about arranging a donation to this hospital. Maybe for the peds floor, the heart unit and critical care. This hospital has taken great care of me and of Killian too. They treat me like a normal guy, not like a rockstar and I kind of like it that way. Although I don't think I would have been able to talk them out of so many Jell-O cups if I were just a regular guy.

I text Jax and ask him to find out about the paramedic who saved me. I'd like to do something nice for him too, maybe send him to Disney World or some place with his family.

Seth drops off two green and one orange Jell-O and heads right back out. I settle in with my white plastic spoon and remote and find out what's happening on Days of Our Lives. Because what else do I have to do with myself until Mav gets here with my clothes.

I've watched this soap for three days now. Something shady is going down with Steve, and I've got to find out what it is. My door opens and shuts, but I don't pay attention. It's not Mav with my clothes. He's noisy when he comes in because of those boots he wears that have chains on them, so I'd have heard him coming down the hall. It's probably just another nurse, so I keep my eyes on Steve and what's going down in Salem.

"What the fuck are you watching?" Killian's voice startles me, and I drop my fucking Jell-O right on my sheet, which makes a big mess because, of course, it lands upside down. He chuckles at me as I curse and try to clean it up. He flops into my plastic guest chair.

I don't know what I expected to see, but it wasn't this. He looks good. Like regular ol' Kill. There are slight bags under his eyes, but other than that, he looks like he always does.

"Kill." I gasp and feel the emotion clogging my throat. He's here. He looks fine. And he helped save my life. How do I thank my best friend for saving my life?

"Hi. Uh, are you even supposed to be here?" I can't get the words out right. I want to thank him, not question him.

"I got my walking papers." He removes a folded-up set of

papers from his back pocket and begins to unfold them. "Along with five pages of aftercare shit. And three different follow-up appointments." He rolls his eyes, then glances back up at the television.

"Is this a fucking soap opera, Sam? Are you sure you didn't get brain damage from lack of oxygen or something?" He rolls his eyes again and then looks me over, his eyes zeroing in on the electric green Jell-O stains on the white sheet that covers my crotch.

"You realize it looks like you pissed antifreeze all over yourself, right?" His laugh starts off as a slow, deep chuckle, but soon it's higher pitched and bordering on hysterical. It's the kind of laugh that you have or else you'll fucking cry because your emotions are so bungled up inside that you don't know what end's up.

By the time Mav walks in a few minutes later, we're both laughing so hard we have tears running down our faces, and my fuckin' ribs are smarting like a son of a bitch, all because of green Jell-O and the soap opera.

He stops in the door and looks at us like we've lost our melons, then sets a paper bag down on the bed between my legs.

I cough a few times while trying to suppress my laugh, lungs still irritated from having so much water in them. Mav eyes me, his forehead wrinkling.

"I'm fine," I cough out. The respiratory therapist told me that I'll probably have a cough for a couple of weeks, but I'll need to watch it and if it gets worse, go to the doctor before it turns into an infection.

"I hope that's okay. I never realized most of your clothes are all the same." He moves over to the windowsill and leans against it. His worried eyes take us both in slowly, assessing us each. He looks a lot less tired, but there are still creases in his forehead and around his mouth.

"I'm sure it's good, whatever you brought. Thanks, man."

He nods at me, then looks to Killian. "When'd you get released? Does Cal know?"

"I dunno, twenty minutes ago, maybe thirty? I texted him right before I came down here. He said he'll be up soon. I told him not to hurry. If they release Sammy too, we can all just go together."

Mav nods, still eyeing Killian skeptically.

"Look, I have my papers if you don't believe me, even my follow-up appointments." He flashes Mav the same thick folded paperwork that he showed me.

"I'm okay, Mav. Really." Kill's voice is low, and he picks at the arm of the chair, not meeting his gaze.

Mav eventually nods and looks over at me. "You're sure you want to stay with Cal and not me?" He chews on the corner of his lip. Shit. I've stayed interchangeably with each of the guys over the years. But I've probably stayed with Mav the most between him and Cal. I don't want to hurt his feelings.

"It's not personal, Mav." I can't explain it, I just need to be around Kill for now.

"I bet Cal $50 bucks you'd pick me. No worries, though. I'll win it back from him somehow. I always do." He looks sheepish for a second, then wiggles his eyebrows.

"Speaking of money, I've decided to donate some to this hospital. I'm thinking to the critical care, heart, and pediatric units. Kind of a thank you for taking care of me. Of us." I kind of blurt it out without meaning to. "I don't want it to be flashy. It's not a 'look what I did' kind of thing. I'd prefer if the media didn't get wind of it at all, but I don't see that happening since everyone knows I've been here. The fans are still sending flowers even though I asked on Insta that they stop."

Mav watches me. "You know you don't have to, right? Donate money."

I nod. "I want to. They saved me here. I want to help them save more people. But I don't want it to become a stunt."

Mav nods. "I understand that. Wait a couple months, and talk to Barry. He'll help with it. That's kind of you, Sammy." Barry is our band's financial manager. Mav squeezes my leg. "Of course, you can also consider doing something like what Kady and I have done with the Monumentus Festival Survivor's Foundation. Encourage fans to donate. It could double the money you donate. Just something to think about."

"I want to do something nice for the paramedic who saved me, too. Maybe send him on a vacation or something. Jax is trying to find out who he was."

"I'm sure he doesn't expect anything," Mav says.

"I know. I want to do it. He saved my life. He should know I appreciate it." I shrug and look towards the outside as a bird flies past my window.

Killian lets out a nervous laugh. "It wasn't a 'he,' doofus. It was a 'she.'"

"Seriously? Did you get her name?" He has my full attention now. Maybe if he knows, I can contact her without having to go through Jax.

"No, Sam, I didn't ask her name. I was a little preoccupied with you being nearly dead and all." Killian scowls, his expression darkening across his face.

My nurse comes back in. "Good news. Doctor says I can remove your monitors so you can go up to see your friend." He starts busying himself removing my monitors and then takes out my IV.

"Thanks, Seth, but my friend was just released. He's here." I nod to Killian.

"Oh, good. Our Sam's been quite worried about you." Seth gives me away and I grimace a little.

"And I'm sure you've been worried about him too. I'll just go get some more Jell-O. It'll probably be a few more hours before the paperwork processes."

Three hours and eight Jell-Os later, Killian and I walk into Cal's house in the Hollywood Hills.

Ari hugs me so tight that I can't breathe as soon as I hit the threshold of the house. "Oh, Sammy. It's so good to see you out of that hospital."

She then repeats it with Killian.

"Gibs is napping. He helped me prep your rooms, and he left you each a buddy to sleep with. It was totally his idea." She holds up her hand, indicating her non-involvement. "He knows you were sick and just wants you to both feel better." She smiles at the thought of her stepson doing something so caring. Gibs is an amazing kid, but he's lucky to have Ari in his life. We all are. She's another one of my guardian angels.

"Sam, you're across from Gibs's room, like always. And, Kill, we put you across from the one my sister is in now." She smiles.

"Ugh, I just want to take a shower. I feel like I have hospital germs crawling all over me." Kill gives a shudder before taking off upstairs.

Cal follows me upstairs and into the room I'll be crashing in. Sure enough, there's a stuffed dinosaur on my bed and a small matchbox Jeep on my nightstand. It makes me smile that he not only helped Ari, but that he wanted to leave me stuff to make me feel better and he identifies me with my Jeep. He's an amazing little dude.

"Hey, Sam, um, I want to ask you a favor." Cal leans back through the doorway to glance into the hall, then moves back into the room with me. "Don't mention seeing Sev to Killian. Please. For me." There's a strain on Cal's face and his tone is serious. His stress radiates off him. He's holding on so tight to the stress that if he's not careful, he'll be in the hospital next.

"Kill's okay, right? You said the tests and scans all showed there wasn't any permanent damage." My own heart starts racing again. Was he lying about that for my benefit? I don't like being handled with kid gloves and I know Kill won't either.

He nods. "He's okay, Sam. His heart's good. I just don't want him thinking about Sev right now. Her death really messed him up. I don't want him falling back into that weird depression and totally blocking me out of his life." He closes his eyes when he says my sister's name.

"He'd want to know." Sev and Kill had a connection that we weren't supposed to know about, but I'm pretty sure they were a thing. They didn't tell me as much and I've never asked Kill officially, but I'm pretty sure.

Cal's face hardens, his lips now a thin line. His eyes narrow and assess me coolly. "I'm asking you to just let it be, Sam." His tone is no nonsense before he looks back up at me. "Thank you." He turns quickly on his heel and leaves down the hall to stick his head in the bathroom to check on his brother.

# R

I'VE ONLY BEEN at Cal's for a few days and I'm already going bat shit crazy. Dude won't let me do a damn thing and it's driving me fucking bonkers.

He won't even let me play. At all. The doctor said to take it easy and to watch for the cough getting worse, but he didn't say I couldn't play. Even when I promise to go easy, Cal refuses to let me and has threatened to lock the door to the music room. Asshole.

Maybe I should've stayed with Mav, but I have a feeling he'd be just as bad. And I wouldn't have Killian to hang out with. Besides, Mav's over here to check on us nearly daily anyway. And on the rare day he doesn't come, he texts me about fifteen times a day.

"Shammy. Play?" Gibs holds out a green pickup truck towards me. I slide off the couch and onto the floor next to him, accepting his truck. Luckily for me, playing with Gibson is one of my few Cal-approved activities.

It's funny. Gibs calls Killian Unka Kiwi, and he calls Mav Unka Mads. But he calls me Shammy. No uncle prefix, just Sammy. I like it that way. He's just as much my nephew as Killian's in my heart, but I don't need the stuffy formal title.

We roll trucks around the floor side-by-side and use his blocks to build an elaborate fort around them. Okay, maybe I do most of the fort-building. But he likes me for my preschool engineering skills.

"Where Unka Kiwi at?" He looks around for his uncle.

"Your dad took him to the doctor." The first of his three follow-ups. Cal went with him. Ari's around here somewhere. At least she doesn't watch me 24/7 like Cal.

"Aww betta." He stands up and hugs me around the neck. He pets my hair and looks at me. "Aww betta, Shammy."

I wrap my arms around his little warm body. "Yeah, I'm all better buddy."

He puckers up and kisses my forehead. "West, Shammy. Kay?"

"I'm all rested up. Thanks, buddy." I hug him back and pat his back. "I'm all good."

"Aww good," he repeats back to me, nodding with a serious expression.

Ari appears in the doorway, a soft smile on her face. "You guys want some lunch?"

"Shicken pease." Gibson gets back to playing.

"I'll help you." I stand and make my way to the kitchen area.

"Cal and Kill are on their way home." Ari cuts up some watermelon.

"Here, let me do that." I take the knife and start cutting the watermelon. "Is Killian okay? I have this feeling that Cal's not telling me something, like he thinks I can't handle it."

Ari stops making Gibson's chicken and looks over at me.

"Sammy, Killian's fine. They're just follow-ups because they need to walk him down off some of the meds they gave him at the hospital."

She puts down the chicken and comes over and gives me a hug.

"He's fine. Just like you are. You're both fine," she says quietly. "And thank God for it."

I nod and turn back to the watermelon I was cutting.

The door opens and Cal walks in, followed by Killian, who doesn't greet us. Instead, he turns at the staircase and stomps upstairs, slamming his door when he reaches his room.

"What's going on?" My heartbeat accelerates.

"He's just upset. He'll be down in a few minutes."

But Killian doesn't come downstairs, not for lunch. Not even when Gibson taps on his door and asks him to come out.

"Sammy, wanna swim with Gibs and me?" Cal holds up Gibson, whose face is still smeared with ketchup.

"Sim Shammy. Sim!" Gibson squirms in Cal's arms at the excitement of swimming. This kid loves the water just like me.

My stomach churns and my heart races. Is this because of going into the pool? It's nothing like the ocean, but I just can't do it. I shake my head as a wave of nausea hits me out of the blue, and then lightheadedness. Like, I might throw up and pass out at the same time.

My face must say what my lips can't because Cal's brow furrows. "Dude, you don't have to. It's okay," Cal says.

"Sim. Sim! Shammy! Sim!" Gibson starts to get impatient because he loves to swim, and I used to love taking him into the pool.

"Uh, I, uh, I just can't. Sorry." I jog up the stairs and head right for my room, shutting the door. I flop onto the bed and throw my arm across my eyes. A few minutes later, I'm treated to the muffled squeals of delight coming from outside as Gibson messes around in the pool, while my heart's still

49

pounding in my ears and my breath still comes in strained gasps.

I try to take a few deep breaths to calm my racing heart.

My door opens and the bed dips. "Sam?" Cal's voice is quiet. "I'm sorry, Sam, I didn't think." He puts his hand on my arm that's across my eyes and squeezes. "I just figured you love to swim with Gibs, and he loves to swim with you."

I sit up so fast that my head is a little dizzy. "I need to play."

"I don't know if that is such a good idea. Give yourself another week. Please, for me?" He lifts his eyebrows. I know he's concerned for me and everything, but he doesn't understand. I need to play. Like, *need it, need it.* Because nothing makes sense right now and playing is the only way I can work it out.

"No. Fuck you, Cal. Either I'm playing in your music room, or I'll head to Mav's to play there, or my storage unit. You choose." I don't know who I am with these angry words. That's not me.

He squeezes his eyes tight before reopening them, not used to me being so angry. And honestly, I'm not sure what this sudden fit is about.

He sighs deeply, then looks back at me. "Fine. Play here. But if you start to feel bad, you come see Ari or me immediately. As a matter of fact, maybe I'll jam with you." He gets up.

"No. I want to play alone."

"Sam—"

"Leave me be, Cal. Let me do my thing. I just need to do my own fucking thing." Tears sting my eyes as I bolt and head to Cal's first floor music room. I keep a small-scale kit here and one in Mav's home studio. Neither is anything as impressive as my live kit. But I need to play, and the smaller kit will work.

I get comfortable on my stool. It's been nearly two weeks since I've been behind my drums. I need normalcy and drumming makes me feel almost normal. I slide my hand down to the bag attached to the side of the bass drum and my sticks are exactly where they should be. This is what I need. Things to be exactly where they should be, my life to be exactly how it should be.

I twirl one between my fingers before settling it in my grip. Yeah, that's right. I start out slow, just some basic rhythms. Then I play through some of our older songs. The more I work over the kit, the better I feel.

I've probably been playing a little more than an hour, considering I just played through our entire first album in order. The studio door opens and Killian slips in with a sports drink in hand. He cracks open the drink and hands it to me.

"Thanks." I nod at him before swilling the drink, taking in half of it in one swallow.

He nods wordlessly at me and picks up one of his basses. He fiddles with its tuning and then starts the opening bass-line of the first song on our second album. I join in with just the kick drum first, as I finish my orange drink. Once I'm done, I join him fully. He nods at me, and we start jamming through the second album together.

By the halfway point, Kady and Mav have joined us. And finally, Cal. We don't work through any new music. We work through our second album and then our third. The physicality of playing is exactly what I need to clear my head. Living in the rhythm helps me forget everything that doesn't matter. It makes the fact that I yelled at Callum less important. I'm pretty sure he'll forgive me. Callum has a thick skin. But I normally don't go off like that and now I feel bad for doing so.

What doesn't feel bad is that I'm loose and sweaty. It feels damn good to pound out the familiar beats. Yes, I'm sore as shit. But it's all about the timing of the songs. The stress, the embarrassment of flipping out over something as simple as taking a little boy swimming melts away the longer I play. I'm slightly more winded than I should be, but I haven't played or worked out in half a month.

After hitting the end of the third album, I'm spent and lay down my sticks. I sit on the stool, breathing hard. And I can tell me being winded bothers Cal. He watches me closely for a few minutes before standing to leave, mumbling something about Gibson.

Kady smiles at me before slipping out.

"Good jam, man." Mav gives me a pat on the back and a wink as he chases after his wife.

Kill slips his bass into the stand and stands up, stretching his arms over his head. He then sits cross-legged on the floor and looks up at me as I sit behind my kit.

"How are you feeling?" He tilts his head. "Really, no bull-shit." His eyes narrow at me.

"Pretty good, actually. I really needed that." He nods at me as I stretch my back.

"You know, it's okay if you're not okay." He says it quietly.

"No, I feel great. Seriously. You know me, I have to be moving. Two weeks of not playing between being in the hospital and being here. I needed to play, Kill. I really needed it."

"I don't mean physically. I mean, in your head. I heard you didn't want to take Gibson swimming. And it's okay, Sammy." His eyes bore into me, but I can't meet them. Because it's not okay. It's embarrassing. I shut him down, not liking the way this conversation is heading.

"Look, I just want you to know that I understand if you're not okay." He breathes out quietly. "Do you dream about it? I have, every fuckin' night." He pauses again. Now I understand why he's so on edge lately. He's exhausted as fuck.

I don't want him to feel bad for having dreams. It was obviously more distressing to him than to me. I mostly want to tell him about Sev, but I don't want to piss off Cal, especially if Kill's still as upset by the accident as he just said he is.

"I'm okay. I haven't had dreams or anything. Probably because I don't remember what happened. I just don't want to go in the water anytime soon. But I'm okay. Really."

He nods and rises, but I can't tell if he believes me. "Well, I'm here if you want to talk or if you want someone to go to the pool with you. Or to the beach. You know, to warm up to it slowly or whatnot. Whatever you need, I'm here, man. Okay?"

I nod at Killian, my best friend of all the band members. "You're okay, right? Your heart and all. You seemed kind of upset after your appointment."

Kill looks at me. "My heart is fine. It's my head they are worried about." He rolls his eyes.

"You're head? Did you get a concussion too?"

He barks out a quick laugh. "No. Mentally, you dork. They're making me see a psychiatrist and shit because of how I acted in the emergency room. They've had me on anti-anxiety medication since the panic attack. I don't like how it makes me feel, and I told them as much. They're taking me off it slowly. But Cal lit into me about it all the way home when I said I didn't want to keep seeing the shrink." He shrugs.

"Well, if you need to talk to me, you know you can."

"I'm just grateful you're okay. When I laid you on the beach," his eyes lock with mine. "You were dead Sam. Gone. Just like Sev." The way that he sobs it out makes me grateful that Cal told me not to mention Sev to him. Now I get it.

Killian looks away. "You were fucking dead, Sammy," he whispers thickly, rocking slightly while holding his knees to his chest. "I couldn't have taken that. Not losing you too." His inhale shudders as he tries to hold himself together.

I join him on the floor and give him a quick bro hug. "I'm okay. All good. You just saw me play straight through our first three albums. I'm okay. Just used one of my nine lives is all."

He hugs me back. "You're not a cat, man. We don't have nine fucking lives."

I need to pull him out of his head. "You want to go with me to the Venice firehouse to thank them? And then maybe stop by the firehouse of the off-duty paramedic that helped save me?" He smiles at me so big that his eyes bunch in the corners.

"I'd really like that." He sounds much more like the Killian I know. We'll be okay.

"We'll go tomorrow, okay? We'll take them food and some Rebels stuff or something."

# Chapter 5

## *Melody*

"Hey, Mel, thanks for the food yesterday." Jones pats my back as he's on the way out of the firehouse and I'm on my way in. I have no idea what he's talking about. I tuck my duffle under my bunk and head to the kitchen to check-in for shift.

"Mel, these were dropped off for you yesterday." Cap motions to a huge bouquet of sunflowers. Next to it is a half-eaten edible bouquet. There are bright flowers made out of a variety of fruit. I reach over and take a stick of chocolate-covered strawberries topped by a flower made of pineapple.

"And we all ate the lunch they brought yesterday. Too bad you weren't on shift. It was from the Hamburger Hut. It was so good."

"It was for me?"

"Yeah, from the guy you rescued on the beach and his friend. They were so disappointed you weren't on shift, but said they'd make sure to thank you personally. I told him they could do it at your commendation ceremony at the end of next week. Speaking of the ceremony, Clance has already switched shifts

55

so he can be there too and all of us off duty guys are going. We are proud of you, kid."

Everyone in the room claps and hollers things like, 'Good job' as my cheeks heat at Cap's words and everyone else's accolades. I can't stand to be the center of attention. But at least it's for something good. But I'm still not comfortable getting a commendation for just doing what I'm trained to do.

But damn, these strawberries are good. I end up visiting the edible arrangement several times throughout my shift, and each time I do, I curse the fact that I wasn't on shift last night. I'd like to see Sampson. Especially when the last time I saw him, he wasn't even conscious.

# R

I FIDDLE with my dress uniform. It's not something I wear very often and definitely not because I'm being honored on stage. Today, everything needs to be perfect since I'll be in front of a bunch of people and representing our firehouse. It's the Tri-City monthly commendation ceremony and I don't want to let Cap down. I won't be the only one receiving a commendation today, but I am the only one from Santa Monica, so everything has to be just right because I don't want it to look bad on our group.

At least I'll have a few people from our house there, including Clance and Sof. The crowd will have some friendly faces. It's a nice feeling to know that there will be people there just for me. It's not something that I am used to.

Thank God I don't have to make a speech or anything. That'd make me hurl. All I have to do is wait for my name to be read, accept my certificate and pin and then carry on off stage. I'm so nervous because there will be a roomful of eyes watching me. What if I fall on my way across the stage to get my certificate? What if—

There's a quick knock, and then Clance opens the door, with Sofie following behind him.

"Hey, kid, you look good." He eyes my uniform to make sure everything's in its right place, but I've gone over it three times. I look down to check my pins one more time. They are all straight. He pulls me in for a quick hug.

Then it's Sofie's turn to give me a big hug, her eyes welling with tears. "I'm so proud of you, Mel. Seriously. You deserve this. I still can't believe you didn't tell us about it at dinner."

"Sof, you're going to wrinkle her up. Save it for after. Because there's totally going to be a celebration after the ceremony. We'll all go to The Bar and have drinks and appetizers on me."

I nod stiffly. "Can I change before the celebration?"

Clance's grin grows huge, and he chuckles. "Of course. We're celebrating you, not your uniform. Now let's get you to the ceremony."

We go in Sof's car since there wouldn't be enough room in Clance's old truck. I smooth out my uniform pants when we get to the parking lot.

Clance grabs my hand with his and squeezes. "Stop fidgeting, Mel. Everything's perfect. You look perfect. Remember to stand tall, chin up, because *you deserve this.* Don't let those voices in your head tell you anything different." He pulls me in again for a quick hug and then we move to walk in together. There are several media stations standing outside.

"Must be a slow news day. They aren't going to put this on the news, are they?" I glance from the media over to Clance.

He shrugs. "Maybe for a special interest piece or something." We enter the hall, and he grabs my shoulder. "See you after. Don't be alarmed when they announce you because I'm going to clap loud. And I might even whoop or something."

"Clancy, don't you dare!" He just gives me a shrug as he and Sofie start into the hall. I find Cap backstage and we walk out on stage together, me taking a seat with the other recipients and he with the other captains.

I scan the crowd when the speeches start, looking for Clance and the others from our house. I finally find them sitting together about midway back on the right-hand side. There's a group of five, including Clance, best I can tell. And I see Jules from Venice sitting next to Clance. So that's six.

They start calling each of us up. The commendation is read, and the emcee talks a little about the situation that it results from. The captain from the house and the person commended go up to get their certificate and pin. Some hands are shaken, pictures taken with the commendation and pin, and then the person sits back down and waits for the next one. Seems easy-peasy, so I don't know why I can't seem to sit still. It's like I have jumping beans in my pants or something. I shift slightly trying hard not to bounce my knee like I really want.

"And finally, we have a lifesaving commendation for Melody Tanner from Santa Monica Fire for her off-duty perfor-mance of CPR on a drowned surfer off of north Venice beach. Her quick thinking and command of the scene saved the life of the surfer." I stand and walk tall across the stage like Clance told me to because I deserve this. I really did what the announcer spoke about.

I shake the commissioner's hand, then Cap's hand and when he and I turn to face the audience for the pictures, Clance and the rest guys from the house, including Jules, all stand and start making a scene by clapping, whistling, and whooping. My cheeks heat, but Cap's hand squeezes my shoulder as we smile for the cameras, like he knows I just want to bolt off the stage. But I keep myself calm and here, even though the side of the stage beckons me.

Then a group of six or so people on the other side of the hall start doing the same thing and my cheeks get even hotter. I can only assume they are more people from the Venice Firehouse, maybe, because I can't really see them from where we are. I just really want this thing to be over already, because the one person I wanted to be able to be here couldn't be. It's why I don't deserve to be on this stage. There are some more pictures taken. Cap pats me again in a quick but gentle motion and then we head back towards our seat for the rest of the ceremony.

When it's over, I jump up to make my way offstage to find Clance so we can get the heck out of here. Cap grips my shoulder and leans in. "Don't leave yet. I have some people who want to meet you." I really don't want to do the after-ceremony mingling. I want out of my dress uniform and shoes so much.

"I'm just going to say hi to Clance and the guys." He nods and lets go of my shoulder.

"Congrats, kiddo! I'm so freaking proud of you." Clance gives me a big one-armed hug. A few of the fire guys and my temporary partner Stephen are also here. Everyone wants to give their congratulations and take pictures with me and my commendation. I'm about to beg Clance to sneak me away from here when Cap approaches our little group.

"Sorry, guys, I'm going to have to steal Mel for a minute. Some people want to meet her." Cap stands tall next to me and puts his arm around me. He turns me, and we head to a small group of people standing in the far corner.

"Gentlemen, this is Santa Monica Fire Paramedic Melody Tanner. Melody, this is Sam, the surfer you saved and his friend Killian, who was with him that day."

I look up at them. "Hi." My breath is stolen from my chest seeing him again. He looks good. So much better than he did on the beach that day. "Sampson."

I am suddenly enveloped in a tight, strong hug from a very grown-up Sampson, his long blonde curls in my eyes. He rocks us back and forth and then his friend hugs us both. Sampson pulls back with a gasping sob.

"Thank you for saving me, Mel." I can't help but reach out and squeeze his arm, his relief palpable.

His friend grabs me again and hugs me tight. "Thank you for saving my best friend. I didn't know what to do. Thank God you were there." His voice shudders as he rocks me. And part of my brain realizes that if I saved Sampson, then this must be one of his bandmates who is hugging me. One of *the* Blind Rebels is hugging me.

Of course, I know who they are. They stole my Sampson. I tried to keep from watching their rise to stardom because I was so pissed off at him for leaving me.

But I can't take my eyes off my Sampson. He's all grown up. He's taller and thicker than the boy I loved in high school. His hair's still blonde and curly, but it's even longer than it was back then. And those eyes. They are the same big, expressive blue eyes. He breaks his gaze on me to look up at his friend, his forehead wrinkled. I venture a look up at the man hugging the stuffing out of me.

It's Killian Donogue, bassist from The Blind Rebels, the other surfer from the beach that day. Rebels lead singer, Mavrick, pulls his friend away to take his turn with me.

"We all want to thank you for saving our Sammy." He leans in and gives me a hug too. There use to be a time I called this man, the ring leader of the Blind Rebels, the devil for stealing Sampson away from me. His wife Kady, who I only know from the tabloids, also gives me a hug. Meanwhile, Sampson stands, watching all his friends hug me.

Callum, Killian's brother, comes forward and gives me a brief hug. "We'd like you to have dinner with us as a thank you. You can bring your friends if you'd like. We all insist."

"Oh, uh…" I am still speechless because that's my Sampson, and the guitarist of one of the hottest rock bands in the United States is standing in front of me, asking me to go to dinner with the band.

But mostly because that's *my* Sampson. I've always imagined what running into him would be like. Before the day at the beach, the last time I saw him in person was years ago, when his sister died. I saw him at the graveside service from a distance. But now here is my Sampson, and he smells exactly like he did in high school, of beeswax and maple. It brings me back to happy, carefree days at the beach.

Someone squeezes my shoulder. "We'd love to," Clance says over my shoulder. "Right, Mel?"

I just nod because I still can't believe that Sampson is standing right in front of me.

Sammy comes back to me and puts his hands on my shoulders. "Damn, Mel. I can't believe it's actually you. That *you* saved me. It's so fucking good to see you." He squeezes my shoulders and then pulls me in for another hug. "You look amazing. How can I ever thank you for saving me? I miss you. So much."

His words throw me. *He misses me?* He says it like it's been a month, not over a decade. He says it like he misses me the way I missed him for years after he left. I waited for him to come back, but he never did, and I had to leave.

Mavrick Slater interrupts. "I hate to do this, but the media wants a quick interview. Do you mind? Just you, Sam, and Kill."

"Oh, I dunno." I pull away. I don't want to be on television. "I need to change before dinner and stuff." I look down.

"Go on, Mel," Clance says. "We'll still have time to get you to your place so you can change before dinner."

There are a couple of TV cameras and one of the local news people set up on the stage. I take a relucent seat in between Killian and Sammy.

Sammy's leg bounces while their sound person makes sure we are all wired with microphones.

Jodi Seavers from the local news channel is sitting in front of us. This all feels both surreal and nerve-wracking and hot under all these lights.

Sampson starts by talking about how they were surfing the storm surge that day. Killian talks about seeing Sammy get knocked out by his board and about paddling him in. The tone of his voice is so gut wrenching, I can't help but remember the feral cry he let out on the beach while I was giving Sampson CPR. I almost get teary.

"So, Melody, what had you on the beach that day?" She turns to me, but I can tell she's not as interested in me as she is in Sammy and Killian. Nor should she be. I am not that fantastic.

"I was running. I run almost every day. Usually, I run north from the Santa Monica Pier and later in the morning. But I woke up early, and while I was running, decided on a lark to run towards Venice instead."

"And what did you see?"

"I saw Killian ride his wave in and then paddle back out. And I saw Samp, uh, Sammy take a wave and the board shoot up. It looked like it clipped him in the head, so I stopped to watch Killian bring him in and could tell that Samp, uh, Sammy, was in distress. I yelled at another jogger to call 911 and I ran out to help Killian get, uh, his friend down on the sand and then I started CPR until the Venice rescue squad showed up."

"She was amazing. Right before the ambulance crew arrived, he spit some of the water out and she rolled him on his side and hit him on the back and more water and stuff came out," Killian says, a slight awe to his voice.

"Did you know who you were saving at the time?" Jodi prods.

"I was more concerned about getting Sammy breathing again by keeping my chest compressions strong and the right rhythm than who he was." I don't want them to know I know

Sampson. I don't want that notoriety, to be known as the girl that Sampson left behind because she wasn't enough for him.

"They were strong, alright. My chest is still bruised." He chuckles and rubs at his chest. "She might be small, but she broke two of my ribs in the process," he adds. He's very much the confident rock star I've seen on television, so comfortable with all the attention. He swings his arm over the back of his chair as he looks across me towards Killian. I feel ridiculous sharing the stage with them. They're both larger than life on this little stage and I'm the nobody in the center.

To me, he's just Sampson, the kid I knew and loved in high school. The one who broke my heart when he and my best friend, his sister, both left.

"It's important to make sure to keep the heart pumping to keep the brain oxygenated and alive."

Jodi is captivated by them, but finally swings her gaze my way.

"Well, I'm not sure you succeeded there." Killian chuckles. "Just kidding." He reaches over me and tousles the curls on Sampson's head.

"In all seriousness, though, Mel here saved my life. I can never thank her enough for that." Sampson reaches out and squeezes my knee, and that zap of electricity he's always given me zings through me like he's never been gone.

"She saved his life, and *we* can never thank her enough," Killian corrects and throws an arm over my shoulder and squeezes, his eyes watery and his voice a little rougher than it was minutes ago.

"Anything you'd like to say?" Jodi asks me.

"I'd just like to encourage everyone to take CPR and first aid classes. They're available through the Red Cross, most local community centers, and even most of the community colleges and adult schools offer them as well."

They take a couple of still photos of me standing between

Killian and Sampson, holding my commendation. And then it's finally over.

Mavrick and Clance are in a deep conversation when we rejoin them.

"Let's go get you changed." Clance puts his arm around me and leads me and Sof out the door.

"Wait, Mel," Sampson calls out to me. I turn and he gives me another huge, strong hug. "I just needed to hug you again. Fuck, I still can't believe *you* saved me." His words are so soft that I'm the only one who hears them. Then he pulls away and smiles at me softly, and it's here that I see reminders of the boy I knew in high school. "See you at dinner. We can catch up."

Clance drives me to my place and drops Sof and me there. "I'm going to change out of my uniform. I'll be back soon."

Surprisingly, Sof waits until my door is shut before she lets loose with a squeal so loud that I am sure it would wake the dead.

"Dang, Sof, even Mrs. Chamske could hear that, and she lives across the hall and is half-deaf."

She grabs my shoulders and squeals again. "We're having dinner with The Blind Rebels!" She jumps up and down. "You saved the drummer of The Blind Freakin' Rebels!" She continues to pogo stick while holding on to my arms.

"Why aren't you excited? And why did you act like you knew the drummer?" Sof's eyes squint at me. "How do you know him? Oh. Em. Gee. Are you dating him? Have you been dating him on the sly?"

I can't help but chuckle at her ridiculous claim.

"I knew him way back in high school, Sof. We were friends once upon a time. I don't know him now, and I'm not dating him or anybody else. You'd be the first to know if I was." She looks at me like I've grown reindeer antlers or something. "So, do you know where we are going? I'm not sure how to dress."

"Casual is all they said. Mavrick said he'd send a car here to pick us up. How cool is that? A car. Do you think it'll be a limo? I wonder where we are going. Did they say anything to you about where?"

I can't help my giggle. Sofie is on ten and I can't get her to turn down. I've never seen her like this. She's star-struck, rock-star-struck, that is.

I carefully set the pieces of my uniform down on my bed as I strip them off. I pull out my favorite pink top and my best pair of jeans and slip on my tennis shoes.

"How's this for casual?" I pop out of my walk-in.

"Too casual," Sof says.

"I don't want to feel overdressed," I counter. I relent and let Sof pick me a new shirt, but these are my favorite jeans, and they make my ass look fabulous, so I am not letting her put me in the skirt she wants. She even swaps out my shoes for my ballet flats, which make me look even shorter than I am.

"You need some jewelry." She rifles through my box and picks out some bracelets and earrings.

"I'm not wearing those earrings." She holds out a pair of simple flower shaped earrings.

"But they are so adorable, and they match the shirt." Sampson bought me those earrings for my birthday in high school. He saved for months to buy them, and I refuse to wear them now. It would crush me to lose one. To me, they're still irreplaceable, even though Sampson basically taught me I, on the other hand, am quite replaceable. Plus, I don't want him to know that I still have them. That's a little too much.

I wonder if he even remembers giving them to me, or if he ever wishes he'd stayed. No. How could he wish that? If he'd stayed, he wouldn't be the drummer to one of the most iconic rock bands of our time. While I know that Sammy Denton of The Blind Rebels was my Sampson Denton, it just doesn't reconcile in my brain how my shy Sampson was the same guy I was on stage with just hours ago.

Although when he hugged me, really hugged me, he felt like my Sampson. Smelled like him too, a unique mixture of beeswax, maple, and him. It felt like home, almost like he'd never left. How I wish that was true. Maybe tonight we can fix that.

"No can do, Sof. These studs are fine." I put my foot down. She doesn't like it, but she acquiesces when she figures out I am not going to budge on wearing the flower earrings.

"Hey, ladies, you decent?" Clance calls as he walks into my apartment. I have a dressing screen and a walk-in closet, but he's still careful after that one time they walked in on me changing.

"We're good." Sof peeks out to check out her husband.

"I'm all done being redressed by Sof since what I picked out wasn't up to her standards." I wink at him.

"I just didn't want her to be too underdressed." She throws her hands up in the air. Clance gives her a once over and then me.

"Well, you both look fine to me." He flops onto my couch. "Any idea where we are going to dinner?"

Sof and I shake our heads. "We were just discussing that. I almost wish I thought to ask for Samp- ugh, Sammy's phone number, so I could call and cancel."

Clance eyes me again. "What is it with you and his name? It's like you know him or something."

"New development!" Sofie holds out her hand to her husband, shaking it with bubbly excitement. "She does know him. They were friends in *high school*. I just don't know how she forgot to mention she knew the drummer of The Blind Rebels. We've known her for almost, what, ten years now and this never came up?"

"It's not a big deal. We used to be friends in high school. Then he went and joined the Rebels and, well, I am here." I shrug, but they both eye me like they aren't convinced that's all there is to the story, and they'd be right. But it's not their business.

Clance gets a text and then tells us the car is at the curb.

"Wait, did you exchange numbers with one of them?" Sofie eyes her husband.

It's now Clance's turn to shrug. "I might have Mavrick Slater's digits. No big." He winks at me.

# Chapter 6

## *Sammy*

I inch towards the door to the stairs down to the studio. I'm seriously considering sneaking down into Mav's studio to hit the skins. I need to release some of this nervous energy buzzing through me. I can't believe that Mel will be here soon.

*My Mel.*

I couldn't fucking believe it when I saw her take the stage at the ceremony. Jax told me who saved me. It didn't even take him a day to find out. But I couldn't wrap my head around it until I actually saw her on that stage today, dressed up in her uniform, head held high.

I haven't seen her since fucking high school. Eleven years, but I recognized her right away. She still has the same big brown eyes and hair that's not quite blonde but not quite brown either. And those lips. She breathed life into me with those lips that I still fucking dream about. I think I must have gasped when I saw her, because Killian grabbed my arm and squeezed it.

And now she'll probably be here in about half an hour, and I can't fucking sit still because of it.

"Shammy. Wook. Diney." Callum's son thrusts a small stuffed dinosaur into my hand. "Hugs Diney!"

I hug Gibson's dinosaur and pick up my little buddy. "Wanna see if it's okay to go down to the beach?"

He nods.

"Ar? Is it cool if I take Gibs down to the beach?" She looks up at us and smiles, and it's a relief to see her smile and the light back in her eyes.

"Sure, go ahead. Have fun. But don't forget your guests will be here in half an hour or so." She's so much a mom. I'm glad she's finally doing better. She and Callum were both devastated when they lost their baby. I've never seen Ari in such a funk like that. And Callum was a damn mess between worrying about Ari and trying to grieve a baby that never was.

I head towards the patio, and Kill is hot on my trail.

"Can I come too?" he asks breathlessly as he catches up.

Gibson nods. "Unka Kiwi at da beesh."

We head down the stairs that lead to Mav's private gate to the beach. Kill opens the door and the briny ocean smell causes Gibson's nose to curl up.

"Shtinky."

I freeze just outside the gate. Kill puts his hand on my shoulder, but I can't fucking move. My heart is racing, pounding so hard it feels like it might escape my chest or die trying. What the fuck was I thinking coming down here? As the waves gently crash against the shore yards away, it competes with the sound of the blood rushing through my ears at break-neck speed.

"It's okay. We'll stay up here and build a big sandcastle, right Gibs?" Gibs nods and starts trying to take off his shoes while I'm holding him. All I can focus on is the roar of the ocean and holding him tighter to me.

"Shammy. Squishin' me. No shoes. Pease. Off." He throws

himself half over my arm, trying to take his shoes off but can't quite reach them because of my grip around his middle.

"No shoes!" he whines, trying to reach his feet again.

"Here, I'll get 'em off for you." Killian busies himself with taking off his nephew's shoes, but he's keeping a watchful eye on me. And I'm watching him watch me because I cannot fucking move. My eyes widen slightly at Kill, and he nods like he understands. I'm glad someone does because I sure as fuck don't understand why I can hardly breathe. What the fuck is happening to me?

After he's taken off the shoes, he slides Gibson out of my arms and into his own.

"Just sit on the sand, Sammy. It's okay. You don't have to go any farther." He coaxes me quietly, so quietly I can barely hear him over the blood still racing through my ears.

"Jus sit in sand, Shammy." Gibson points to the ground.

I drop onto the sand and sit cross-legged. Killian sits facing me, and Gibson sits happily between us, digging for 'tweasure' in the sand. We aren't anywhere near the ocean. Even if the tide was a king tide, it still wouldn't reach us. But even way up here my chest tightens, and I can't breathe.

"It's okay not to be okay, Sammy. Just take a slow breath." Killian repeats his mantra and pats my knee. When I don't say anything, he leans over Gibs to give me a strong pat on the back, causing me to gasp in the breath I didn't realize I was holding.

"S' okay not okay, Shammy." Gibson parrots his uncle and pats my other knee. "S' okay." Then he stands up and wraps his arms around my neck. "S' okay, Shammy. Aww. 'S okay." His little hand pats my head as he attempts to soothe me, the way he's been soothed many times. But that just makes it worse.

Tears are running down my cheeks and I didn't even know until Gibson tried wiping them away.

"No cwy. It ohhhkay."

Fuck, I'm crying like a little bitch on the beach in front of my best friend and his nephew and I don't even know what the fuck is wrong with me. I haven't cried since Sev died.

I love the ocean; she's my peace. There's something healing about the sand and the smell and how it makes whatever my problems are seem insignificant in the greater scheme of life.

As much as I need that peace, as much as I need to be in my happy place, I can't be. My brain is telling me if I don't get the fuck out of here, I'll pass out, that the water will get to me and I'll drown all over again, only this time Mel won't be here to save me.

The intuitive need to flee is just so strong. I've never felt anything like it before. That this is the one place I've always found soothing upsets me even more. It makes the tears come harder. There's no sound, but Gibson seems to sense that I'm not as okay as I should be.

"S' okay, Shammy. Pomise." His little arms squeeze tight against my neck, making the not breathing thing even worse for me.

And over his shoulder, my eyes lock with Killian's.

"Uh, I need to get back to the house. I need to go." My voice is shaky and doesn't sound like me, but I try to pull Gibson off me, which makes him clutch my neck harder.

I don't know if it's the weird sound of my voice or the look on my face or maybe the sudden rivers rolling down my cheeks, but somehow the urgency of my request is understood by Killian, who pries a consoling Gibson off of me.

And I don't wait. I can't. There's no checking to see if they're following, no holding the gate open. I don't even remind Killian to pick up Gibs's shoes. I bolt straight for the house and right into the upstairs bathroom. Do not pass go. Do not collect sympathetic concerned looks.

The all-encompassing need to get far away from the ocean that I've always loved doesn't ebb but propels me further, away

71

from all the eyes of concern, away from the deep shame that sits low in my belly and burns on my face.

I don't know how long I'm in the bathroom quietly freaking out about panicking at the beach. How can water do this to me when watersports have been my life since I was old enough to walk to the beach?

Kill's right. *I'm not okay.* Maybe he's right, and I did suffer brain damage or something from when I drowned.

There's a soft knock on the door. "Sammy? It's just me. Kady. Um, can I come in?"

I quickly wipe my face on one of her matching monogrammed hand towels and then reach over and flip the lock quietly.

The door eases open, and then she shuts it and locks it behind her.

I lean nonchalantly against the sink counter, and she walks over, quietly placing her arms around me and gives me a hug. When she does, I relax against her even though I didn't realize there was so much tension in my body. She says nothing. Just hugs me a little tighter to her.

"Hugs help me sometimes," she says quietly. "They ground me and remind me that I'm okay. I thought it might help you. And it does get better. Sure, they still sneak up on me from time to time, but it's also about how I react to them."

I say nothing, and she finally releases me.

"It's different for everyone. The panic and how it manifests. You can learn to work through it in therapy. It's helped—"

I pull away from her.

"I'm fine. I don't need help." I turn to wash my hands.

"Sammy, I—"

"I said I'm fucking fine, Kady. Drop it. I'm not some head-case like you." She steps back as if I slapped her. And I may as well have. She turns her head to try to hide the tears I've caused, but it's too late. I've seen them.

*What the fuck is wrong with me?* How could I say something like that to her? Mavrick will kick my ass. He *should* kick my ass. Hard.

I fling the door open and head back downstairs just as quickly as I went up. Now I really need to sneak down into Mav's studio to blow off steam before Mav catches on to what just happened between Kady and me. I can't believe I just said that to Kady, of all people. Kill's so right.

I'm not okay.

# Chapter 7

## *Melody*

A ll three of our jaws drop when the limo we've been riding in pulls up to a fancy metal gate at a beachside property in Malibu.

"Holy shitake mushrooms," Sofie mutters. "Casual dinner is at one of their houses. Is this Sammy's house?" She looks over at me as if I have the answer, which I don't. All I have is this deep sinking feeling that I am not just in over my head, but that I really don't belong in Sampson's world, especially if this is his house. I shrug because I have no idea whose house this is. Even if it's not Sampson's house, it goes beyond anything I'd ever be able to even dream about.

The car pulls up to the front of the house and the driver opens the car door. We slide out and just kind of stand in front of the two steps that lead into the house. Clance grips my shoulder as if he senses my hesitation. My desire to hop back in the limo and go back to my little apartment in Santa Monica must be written all over my face.

"Shall we?"

As we approach, the door swings open, and Kady Slater greets us with an adorable baby on her hip and a huge, welcoming smile. "I'm so glad you're all here. Come on in." She hooks her head to the inside of the house, and we file in.

"Hey, everyone, our guests of honor are here," Kady calls out as we follow her out of the stunning foyer and into what I can only guess is considered a great room. It's a huge living room that opens into an amazing kitchen space. There's a wet bar in the corner of the room near the kitchen area. Beyond is a patio with a stunning ocean view.

As we enter, everyone in the room turns to look in our direction. An adorable blonde boy of about three peeks up over the couch from between Killian and Callum Donogue with a toothy grin and then hides back behind the cushion. Callum stands and walks over to us.

"We didn't meet properly at the ceremony. I'm Cal." He holds out a hand to Clancey first, who shakes it.

"Clance, and this is my wife, Sofie." Cal takes her hand and shakes it.

"Nice to meet you both," he says, and when his eyes meet Sof's, I swear she practically melts on the spot. Callum then moves over to me. "And you need no introduction. Melody Tanner, saver of our Sammy."

I expect him to hold out his hand for me to take, so I lift mine, but instead Callum leans in and wraps his arms around me in a friendly but tight hug.

"There aren't enough words to thank you for that." His voice is low so only I can hear and punctuated with an extra tight squeeze before he pulls away, making eye contact with damp eyes.

When Cal reclaims his arm, Mavrick Slater is introducing himself again to Clance and Sof. He then grips my shoulders. "You. Thank you. Again." He takes a deep breath. "There can't be enough thank yous for what you did." He leans down and gives me a brief hug as well.

"You're part of our family now." His words, quiet in my ear, are a salve on my burned soul.

He has no idea how much his words affect me. It's what I've always wanted. A family.

Arm still around my shoulders, Mavrick looks back at Clance and then at me. "Is he your brother?"

I shake my head and giggle nervously. "No. Well, like a pseudo big brother, I guess."

Mav gives a chuckle. "He definitely gives off big brother vibes." He squeezes my shoulder again. "Come on in. Make yourselves comfortable. Can I get you all anything to drink?"

"I'll take a beer," Clance says. "And a glass of wine, red, if you have it for Sof?" Clance looks over at Sof, who nods. She's still quiet, the awe on her face obvious to me. "Please and thank you," she says.

Mav nods. "You got it." He turns back towards me. "How about you? What's your poison, Melody?"

"A soda. Diet if you have it." He nods and heads to the wet bar.

Killian stands and offers me his seat on the couch, so I take it. "I'm not sure where Sam got off to." He looks at Mav who shrugs as he brings back Sof's wine and my soda.

Callum's eyes move to a small hallway off the room we are in, and Killian starts that way. Meanwhile, the stare of the small boy who I'm sharing the couch with is heavy on me.

I turn slightly so I'm facing him and Cal. The blonde boy stands on the couch, mostly facing Cal. He gives me a curious side-eye while weaving his little fingers into his dad's long dark hair. When I smile and make eye contact with him, he buries his head into the crook of Cal's neck, his soft blonde curls a stark contrast to Cal's dark, straight hair.

Cal hugs his son to him reassuringly and chuckles at me over his head. "Gibson's a little shy at first. Especially when he's tired."

I can't help myself. I reach out and pat the toddler gently. "That's okay, Gibson. I'm a little shy at first too."

A cute blonde woman approaches and holds her hands out to Cal. "Let me put him down for a nap, so he'll be happy for dinner."

Gibson goes to her quite willingly. "Stowee."

"I brought your book, buddy," she says into his hair, and he weaves his fingers into hers.

"Before you go, Ari, this is Melody Tanner, the paramedic that saved Sammy, the one that was on the beach. Melody, this is my wife, Ari. And her sister Vi is around here somewhere too."

"Nice to finally meet you, Melody." She squeezes my shoulder.

"Please, call me Mel. Everyone does."

She nods and pats Gibson's back. "I'll be back down in a bit." She takes the adorable little boy upstairs with her, Cal's gaze never leaving her until she's out of view.

"Found him." Killian returns from the hallway with Sampson following. Sam's slightly out of breath, his black t-shit tight around his forearms. He's got drumsticks in one hand that he slips in his back pocket. Good to know that old habits die hard. His face is dark for a moment before he slips on an easygoing expression like a mask.

"Hey." He nods to Clance and Sof. "Good to see you guys. Sorry I lost track of time downstairs." He lifts his shoulders.

I'm hit by a memory from back when he was my Sampson.

*"I want to kiss you, for reals this time." Sammy's bright blue eyes meet mine, his dark lashes fanning down on his cheeks as they redden. His hair in damp ringlets not quite to his shoulders. Him leaning in. His lips.*

I shake the memory away.

He seeks me out. "Hey, Mel." His smile to me is soft, but

there's a stiff awkwardness in it and I can't tell if it's something on my end or his.

"Hi." I give him a little wave from where I sit next to Cal on the couch. "Thank you for having us over."

Sampson gives a little shrug, indicating that it's no big deal. "It's Mav's house. He's the one you should be thanking."

*Ouch.* So, he doesn't want me here. Rejected again, just like our first kiss way back in high school. I stiffen and look over at Mavrick.

"You have a beautiful home. Thank you for inviting us." I set my hands in my lap and concentrate on not fiddling with my rings as Mavrick says something to me about being welcome in his home anytime as he hands me my diet soda. There's a slight sharpness at the end of whatever he said that causes me to look up in time to see him send a look in Sampson's direction that doesn't seem to hit its intended mark.

Sampson's aloofness surprises me and puts me on edge. He seemed to want to see me again at the ceremony. He mentioned wanting to catch up. But now he's cold and distant. I knew we shouldn't have come. I don't belong in his life anymore. I probably never did, and the grandness of this house doesn't help matters. It only reminds me that I do not belong in his world anymore.

Mavrick subtly kicks Sampson's foot on his way over to me. Sitting between me and Cal, he looks over at me. "It's the least we can do. So, tell us about you, Mel."

Ari returns from downstairs and sits on the arm of the couch near Cal, who puts his arm around her.

"I'm not that interesting. I'm a paramedic. I run on my days off. I like to read." These are things they already know, but I can't think of anything that a rock star would find interesting about me. I'm pretty boring overall. I shrug a little. "Is there something specific you want to know?"

"Yeah," Killian says from his perch at the breakfast bar. "How did you learn to do that, you know, CPR?"

"It's all part of paramedic training. You learn a lot of life-saving techniques. Paramedics train even longer than EMTs. But anyone can learn CPR. As a matter of fact, I give classes on CPR and first aid a couple of times a month on my days off." I won't go there with virtual strangers. It's too much to give them the real reason I'm a paramedic, and why I'm passionate about getting others trained in CPR and first aid.

Cal perks up at that little tidbit of information. "You mean like we could hire you to teach us? All of the band, wives, and our security people? I think it'd be a great idea."

I nod. "Absolutely. Let me check my shift schedule tomorrow and I'll be happy to throw some dates out for you guys. We can do it here if you'd like. I can bring the equipment we need. It's something I'm very passionate about. Anyone can make a difference before paramedics arrive."

Cal and Mav chat about it, then come back to me. "Please let us know. This whole thing has been kind of a wake-up call. Two of us are parents now. It'd be nice to have that in our tool belts. Just in case." Mav definitely seems to be on board with it too, as he nods vigorously.

Killian looks skeptical and Sampson is just sitting there, knee bouncing and biting at his finger like he can't wait for the whole ordeal of us being here to be over and he can go back to doing whatever he was doing before we got here.

Any grand delusions I had earlier of a reunion with Sampson have most definitely been squashed, but it would be nice if he'd show at least a little excitement to see me. He seemed excited back at the awards celebration. If he'd acted this way at the ceremony, I wouldn't have agreed to come. It makes me wonder what the difference is between then and now. The only thing I can think of is that maybe he was worried about how it would look if he just dismissed me at the ceremony, since all the media were there.

Mav moves things out onto the patio as they start to grill in the outdoor kitchen. The patio has an amazing infinity pool and what looks like a private staircase down to the beach. But the view of the coastline from the patio is beautiful and the scent of the salty air relaxes me.

The band members all interact with each other and work to incorporate us into their conversation. Except for Sampson. I want to pull him aside and ask him if he'd rather I left. It's so obvious that he's purposely avoiding me. I'm embarrassed to be here. Any time I work my way towards him, he moves away. I eventually break away and catch Kady to have her point me in the direction of the restroom before dinner.

On my way back out to the patio, I stop in my tracks when I hear voices. "What the hell is going on with you? This was *your* idea, Sammy. And now you want nothing to do with your own guest." Mav's voice is a harsh whisper. "You haven't said anything to her beyond 'Hey.' You're never such an ass. Ever. So, what gives?"

I stop and eavesdrop because I can't just walk out there; it's the only way back to the patio. And now I want to know the answer too. I don't know Sampson as a man. I knew him as a teenager. I'm curious too, but sadly, I can't make out Sammy's response, just a low grumble.

"You're worrying me, man. This isn't like you at all."

There's a cry from upstairs, so I back down the hall a bit so it will look like I'm just coming from the bathroom in case whomever goes upstairs catches sight of me.

Kady catches me in the hall and smiles at me brightly. "Want to go up to get Brio and Gibson with me?"

"Sure. But I have to warn you, I don't think Gibson's too sure of me yet."

Kady giggles as we walk right past Mav and Sampson, who

regard us quietly as we continue up the stairs. "Don't worry. He'll warm up to you. You can carry Brio. He's in an 'I love everyone' stage right now."

Turns out when Gibson wakes up, he too is in an 'I love everyone stage' and that includes me. He takes me by the hand and motions for me to sit on the floor and then goes over to a bag of toys that I assume are his. He pulls out each toy and shows it to me, while Kady changes Brio.

"Twuck. Cow. Mooo. Pig. Oink. Daddy's twuck." He hands me the plastic cow and looks at me with big expectant eyes.

"Mooo?" I'm not sure that's what he wants to hear, but I must have been right because his eyes light up and he nods his head.

"I think you've made a new friend, Gibs. Go show her to your dad." Kady winks at me as Gibson holds my hand and walks me through the house, out onto the patio and right to his dad, who's standing near an outdoor bar with Killian.

But what's caught my eye since returning from upstairs is that Clance is with Sampson. Mav is standing between the two of them on the other side of the Slater's infinity pool. Clance appears to have his chest puffed out in defense and Sof is looking on, fiddling with her straw as she sits on the edge of a chair, looking like she's about ready to jump up. Mav says something and both Clance and Sampson look at me. Sampson steps back, kind of behind Mav, and Clance smiles at me. But his jaw is still tense.

"Daddy. Wook. My fend, Mail," Gibson announces, looking up at his dad, uncle, and Sampson. His chubby hand pats my leg.

Callum grins at me and picks up his son. "Did you make a new friend, bud?" Gibson nods with a serious expression.

"Fend. Mail my fend." He reaches over and pats me on the shoulder this time.

Killian grins at me too, but Sam just regards me with the same coolness he has since I arrived.

"Mail sim?" He looks up at his dad and then side eyes me.

"No swimming today, bud. I'm sure Mel doesn't have a suit with her. Maybe another time." Cal looks at me. "He's half fish this one, thanks to Sam. It's one of the reasons I think training us in CPR would be a good thing. I've had nightmares about him falling into our pool at home since he was born."

"I'd be happy to train anyone who's interested. Just get me a head count so I can make sure to bring enough equipment."

"Time to eat, guys." Mav calls us all to the table. There are burgers, hot dogs, potato salad, green salad, and condiments galore. I sit between Clance and Ari. We eat and talk. Well, they talk. The conversation is driven by Mav and Cal, with occasional comments from Killian or exclamations from Gibson. Sammy, who's sitting as far from me as possible, is quiet and has said nothing for the entire meal.

"This is delicious. Thank you," I say to Mav, who seems to be the unwitting host of this whole thing. I assume that Sampson wanted him to host so he didn't have to divulge his address, because he's that worried I'll want to be part of his life again.

"Honestly, it's the least we could do," Mav says, looking at me. Clance grabs my leg and squeezes it. Sampson remains mute, which earns him a glare from Mav. As interesting as this has been, I really want to leave. My head gives a dull thud, reminding me that I am not good at small talk and the stress of the day is catching up to me.

"Don't forget, Ari brought cupcakes for dessert," Kady announces as our meal is winding up.

"Oh, none for me. I'm so full." My announcement surprises Clance, who gives me a WTF look, but thankfully says nothing. He knows I'd normally never look a free dessert in the mouth. Not without putting it in my mouth. I give a small smile.

"I'll give you some to go," Ari says as she lays out a plate of cupcakes. Sampson is the first to lean over and grab one, shoving half of it into his mouth.

"Speaking of going, I really should go. I'm on shift tomorrow." I stand, and Clance and Sof follow suit. We say our goodbyes. Gibson seems bereft that I'm leaving now that we've become best friends. I give him a little hug and rustle the hair on his head. I probably won't be seeing him again. But he's so cute. "Thank you again. It really wasn't necessary, but it was nice of you to go through all this just for me."

Mav, Kady, and Cal follow us out to the limo that is still waiting. They each give me a hug. "We'll be in contact about the class." I nod, but I'm not sure that the class is such a good idea or if it's just empty platitudes.

"Wait." Ari comes jogging down the walkway with a pink bakery box in hand. "These are for you guys. I always buy way too many because Sammy usually eats a ton of them."

"Thanks." I take the box from her.

We hop into the limo and start our drive home.

"Do you guys want these?" I motion to the box of cupcakes.

"Nah, you should enjoy them." Sof reaches over and squeezes my arm.

"I'll take them to the firehouse tomorrow. Those guys will eat anything." I set them on the seat beside me. "I dunno what's wrong with me today, but I'm exhausted. Guess maybe the nerves from the ceremony are catching up to me." I lean my head back and shut my eyes.

I don't sleep, though. No, I think about Sampson. The Sampson at the ceremony was so different than the Sampson at the house. There can be only one answer. *Me.* He probably planned the dinner before realizing that I was the one who saved him. It's me. It's always been me. I've never been good enough for him. I wasn't back in high school and obviously not now. Either that or it was because there was media milling about and he wanted to come off looking good.

When the limo pulls up outside of my building, I have to stop myself from running up to my apartment and just throwing myself on my bed. Instead, I hug Clance and Sof and thank them for going with me. For spending the day with me.

"Text me tomorrow," Sof calls as Clance leads her over to his truck. When they get to the truck, Clance turns and waves, and when I turn my back, I know he watches until I'm into the residence's door. Because that's just how Clance is.

# Chapter 8

## *Sammy*

I really fucked up. Again. What makes it worse is that it was with Mel. Again. *My Mel.* Well, not really *my* Mel anymore, and with how I treated her tonight, that pretty much solidified me in the asshole hall of fame. With that comes knowing that she has no reason to even give me a second thought.

I roll over again in the bed in Cal's guest room, but I know I won't get to sleep tonight. Part of me wants to get dressed, get in my Jeep and head to the beach. That's what I'd normally do if I was upset like this. But with how I freaked out at the beach yesterday with Kill and Gibs, that's a no go. What if it happens again and no one's there to talk me down?

"Fuck." I reach over to the nightstand and pull off my drumsticks and beat a quiet rhythm on the mattress in the dark. It's not as satisfying as full-on drumming, so I try hitting the bed a little harder. I don't want to wake up Gibson across the hall, but I need to move. This lightly drumming in the mattress isn't doing anything for me. I need to pound my drums. Hard.

"Dammit." I get up and pull on some sweats. Not wanting to wake up anyone, I make my way quietly downstairs, standing in the hall and debating with myself... gym, or music room? Either could be satisfying. I turn right into the music room, making sure I close the door before I flip on the light.

I make my way to the stool and just start pounding. I'm not playing anything specific. I'm just drumming for the sake of hitting the skins, needing the physical release drumming gives me. I drum hard and fast, trying to shake out the demons from my head. And soon there's nothing in my brain but the beats. There's no Mel, no panic attacks, and no looks of pity. Nothing but the physicality of working the set over and over and over until everything blanks the fuck out.

# R

"FOUND HIM. AGAIN." Killian's loud voice wakes me up. I rub my hand down my face without opening my eyes. When I finally open them, I'm on the couch in Cal's music room and Kill's looking down at me. I don't remember moving from the kit over to the couch. But at some point, I must've because here I am. The shirt I was wearing is flung over the back of the couch as I lay here shirtless.

"You keep disappearing and every time I go looking, you're in someone's music room. Last night it was Mav's, today it's Cal's. Why'd you come down here when you've got one of the best beds on the market upstairs? You know Cal, there are two things he doesn't cheap out on, beds and Gibson."

Killian sits cross-legged on the floor of the room close to the couch. "Late night drumming?"

"Late night, early morning." I pull my shoulders up in a shrug.

"It's how you work shit out." Shrugging, he looks me over. "What's going on with you? You're not yourself. Talk to me, Sam."

I sigh and look at the ceiling over me. How can I talk to Kill about it when I don't know what *it* is? I'm all mixed up. I want to tell him about seeing Sev and about being scared in the only place I've ever felt peace that wasn't behind a kit.

Cal pops the door open and peers in at us. I'm still lying on the couch. His brow pulls together. "You okay?"

I roll up to a sitting position and shrug. "Okay is relative."

"Ar's made you fools breakfast. You need to come eat it and thank her for making it." He leans against the door, arms crossed over his chest, just watching us, me mostly.

"'Mon, Shammy. Bekfist time." Gibson comes running in under Cal's arm that's propped on the open door. He's not allowed in the music room, so he looks around for something to get into, his eyes sparkling with mischief as they land on my drum kit.

"Hold up. He's interested in my kit." I pick him up and set him on my lap as I sit on my stool. I carefully place a set of drumsticks in his hands and lightly grip them, my hands carefully over his.

"Okay, let's start off with just the snare drum. Okay, bud?" He nods like he understands what I'm saying. I tap out a rhythm with right, right, left, right. Right, right, left, right. He bobs his head while doing it. Concentrating, his tongue pokes out between his lips, just like his father's does when he's song-writing.

"That's it, buddy, you're doing it," I encourage him as I let go and move my hands to ruffle his hair and he keeps the beat going all on his own.

He nods, his head bobbing up and down with the beat. "Doin' it."

I look up at Cal. "Dude, your kid's a freakin' drummer." I can't help the grin that feels like it might split my face. My first genuine grin since I saw Melody at the ceremony.

Killian nods his head along with the beat Gibson's drumming out on my kit. It's a little slow, just a tick off, but fuck if he's not drumming it out pretty good. He's a damn natural and why wouldn't he be. He's been around music making since he was born.

Ari slips into the room, hooking her arm around Cal's waist as Gibs continues to push the beat. He finally stops.

"Did it!" He looks up at me and smiles. I hug him to me.

"You certainly did. You're a drummer, just like me."

He nods. "I dummer like Shammy."

Killian explodes in laughter at his nephew's mispronunciation. "If that ain't the truth."

Cal playfully punches Killian in the gut. "That's my kid you're talking about."

"Actually, I was talking about Sammy. Gibs is only three. He has plenty of time to learn." Killian snorts and then starts laughing again, a quiet laugh that rolls through his whole body.

Gibs slips off my lap, keeping my drumsticks as he runs off. "Bekfist time! So hungwy."

We follow. He climbs up into his chair and sits on his knees as we sit around him and eat the breakfast Ari made. It might be slightly cold but it's so good. She's a good cook.

"Thanks for breakfast. I'm going to head out for a little while. I need to pick up some things. Including a child's drum set." I shovel the last of my pancakes into my mouth.

"Sammy, you don't—"

"He's three, Cal. Three." I hold up three fingers to accentuate my point as I swallow down the last bits of pancake. "And he pretty much held the beat after I let go. That's the first time he's ever sat at a drum that I know of, and he held the fuckin' beat, at three years old." I've always loved Gibs. He's amazing and I love watching him grow and learn and God, do I love my little chats with him.

I don't think Cal realizes his kid might be some sort of musical genius. I don't know much about kids and musical ability at three, but that was freaking awesome. How could I not encourage that? Fuck, I'd buy him a full-size kit if I thought he'd fit into it. If I thought Cal'd let him play it. I know they make real, small-scale kits for children and Gibson's getting one. And I'll happily sit with him any time he wants and help him learn.

"Sammy, you spoil him," Ari says, wrapping her arms around me in a quick hug.

"I'm supporting him; there's a difference. He's genuinely interested in drums. Of all the instruments in that room to choose from, he picked my drums. Fuck, I'll support that all week long." I shrug as I wipe my mouth. "Anyway, thanks for breakfast. I'm going to head out for a bit." I stand.

"You want company?" Killian stands when I do and picks up his plate to carry into the kitchen.

"If you wanna come, you can. But I'm leaving now." He sets his plate in the sink and joins me at the door.

We take my Jeep.

Killian chuckles. "I don't think Cal's too keen on you getting Gibs a drum kit."

"I don't care. He's getting a kit. That kid has talent already, Kill, you saw him. I mean, Cal's his dad, so it's not a surprise. But why not foster it instead of squelch it?"

Kill nods. "It was amazing to see him keep time like that." He shakes his head. "He's lucky to have you as an uncle, Sam. We are all lucky you're in our lives." He pats my leg. "You know that, right? We all love you."

I nod. Kill's been unusually touchy-feely lately. It started right around the time that Cal got engaged. But it's been even more so since the surfing accident. I came away with an intense fear of water and he came away with an intense fear of loss.

"Ever since the accident, you're different. I'm more than a little worried about you, Sam. Of all of us, you've always been the easiest going. But you seem really uptight lately. No, not uptight. Just different. Anxious. Nervous. Snappy and even angry sometimes. I mean, you fell asleep in Cal's music room. I know you hit the drums all night. We all know it's how you work your shit out." He pauses and looks out the window as the Hollywood Hills turns into downtown Los Angeles.

"I have trouble sleeping too," he sighs. "I keep seeing you on the beach." He shakes his head. "If you need someone to play with or just talk to, I'm here. Just send me a text and I'll meet you down in the music room or wherever." I feel him eyeing me.

I swallow the lump in my throat. "'Preciate it. I'll probably take you up on that at some point."

There's an easy quiet between us as I continue our drive down to Sunset.

"I was a jackass yesterday to Mel," I admit to him.

"Yeah, you really were. You hurt her feelings. That Clance guy wasn't thrilled with you, man. He's like her brother. I thought I was going to have to jump in between you, and I wasn't looking forward to it because that dude is big."

I nod, remembering the angry tone of Clance's voice when he demanded to know what my problem was at the barbecue. "I have a history of doing that with her, hurting her."

"So you do know her." He turns in his seat to face me.

I nod and don't take my eyes off the road. "We went to high school together. Started off as friends. Then were more than friends. Then I left to join the Rebels. I cut off contact with her. It was stupid because I've always lo — uh, liked her." I sigh. "Always wondered what happened to her. Seems like she's done well for herself. I never pictured her as a paramedic. Although back then I didn't picture her as anything but my girl." I shrug. "Until she wasn't."

"And what about now?" Kill's eyes pierce me with their unrelenting gaze.

"What about now? I doubt she wants anything to do with me now." I chuckle, but there's nothing humorous in it. I treated her like crap yesterday. She won't want to give me the time of day. Nor should she.

"Do you want anything to do with her?"

I don't answer him. I want *everything* to do with her. She's my Mel. But I lost that right when I left her with her shitty mother. I knew she wouldn't be destitute like Sev and I basically were. Her mom, at least, kept her in groceries. It was attention and love that Mel lacked. I should have brought her with me. But I could barely keep myself and Sev fed and a roof over our heads with the band as my roommates. Adding Mel to that would have brought us down even further.

Even after success finally started rolling into my bank account, I sunk most of it into trying to get and keep Sevenya clean. And truth be told, I'd do it all over again if I thought I might save Sev. I miss her. But it doesn't mean that I didn't miss Mel and feel guilty as fuck leaving her with that piece of work mom of hers. That lady was cruel to Mel. I don't know if it's just how girls are with their mom, but she never really seemed to stand up to her mom either. Not that I saw. Instead, Mel seemed to just shrink in every time her mom cut her down. I came in twice on her mom being physically abusive to her. It got me wondering what was worse, a mom who was so addicted to pills that she left her children destitute and hungry or a mom like Mel had. Sure, Mel was provided for and had all her needs taken care of, but that woman was cruel and mean. I'd stepped between Mel and her mom twice. And I don't regret doing it in the least. Someone had to show Mel she mattered. I can't even think about what it was like for her after I left with Sev or how long she stayed living at her Mom's.

Pulling up in front of the Rock Shop brings me back from being all in my head. I've done business here since high school. I haven't been here in probably a year, maybe even more. I hope Chuck is in. He owns this place and I prefer to work with him because he keeps me grounded. He remembers where I came from.

I flip my sunglasses onto my head as we walk into the darkened shop. It smells like varnish, beeswax, and maple in here, like home. I glance at the counter and there's some teen working. My eyes work the back of the shop and I see Chuck talking with a client. He glances my way and I give him a chin lift as Kill and I walk further into the store.

"Well, lookie here, damned if we aren't graced by one the greatest rock drummers of our time. Sammy Denton as I live and fuckin' breathe," Chuck calls out as he approaches us. "How the fuck are you, man?" He reaches a big hand out and I slap mine into it as he pulls me in for a quick bro hug.

"You know how it is," I mumble into his shoulder. "You've met our bassist Killian before, right?" I move aside as Chuck repeats his man hug with Killian.

"What can I do you for guys today?" We walk back towards the starter kits.

"I need a youth kit. Standard, maybe a little extra. Double bass if you have one. Sticks in several sizes. Adjustable stool, but I need it to start off real low, the kit too."

"There isn't a premade youth kit like that, Sam, not with a double bass, but fuck, for you, I'll make you one myself. I can have it ready in a few days. What age range am I looking at?"

"He's just starting. He's three." Chuck's eyes widen. "Sat him on my lap today behind my kit and just showed him some basic shit. And he fuckin' kept time." I shake my head, still not believing little Gibs taking over the sticks.

"You have a three-year-old?" Chuck looks at me in surprise.

I shake my head and laugh. "No and thank fuck for that. I can barely keep myself alive. It's Cal's kid. I think he might be a drumming genius or some shit. And Uncle Sammy's going to support the hell out of that, whether Cal likes it or not."

Chuck laughs a high-pitched giggle, one that tells me he's

tickled with my determination to get Gibs a kit, much to his father's chagrin. "You got it, man. Like I said, give me a couple of days and I'll throw it together for you. Anything specific?"

"Give him my cymbal set up for now. A pair of small noise-canceling earmuffs in green. Make them the best quality out there. I think he has a pair for when we're on tour, but they're probably packed away and I don't want to give Cal an excuse to say no. Oh, and if you can manage to make the kit green too, that'd be perfect." Chuck takes notes on his sales write up sheet, nodding with everything I say.

I spend a couple more minutes just shootin' the shit with Chuck, Killian, and the teenager behind the counter, whose name is Calvin. He's a cool kid. I take a selfie with him so his friends will believe he actually met me. Being recognized still tickles the fuck out of me. That someone would want their friends to know they met me... it's still kind of surreal, even after all this time.

I shake my head as we walk out of the Rock Shop and Kill throws his arm around my shoulder. "You're the coolest guy I know, Sam. You made that kid's fuckin' month, I think."

I shrug my shoulders and pull away. "It was no big deal."

"To you, it's no big deal. To that Calvin kid, it's a huge freakin' deal. He had that picture texted out to all his friends before we left the store. That you took some time to actually just talk to him. That's the shit to that kid."

We get into the Jeep and before he's even buckled in, Kill turns to me and rubs his hands together. "So now that that's out of the way, how are we going to fix things with Melody?"

I sigh. Do I want to fix things with Melody? Hell yes. I'd love to have her in my life again, even if it's just as a friend. Do I think things are fixable between Mel and me? No, not really. I frown at the thought. It makes my chest hurt that I've left things like this between us a second fucking time. But I'm not going to tell Kill that.

"Come on, buddy. You can do it." Kill winks at me as he throws my own words to Gibson back at me. "Let's go to the Burger Shack and plot out how to fix this. It'll make you feel better. And keeps us out of Cal's overprotective shadow just a little longer. You'll feel better after some onion rings."

Kill was right. I do feel better after the onion rings, burger, and chocolate shake that I'm still nursing as I tip back on the back two legs of my chair. We're eating in the private dining room and are the only two back here. It helps that Mav's on the in with the owner. We can pretty much eat here whenever and not have to worry about interruptions.

"Back on track, man. Melody. You were an ass to her yesterday. We need to fix it." Kill pops the last of his bacon cheese fries into his mouth, closing his eyes for a second as he enjoys it. If Cal saw him eating those, he'd throttle him, and then throttle me for bringing him here.

Ever since Kill's heart issue, Cal's been all over him to eat better, exercise more, and just be more like Cal. Even though his doctor specifically told them it was most likely due to a side effect from the medication he was given at the hospital, and he has no damage to his heart.

Cal's super overprotectiveness has been getting on both our nerves. I'm surprised he didn't insist on coming with us today, since he often doesn't let either of us out of his damn sight for very long.

"So, Mel." He settles his dark blue eyes on mine. "What does she like? How can we get you back in the good with her? Come on, you're Sammy Fuckin' Denton, man. You've got to get the girl."

"I don't know. I'm not sure how to navigate a grown-up Mel. I know high school Mel, and she's obviously changed a shit ton since then. I wouldn't even know where to start." My sigh is heavy at the thought. I used to know Mel better than anyone, and it's hard to admit that I don't know who she is anymore.

Kill shoots me a cocky smirk as he pulls out his phone. "Luckily, I know someone who does."

He starts typing on his phone and shows me the screen.

*Kill: Hey. It was great meeting you yesterday. I happen to know a jackass drummer who wants to apologize to a certain paramedic you may know (not your husband). Any specifics you can give us for preferences would be greatly appreciated. Thanks a ton, Sofie. BTW this is Killian.*

# Chapter 9

## *Melody*

The grime of a hard shift is still imbedded in my skin and the scent of charred flesh is not a perfume I want to wear any longer than I have to. It's the worst smell associated with being a fire paramedic. An injured firefighter and a severely burned patient on the same fire call, it was an intense and hot scene. After treating the burned patient towards the middle of my shift, the scent is still so thick on me I can almost taste it, despite changing into my back up uniform at the house.

Then, of course, there were the other calls. A dead infant, probably due to SIDS, and the anguished howl of his mom still ringing in my ears. A three-vehicle accident with transporting injuries, one that required coordination with a heli-evac. A drug OD and two people who were too drunk to take care of themselves and required rides to the hospital so they could be supervised while they dried out. Two gunshot victims, one that was DOA, the other was a twelve-year-old girl caught in the crossfire.

It was a shitty shift with the calls timed, so I couldn't even grab a satisfying nap in one of the bunks at any point, so my bones ache with exhaustion.

Shower and sleep are the only things I need right now. Although maybe a snack too. That's it. Shower. Snack. Sleep. In that order. I'm ready to close my blackout curtains and just slumber.

When I head down my hall, I find a pink pastry box sitting on my welcome mat. If there are brownies or cupcakes in that box, I am kissing Clance or Sof, whichever left me the gift. Probably Clance, since I know he listens to our radio even when he's not on call. He'd know it was one of *those* kind of days.

I scoop up the box and head into my apartment, eager to sample whatever's inside. I set the box on the breakfast bar and pop it open to find a note scrawled in blue ink in a handwriting I recognize but haven't seen in a decade on the underside of the lid.

*Mel- Stopped by with a peace offering. Guess I missed you. Enjoy these treats. I'm sorry for being an asshole. Let me apologize in person. Call me 555-726-7766. (heart) Sam*

*PS. Mrs. Chamske thinks you hang the moon. I had to borrow this pen from her. Also sorry for eating one of the brownies. I tried to wait for you and got hungry (Smiley face with tongue hanging out).*

In the box are four different cupcakes, four huge chocolate covered strawberries and three brownies. All from my favorite bakery, Angelina's, down in Venice. Did he somehow find out I love Angelina's, or was it a coincidence? Maybe he lives in Venice. After all, that's where he was surfing.

I don't know how he's figured out where I live. Sofie's doing, no doubt. Not sure how I feel knowing Sampson knows where I live now.

I shove one of the strawberries in my mouth, then shower away my shift. I want one of the cupcakes, but I also want sleep.

Since the bed is closer to the bathroom than the pastry box, I choose sleep.

*Sammy and I are wrapped together in a blanket, me between his legs, his strong arms wrapped around my front. His stubbly chin is on my bare shoulder, him holding the blanket closed around us. We're both quiet, just watching the waves roll in at our spot. The sun is low on the horizon, casting long shadows across the small, secluded section of beach we've claimed as our own. The breeze is cool and we're both still damp from bodyboarding, so we huddle together to warm up. But let's be honest. I love the comfort of his warmth against me. The safety of arms enveloping me. Especially today. Especially after last night.*

*My mom was in a stellar mood when I came in from my date with Sampson yesterday.*

*"Off whoring yourself out to that long-haired miscreant again, Melody?" The words were out of her mouth before I had even had a chance to set my backpack down.*

*"No one will want to buy the cow when you give the milk away for free. And in case you're too dumb to understand, you're the cow, Melody."*

*I move through the living room quickly, my hands gripping so tightly around the straps to my backpack that they hurt.*

*"Don't you walk away from me when I'm talking to you." She grips my shoulder hard and spins me so fast, the weight of my backpack unbalances me until I let it slide off onto the floor. Smack. My cheek burns and tingles. The slap was such a surprise that I bit my tongue and my feel the blood in my mouth. I can't help but wince. She usually doesn't hit me where it will show, so I'm stunned.*

*"You're just like him. Just like you fath... er." She gasps as she grabs me around the neck and struggles to get me to the ground. I struggle to stand upright, but she's taller than me and has the advantage. Soon, I'm flat on my back as she straddles me, continuing to pound me in the stomach, screeching her hatred for my father dying as she goes. It hurts, and my stomach tightens and churns trying to*

*protect itself. But it's too much, and I turn my head and vomit up the dinner I had with Sampson all over the hardwood floor.*

*She finally rolls off me, getting up with one last push to my abdomen. "Clean that shit up before you go to bed. I don't want to see your face until tomorrow.*

*He leans closer to my ear, the soft scrape of his stubble bringing me back to the beach, in the safety of his arms. "Someday, we'll have a beach house of our very own." He pulls me into him tighter and his banana-scented sunscreen mixes with the surf. It's a comforting scent and what I imagine a normal home is like. I snuggle into him tighter.*

*His breath warm and damp on my ear, he whispers, "I want to kiss you, Mel. For reals this time."*

"Mel?" There's a rhythmic pounding that I can't place.

"Mel? It's me. Sammy, uh Sampson. I know you're pissed, and I deserve that. I do. Can I come in just for a minute so we can talk? Please, Mel? Let me in."

It takes me a second to orientate myself, but I'm in my room. I grab my phone and see it's just after three in the afternoon. Shit, I've been asleep for almost six hours. Sadly, I probably could have slept another three, except for the sound of drumsticks tapping out an annoying beat on my door. It's a sound I'm more than familiar with.

"Mel?" He taps a few more times. I get up and grab some sweatpants as I head towards the door.

I curse So for slipping Sampson my address.

When I open the door, he's not there. I peek down the hallway to see him walking down the hall, about to turn the corner to the stairs, drumsticks tucked in the back pocket of his dark jeans. I guess some things never change.

"Sampson?" I've always called him Sampson, and I'm not stopping now just because the world knows him as Sammy.

He turns and a huge smile, the smile from our childhood, the one that shows off that one dimple in his cheek, spreads slowly across his face. My traitorous heart sputters at the sight of that smile. It used to make any day better. Now it breaks my heart a little bit more because I can't call it mine anymore. Because I wasn't good enough for Sampson. I sigh a shuttered breath.

"Mel! I thought I missed you. Again." He trots back towards my door.

"Yeah, sorry. I was asleep." I'm sure he can tell because my hair feels like it could be advertising special move-in rates for birds. I don't even bother to try to pat it down.

His lips pull down in a frown and his brow wrinkles as he looks me over. "Oh. You feelin' okay?"

I nod. "Yeah. Well, just a little tired. It comes from working twenty-four-hour shifts. I got home about 9 this morning."

"Oh, shit. I didn't think about that." He slaps his hand to his forehead. "I can come back later or another day or whatever." He backs up from the door like he's about to head back down the hall.

"I'm awake now." I pull my door open and motion that he should come on in.

"Thanks, Mel." He walks into my apartment tentatively and shoves his hands into his pockets.

As I watch him take in my place, I try to see it as Sampson would it. It's a one-room studio, but it's generous for that. The building was newly remodeled when I moved in. The bed in the right corner is cordoned off with a couple of decorative dressing screens. If he could see the bed, he'd find it unmade, since he did just wake me up. There's a good size bathroom near the bedroom area and there is a small walk-in closet on the other side of it.

The living area is sparse. A small TV that I almost never turn on sits on the wall, a gift from Clance and Sof when I moved in. The couch is a very comfortable brown leather over-stuffed one, also from Clance and Sof, a cast-off from when remodeled their place last year. There's a soft fleece throw blanket over the back that I change out depending on the season. A small glass coffee table sits in front.

The kitchen area is small and tidy, but the breakfast bar contains the pastry box he left on my stoop.

My place is small and plain. Nothing like the palatial ocean-side mansions that Sampson's probably used to.

"Have a seat. Do you want a cup of coffee?" He shakes his head. I shrug. "It's no big deal. I'm having one."

"Nah, I don't like coffee that isn't sugared up until it no longer resembles coffee. Like a caramel frappe with extra, extra caramel and light on the coffee." He smiles at me and then shrugs those strong-looking shoulders. "I guess I never developed a taste for it."

He slides onto one of the barstools at my breakfast bar and I turn my back to him as I slide a coffee pod into the machine and select my favorite mug, a blue one that says 'professional badass' on it. A gift from our firehouse's secret Santa exchange last year.

The pastry box rustles as Sampson helps himself to the bakery yummies he left me.

"Yeah, well, I don't love it for the taste. I love it for the caffeine." I turn after the coffee's done brewing to see him chewing the last remnants of a brownie. I lean against the counter behind me.

"Why are you here, Sampson?" I pull my mug to my lips and blow slightly over the scalding liquid before I take a long sip. He shifts on his barstool and doesn't make eye contact.

"I was rude to you at Mav's the other evening. I didn't mean to be, Mel." He picks at the chocolate on one of the strawberries in the pastry box.

I shrug. "It doesn't really matter, Sampson." And it doesn't. I was stupid to think he might want to be part of my life again. *Childish dreams.* The invitation was all for show in front of the media, who were no doubt milling around hoping to catch a piece of gossip. Sadly, with Sampson's fame comes the fact that the walls will always have ears.

His head snaps up to look at me. "It matters to me. It was rude to invite you over, then ignore you. I'm not that person."

"Actually, you're exactly that person, Sampson. You walked out of my life and never looked back. I consider that a big ignore. I waited for you to come back for me, and you didn't, so I've moved on. I'm not the same little Mel that you remember." His body hunkers down on itself, and he won't meet my gaze.

"I'm glad you have the band and your success. I know you worked hard to get where you are." I shake my head and try to stay the course and not let years of hurt fester into the hate that's boiling in me, almost ready to erupt. "It was nice to see you again. I consider the cupcakes your apology or whatever you needed to get out of this." I wave my arms between us. "Maybe I'll see you around in another decade, Sam." I enunciate the last letter of his name with a pop as I push off the counter.

His face pulls down with his frown. "Wait, Mel, that's—"

"Exactly how this ends. Goodbye, Sam. Sampson." I walk over to the door and hold it open.

He shoves his hands into his pockets and hangs his head as he shuffles towards the door. Hitting the threshold, he turns and looks up at me with those blue eyes of his. "I wanted to fix things between us," he says quietly.

"There's nothing to fix. Maybe you should have tried that, I dunno, ten or eleven years ago. I've moved on and accepted that our relationship wasn't what I thought it was."

He looks at me like I kicked his puppy. My heart clenches as he turns and retreats down the hall, making me almost call after him. Almost.

That night I dream of Denise. I haven't dreamed about her in a while. It wasn't so much of a dream as it was memories of that night back in college playing on repeat while I tried to sleep. Flashes of the frat party. Of being so sloppy drunk. Of finding her the next morning in our bathroom. Of the vacant look in her eyes that told me she was already gone. That I was too late.

I'll never be too late again.

# Chapter 10

## *Sammy*

I don't know what I expected when I went to see Mel, but being kicked out on my ass wasn't it. I get in my Jeep and drive to a vista point out by the ocean. Usually when I'm bummed out like this, I go down to the beach. Most often, that means heading to the beach Mel and I found back in high school. *Our spot.* Each time I'm anywhere near the water now though, it's the same fucking thing. It used to be my favorite place. It still is my favorite place. But my brain and body don't seem to understand that anymore.

Sitting on the bumper way up here, where I can see the water from afar, is not the same. I only faintly smell the salty air. Barely hear the roar of the ocean. There's no peace settling into me and releasing all the tension in my body. There are no feelings of home. The beach used to bring that, but now it causes the tensions already building in me to worsen quickly. Fuck. I hate this. I don't know where to go or what to do with myself. I'm all over the place and have no way of bringing the pieces of me back together.

I head for Mav's place, mostly because I'm sick of Cal's overprotective shit and don't think I could stand Kill's disappointment in what happened with Mel. I don't understand his weird, vested interest in what goes on with me and Mel. I don't need that pressure from him on top of everything else. This is even worse than when the band broke up for that year. Back then, I was pulled apart. Team Mav or Team Cal, when all I really wanted was Team Blind Rebels like always.

I enter to the gleeful screeches of Brio and the hideous sounds of a piano being pounded on. Mav never locks the door since he has security and the coded gate. I know I'm always welcome here anytime. Just like at Cal's or Kill's. Although Kill's still staying with Cal for the time being.

I search out the cacophony and find that Brio's sitting with Mav on the floor of the living room, pounding on one of his old keyboards.

"Hey, Sammy. What's up?" Mav lifts his chin at me while keeping his hands supporting Brio, so he doesn't go face first into the keyboard.

"Hey." I flop down on the floor and hit a few of the keys from my side of the keyboard. Brio grins and mimics me by banging his fists on the keys. "I was just in the neighborhood. Thought I'd swing by."

"Bullshit," Mav says.

"Language, babe," Kady calls from somewhere down the main hall. "Hey, Sammy, I'll be out in a few."

"Bull crap," Mav corrects himself.

"That's not any better," Kady calls. "We don't want his first words to be cursing, Mav. Seriously," she huffs, still out of sight.

"Let me guess. Cal's being overprotective and Kill and he are about to go to blows over it and you didn't want to be in the way." His eyes sparkle because he likes knowing he's always right. That's Mav.

"Something like that," I mutter. "Cal's being super controlling of me and Kill both. I just needed out for a while. By myself." Mav nods and encourages Brio to hit the keys some more. He screeches and obliges.

"He really takes after you, huh? With the whole screeching thing?" Mav chucks some sort of soft book at me, and I duck out of the way.

Brio takes this as a sign to throw his toys around and picks up some of his squishy blocks and tosses them around, laughing deep baby belly laughs as he joins in on the fun. It's the kind of laugh that's infectious, even if you're an adult. We all throw a few in the air too and chuckle together.

Kady sits on the couch nearest us and watches the three of us play.

"Mav, it's time for Brio's nap. Put him down for me?" She doesn't have to ask him twice. Mav is up and taking Brio upstairs before I pull myself up off the floor and sit on the couch.

"Hey, Sammy." Kady smiles, but both her body and smile are tight.

I've been so preoccupied with trying to get Mel to forgive me that I almost forgot I was disrespectful to Kady the other day too. Fuck disrespectful, I was downright mean.

Damn, I was in fine form that evening. And if anyone doesn't deserve that kind of treatment, it's Kady. I shake my head slightly at myself, but I think she takes it the wrong way.

"I'm sorry. I shouldn't have come into the bathroom at the party the way that I did. I shouldn't have done that." She looks at her hands and then back up at me.

Fuck me, I was a complete dick to her and yet she's apologizing to me.

"We see things through the lens of our own experiences, but sometimes that clouds what we see. I *assumed* you were having anxiety issues because I have them." She looks up at me and her eyes are watery. "Please don't stay too mad at me. I was just trying to help."

I sigh and reach over and take one of her hands. "Kady, I'm the one who should be apologizing. I shouldn't have been a such a jackass. You were trying to help me. I just..." I glance towards the staircase to make sure Mav's still upstairs. "I keep having these episodes. I don't know if it's anxiety, or I'm just crazy or what, but each episode involved water." I run a hand through my curls. "I've always loved water, but now it seems whenever I go anywhere near it, my brain freaks out and I just need to get away from it as soon as possible." I leave out the fact that I practically hyperventilated in the fucking shower this morning.

I blink my eyes a few times, trying to keep my weird, unexpected tears at bay. "Maybe Kill's right and I suffered brain damage or something. Water used to be my sanctuary, my happy place, my peace. Now I can't get anywhere near it. It makes me an asshole because I feel like I can't go anywhere without worrying about freaking out and making a spectacle of myself again."

I brush the back of my hand across my eyes quickly. "I had to ditch Gibson and Killian and get the fuck off the beach before Mel got there. I was upset and pissed at myself for being weak. It's no excuse for what I said. I'm sorry I snapped at you. You didn't deserve me being shitty to you for my own bullshit." I try to tap down the sob threatening to come out. I'm a fucking mess. "I didn't mean what I said. I didn't. I swear. Please don't hate me."

"Oh, Sammy." Kady throws her arms around me, pulling me to her tight. "That wasn't you talking, it was the anxiety. I could never be mad at you for that. It triggered your fight-or-flight. If anyone gets that, it's me. You *can* learn to work through it with a therapist. That's what helped me anyway." She pulls back. "I can help you find someone to talk to, if you want."

I stiffen at her words and shake my head. "No." My voice sounds weird, even to me. I want to fix this, but not that way.

I can't see a therapist. No way. I'm not crazy. Or am I? Even if I am, I can't be medicated like our mom. Maybe I did injure my brain, and this is Kady's way of trying to tell me I'm not the same anymore. People keep telling me I'm different, not the same, that they're worried about me. What if this is the new me?

"It's nothing to be ashamed of. I've seen a few. One right after the shooting. And one recently, actually. It's helpful to have an unbiased person to talk to sometimes. No one would think any different of you. I promise." She squeezes my shoulders. "It's okay to ask for help, Sammy."

I shake my head. "No. Just no. I don't need it." I stand and walk towards the stairs to Mav's studio.

"I'm gonna hit the skins for a bit." I jog down the stairs and take my place behind the kit. Everything just happens. Even mistakes. Sometimes the mistakes become whole songs in themselves.

There are no windows down here and I don't have a watch or anything because I left my phone upstairs.

It's not until I finally feel the fatigue in my muscles, that I realize I've been drumming on automatic pilot for a while, wondering about Mel. What's gone on with her since I knew her. She's a different person than the girl I left behind. I want to know what's shaped her into the person she is now. Like the whole paramedic thing. It doesn't seem like something high school Mel would have considered as a career. What made her pick that?

I finally start to slow. Today's session was a good burn, a tiredness I've earned. That helps keep the need to flee at bay sometimes, I'm finding.

Someone clears their throat and I look up to Mav leaning against the doorjamb of the control room.

I nearly jump off my stool at the sight. I didn't hear him come down the stairs, that's how wrapped up I've been in getting out all these feelings, emotions, whatever the fuck they are, out in the beats. I wonder how long he's been there watching me come unglued in the only safe way my body understands.

"You've been down here nearly two hours." He tosses me a sports drink. "What are you doing, Sam?"

I twist open the beverage and down about half of it. "Just messin' around." I shrug and then stand up and stretch. "I should probably get back to Cal's before he sends a search party out."

Mav's face pinches and he sighs. "I let him know you were here over an hour ago." He sighs and looks at me with that look. It's part concern, part pity, and it's the pity part that pisses me off. I don't want anything to do with pity. I'm stronger than that. I always have been, but why doesn't anyone else see that in me?

"You know we're here if you need to talk, right? Kady or me. We're both here for you. Whatever you need." He clasps me on the shoulder and squeezes hard. I just want people to leave me alone, but not. It's hard to explain.

When I just nod, his face pinches even tighter. "Cal's worried about you, man. So is Kill and because Kill's worried, Cal's worries even more, you know how his brain works. But the worry is valid. You're not yourself, man. Talk to someone. If not any of us, a therapist or something. We'll help you, no matter what you need." He squeezes again, not as hard this time.

"I'm good." My words come out scratchy and don't sound believable, even to myself. I pull away from Mav and turn to head towards the stairs.

"We love ya, Sammy. You know that. All of us do." His voice

scrapes with concern and is laced with more emotion than normal for Mav. "We just want to help."

I clear my throat and look at my feet for a minute or two. I know he loves me. I know they all do. But I also don't know that I'm fixable right now. And what's more, I don't know if I want to be fixed if it means being medicated. But I do want Mel.

# Chapter 11

## *Melody*

There are so many bouquets in my little studio apartment that it's starting to smell like a floral shop, one with too many different kinds of flowers so your nose can't pick out the individual scents, so it's just one florally smell. And these don't include the ones that keep getting delivered to the firehouse. The ones there are embarrassing.

There's a knock on my door and I open it up to yet another delivery. This one is probably the prettiest of them all; it's a wildflower bouquet. I tip the delivery guy a few bucks and put the newest bouquet on the breakfast bar. Every surface of my house, including the bathroom, has at least one flower arrangement. I can't even see the TV from the couch because they're also on the coffee table. It gives me a headache on the days I stay in.

Sampson has to stop this. I can't believe all these flowers. When I got the first couple, it was endearing that he was trying to apologize with flowers. It reminded me of the Sampson from high school. The boy I was so in love with. I almost called him.

But it's gone from endearing to out of control and reminded me that I don't know rock star Sampson. And the shy boy from high school died in my eyes when he abandoned me, much like everyone else in my life except for Clance and Sof.

As much as I want something with Sampson, being with him is a slippery slope my heart can't risk. The dinner at Mav's reminded me that he tore me to shreds once by leaving and that he could very well do it again. I can't subject myself to that kind of soul-crushing disappointment again.

I pick two of the gaudiest arrangements and walk them across the hall to Mrs. Chamske.

"Thank you, dear, they're so pretty. Can you put them on my table?" She holds the door for me, and I walk them in and put them on her dining room table. Even though I know this building was renovated, her apartment looks like it's something out of the seventies.

"Thank you for sharing. I noticed you've been getting a lot of flowers. That nice young man with the baked goods?" She smiles up at me, her wrinkles multiplying the bigger her smile gets. Her silver hair is perfectly styled, not a hair out of place.

"Yes. He's being ridiculous." I shake my head and fight the urge to sit down with Mrs. Chamske. She's the grandma I never had, and I've gotten sucked into the time warp that is her home on more than one occasion.

"I think he's trying to prove a point." She grabs my arm and squeezes it. "He's being romantic and all that. Just like my Arthur used to be. You should accept his apology."

"Well, I don't know about that."

"I do. Trust me. I've been married three times. Arthur was my last husband. That man could frustrate me to no end. But he always made up for it with flowers. And by being good in the sack." She gives me a shrug, the type that tells me she knows what she's talking about and is willing to throw it out there purely for the shock value.

"Mrs. Chamske!" I about choke on my tongue. One thing I don't want to think about is Mrs. Chamske in the sack, the bed, or in any kind of intimate setting at all. The very thought is burning holes in my brain.

"What, dear?" She looks at me and I can almost see the devil horns holding up her halo in her long silvery hair. "A good sexual relationship is important in a marriage. He'd do this one thing—"

"I've got to go." My voice raises at least two octaves, and my cheeks must be red because I can feel the heat burning in them as I bolt towards her door. "I'm on shift tomorrow and have so much to do." I beat it out of there before I get sex advice from my seventy-nine-year-old neighbor.

When I get to the firehouse the next day, three new bouquets are there too. I roll my eyes when I get in.

"Mel, you got some deliveries while you weren't here," Jose from the ladder engine announces.

"So I see." I throw my duffle bag under my bunk and come back out. "Am I cooking tonight or are we going to let Stephen give it a go?"

"Negative to both. We have someone catering dinner tonight," Cap calls out from the couch in the TV room.

"Catering dinner?" I turn around in the kitchen.

"Yeah," Cap shrugs. "I got a call last night that dinner tonight would be catered, paid for by a private party wanting to show support of first responders. They are doing it to all the houses in Santa Monica, Malibu, and Venice."

"Wow."

I head back to my bunk and grab my phone.

**Me:** *You need to stop with the flowers and the food.*

**Sampson:** *I don't know what you're talking about.*

**Me:** *My house looks like a mortuary. As does the firehouse. And the catered dinners? It's too much.*

**Sampson:** *Again, don't know what you're talking about.*

I send him a picture of my apartment filled with flowers that I sent to Sof.

**Me:** *You signed all the cards, dumbass.*

**Sampson:** *They're not from me. It's probably Kill. I'll get him to stop. Sorry. He's trying too hard to get you to like me. I'll explain to him again that I broke us a long time ago. Have a safe shift.*

I'm not sure how he knew that I'm on shift, but I guess I'll give him the benefit of the doubt there. The alarm goes off for the ladder and the paramedics. It's a car accident. If they called for the ladder, they must need the jaws of life. I grab my gear and head to the ambulance.

When I get back, there's a text waiting for me.

**Sampson:** *It was Kill. He said he was trying to help my case. Did it work?*

**Me:** *No.*

# Chapter 12

## *Melody*

After an action-packed night, the early morning part of my shift drags and I actually get some sleep in my bunk, a solid two hours. When I finally get off shift, I head over to Clance's to borrow his truck before heading to the community center. I'm giving the CPR /First Aid class to The Blind Rebels group this evening, so I came here for my supplies. Then it'll be home to take another nap.

I considered turning down Mav's request, but having people learn CPR and first aid is my passion. I made a promise to Denise that I wouldn't let her death be in vain. It changed my entire career trajectory. It didn't hurt that Mav stressed again how much they wanted this training because of his infant and Cal's toddler. I couldn't turn that down. If something happened to either of those boys after I had refused, the guilt would be too much.

I throw enough of the resusci-dummies into the back, along with some first aid kits for practicing splinting and such, and enough of the official books for everyone to have their own.

After catching some more sleep and a shower after my afternoon run, I take off towards Malibu. We're meeting at

Mav's house. I wonder if Sampson is going to be there or if it's too weird for him. Between me being the one that saved him and the weird hot/cold thing he has with me, it might not be something that he's interested in. I pull up to the gate and press the button.

"Hey, Mel, park close to the door. Mav will help you carry the stuff in." Kady's disembodied, yet cheery voice comes out from the speaker box and the security gate to the house starts opening slowly.

As soon as I pull up, the door is open and Mav's there to help carry the dummies in. We make several trips to carry the stuff in, and during the last of them, a large white SUV with darkened windows, followed by a beautifully restored classic black pickup pulls up. The SUV door swings open, and Cal, Ari, Sampson, who's holding Gibson, and a gentleman I don't think I've ever seen before, pour out of the SUV. Killian and another gentleman come from the black pickup. Mav did mention that there would be some of their security detail coming as well. The more the merrier, I say.

"Mail! Hi, Mail. Hi!" Gibson waves at me, and I can't help my grin that he remembers me.

"Hi, Gibson. Who do you have there?" I nod to the stuffed lion tucked protectively under his arm.

"Rawr! Dis my Wyon." He holds it out so I can see it better.

"Ooh, he looks mean. I'll stay away." I take an exaggerated step back from him and his lion. Meanwhile, Sampson refuses to even make eye contact with me.

Gibson cackles. "He not weal, Mail. He my buddy." He hugs the stuffed animal back to him. Sammy carries him in, and I carry the last of the first aid manuals.

The Slaters have rearranged the great room from the last time I was here. The couches have been moved so they are at the edges of the large room and the tables are completely missing so now there is a big empty space in the middle. I knew the room was large before, but it looks even larger with the new furniture configuration.

"Uh-oh! What happen here?" Gibson surveys the new layout of the room after wiggling free from Sampson.

Kady laughs and squats down to his level. "We moved everything around for tonight. We're taking a special class, while you and Brio get to hang out upstairs with Elsie and watch Cars. How does that sound?"

"Where SeeSee and BeeOh at?" He looks around.

"SeeSee is what he calls Elsie, Brio's nanny," she says to me before looking down at Gibs. "She's up to date on her CPR and first aid. I'll take you to them, buddy." She takes his hand and leads him and his lion upstairs.

While everyone else mingles, I start setting everything up. I lay out one mat for each resusi-dummy, along with a first aid kit and two books per station. I have a few baby resusci-dummies too that I lay out at the front of the class along with my own resusci-dummy. I don't ask any participant to do anything I won't demonstrate myself.

Everyone pairs off, two to a dummy. We have Mav and Kady, Cal and Ari, Kill and Sampson, Jax and Aiden, and Russell and Jeff, who were here when I arrived. I was introduced to the people I didn't know. Jax, Aiden and Russell are all security and Jeff is a road crew manager.

"I know you're all anxious to get to the CPR portion of the course, but I'm going to go over some basic first aid first. That'll be about an hour and a half. Then we can take a break before we get into the CPR portion. After that, you'll all be certified in CPR and first aid. I have cards for you and everything."

I start by going over basic first aid for lacerations, burns, broken bones, and choking. I get to hear about how Ari saved Sampson from choking on a taco with the Heimlich maneuver. This is real life experience, and these kinds of situations are the best for urging others to learn first aid. I have Ari and Sampson come to the front and have her demonstrate what she did, and also demonstrate other techniques for what to do when you're much shorter than the person needing help. And what to do if you are alone and find yourself choking.

Afterwards, we have a break. I use the restroom and by the time I've come out, Kady has laid out a nice spread of snacks and Sampson's disappeared. He seems to do a lot of that when I'm around.

It was hard knowing that Sampson was choking, and I wasn't there to help. Thankfully, it wasn't his time and Ari was there and skilled. She had to be super-skilled because Sampson's way taller than she is. I'm surprised she didn't have to stand on a chair to help him. But he's still here, thankfully. And even though I seem to bring up something bad for Sampson, I am glad he's still here. My heart beats with hope that maybe one day when the stars align correctly, we'll be something again.

"Thank you again for doing all this." Mav sits next to me at the table. "I've learned so much already. I know Ari's gone through first aid and CPR before. She used to be a nanny like Elsie and their agency requires them to be certified, but she said she was glad for the refresher because it's been a few."

I nod. "I'm glad to do it. It's something I'm very passionate about, obviously."

"I can tell. Is there a particular reason why?" Mav tilts his head at me as he picks up a piece of cheese from his plate.

And just like that, I'm back in our dorm.

*"Come on, Mel, let's go have some fun." Dee pulls my arm towards our shared closet. "It's time you put yourself out there and do something fun for once, girl." We change clothes quickly and she does my eyes for me, because I can never get my eyeliner even.*

"When I was in my sophomore year of college, my best friend and I went to a frat party. She and I both drank way too much. At least one of us should have been sober. Anyway, I didn't realize how much she'd had." I fiddle with my cracker.

*The rhythmic pounding in my head reminds me of Sampson, someone I have purposely put behind me and the anger at him burns fresh in my stomach until I will it away. How drunk did we get last night? I move my sandpaper tongue around in my mouth and risk opening my eyes. Our blinds are pulled, but the light streaming in makes the pounding harder as I sit up. The room spins slightly, and I look over at Dee's bed. She's not in it, but the bathroom light is on.*

*"How can you be in there with all that light, Dee?" I knock on the door. She doesn't answer. "Dee?" Nothing. No noise at all, not even the slightest stirring. I turn the doorknob and the door pushes open. Dee's sprawled out on the floor in front of the toilet and sink. The acidy smell of vomit and urine pierce my nose and cause me to gag. Her hazel eyes are open and so vacant.*

*"Dee?" I drop to my knees and grab her hand. It's cold and her fingernails are blue.*

*"Dee! Fuck. Dee!" I shake her shoulders and scream her name.*

*When I shake her, there's a smear of red on the tiled floor underneath her. Then there's a piercing scream. It takes me a few seconds to realize it is coming from me.*

"She, um, passed out in the bathroom of our dorm that night at some point, cracked her head on the toilet, vomited and aspirated."

*"There was nothing you could do. She's probably been dead for a few hours. Don't blame yourself." The paramedic completed my IV in the ambulance as we pulled out. "This is just a little something to relax you a little bit. You kind of wigged out on us. Totally understandable." I remember the kindness in his Hershey's chocolate eyes as he patted my hand. If I hadn't passed out myself, I would have known what was happening. She wouldn't have died. I would have been awake to help her.*

"It was already too late when help got there." The guilt I've worked years at keeping stuffed into a tiny box in my head starts to crawl out. I take a breath, then a drink.

*Dee's parents stand at the front of the church and every so often her mom, Angela, lets out a devastated sob that pierces through me, causing my shame to bleed out of me from all my pores. It's too much. I can't do this.*

"After her funeral, I decided I'd never let myself be in the position where I didn't know what to do. In all honestly, she would have probably died anyway. I didn't hear her pass out because I was sound asleep. But it's at least part of what drew me to being a paramedic, I think. It's also why I don't drink." I take a shaky breath.

*I take the few steps out of the row, even though it's in the middle of her service. My best friend is gone, and it's my fault. As soon as I get to the aisle, I turn and run straight out of the church, down the steps and halfway across the lawn before my knees give out and I drop onto the vast green ground. My sobs echo against the stone façade of the church.*

*I'm vaguely aware of someone dropping onto the lawn next to me. There's a light rub on my back.*

*"You don't have to let your friend's death be in vain." His voice is familiar. Looking at him through blurry eyes, I recognize the paramedic from the ambulance. "The way I see it, you can let your friend's death destroy you, or you can figure out what you want to do with your life and do it for her."*

"Fuck, that must have been traumatizing." He reaches over and touches my arm.

"It was." I nod, the mood at the table now bleak. "She was my best friend and losing her changed me. I was in a dark place after, but thanks to someone who made it his mission to make sure I was okay, I was eventually able to use my trauma to better the world in the ways I knew how." I shrug at Mav as I try to push the sadness and guilt away. "Try to keep someone else from feeling the guilt that I did. Do." I don't talk about Dee much, but there is just something about Mavrick Slater that makes me comfortable doing so. It's not something I'd expect before meeting the lead singer. There's just something welcoming about him, about the whole group of them, really. They've made me feel like I belong in their life. Like I'm important.

I don't even think that Sofie knows the full story of when I met Clance the first time. I didn't see him again until the day I was placed as a trainee on his bus. We've never spoken of that day at the church. Maybe he doesn't even realize that college girl was me.

As I take a deep, fortifying breath, Cal joins us with his plate of snacks. "Thanks for doing this for us."

"I was just telling Mav that I'm happy to do it. Educating the community in CPR and first aid is something that I'm passionate about. It's something everyone should know. I commend Ari on keeping up to date with it." He nods.

"I guess we should reconvene for the CPR portion."

First, we go over all the parts of the resusci-dummy and how they work. I pass out individual mouth/nose pieces. I demonstrate a proper mouth sweep, how to tell if someone is breathing and how to measure for a pulse.

"If it's easier for you, you can also straddle the body." I swing my leg over my dummy. "This is a move that's commonly done on a moving stretcher but can be helpful if you're small in stature and the person you are working on is larger."

"Now I want you to work together. Three rounds of CPR each. Then switch off. I'll be working around the room to help and correct you all on posture, angle, and force of compression. You have to press down a lot harder than you'd think. The thing to remember when you are doing this in real life is that you'll probably feel bones break. And that's okay. Do not let it dissuade you from continuing." Sampson visibly cringes at my words.

"If they are not breathing and have no pulse, then you're the last chance at life until an ambulance gets there." My rapt audience nods.

"Okay, let's do this. Start with the evaluation. Remember your ABCs. Airway. Breathing. Circulation. Sweep the mouth. Two rescue breaths. Thirty compressions. Two rescue breaths. Thirty compressions. Count out loud. It's helpful to the first responders arriving so they know where you are at. Let me know if you have any questions when I get to your group."

I walk around and help people get their mouth pieces secured on the dummies and answering questions about hand placement and how hard to press. I stop by Sampson and Killian's station and watch as Sampson gives CPR to their dummy, while Killian watches.

"Actually, press a little harder, but that's a good rhythm you have going there." He nods and starts again, pressing harder this time. "Good!" It's hard being here close to him, but with a distance between us. It's on me- I threw him out. But it doesn't make me feel any better.

I glance at Killian to check to see if he has any questions before it's his turn and realize he's gone totally pale. I squat beside him and put my hand on his shoulder. He's completely stiff but also shuddering. "Hey, are you okay?" I ask quietly so as to not draw attention.

His breathing is fast and shallow, and he rips away his eyes from watching Sampson to look at me. In just that brief eye contact, I see the terror screaming through his dark blue eyes. He shakes his head slightly at me. "Bad memories?" I ask, and he nods ever so subtly.

I squeeze his shoulder and reach over him to grab one of the sealed bottles of water near their station. I open it and hand it to him. "Take a few sips." He does, closing his eyes.

I position myself between him and Sam, so when he opens his eyes, he's forced to look at me and not Sampson practicing

CPR. "Remember, this isn't Sammy at the beach. That's over." He nods at me, his eyes, still round as saucers, don't look away.

"This is what *you* can do if something like that happens again. This is reclaiming a scary situation and giving yourself the ability to say that you did everything in your power to give them the best chance at life until help gets there." I squeeze his shoulder again.

He's loosened up a little, his breathing is slower and his color's coming back. But now we've caught the eye of a couple of the other pairs of people, specifically Cal, who looks like he's moments away from leaping into the middle of us. That's the last thing the poor guy needs right now. Over Killian's shoulder, I give our audience a brief nod, trying to convince his brother that he's fine.

"It's just a little flashback. I've been doing this for years and I get them too. It happens. Nothing to be self-conscious of." Killian nods and takes a couple of self-regulating deep breaths. By now, Sammy's done with his compressions and is sitting back on his heels, watching Killian and me.

"Let's switch out, everyone," I call to the class. But I stick near Killian, keeping my hand on his back as they switch places. I assist him with getting his face piece snapped onto his dummy since his hands are still a little shaky.

I remind him to do the airway check, mouth sweep, and then help him position himself for compressions. He looks up at me and I nod my encouragement. He starts his first set of compressions, and I'm proud of him for going through with it.

"Sampson, can you help Killian get into the right rhythm now that he's got the right posture?" He moves next to me and talks Killian through the compression rhythm.

"I'll be back to check on you guys in a minute." I move back around the group, correcting postures and compression strengths. I squat down and watch Ari doing CPR like a pro, and speak softly to Cal.

"He had a little flashback to the beach. He's okay now, I think." I nod towards Killian, who's stopped compressions to give his dummy breaths and then back again.

"You all are doing amazing." I observe as I stand back up. "I don't have enough infant dummies for every group to get their own. But seeing as how we have a baby and toddler in the group, I think it's wise for everyone to get a chance on one of the two I brought with me."

Everyone works through the baby and toddler versions of both the CPR and choking. It's here where we spend the most time. I want these parents and their friends to be completely comfortable with manipulating a child for resuscitation, because it's different and counterintuitive to treat a child almost roughly like you have to do to perform lifesaving aid on someone so small. Hopefully, they'll never have to use it, but it's in their back pocket if they need it.

After the last person finishes up with the infant dummies, I start packing everything away and rolling up the mats so the Slaters can get their living space back.

"Dat your buddy?" Gibson watches me put away one of the resusci-dummies back into its case.

"I guess you could call it my buddy. He helps me teach people about how to make owies all better." I try to put it on his level without scaring the hell out of him. I don't need to be accused of giving a three-year-old nightmares.

"He seeps in your bed like UffUff?" he asks curiously. I can't help but chuckle. I'm not sure who UffUff is, but I take it that it's some sort of stuffed animal he sleeps with.

"No, bud, he sleeps in this box. No buddies are sleeping in my bed." I show him how the dummy fits in the box and then let him help me put the next one in. He helps until we have them all in their cases.

"Aww done." He brushes his hands together in an adorable, finished gesture. So adult, yet adorable from the toddler.

"Yep, we're all done. Thank you for being such a big help." He smiles and gives me a big hug.

"Welcome!" He turns and rushes off somewhere behind me. I carry the cases out, making several trips and secure them in the bed of Clance's truck and head back in to say goodbye.

"Thank you so much for letting me share my passion with you and your friends and family. Everyone took it seriously and I feel really good about what I saw in class today. I hope you feel that way as well." I offer my hand to shake, and Mav takes it and pulls me into a big hug.

"Thank you, Mel, for helping us learn what to do in an emergency. Please join us for dinner. It's going to be informal. It'll just be us and some steaks and chicken on the barbecue, nothing fancy."

I shake my head and give him a sad smile. At least I'm hoping that's my expression. "As awesome as it sounds, because judging by your delicious snacks and the barbecue last time, the dinner would be amazing." He chuckles. "But I'm exhausted. I worked a twenty-four-hour shift and got home around 9 this morning. I need to get the dummies back to the community center, and then head home to crash for the night."

He nods understandingly. "Another time maybe."

I just nod because in my heart I know there isn't going to be another time.

"I'll walk you out. Did you get everything?" I take a quick look around, then nod and he escorts me out to my car.

He leans against Clance's truck and looks back up at the house. "Thank you for whatever you did with Killian this evening."

"He just had a little flashback to the beach. He got it under control."

His brow pulls together at my words. "We're worried about them both." He runs a hand over his face. "Neither Kill nor

Sammy have been acting like their normal selves since the accident."

"They'll be okay. Heck, I still have flashbacks to certain calls. It's normal after any traumatic event," I reassure him, leaving out the first-hand knowledge that the closer the person is to you, the worse they can be.

"Are you sure you're safe to drive, Mel? I'd hate for you to fall asleep driving. I'd be happy to drive you. My security detail can follow and drive me back."

"I'm fine, really. Thanks for the sweet offer, though." He holds the door open as I get into the truck.

"Please text me when you get home. I'll feel better knowing you've made it safely," he asks.

"I can do that." I smile as he shuts the door, then I head back to Santa Monica.

The drive is long, and the weekend traffic is not kind. I get the dummies back to the closet in the community center. The whole time I'm putting them away, I'm thinking of Sampson. He didn't say a word to me this entire evening. It's probably better that way. But I did notice him watching me coaching his friend through his flashback. His friend is clearly haunted by what happened on the beach. Maybe Sampson is too, and maybe I should cut him a break. I must be tired. Sampson doesn't want anything to do with me.

As much as I didn't want to notice, though, I saw the dark marks under Sampson's eyes as he carried Gibson into the house when they first got there. I wanted to tell him if he needed to talk to someone, he could talk to me. But every single time we had a break, he seemed to disappear like he was avoiding me. Even when I was leaving, he was MIA, and I didn't want to wait around for him. I did that for two years after he left. He never came back. Maybe I should text him, though, give him the olive branch. Be the bigger person. No, I can't. If he wanted to talk to me, he would have made the effort and I won't wrap my life in his again.

I grab my phone and consider texting Sammy, but instead, text Mav.

**Me:** *I'd forgotten about traffic on Saturdays. Hope you weren't worried. I'm home. Thanks again.*

**Mav:** *Thank goodness, I was starting to get worried. And we should be the ones thanking you. Sleep well.*

# Chapter 13

## *Sammy*

When I return from the restroom, I can't find Mel anywhere. I want to ask her to have coffee with me or something. I need to figure out what's going on between us. If anything.

"Have you seen Mel?" I ask Mav when he comes in from out front.

"She just drove off. Why?" He narrows his eyes at me.

I shrug. "I was just going to thank her for helping Killian with the CPR thing." And I really was; she was great with him. He was so freaked out, he was shaking. He looked exactly how I feel when I'm near water. That wasn't the only reason I wanted to talk to her, though, and I don't need Mav sticking his nose in my business, like Cal and Kill do.

"Sorry, man, she left. I invited her to stay for dinner, but she said she was too tired." He sighs a breath in the dramatic way only Mav can. He looks at me. "Part of me wonders if that was just her polite way of not wanting to be around in case you decided to put on another asshole show like the last time we had dinner with her." He stares me down.

"It's possible, but she was on duty last night, so it's also possible she really was just tired." He quirks an eyebrow up at my explanation. "What?"

"You know her schedule."

I shrug. Yeah, I know her schedule. Sofie texted it to Killian, who forwarded it to me, and I memorized it. There's nothing stalkerish about that, right? "So?"

"I think she likes you, but is afraid of you—"

"She's not afraid of me. She's mad at me. I hurt her years ago. So she doesn't want anything to do with me now. My jackass behavior at the barbecue didn't help prove I've changed much."

His eyes narrow on me. "Have you?"

"Changed? Haven't we all? It's been years. I'm sure she's not the same either."

He nods and looks over at Kady. "That's for sure." His eyes settle back on me. "Don't pass up something because you're afraid. That's all I'm going to say. I'm not Cal. I'm doing my best not to worry over you and Kill, despite you both giving us every reason to. I'm trying to be the cool friend. The one who lets you into his house at all hours to drum until you pass out from exhaustion, if that's what you need to do to get some sleep." He locks eyes with me to make sure I understand what he's offering. I understand, just like I know that he gets I'm not sleeping. We all know each other so well, sometimes we don't have to ask for the things we need. Like forgiveness. Or a place to crash.

"Just make sure you lock the door if you come in and the place is dark. And don't venture up to the second floor late at night, if you get my drift." He winks at me and strolls over to Kady, taking Brio from her arms and nuzzling him before blowing raspberries on his stomach until he squirms in his grip and giggles.

My brothers have the families I've always wanted. Lucky fuckers. But what good could I be to a family? I couldn't even save Sev when she needed me.

I still don't understand why Kill's never mentioned his thing with Sev to any of us. Only thing I can figure is that he thought we'd be angry with him. I wasn't so nobody else should have been either. We are too tight for lies.

I was fine with them as a couple; they were good for each other. If either one had told me, that's exactly what I would have told them. It wasn't his fault Sev was like our mom. I saw that he tried his damnedest to save her too. I tried everything to fix her. But because I couldn't. I lost my sister and it broke my best friend. This is exactly why Melody and I are a bad idea.

But all that doesn't stop me from wanting her. Ever since our hug at the ceremony, I've wanted that connection we've always shared on a deep, visceral level.

I realized the moment I put my arms around her after the ceremony that our connection was still there. It zipped between my chest and hers and suddenly I was calm and wanted to sag into it. Mel's always given me that inner peace, one even deeper than the ocean used to give me.

Maybe that's why I'm drawn to Mel. Because of this thing between me and the ocean. Because she comforts me in a way I used to only get from the water.

Fuck this anxiety or whatever it is. I refuse to give into it. I won't be a medicated zombie for the rest of my life. That's what happened to my mom, and it turned her into an addict.

# R

A FEW NIGHTS LATER, I slip into Mav's quiet, darkened house. It's half past midnight and everything is locked and dark. I lock the door after myself and use the flashlight on my cell as I walk quietly to the stairs that go down to the studio. Carefully and quietly, I snap the baby gate shut at the top of the stairs.

Part of me feels guilty for leaving Cal's in the middle of the night. But I know that if I used his music room, I'd end up getting another lecture about how I need to talk to a therapist, blah blah blah. I just want to play my drums.

I flip on the studio light. My drum kit is in the other room. But in the control room there's a folded-up blanket and a pillow sitting at one end of the old couch that used to be in our shared apartment back in the day. My favorite sports drinks are stocked in the mini-fridge, and in the door are some cheese sticks I know weren't there the last time I was down here. A box of granola bars sits on top of the fridge.

I pull off my shirt and walk into the room we record in. Sitting on my stool, I notice a sticky note on my snare drum in Kady's curly handwriting.

*We love you, Sammy. K & M.*

I fold it up and stick it in the wallet in my left rear pocket. I reach for my sticks and play. Nothing in particular. I just let the rhythm take me where she wants to go. And tonight, she wants hard and fast.

I punish myself and the kit with a rhythm that would never fly in a Blind Rebels song. It's something you might hear in a death metal band or something. I don't care. I just go at it until my hair's matted to my face thanks to the sweat rolling down my forehead.

I play until I have nothing left to give, until my arms finally give out and I rest my head on the snare for a few minutes. After I've caught my breath, I curl up under the blanket on the couch in the control room.

*I'm at our beach. I'm not alone or afraid because Mel's here. The ocean breeze carries a light mist from the incoming fog bank, keeping us damp. I wrap our blanket around her shoulders and then snuggle into her. My Mel. She smells like coconut and sunshine.*

*"I want to kiss you, Mel. For reals this time." My words come out in a whisper.*

*She turns her head and looks at me with those big chocolate brown eyes of hers. Eyes that beg me to rescue them for what they've* endured. *And I want to help her so much. I saw the new bruises. The ones that look suspiciously like fingers on her upper arms. The big one on her side when her shirt flew up before she'd yanked her wetsuit all the way on. The one she tried to cover with makeup on her cheek.*

*She didn't have to tell me, though. I can always tell when it was bad the night before because she's unusually quiet the next morning, not herself. She doesn't think I know she's slowly breaking apart on the inside. I can't fix this for her, and it fucking kills me. Her mom blames her for her dad's death. Which is totally stupid. It was an accident on the movie set where he was a stuntman.*

*So when her mom's not working all hours and ignoring Mel completely, she's beating the fuck out of her. And Mel won't fight back. I jumped in between them a few weeks ago. I just needed her to stop hitting my Mel.*

*I want to get her out of there and bring her with Sev and me when we take off at the end of the school year, but I'll be barely out of high school with just my shitty job at the restaurant across from the Rock Store. Anything that doesn't go to our part of the rent or food will have to go towards band things. Gas for getting to gigs and other band incidentals.*

She shakes her head and glances back out at the ocean.

"Please, Mel. Let me kiss you. For reals." I brush a kiss against her cheek, ending up by her ear so I can continue my plea.

She turns towards me and her lips part as she leans in.

# Chapter 14

## *Sammy*

"Yeah, he's here," Mav rasps sleepily into his phone in the short hall outside of his studio. "You're going to give yourself an ulcer if you don't lighten up with Sammy and Kill, man." Mav sounds irritated as he closes the door back over softly.

I'm wide awake now and my heart's beating so fast it might jump out of my chest. I concentrate on the egg carton pattern of the soundproofing on the ceiling and try to slow it down.

"He's got a key. He's always had one. Whoa Cal, slow your roll man. Dude, seriously stop. Sammy's always welcome to crash here. Always. And he knows it."

A partial huff of a sigh comes out from Mav, still behind the almost closed door. "Look, I love you, Cal. And I get you. I do, man. He has to work through his shit in his own time. If coming here in the middle of the night helps, then so be it. I'd rather he be here than who knows the fuck where, doing God knows what. Feel me?"

I hate that they are arguing about me, but I also love Mav for giving me a freaking break and defending it to Cal.

"Yeah, I won't be doing that. No." I can almost picture Mav

133

shoving his hand through his hair. As much as he loves to say he's an asshole, it's more that he doesn't do well with conflict, especially when it's with his chosen brothers.

"I said no, Cal. He's still asleep anyway, and he probably needs that more than anything." There's a brief pause. "Don't make me change your fuckin' gate code, man, because I so will. Give him some fuckin' space. Yeah. Later." He sharply barks out the last word.

Mav stands on the other side of the door muttering to himself. I can't hear his words, just the deep, quiet timber of his voice.

The door swings open, and he peeks his head in. "Sorry, I woke you. I just wanted to be sure you were down here before I told Cal you were."

I sit up on the couch and Mav slips in. He's wearing pajama pants with Paw Patrol characters on them and is suffering from a nasty case of bed head. It's obvious he rolled out of bed and slipped his PJ pants on to come look for me. So now I feel shitty. Guilty for disrupting two households.

"What time is it?"

He looks at his phone. "A few minutes after seven."

I groan. "Only Cal gets up that early."

"No, actually, we do too. Brio's already up. It's a parent thing. Go back to sleep, man. You look like you need it. Cal should leave you alone long enough for you to get a few more hours in."

"Thanks, Mav, for calling him off of me." Everyone's worried about me and that should make me feel good, make me feel loved. Instead, it makes me feel like hell because I'm not worthy of the worried looks or the furtive conversations when they think I'm out of earshot.

He nods and furrows his brows as he watches me settle back down onto the studio couch. "Whatever you need, Sammy. I mean it."

134

He watches me for a few minutes and then closes the door.

By the time I wander upstairs a few hours later, Killian's on the floor with Brio, playing and interacting with him like it's second nature. Fuck, he'd make a good father. I hurt for him because since Sev died, Killian's never been the same. He won't get close to anyone. He even holds us out at arm's length most of the time.

It would destroy Cal if he saw Kill playing so openly with Brio, but there's a big difference between Brio and Gibson. When Gibson was born, Killian wanted nothing to do with his nephew, and Cal took it personally. He didn't realize that seeing his twin with a baby was re-breaking Killian's heart. Kill's hinted around that he's jealous of Cal's relationship with Gibs and even his relationship with Ari. And he is, deeply jealous of it. I think he wanted the family he never had, and he thought he might have a chance at that with Sev. If she would have only let him in or come to us when she started using again.

"Hey." He lifts his chin as I drop down on the floor with them. "Just to warn you, Cal's super pissed right now. He's livid with Mav because he told him not to come check on you. So, I got sent instead." Kill shrugs and hands Brio another toy to play with.

"I just gotta say, I'm with Mav on this. If coming here to drum in the middle of the night helps, keep doing it. Maybe you should think about staying with Mav." He looks at me and shrugs, but it almost seems like me leaving Cal's isn't something that he wants. It's not something I want right now either.

I shake my head. "I just needed to play. I don't want to leave Cal's." I sigh. "Playing hard helps me work the shit in my brain out of my system long enough to let me sleep. It's easier here when I need it. I don't feel as judged as I do at Cal's when I do it."

Kill reaches out and squeezes my shoulder tight. "Whatever you need."

After helping Brio stick a plastic triangle in his puzzle box, he looks back at me with mischief in his eyes. "So, how are we doing on Operation Mel?"

"I was thinking about asking her to have coffee with me so we can talk some shit out."

Kill practically bounces as he sits on the floor with Brio between his legs. "That's a great idea, Sammy. Do it. Do it now."

Brio picks up on his exuberance and starts clapping, and I have to wonder where the hell Kady and Mav are. And in that spooky way of his, Killian answers my question without me even asking it.

"They ran to the store together, gave me some shit about never going to the store without..." He points to Brio and then shrugs.

I pull my phone out of my back pocket and set it down in front of me. "Why is my relationship with Mel so important to you?" I tilt my head while I watch him pick the area of his shoe where the sole meets the side while Brio slaps his hand against Kill's leg.

"She makes you different. Happy doesn't seem like the right word, because let's face it, you are the happiest of the four of us. But it makes you feel settled. Like you've always been missing something and now you've found it again." He shrugs. "I want good things for you, Sam. For you to be like you were before we lost Sev."

I can't not tell him anymore. My stomach turns, because I don't want to go against Cal's wishes, but I need to talk about this, and Kill would understand above anyone. He needs to know.

"I saw her, Kill." I try to look him in the eye, so he understands I'm serious. But his concentration is still on his shoe.

"Who, Mel?" He looks at me confused, but I think in his heart Kill knows.

I shake my head slowly. "No. Sev." I sigh.

"When I was, um, in the hospital, I was talking to her. I tried to hug her. She looked so good. Like she did before she started using so much. I was talking to her, then she disappeared, and her voice changed into Mav's voice. And then I woke up in the hospital."

His mouth is slightly open, and he just stares at me. "That's not funny, Sam."

I shake my head. "It's the truth. Cal didn't want me to tell you. I'm not sure why. I think maybe he was worried about how'd you take it?"

Kill slowly shakes his head. "Was there a baby?" His voice breaks and it guts me. They didn't say anything about her being pregnant on the medical examiner's report. I'd have remembered that. Maybe Cal was right, and I shouldn't have brought this up.

Kill's desperation and hope laced voice stabs me in the heart as he reframes his question. "Was there a baby with her?"

"No. She was alone. There was no baby. Just Sev." I want to ask him why he thought she would have a baby with her.

"There was nothing about her being pregnant in the medical examiner's report. I read it." Once. And then shoved it in a drawer somewhere in the condo and never looked at it again. I never want to.

His body slumps into itself, and I hate this version of Kill. The one he's worked hard to move past. The one he doesn't even let his brother see. But I've seen it. "But she was okay? Sev was okay?"

"She looked good. Seemed good." I reassure him. "She just kept telling me I didn't belong there and that I needed to wake up. I asked her where you were, and she said you weren't there and that you didn't belong there either. She was so real, Kill. I mean, I know it was just my messed-up head. But she was so fuckin' real."

Kill nods and goes out on the patio, leaving me with Brio, so

I pick him up and snuggle him. Kill needs a few to himself. He slips out Mav's gate onto the beach. I wish I could follow him. But I can't. I won't. I don't want to risk having another meltdown.

About twenty minutes later, Mav and Kady come back from their shopping expedition with no bags, but big grins. Trader Joe's my ass.

Kill rides with me to the cemetery in the valley that we buried Sevenya in. When I say we, I mean the whole band. We'd just finished our first tour. We weren't headlining yet, but there were rumors of it. I had a shit ton of debt from trying to get Sev the help she needed. So they chipped in to help me get her this plot and headstone. More the three of them than me, since most of my money at the time had been sunk into two stints in rehabs, especially that fancy one in Montana that I was sure was the answer. I was a freaking mess after she died. Thank God, I had the guys.

Kill gives me some time to talk to Sev, and I give him some time with her too. Together, we clean off her headstone and leave her flowers. As we're about to leave, Kill sticks a guitar pick in the metal vase that holds the flowers we brought. He always leaves a little piece of him when he visits her. Sometimes it's something physical like a coin or a pick, but every time he leaves a tiny part of his heart too. I'm beginning to wonder if there's anything left where his heart should be. I should have told him I suspected he and Sev were together. Maybe it would have lightened the load of shit he keeps locked inside.

As we head back to my Jeep together, he swings his arm over my shoulders. "You text Melody yet?"

# Chapter 15

## *Melody*

I pull into the nondescript parking lot of the burger joint. Taking a deep breath, I get out of the car. The breeze off the ocean carries the salty smell over the exhaust of the cars that travel the highway between my car and the ocean.

Why I agreed to meet Sampson here, I don't know. Clance made it clear he wasn't a fan of the way he treated me the at the Slater's house, even after I explained that I knew Sampson, but I don't know Sammy. Clance didn't seem to care or understand, but he's definitely no Blind Rebels fan, that's for sure, and so I didn't tell him or Sof that I agreed to this meeting.

I text Sampson that I'm here and make my way into the restaurant. As I enter, the hostess asks me how many in my party. As I'm about to answer, Sampson appears.

"She's with me, Ang. Thanks." Sampson knocks on the hostess stand, then takes my hand. "Come on, Mel, we have the private dining room to ourselves." He pulls me through the restaurant, and we end up in a small dining room off the main one. He didn't lie. It is just the two of us. The other four tables are empty as we sit at one by the window.

"Mav knows the owner, so they treat us well here," he

explains as he sits across from me. He's smart; our meeting is public but private at the same time. I thought we'd be on equal ground meeting somewhere in public.

"We could eat out there, but I can't guarantee that we won't be interrupted by fans. This way we can talk. About anything. About everything." Sampson hands me a menu.

"First, let's order." The waiter seems to be on the same wavelength as Sam and shows up shortly after. I order a salad and a milkshake. He orders a bacon cheeseburger, onion rings, and a milkshake as well.

After the waiter returns with our drinks and leaves us again, our chit chat dies out.

"Why am I here, Sampson?" I look over at him.

"Because I need to get some things off my chest." His gaze turns from the cars zipping past the window to mine. His eyes connect with mine and I can tell that whatever is coming is something he needs to say, whether I want to hear it or not.

"Well then, go ahead," I encourage. The sooner he's done baring his soul or whatever he's going to do, the sooner I can get back to my life.

"First, I'm sorry for how I treated you at Mav's after the ceremony. I know it came off like I didn't want you there or that I didn't appreciate what you did. That was not my intent—"

"No. You came off as callus. As if you only extended the invitation because media were milling about the ceremony and might overhear your generosity," I huff out angrily. "You ignored me during the CPR training. All that tells me exactly where I stand with you. I don't belong in your world, Sampson. I obviously never did."

He opens his mouth to reply, but our waiter comes back with our lunches and sets them in front of us. "Can I get you anything else?"

I shake my head. "No thanks."

Sammy looks up at him. "Just some privacy."

Our waiter nods and walks out of the room.

I push my salad away from me slightly, no longer hungry.

"You're not going to eat?" Sammy looks up from adding ketchup to his burger.

I shrug. "I'm not hungry." I push the plate even farther into the center of the table as I slink down in my seat. I want to leave. I shouldn't have come. Maybe I should dump my shake all over the table to distract him, then slink out.

He straightens his spine and looks at me. "Hey, I never said anything about you not belonging in my world. Not back when we were younger or now. That sounds like something your mom would say, Mel. Since when do you listen to her?"

He wants to ask about her, but I cut him off, not wanting to open that can of worms in front of him. Not right now, probably not ever.

"I still don't understand why we're here. I probably shouldn't have come." I lean back in my chair, hoping to catch the eye of the waiter so I can get a box for my untouched salad.

"I couldn't have taken you and Sev both, Mel. I was a still a kid myself. I had a shitty job and could barely afford the rent with the band split four ways and have enough left over for food for Sev and I. Big dreams didn't pay the bills back then. I knew she was hurting you, Mel, and I wanted to bring you with me. I just couldn't afford both of you." His words break towards the end and his eyes are locked on to the table and not me.

"And I understood that. What I didn't understand was how or why you cut me out of your life. It was like I never existed in the first place." I shake my head. "You didn't even stay long enough to say goodbye, Sampson. Not a call, a text, or anything. I mistakenly thought I meant something to you." The hurt in my heart comes back as an aching gap in my chest.

"I waited for you for two years," I whisper. Two years that I'll never get back. Two years of pain and bruises until I couldn't take it anymore.

I sniff and sit straight, trying to regain my composure. I will not let Sampson break me again. "Excuse me if it's hard to reconcile the Sampson, who left me without a word, to the famous Sammy Denton from the Blind Rebels." It comes out so bitter sounding, I wish I could take the words and shove them back in my mouth and swallow them whole.

He doesn't look at me and instead watches the cars passing by on the Pacific Coast Highway again.

"I don't have an excuse for leaving like that. I'm sorry, Mel. It wasn't fair to you." He shreds the coating from one of his onion rings.

"When Sev and I left San Fernando, I was young and struggling." He shrugs. "Sevenya's always had issues, even more than I realized at the time. But when we left for L.A., she turned to drugs to deal with them. It didn't get bad until the band was starting to get a footing in the rock scene. My first record advance only paid for half of her first stint in rehab. She was my only family, Mel. I'd sunk nearly every dime I had into trying to get her the help she needed. But in the end, it wasn't enough. And what do I have to show for it now? Some record awards, a dead sister, a broken best friend." He shrugs. "A condo I can't bear to get rid of because it holds the last of her things, but I can't stand to live in either because I can't keep walking past the room she overdosed in. So when we're not touring, I couch surf between Mav, Killian, and Cal. Yeah, life is just fucking peachy over here."

My stomach drops. It makes sense Sampson still grieves his sister, but I had no idea he still had the condo she died in.

Sampson spikes his napkin into his plate. "Fuck. I'll be back." He jumps up from the table and heads towards the entrance of the private dining area.

I wish I could go back in time and not make the comparison to the Sampson I knew and Sammy now. It wasn't fair of me. The waiter comes back while he's still in the restroom, so I ask for some water and a box and he comes right back with them from the kitchen. By the time the waiter leaves, Sampson is heading back to the table.

He returns to his seat and looks me directly in the eye. "I want to fix us. That's why we're here."

I don't see this working out and he must be able to tell that I am about to turn him down because he sticks his hand out, shutting the box I was about to scoop my salad into.

"Before you shoot this down, Mel, I'm only looking for your friendship. When we were younger, before I left, you were the one person I could talk to about anything. The one person who made me feel better just by hanging out with me." He sighs and glances out the window again.

"I want that friendship back, Mel. I've fucking missed you." He sighs a long breath out. I've seen the band interact together, so I know he has his bandmates and I'm pretty sure they'd do anything for him, including being that listening board he says he wants. There is still a sadness around him, however. He turns his gaze back to me.

"I didn't realize how much I missed you until I saw you. Yeah, I was a jackass. But you should know I'm having some other things, other issues, I guess, that don't have anything to do with you that caused my behavior at Mav's."

He glances out the window and then back at me. "Look, can we just hang out together a little? Have some pizza and shoot the shit like we used to. See if we can be friends again? All I'm asking, Mel, is for a chance to get my best friend back. Do you think we could try?"

With his chin tilted down, he looks up at me through his dark, thick eyelashes.

I shake my head, but not at his request. At myself. "I never could say no to you, Sampson. Friends." I stick my hand out across the table at him to shake his hand. He shakes it back.

"Friends. So, what should we do first? As friends. I want to do something fun together. Something where we can just catch up. Learn about each other's lives now. And please don't recommend surfing. I'm not ready to go there yet." He smiles softly at me.

"Want to hit the gym with me tomorrow? I go to this one in Santa Monica. It's a small gym, nothing fancy. Clance comes with me most of the time, but he's on shift tomorrow. We could meet at my place, walk or run to the gym, and do a circuit or two together and jog back?"

His smile gets a little bigger, reaching farther up his face. "Sure. I'd like that."

He puts a small, white jewelry box onto the table. "This is something I've been meaning to give you since the ceremony. It's just a little token of thanks for saving me. I made it before I even knew you were the one who saved me." He shrugs as he slides the box towards me. "Go on. Open it."

"Sampson, you didn't need to." My fingers fiddle with the smooth box.

"It's nothing big, Mel. It's something I made. Don't get too excited. Like I said, when I made it, I didn't know it was you that saved me." His cheeks turn a light shade of pink that looks odd on him.

I open the box and remove the small pieces of protective cotton to find a silver charm bracelet. On the bracelet is an angel wing charm, a blue stone that has TBR logo engraved on the other side and a drumstick.

"You made this?" He nods. "Seriously made them with your own hands?"

He chuckles. "A while back, the band took a year-long hiatus of sorts. I took up metalworking to keep me busy. You'll notice each of the guys and Kady have a pendant with TBR carved into it with their own colored stone. I made those too. And the bracelet Ari wears. I made that, too." He looks at me.

"It's a lot like yours because she saved my life once, too. I was choking. That was back when she was Gibson's nanny."

"Nanny?"

He gives me a look. "Didn't Cal tell you she used to be his nanny before she was his wife?"

"I didn't realize they weren't blood, her and Gibson." They are as close as any mother and son I can think of.

"Cal fell in love with his nanny. Actually, Gibson's birth mom was Mav's fiancé when he was conceived. I'll let you ruminate on that for a few." He chuckles and sits back, popping another onion ring into his mouth while I think about that. "Yeah, so that is why there was a 'hiatus.' Mav and Cal were at each other's throats for a good while."

I slip my bracelet on while Sampson settles the bill, and we head back towards our vehicles with our to-go containers of barely touched food.

"So, tomorrow, either bring me breakfast, I prefer donuts, or you buy pizza afterwards," I tell him before we split away going to our separate cars.

"What if I want both?" he asks.

"Then you bring donuts and offer to buy pizza after. But you may not want to after the workout," I throw at him saucily.

"Text me the time. See you tomorrow."

# Chapter 16

## *Sammy*

**M**el: *Is 8:00 too early for you?*
 **Me:** *No, not lately.*
 **Mel:** *Don't forget the donuts. You can park in my spot in the covered residents' parking. Spot 307.*

I pull my Jeep into spot 307 and take the pastry box up to her third-floor studio apartment. I'm just about to knock when Mrs. Chamske's door opens.

"Young man. Can you help me change a light bulb? It won't take but a second."

"Sure Mrs. Chamske." I turn into her apartment and breathe in the smell of sugar cookies and roses. I notice a bouquet on her kitchen table. Pretty sure that's one of the many Kill sent to Melody on my behalf. They look like they are on their last legs. I'll have to send Mrs. Chamske a new bouquet. She turns to me, her glasses slipping down her nose like a librarian and her long silvery hair in a messy bun.

"It's the one in my bathroom. I have a stepstool, but I shouldn't be up on it with my dizzy spells." She shows me where her stepstool is. I take it into the bathroom and turn the light off.

"Melody's a lovely girl." She's fishing, the cagey old lady. When I look down, she's leaning against the wall watching me.

"Yes, she absolutely is. I've known her a long time. She's a nice girl."

"If you've known her for so long, how come I haven't seen you before these last couple of weeks?" She holds on to the stool while I remove the covering over the light to get to the bulb.

"Well, ma'am, that's my fault. I knew Melody back in high school, but then moved away with my younger sister and we lost touch. But she saved me actually, at the beach. I drowned, and she did CPR on me. Saved me."

"She's your guardian angel." I nod because Mrs. Chamske is absolutely right about that. Melody is without a doubt my guardian angel, always has been.

"You have to apologize and get in her good graces. She needs a good man. I was married three times, but my last husband Arthur, he was the best of them. Always brought me flowers and was really good in the sack."

I nearly drop the new lightbulb. I screw it in as quickly as possible, reattach the light's cover and then hop off the stool.

"You should be all set, Mrs. C. I really need to get over to Mel's. We're heading to the gym. Do you want a donut before I go?" I return to my donut box and open it for her.

"Ooh, a maple bar would be lovely if you have one."

I fish her out a maple bar and set it on her table. "See you around."

I shut her door behind me and turn around to see Mel standing in her door. "There you are. I was thinking you changed your mind. Why are you so pale? Were you over at Mrs. Chamske's?" The area of her nose between her eyes wrinkles up.

"She asked me to change a lightbulb. I think she was watching for me."

"She likes you, so she probably was." Mel takes the donut box from me and returns to her apartment, leaving the door open for me to follow.

"She was telling me all about her husband, Arthur."

"Oh, no." Melody laughs as she starts perusing the box of donuts. "Did she tell you all about how he was good in bed?"

I nod and she laughs harder. "Be glad she skipped over the story about how he died." Her brown eyes are twinkling with humor, and I love the way her lips are curled up. Makes me want to kiss them. *It's way too soon for that,* I scold myself.

"You got my favorite." She practically cries out with glee as she digs out a pink-iced strawberry donut from the box. She immediately takes a bite, shutting her eyes as she enjoys her doughy confection.

I fish out an old-fashioned with chocolate glaze.

"You got ripped off, though," she says as she looks back into the box.

"I did?"

She nods. "They only gave you eleven!"

I laugh. "I offered one to Mrs. C. She took the maple bar."

"That's okay, those are my least favorite." She pulls another donut out. "Don't judge me, Sampson." She wraps it in a napkin and sticks it in her microwave. "It's for later. The rest will go to the firehouse with me tomorrow."

She runs us through some warm-ups and then we lock up and jog the few miles to her gym. It's a bare-bones type of place. It's a warehouse with some state-of-the-art equipment, but also some old school stuff.

I follow Mel's lead as she works us through a circuit training that includes cardio and strength training. It's not hard for me. But while working through it, I learn that Mel's a beast when it comes to working out. She attacks the circuit hard, giving it her all. She's not here to stand around and look good in her workout gear, which she absolutely does.

I watch her as she sets us up for some resistance band work. The muscles in her arms flex as she hooks them up. Muscles. My little Mel's got muscles now.

We work through the circuit together three times, stopping between each circuit to drink some water. A lot of the patrons seem to know Mel and take time to stop and talk with her. She introduces me as an old friend and fuck if that doesn't make me smile.

"Race you back to my place. Loser buys dinner tonight." Her smile is huge as we head out of the gym after our workout.

"You're on, Mel."

"Go!" she shouts as she takes off towards the downtown area she lives in.

"Hey!" I take off after Mel. She's fucking fast. I could probably catch her if I wanted to. I just really want to take her to dinner tonight. Although I'm not going to let her think I'm not trying. I push to catch up to her. And just as I do, she pours on the juice and takes off on me again. When we turn the corner to her street, she seems to have extra boost, and I run full out and don't catch up to her. She slaps the resident's door of her building, but I'm still five steps behind her as she does.

"I win!" She's out of breath and bends against the door, trying catch her breath.

"You did." I finally catch her. "Damn, you're strong *and* fast. You're almost at superhero status, I think," I pant out and she giggles.

"Come on up and catch your breath. Have a soda or sports drink or something." I follow her up to her apartment and don't feel bad about the view. She's all curves. She's hard and soft.

"What's your poison, Sampson?" She has her fridge open.

"Sports drink. Orange or red if you have them." She tosses me an orange one and takes a red one for herself.

"So you're taking me to dinner? Are we doing pizza?" She polishes off half her sports drink in one go.

"What do you feel like, Mel? I'm not picky. I'll eat anything."

She snorts. "Yeah, I remember. You choose. Pick me up by 6:30, I'm on shift tomorrow so I can't be out too late."

"Okay. I'll be back."

"I'm counting on it, Sampson." And there is something about her voice that tells me that she's serious. That she's counting on me to make up for my past mistakes with her. I vow internally right then and there to do just that.

# Chapter 17

## *Sammy*

### A month later

I know it's here somewhere. I flip through the shirts that I've hung in the closet next to Gibson's old portable crib at Cal's. I know it was here. It's always in my backpack when I move between Cal and Mav's, so it's always with me. I've checked my backpack. I've even looked under the bed. I know it's got to be here. I turn to hit the laundry room to see if it's there when Kill pops his head in my room.

"What didja lose?" His forehead is crinkled, and I must look dumbstruck because how the fuck does he know I've lost something?

"I can tell by the look on your face you're looking for something. What is it? Maybe I can help you find it." He nods at the contents of my backpack spilled all over the bed.

"My Motley shirt. I can't find it. I want to wear it today." It's my favorite shirt. It was the last present Melody ever gave me. She bought it for me at a concert we went to for my birthday. It's been my lucky shirt ever since. I even wore it the day we signed with Monumentus Records. I always wear it when I feel I need a little extra boost of confidence, and Killian knows this.

His eyes narrow on me. "That's your lucky shirt. What's going on?"

"Mel invited me to dinner over at that Clance guy's house. I'm not his favorite person." Mel thinks that by going to this cookout with her, maybe Clance will ease up on his anti-Sam campaign.

Kill snorts. "That's for sure. I thought he was going to punch you when you were shunning Mel that evening. You really think that your old, threadbare Crue t-shirt is going to impress him, Sam? That shirt's more like a security blanket. And honestly, it looks it. It's too well-worn to be worn out of the house anymore." He shakes his head and moves into my closet. He flips through some of my shirts. "Wear this shirt instead. And change into your blue chucks. You'll be good."

I take the shirt from him. It's a black and blue button down that I think I wore during a music video or something because it's definitely not a shirt I'd wear on the daily. "You sure?"

He nods. "It says casual, without saying I'm wearing an old shirt because I'm insecure. You're a damn rock star, Sam. So the fuck if he doesn't like you. Mel likes you enough to invite you, right? Just don't go out of your way to be an asshole and it will go alright."

"Okay." I slip the shirt on and change my chucks out for the blue ones.

"How is this thing going between you and Mel? You seem to spend a lot of time with her." He sits on the edge of my bed and watches me tie my shoes.

"We're friends now, I think. I'm glad because I've really missed her in my life, Kill." I sigh. "I think if I can get Clance to like me, it will go a long way with Mel. He's legit like the big brother she never had. And she looks up to him."

"So you like being friends with Mel, but want more?" He tilts his head as he watches me like he always does.

"Yeah, I guess you could put it that way. But I'd rather be

just friends with her than not have her at all. So if the more thing doesn't work out, I'm okay with that as long as she's still my friend, I guess." I shrug. These last few weeks have been especially good. Mel's light has made such a difference in my life. We laugh like we used to.

"Have you two, you know, kissed or anything?" Kill peeks out from under his jet-black bangs.

I feel my cheeks get a little warm. I nod. "We kissed a little bit the other night. But nothing too intense. Not that I don't want to kiss her more, you know, intimately. But it feels like I should let her take the lead on that part of us. At least for now."

"You're a great friend, Sam. She's lucky." He pats my shoulder. "I see a difference in you. We all can. You're happier. I don't know if you've noticed, but Cal's even lightened up on you. It's because you smile now and just seem more upbeat." He pauses. "I think it'll work out the way you want. You just got to give it time."

"I hope you're right." I nod, knowing he probably is.

"I am. By the way, I know where your Motley shirt is." Kill has a sheepish smile on his face and shrugs his shoulders a little bit.

I look at him and raise an eyebrow. Fucker's holding out on me. "Did you take it?" I swear if he did, I'll nut punch him because that's so not cool.

"Gibson's been wearing it to bed or out by the pool most of the week. I thought you gave it to him. It's like his favorite shirt right now, although it's more like a floor length dress on him. I'm surprised you haven't noticed. Dude, you need to give up the shirt. It's old."

"That little sneak stole my favorite shirt." As much as I miss that damn shirt, I can't possibly take it back from him. It's starting to get a hole in the right armpit anyway.

"I thought you had given it to him. Let the kid have it, Sam." He pushes his bangs out of his face. "Go easy on Gibs. He's feeling out of sorts, picking up on Cal's worries. On all our worries. He might only be three, but he can tell something's off. He can tell you're gun-shy around the water. And now you're not around as much as you have been, and sometimes even when you're with us, you aren't with us, if you know what I mean. You know, daydreaming or worrying or whatever you do in that head of yours. Gibson's a smart cookie. Anyway, you probably left your Crue shirt in Cal's music room or somewhere and he just wanted to feel closer to you, so he snagged it." Kill pauses.

"He's looking forward to his next drumming lesson. He told me all about it yesterday. I know Cal was resistant to the drumming, but he's impressed at how fast Gibs is catching on. Hell, I am too, Sam. That small drum kit was a good call." He nods at me.

"We're on tomorrow for more drumming. You should jam with your nephew. He'd get a kick out of it. He likes to show off what he can do." I grin. Exposing him to making music with the other part of the rhythm section can only further his interest. He knows we all play together.

I love sitting on the floor next to his kit as he mimics what I do. He's got a natural talent. It's in his genes. Cal is not just a hell of a guitarist and songwriter, he's got an incredible ear for harmonies and rhythms. Being around music and musicians all the time probably doesn't hurt Gibson's interest. We've been writing music around him since he was born.

"I might do that." He smiles at the idea. "You don't think it'd throw him off?"

"Nah. It'll be fun." It might throw him off a little, but it'd be a good experience for him. Hell, we should invite Mav over too. Give the little dude the whole experience.

"I got to get to Mel's so we can head over to Clancey's." I can't help but grimace and Killian laughs.

"Loosen up, and just be yourself. Show them the real Sam,

not the asshole Sam from the party. They'll love the real you because you're good people, Sampson. The best." He slaps me on the back as he heads out to the pool, and I head over to pick up Mel.

She's waiting by the curb, wearing a cute yellow sundress that accentuates her tanned legs and her hair that's somewhere between blonde and brown. I'm glad that I dressed up a little now. She hops up into the Jeep before I can get out to help her in.

She gives me the address and I program it into my GPS. We make small talk and I even tell her about Gibson stealing my favorite shirt to sleep in.

"He's so cute." She smiles. "Wants to be just like his Shammy." She repeats Gibson's lisp of my name.

"He'd love to see you again. After all, you are his fend Mail. You should come over and see him play his drums." I can't help it. I'm proud of him.

"He plays the drums?" She turns to look at me.

"Yep, and he's good. He's only three, and he's been playing for like three weeks." I know my smile is wide; it always is when I talk about Gibson. You'd think he was mine the way I talk about that kid.

"Oh, here we are, the gray house. You can park in the driveway."

"Wait there," I tell her and then grab the wine out of the backseat and go over to help her out. Yes, she can get out by herself, but it doesn't mean she should.

"You brought wine. Sof will love you forever." She smiles at my gift. I know enough not to show up to someone else's house with no offering of a thank you for inviting me. I'm definitely not showing up at Clancey's without it. I want this to go well. I've already given him enough reasoning not to like me.

I follow her to the front door. She knocks and then opens the door like she lives there. Just like I do with Mav and Cal.

This is her family now. I still wonder what's going on with her mom, but I haven't had the nerve to ask. Maybe next time we have lunch.

"We're here," she calls out in a sing-song voice.

"Mel-lah-dee. Get thy ass in here," Sofie calls from somewhere deeper into the house. I follow Mel into a kitchen and Sofie has my Mel in a hug that rocks her back and forth.

"Look at you," Sof says. "Every time I see you, Mel, you look even better. Doesn't she look nice, Sam?" She looks over at me, and I can see the sparkle in Sofie's eyes.

"She looks great! That dress is beautiful." I don't mention that I nearly fell out of my Jeep when I saw her waiting for me outside her building.

"I brought wine," I say, holding up the bottle and feeling suddenly awkward, like Sofie can tell how much I love Mel. Even though I'm doing everything I can to keep this thing between us firmly in the friendzone, the more we hang out, the harder it is for me to keep her there. I really don't want to jeopardize what we have by showing her my true feelings.

"Oh, you've trained him well already, Mel." Sofie winks at me and takes the bottle.

"Clance is out on the patio doing things to the grill that I don't understand. Go on out, both of you. I'll be out in a few minutes." She shoos us through the kitchen.

Mel stops and grabs a beer from the fridge. "Want one? Grab it. This is for Clance." I reach in and grab a beer and follow.

It's obvious they spend a lot of time out here. There's some cornhole set up on the grassy area. The patio has a grill on one end and a small dining area on the other. There are flowers all over in the beds that line the yard as well as in pots on the patio.

"Hey, you." Mel approaches Clance and hands him a beer.

He smiles at her. "You're here. For some reason, I expected

you to be late. I haven't even fired up the grill yet. I was hiding so Sof didn't make me chop shit in the kitchen." He gives Mel a one-armed hug.

I get a chin lift as I tip my beer to him in greeting. "Hey, man. Nice to see you." He doesn't seem too put out that I'm here. So that's a good sign.

"You too. That's quite the grill." I nod at it. I don't know much about grills. I don't know much about cooking. But if Clance is anything like Cal, he'll take it as a compliment. Cal is the king of the grill in the band.

"Thanks, man."

We walk over to it, and he starts going over the features. "Ugh. You guys and your grills." Mel rolls her eyes. "I'm going to see what's keeping Sof."

I can't help but watch her in that dress as she sashays her way back into the house. And I'm busted by Clance while doing it.

"So, what's going on with you and Mel?" He folds his arms over his chest as he leans against the railing on his covered patio and assesses me.

"She invited me, and I like spending time with her. So I came." I shrug. I know damn well that's not what he's asking.

He rolls his eyes. "You know what I mean, Denton. What are you doing with Melody?"

"We were friends a long time ago. I'm just trying to rekindle the friendship."

"That's it? Just friendship?" His eyes roll when he gets to the last word. Like he's fighting not to put air quotes around it or something.

"Mel's always been special to me. I didn't treat her in a way she deserved in the past. I'm trying to show her that I've changed. Would I like another chance at a relationship with her? Hell yes. But I'm content just being in her orbit if she'll have me." Kill would be proud of my answer, I think. I just laid it out for Clance. I give him a little shrug.

He pulls his lips back as he considers my words. It's not quite a smile, but it's not a frown either. I guess he's still on the fence with me. And I'm okay with being on the fence for now.

Sof and Mel come out, Mel carrying a cheese tray in one hand and a coke in the other. I take the cheese tray and set it down on the table. "Thanks."

When she makes eye contact, there's a question in her eyes. Am I okay? I answer her with a smile.

Cornhole is played and I find out that both Melody and Clance are fiercely competitive, especially with each other.

"Best out of seven!" Clance demands as he loses another game to Mel and collects the bean bags from his end of the game. Melody laughs a lighthearted laugh that makes me inexplicably happy.

"Those two are like siblings. The competition gets fierce with them. Once Melody won some ridiculous trivia game over Clance at the firehouse back when they were both on the same bus, and he refused to speak to her for like two weeks. Which sucked for me because it's like best friend versus husband." Sofie motions, weighing them with her hands as if she were a scale, then laughs while shakes her head. "Plus, she had just started living with us at the time."

"I can see that. It surprises me. The Mel I knew in high school wasn't competitive. Of course, I didn't spend much time playing board games or bean bag toss back then, so maybe it was always there." I shrug.

Sofie shakes her head. "I don't think it was. I think it comes from working in a mostly male firehouse and having to prove you're just one of the guys. The Mel you see today is a very different Mel than the one that Clance brought home like a stray puppy. Back when Mel was still a probie, new at the firehouse, Clance was her mentor. They were partners, geez, probably for three or four years, riding on the same ambulance."

She's piqued my curiosity. "How was she different?"

"She was extremely shy and quiet and took things far too deeply to heart. The first week Clance was working with her, he came home and said, "Sof, this new girl, she's either going to be a hell of a paramedic, or she's not going to make it past probation, and right now, I'm leaning towards the latter." She chuckles to herself.

"Clance was up for the challenge, though. Took her under his wing. The shitty place she was living in got condemned. She was in a panic trying to find a place to live before she had to be out, but hadn't received her first check yet. Clance noticed something was up with her and eventually cajoled out of her that she was on the verge of being homeless. He insisted she stay with us." She looks up and watches the two of them still throwing bean bags.

"God, I was spitting mad at Clance. I didn't talk to him for nearly a week, which considering their shifts is really only three days. Here I was, I hardly knew this girl, and he comes home from shift announcing that she'll be staying with us. Didn't ask me, mind you, just announced it like he was king of the castle. I was sure she had designs on Clance because he's awesome. I couldn't have been any more wrong. She was so withdrawn at first. But between working with Clance and living with both of us, that shell she had built around herself didn't stand a chance of not cracking, eventually."

She turns to me and grins. "Now she's my dearest friend. You'll understand if we're both a little protective of her."

I shake my head. "I'm glad she has people like you in her life. She needs good people in her corner." Mel deserves to have the chosen family of her dreams since the one she was born with didn't turn out so stellar. I know that Clance doesn't trust me yet, but I'm glad that Mel has them in her life.

During dinner, they tell me funny stories about the goings on at the firehouse and I feel like I know some of these characters with the way Clance and Mel describe them. I also found out by a slip of the tongue from Sof that Mel had a long-term boyfriend named Grady, who was a police officer. From the way Clance was grinding his jaw, he wasn't thrilled with this Grady guy or how he treated her. So maybe Clance is just protective of her with anyone she dates.

"So, Sam, you hit the waves lately?" Clance tips back in his chair and tugs a drink from his bottle of beer as he watches me.

I shake my head and try to silently force the sudden acidic churn in my stomach away. It was just a question about it, for crimeny's sake. "Nah. I haven't felt the call since Mel saved me."

I shrug it off and pray he leaves it alone. I've been really trying to be myself and I don't want to discuss my issues with water with strangers when I won't even discuss them with my best friends.

"Oh yeah, guess that'd do it." He grimaces. "I rode those storm waves later in the afternoon. I didn't know about your accident when I did. They were rough. The fourth wave of the sets were total board eaters."

I take a breath and try to quell the sound of the blood rushing in my ear. A sound that mimics the surf. "Yeah, that's the mistake I made, I think. That's what Kill tells me. I don't remember much of it. They say the knock to the head will probably keep me from remembering much about the accident itself. Well, that and the fact that I was basically dead when Kill pulled me out of the water."

The heaviness settles over the table. I look across the table at Mel. "Thanks again for saving me. I can't say it enough." My voice catches slightly, and I look down at my lap quickly to get the emotion under control quick before anyone notices.

She bites her lip but says nothing. I think Sev put her there for me that day. It's the only thing that makes sense. She said herself that she normally runs later in the day and usually goes north on the beach, not south.

"You're welcome." She says it quietly, the rosy tint darkening on her cheeks.

"Did you know there are videos of it? Of your resuscitation, on the internet?" Clance asks nonchalantly. Sofie gives him a look and probably a kick under the table, judging by his sudden jump.

I nod. "I haven't watched. I don't plan to. Honestly, I can't." I don't want to see myself like that. I don't know why. I just can't. "The fans sent flowers to the hospital. Gosh, there were so many flowers, because they saw the videos. I have all the cards. But they couldn't fit all the arrangements in my room. Mav had the nurses give them to other patients. I keep wanting to go through all the cards, but another part of me doesn't want to. Because it makes it more real, I guess. It was scary, but not for me. I don't remember any of it. But the way that it affected Killian, Callum, and Mav, seeing them deal with it, living it through their eyes, has been difficult." I say the last part so quietly I don't know if they can even hear it.

Clance nods. "I can see that. It's a similar thing for us paramedics, right, Mel? There are cases where you want to know the outcome. But you don't check on them because if it didn't turn out the way you hoped, you know you'd be wrecked because you gave it your all and it didn't prevent the bad outcome. It can eat at you."

Mel nods, her expression darker than normal. "It's an easy hole to fall into. I don't check anymore. I go all-in to each call, knowing that I did the best I could for the short time they were my patient and I leave it at that. But you still have cases you wonder about. Yours was one of them, actually. I wondered if it had been enough, hell I even dreamed about it a few times." At the mention of the dreams, Clance glances at her, his posture suddenly stiff.

"Mostly about Killian's reactions to what was happening. It was gut-wrenching to hear. My brain remembers it, but I couldn't react or respond on scene because I had a more important job to do at the time. But the brain doesn't forget." She looks like she wants to say more, but she doesn't.

"Yeah. He's still pretty messed about the whole thing. I mean, we both are in our own ways, I guess." I shrug. "We each came away with an unhealthy dose of fear." I blurt it out, not meaning to. I don't know these people. Kill would murder me in my sleep if he knew I was telling his secrets. Right now, it's the only way I can keep the pressure off myself, by distracting them with tales of Killian. Fuck, if Mav were here, he'd probably be kicking me under the table. Sometimes I just say the first thing that pops out of my mouth without thinking about the consequence of what I've said.

"Who wants dessert? I made brownies." Sof starts to stand.

"Me," Mel and I say in unison and then laugh.

"I'll help you clear this stuff." I stand and start collecting stuff and Mel does the same thing.

"You're our guests," Sof complains as Mel and I continue to gather the used utensils from dinner.

"Sammy and I can clean this up. You concentrate on brownies," Mel says to Sofie, who just laughs.

# Chapter 18

## *Melody*

C lance pulls me aside as Sampson and Sof discuss the merits of corner brownies over center brownies as they both stand over the still warm dish. I have to admit, I'd rather be with the brownies than with Clance because I know he's going to have something to say about Sampson and I have a sinking feeling it's not positive.

"How do you want this thing with Sampson to play out?" He looks at me. "Because I've talked to him and—"

"You didn't, Clance! I just wanted you guys to get to know him as a person. I know you have reservations about him, and Sampson realizes this too. I just thought it would be good to hang out with him a bit, maybe ease your concerns. He's not the guy you saw at the party." I can't believe Clance talked to him about me.

"You might find it interesting that he's willing to give up on any romantic leanings he has towards you as long as you'll stay his friend." Clance watches as my face turns red. The flame works its way from my jaw and burns across my cheeks.

"Clance, what did you say to him?"

"I just asked what he wanted out of his relationship with

you." He shrugs. "I needed to make sure that he wasn't here to play with your emotions. Because after he ignored you that night at the barbecue, well, let's just say I didn't like what I saw of him that night." It takes me a minute to realize what he's saying. But he mistakes my silence for being upset with him. "Mel, I don't want to see you get hurt, like with Grady."

I pull Clance into a hug. "You're a good guy." I say to him. "But I'm a big girl." I feel him nod against me.

Sampson's quiet as we leave Clance and Sof's house, but reaches across the Jeep and holds my hand, his callused thumb rubbing over my palm as he drives. He takes me home and parks in my space in the resident parking lot behind my building.

"You don't have a car." It's not a question, but a statement.

"I don't really need one. I can walk, ride my bike or the bus, or ride share anywhere I want." I shrug. "It's an expense I don't need. Most everything I need or want is within walking distance except Clance and Sof's house."

"What's up with your mom?" He looks at me, probably remembering the bruises she used to leave on me, or the times he jumped between us to protect me.

"She still lives in the same place as far as I know. I don't visit. I waited as long as I could for you," I whisper. "When I left, I knew I wouldn't be able to go back home, Sampson. She destroyed my self-esteem. She blamed me for my dad's death. I was a damn kid. He died on set." I shrug. "I haven't seen her since I left." I can't tell him that she cut me off completely when I left. I struggled paying for school and keeping a roof over my head after I graduated and went into paramedic training. The Sampson I know would feel guilty when it wasn't his fault. I wasn't his responsibility. Thank God for Clance and Sofie. For the whole firehouse, really.

"I'm sorry, Mel." He strokes my hair.

Leaning towards me, Sampson leaves a light kiss on my

temple. "Can I kiss you, Mel? For reals this time?" His eyes focus on my lips as his own tongue darts out and moistens his.

His words take me back to the first time we kissed. Sampson and I ran in the same crowd since middle school in the San Fernando Valley. We'd been at a party at a beach bonfire. Somehow, a game of spin the bottle got started. His whole spin seemed to happen in slow motion and when the bottle finally stopped, it landed on me, and my heart pounded. He got up on his hands and knees, leaning over the empty Budweiser bottle, and kissed me. The moment his soft lips touched mine, I literally felt the fireworks zipping between us.

It might have just been static electricity, but my naive teenage heart fell in instalove that very moment. I was all emoji heart eyes and everything. I was a total goner, already head over heels for my curly headed, surfing drummer boy, even though we hadn't gone on a single date.

But then he pulled back and immediately told his friends that kiss we'd just shared, the one that had my heart racing in double time, wasn't *a real* kiss. They laughed about it amongst themselves while I wanted to burrow into the sand like a clam.

It was just because of the game; he didn't have any real feelings for me. I was humiliated because Frannie Alexander witnessed the whole damn thing, and she was the school gossip. I knew by the end of the next school day I'd be a laughingstock and I hadn't been wrong.

Ironically, we ended up a couple the next year, and the first time he tried to kiss me, I reminded him of what he said at the bonfire. From then on, whenever Sampson wanted to kiss me, he told me he wanted to kiss me 'for reals.'

His tongue peaks out from his mouth and moistens his lips again as he waits for my answer, his mouth, those lips totally distracting me.

"Um, Mel? Eyes up here." His mouth pulls back in a smirk

and his eyes glint in the low light of the parking lot. "So, can I kiss you for reals?"

I nod and he leans in and pulls my head to his. First, his lips sweetly kiss the tip of my nose. But then his mouth is on mine, soft and warm. And it feels like the first time. Like all the times before he left.

The familiar zing starts in my chest and is working its way down my fingers and toes. His fingers tangle in my hair and I weave mine into his curly locks. His tongue swipes my lips, testing, and I part mine, inviting him in. The zings grow more intense, and warmth floods me, making it far too humid in his Jeep.

Sampson's kiss is both familiar and completely different than ever before. I capture his moan in my mouth before he pulls away.

"Mel," he pants out breathlessly.

"Come upstairs."

He pulls away at my words. "Are you sure?" His eyes study my face before locking with mine.

I nod subtly. "Yes, I'm definitely sure. Come upstairs, Sampson."

"Stay put," he says as he opens his door and jumps down. He rushes over to my side and opens the door. He takes my hands in his. "Jump on down, beautiful."

My jump from the Jeep ends up being more of a slide down Sampson's body, but there is nothing wrong with being in Sampson's arms, my chest pressed against his as I slide down him like he's the pole in a firehouse. He intertwines our fingers as I lead the way to the staircase for the residential part of the building.

As soon as we're in my apartment, I turn, and he hugs me to him. Sampson smells like the beach. Banana sunblock, coconut spice, sun, and himself. He's no longer the scrawny boy who was always hungry from high school. Now he's all lines of firm sculpted muscles. And these firm biceps, I want to lick them. I totally get the phrase 'arm porn' now because the hard, rounded muscles flex and contract as I grasp them while he moves his arms across my back and up my dress. One bare hand spans across my back, clutching me to him so my body is in full contact with his, while his other squeezes my ass. His mouth moves from my lips down my jaw and neck to that sweet spot between my neck and shoulder.

"Sampson—" His name turns into a moan from my lips when he pulls away and removes his shirt in one fluid motion despite it being a buttoned shirt. And I'm rewarded with Sampson's magnificent chest. I trace his six-pack with one hand as he pulls me to him.

"I need this off." His voice is deep as he reaches towards the hem of my sundress to pull it over my head. As I smooth my hair back down, his eyes narrow as he notices my earrings.

"You still have them." His hand holds my hair away from my head as he examines them.

I nod. "They've always been one of my most precious possessions." I reach up and touch the earring.

"They weren't expensive, you know." He strokes the earring with his finger.

"It's not about how much they cost, Sampson. It was that *you* bought them for me. *You* picked them out. It was the best gift I ever got." He leans in and kisses my ear and then works his way to my mouth. Our tongues dance as he unhooks my bra.

"We should move to the bed." I gasp when he pulls my bra off and replaces it instantly with his hands.

"Yeah." He moves his hands to my thighs and pulls them up to his waist, so that I'm forced to lock my legs around his backside. His arms hold my back as he moves us towards the bed. Once we're behind the dressing screens, he drops me to my feet and slips off his shoes.

I grab him by the belt loops of his jeans and pull him towards me and kiss him hard as I work to undo his button fly.

"Mel, are you sure?"

"Yes, I'm so sure, Sampson," I practically growl at him, and he chuckles a deep baritone chuckle and grins a cocky half-grin I haven't seen from him before. But I like it. A lot. So much I might have groaned a little. He's so much more confident in himself as a lover.

I hook my hand into his waistline and try pulling his pants down, but they're too damn tight. He steps back. "Let me do it."

He wiggles out of his pants and then goes through the pocket and gets a condom from his wallet and sets it on the small table next to my bed.

"Better?" He stands in front of me in just his boxers. He is just as chiseled as I had expected, and then some. I run my hand down his hard chest and take in some of his colorful ink. A red snare drum sits over his heart, emblazoned with a 7 on the side. A ribbon with music notes comes from behind the drum and wraps in a scroll up to his shoulder and down part of his bicep, working into his half-sleeve. I squeeze his biceps again.

"These arms," I say softly and lean in and cave into the desire, licking down his inked left arm.

Now it's his turn to growl at me. I push him back towards my bed and he sits with a bounce. I step between his legs, and he hugs me, his head against my abdomen, the top of his head just under my breasts. It's an intimate position that takes me off guard for a second. Then he turns his face towards me and kisses me. And continues to work his way down to my navel where he stops and kisses me, his tongue playing with my belly button ring.

He stops, looks up at me, and flicks it lightly with his tongue. "This is new."

I nod. I don't want to go there. I got it after Grady. But I don't want to think about him or his betrayal. About how I promised myself I wouldn't get close to anyone again. But this is Sampson. And with Sampson, all bets are off. He's always owned my heart.

"I like it." He continues kissing his way down to my most intimate place, just my lacey underwear between his mouth and me. He leans in and kisses my underwear right *there* so I can feel his hot breath.

"Sampson!"

He looks up at me and smiles as he pulls my underwear to the side and slips his finger down my seam. "Mel, you're so wet for me."

I push against his hand, wanting more, more friction, just more Sampson. I clutch my fingers in his curls.

"I got you, Mel, I got you." He leans in and pulls my underwear all the way down, then leans in and laps me with his tongue in one long stroke. My hips roll of their own volition. My fingers tighten in his curls as he adds a finger while his tongue concentrates on my clit, quickly bringing me to the edge as I roll my hips repeatedly against his hand.

It's everything and too much as he curls his finger at the same time he laves my bud, and I see stars as my climax hits me hard and fast. His arms come up and support me as I start to come down from my soaring oblivion.

He holds on to me, returning his head to my abdomen in a hug. It may be my favorite hug from him yet. One hand holds me upright while the other caresses me gently up and down my back in a soft pattern.

He leans back onto my bed and shimmies out of his boxers, then pulls me down onto him. He reaches over and grabs his condom, ripping it open with his damn teeth like he's in a romance novel or something.

After he's sheathed, he helps me position myself over him.

And even though I just came, I want him again. I want all of *my* Sampson, so I move up to straddle him.

"Easy, Mel." The strain on his face as I slide down him is such a turn on. "Hold on." He holds my hips still as I come to rest, completely sheathing him. "Just give me a minute."

He finally blows out a breath and nods subtly. I brace myself against his shoulders as I start to move against him as his fingers dig into my cheeks. He mutters some curses as he thrusts up against me as I work to tilt my hips down on his, trying to increase the friction I need.

I hook my arms under his so I can roll him on top of me. His arms wrap across my back, holding me to him. "Roll," I hiss in his ear, loving the friction of his hard chest against my tight nipples.

Without breaking our connection, we maneuver so he's on top of me. This is exactly what I was looking for. I wrap my legs around his, digging my heels hard into the back of his thighs. I arch my back and thrust my hips against his. His thrusts come faster, and I'm already building up into an even higher crescendo.

"Fuck, Mel. I can't—" His voice strains and I can see the corded muscles in his neck popping out as he tries to hold back as he hovers over me.

"So close, let go." I drag my nails of one hand across his back as my other is gripping my bedding tight. His jaw clenches as I let go of the bedding and reach between us. It doesn't take much, and I've sent myself off the cliff.

I clench down on him hard.

"Sampson." I draw out the last syllable of his name as he thrusts one more time, chasing his own release, cursing, then finally dropping down on me.

His weight on me brings a comfort I've missed for so long. I concentrate on steadying my breath and my heart. Sampson buries his head in my neck as he works to do the same, his short pants hot on my ear and shoulder. My hand strokes lazy circles across his strong back.

"That was—" He's at a loss for the words but I don't need his words. Sampson has come home.

"Yeah, I know." I continue rubbing his back.

This was nothing like the last time we made love. Before we were just fumbling kids who thought what they were doing was everything. This was so much more.

"Promise me you won't leave me. Not like last time." I hate that the words coming out in this tender moment are so raw and clingy, almost destitute. All things I am not, not anymore.

"Never again," he mumbles against my hair softly and I can't tell if he means it or if he's just placating the needy girl in me. I love the feel of him laying on top of me. Holding me and letting me hold him.

"Shit, sorry. I'm crushing you," he mumbles as he holds himself back up off me, eventually rolling on his side and breaking our connection. He leans his forehead against the side of my head for a minute. It's intimate. It's vulnerable on his part. He finally lays a soft kiss on my jaw.

"I'll be right back." He gets up and walks into my bathroom, leaving me with the glorious view of his toned ass as he retreats.

I roll onto my side, propping myself up on my arm so I don't miss him coming back to bed. *My Sampson.* He's not just some guy. He's the only one my heart has always held close. What I had with Grady wasn't love. I didn't want to acknowledge it, but I think I knew it even then. And I definitely know that now.

But I have to tread carefully where Sampson is concerned. He may think he's all in now, but one day, he'll leave again, without warning. Sadly, my heart is already all in with him and I don't know what to do about that because if he leaves again, I'll be devastated.

He appears in the doorway of the bathroom and gives me

his shy smile this time. I recognize this smile from back when we were teens.

"Wanna take a shower together?" His head tilts slightly as he waits for me to answer.

"Sure." I jump out of bed and head into the bathroom with him. He's got it going and I follow him into my steamy shower. This apartment isn't huge. But the bathroom is amazing for the size of the apartment. My shower is big because I chose the bathroom layout that didn't have a tub. Maybe one day I can afford a place with both. But I love this apartment and I moved in when the building was new, so I'm the only one who's lived here, and that means something to me.

Sampson steps in under the spray, then turns and reaches out to me. I take his arm and he pulls me under the water with him.

He grabs my body wash and starts at my feet and washes me all the way up, paying close attention to every nook and cranny except the cranny that wants his nook the most.

"Sampson. You missed a spot."

He grins at me and looks me over. "I certainly did, didn't I? I better fix that."

After some shower loving and then some more cleaning on both of our parts, Sampson grabs my shampoo and puts some in his hand. "Turn around so I can wash your hair."

He works the shampoo through my hair, pausing at my scalp to massage it in. I don't know what it is about having someone else wash your hair. It's my favorite part of getting my hair done. But my stylist has nothing on Sampson's strong fingers as they work circles around my scalp and then down my hair and back again. He tips my head back and shields my eyes as he rinses the soap out and then adds some conditioner.

"Let me do yours while this stays on for a bit. You'll have to sit on the shower bench." He sits on the bench and turns to the side so that I have access to his hair. I do exactly what he did to my mine. Massaging his scalp as he did mine, his eyes shutting as he lets out a little moan while I do it near his temples.

"That feels amazing!" he groans out as I add a little more shampoo to his hair and repeat the massaging.

"I know, right? What is it about when someone else washes your hair that is just so relaxing and awesome? Tip your head back." He does and I carefully rinse out his hair and apply conditioner to his curly locks.

We take turns rinsing out our conditioner and then towel dry each other and ourselves. "Let me dry your hair."

He pulls my hair dryer and a brush out from the stand and carefully brushes it out a section at a time to blow dry. I dry his, scrunching it as I do to encourage the natural bounce in his curls.

"Now, back to bed," I announce when I'm finally satisfied with the job I did to his hair. He slips on his boxers, and I slip on my Motley shirt. I got it at the same concert where I bought his, the show and the shirt, my gifts to him for his birthday. The same year he bought me the earrings that I adore.

When he sees my shirt, he chuckles. "That's the shirt that Gibson stole from me. I feel like an asshole, but I really want it back. It's my favorite one. Killian calls it my security blanket and I guess it kind of is. I even signed our contract with Monumentus wearing that shirt."

"You did?" I smile, knowing that the shirt I gave him is the one he's deemed as his lucky shirt. Come to think of it, he wore it a lot in the time between when we went to that concert and the time he left the valley for Los Angeles. The distance seems tiny now, but back in high school it was huge.

He nods as he slips into my bed, and I follow. He pulls me so I'm tight against him. "It's always been my favorite shirt because you bought it for me." He rolls on his side so he can spoon me, wrapping himself around me as his big spoon tangles with my little spoon. His chin rests on my shoulder, his nose in my hair. This Motley shirt reminds me of him, but it flips my heart knowing the feeling about the shirt was mutual and that as much as he loves Gibson and would give him almost anything, he really wants the reminder of me back.

"I love the way you smell like your shampoo and you. I've missed it. I'm so glad you use the same shampoo," he mumbles in a sleepy-laced timber as he pulls me tighter to him. "You smell like home."

*He thinks you smell like home.* It makes me realize it took me a long time after he left to find a semblance of home. I only really found it once I was staying with Clance and Sof. It was hard for me to leave them, but I had to get my own place. It was definitely time to stand on my own. How ironic that Sampson walked back into my life after I had just started feeling like I had a home of my own.

I can tell he's dozed off when his arms relax slightly and his breathing evens out. However, I'm wide awake. I can't believe my Sampson is here in my bed, holding me. Sleeping with me, after *sleeping* with me.

My brain keeps repeating he'll leave. That I'm not worth staying for. He'll wait until I'm all in, and then he'll leave. Again.

But my heart wars with it. This is different. Before, when we were kids, he never spent the night with me. We were different people at different places in our lives, just trying to survive in our own crappy circumstances. But now we've moved on. It's been a decade. I've moved beyond my circumstances. I made something of myself when I was constantly told I would never amount to anything.

Sampson's home life was worse than mine, and he had a younger sister to take care of. And I know he'd done his best for Sev. But Sevenya had issues that she tried to self-medicate away. Her self-medication turned into a hardcore addiction. And that addiction and the things she tried to medicate away were what killed her.

I wonder if he even realizes I was at her graveside service. I stayed towards the back on purpose because I was still so angry at him, but there was a time that Sevenya was my best friend. I thought he'd seen me and then he didn't come up to me. That slight at the funeral just perpetuated the hurt that caused the bubbling anger in my stomach. But now I wonder if he wasn't so grief stricken that he didn't notice me in the crowd as he scanned over us.

I roll over so I face him, still in his arms, and snuggle up close to him so I can breathe him in and watch him sleep. His face is smoothed of lines that crease his forehead and the lines around his mouth. I wonder if the surfing accident has changed him. He seems different than the Sampson I'd imagined he'd become on the brief occasions I allowed myself to google him. He always looked happy-go-lucky. I wonder how much of that is just a character he plays.

# Chapter 19

## *Sammy*

It seems like forever since I've slept so well, definitely since the surfing accident. Yet here I am in Mel's bed, having just woken up from a full night's sleep, no tossing and turning restlessly until I'm forced out of bed to drum until I can't anymore.

The only reason I'm awake now is that I've got to pee, but I also don't want to disturb Mel, who's still snoring softly against my chest. It's good to know some things never change. When we dated last time, we never really slept together in the same bed after making love. We didn't have our own places then, so we had ended up doing it at the beach, in our beloved secluded cove. I've held her while she slept, just not in a bed after a night like last night. It was even better than I had imagined as a horny teenager in love with his best friend.

Her hair is fanned wildly out from her head every which way. One hand is curled up between her and I, the other lays across my midsection, one leg thrown over mine. The shirt she's sleeping in has ridden up, exposing that sweet belly button ring. It's probably the sexiest thing I've seen. I've seen belly button rings before, of course, but not on my Mel. *My Mel.* I love the sound of that. It feels natural. Like it should be.

I'm already deeming her mine, when I'm not sure that she's all in yet. I broke us last time, but I won't do that again. I have to show her I'm not the same stupid kid that I was. I shouldn't have ghosted Mel. I should've made the effort to at least keep in touch with her.

She mumbles and rolls away from me. That allows me to go to the bathroom. Her bathroom is probably the cleanest and nicest I've seen in a studio apartment. Its large shower is the focal point. She has the same shampoo and body wash she's used since she was a teen. There's a large sink with a counter with her girlie stuff, all neatly arranged within reach. There's a door that leads into the walk-in that I peek into. It's a typical chick closet, lots of clothes all neatly hung and organized in a way that probably makes sense to her. A hamper. A few racks of different shoes line the bottom. Some boxes. Her surfboard is the focal point at the back of the closet.

"Want to go for a run with me?" Her arms reach around me from behind and she squeezes my back to her front.

"Yeah. That sounds great. I have some clothes in the Jeep. Let me grab them." I turn and hug her to me and kiss the top of her head.

"Hoping to get lucky?" She pulls back, amusement curling her lips.

"Nah, I just always have some clothes with me. I usually bounce between staying with each of the guys, depending on what's going on with whom. So, I always keep the essentials in my backpack." Her face goes serious. Probably remembering our conversation from the burger joint, where I admitted not feeling comfortable in my own condo but not able to get rid of it either.

I kiss her forehead. "I'll be back in a few." I slip on my t-shirt and head down to the Jeep and grab my gear. By the time I've gotten back, she's already in her running clothes.

"Water? I remember you don't like coffee." I nod and down the bottle before throwing on my running shorts and shirt. I slip my Converse into the backpack, replacing them with running shoes. I took up running a couple of years ago. None of the guys have taken it up yet. I thought I'd be able to convince Cal, since he's probably the most health conscious of the four of us. When I suggested it, he laughed and said he runs after Gibson enough.

Mel leads us through the same stretches as we always go through, and then I follow her lead as we run. The next thing I know, she has us heading out to the beach. My chest tightens as soon as our feet hit the sand. We head north along the shore, but I am having trouble keeping up with her suddenly. I can't get enough air in my lungs, my chest on fire with every inhale.

I need to get away from here, up to the street, but I can't find an outlet back up to the road without turning back. Mel's probably a hundred yards ahead of me when I finally drop to my knees in the sand, struggling for breath, my vision darkening on the edges. I'm going to pass the fuck out.

"Sampson?" Mel's arm goes around my shoulders. "Sampson? Talk to me." I feel her hand on my wrist. Her other hand rubbing my back slowly.

"Gotta get out of here," I gasp out.

"Okay, we can do that. Can you stand back up?" She reaches under my arm and helps lift me despite my four or five inches of height over her.

"That's it. You're okay." She keeps her voice calm and soothing, and I want nothing more than to push her the fuck off of me and run flat out for the street.

She wraps her arm firmly around my waist and we head to an alley I didn't see, one that leads up to the oceanfront street. She keeps her arm around my waist despite the fact that the further away from the ocean I get, the easier the breaths come and the easier it is for me to walk unassisted.

I pull away from her slightly and she removes her arm from my waist but captures my hand, holding it tight but saying nothing. She has no idea how much I want to yank my hand from hers and just run as far and as fast as I possibly can and hide. From her, from us. I don't want her knowing, seeing how utterly fucked up I am.

When we hit the street, she turns us to the right, and we head back the opposite way we were running. Only now we're just strolling, her hand still clutching mine tight. We walk past some houses, coming to a stoplight. We cross over and head towards a mini mart. She walks us in and gathers two sports drinks, me just following her mutely while she pays.

Once outside, she cracks the lid on the red one and hands it to me. I sip from it, and we start back up the street.

As we walk, she interlaces her fingers in mine again, this time softly. "You haven't been surfing because you've been having panic attacks. Why didn't you tell me?"

I don't answer. I just concentrate on sipping my sports drink and the feel of her hand in mine. She squeezes her fingers around mine.

"Sampson? Why didn't you tell me? If I'd have known, I would have changed the route." I shrug at her. How can I explain that I didn't want her to know that I'm this screwed up?

"At least tell me you've been seeing someone. Talking to someone. A doctor? A therapist?" I shake my head.

"One of the guys?" I snort at that one. Like that'd help. They'd just drag me to a doctor or a therapist.

"Sampson. There's no need to suffer alone."

"I'm not talking to a doctor or a therapist." I pull my hand from hers and take a step away from her. I need some space. "Just forget about it."

"You can talk to me. You might remember, I'm a good listener." She tries to put her hand back in mine, but I don't let her.

"I should get to Cal's soon. We're working on some writing." I pick up our pace back in the general direction of her place, to the point that she's started jogging to keep up.

"Sampson. Please, just talk to me." I've now worked us up to a hard, steady run, pushing until talking isn't easy for her. Maybe now she'll shut it already with all the 'Sampson, talk to me, Sampson, I'm a good listener' crap. I don't need that. Why can't people just leave me the fuck alone when this shit happens.

I push us harder until we both arrive at her apartment, huffing. I follow her in and grab my backpack and keys.

"You're just going to leave?" She holds out another orange sports drink to me. "Just like that?"

I grab the drink from her, yanking it harder than I should. "I told you, we got a writing session today. And you have shift tomorrow." I shrug. "I'll see ya around, Mel."

I regret the callous tone the minute it leaves my mouth. Her eyes reflect a hurt I vowed I'd never put there again. She takes a half step back and nods, her eyes going to the ground for a second before coming back to mine. And just like that, the hurt on her face is replaced with a blank look.

"Yeah, who knows, maybe I will." Her usual bravado has been replaced with a voice full of hurt feelings and I'm instantly reminded not of the strong woman I know her to be but of the meek girl in high school who let the world step all over her.

I swear I hear her mutter something about eleven years as I close her door behind me. I jog down the stairs, not able to get to my Jeep fast enough. Tossing my backpack into the backseat, I jump in and get the hell out of there.

Music blaring on the freeway, I'm stuck in traffic on my way to Cal's, when my heartbeat finally starts to settle in, and I start thinking clearly again. I messed this up with Melody, again. And of course, I had to do it right before she has a shift. I can't even fix what I did. Maybe I'm not meant to be with her after all.

I promised Gibs a drum lesson today anyway. So the making music thing wasn't a complete lie.

I mute the music and activate the Bluetooth in my Jeep. "Call Melody." The automated voice tells me it's calling her. But I get no rings. Straight to voicemail. Great. I contemplate trying to get over three lanes to get off the freeway and turn around. But I talk myself out of it.

# R

"Shammy!" I'm tackle-hugged by Gibson the minute I walk into Cal's house. He's got his drumsticks in his hand. "Wet's dum!" He holds up his sticks.

"Let me just check with your dad and make sure something important, like naptime, isn't about to happen." I pick him up and toss my backpack in the laundry room as I go by.

"Can we do our drum lesson now?" I ask Cal who's sitting with Ari on the couch. They look like they might have been in deep conversation about something. "'Cause I can do laundry and stuff if it's nap time or if you have something planned."

"It's fine, Sam," Cal says. "Gibs has been looking forward to drumming all day."

He nods his little head. "Aww day, Shammy."

"Cool. Is Kill here? I wanted him to check Gibs out."

"Unka Kiwi watchin me dum!" Gibson jumps around excited.

"He's in his room, I think."

Gibson leads the way upstairs and knocks on Kill's door. He bends over and hollers through the crack at the bottom of the door. "Unka Kiwi. Dum time!"

We spend about 30 minutes with him drumming. Towards the end, Killian grabs his bass and starts to play along with Gibson's drumming. He didn't even skip a beat. I grabbed one of Cal's guitars and plucked along. Guitar's not my best instrument but I can get by. He loved it.

I recorded us playing together on my iPad so that Cal can watch his son jamming with us. Turns out Gibs loves watching himself. He gets that from his uncle Mav.

"Dats Gibson dumming." He points to himself. "Dat's Shammy. Dat's Unka Kiwi and dat's Gibson again." He looks up at me with a grin. "I doin' it!"

I run my hand through his blonde curls. "You sure are, buddy. You're a great drummer! Good job."

He runs off with my iPad to show his dad, and Killian looks at me. Really looks at me.

"You messed up with Mel again, didn't you?"

"How do you do that?" Sometimes he flat out gives me the creeps.

Killian chuckles a deep, hearty laugh. "We knew before you even got home. Mel called Sof, who told Clance, who called Cal. Cal was wondering if you'd go straight to Mav's today."

"I'd never blow off Gibson, he's a kid."

Kill nods. "I know. He makes everything a little better, huh?" His voice has a slight awe to it, and I can't help but wonder if he regrets keeping Gibs at arm's length for so long.

"I knew you'd never blow Gibs off. And speaking of, he's amazing already, isn't he? You've done good teaching him."

"Me? Nah. It's innate for him, in his genes. I'm just harnessing what he's already got."

Kill nods his agreement. "Yeah. But back to Melody. What did you do this time?"

And I tell him, starting with the barbecue and ending with me bailing after flipping out on the beach.

"I tried calling her on the way back here. After I had calmed down. My calls went right to voicemail. Maybe it's just better that I don't see her. I'm pretty fucked up." I don't say the rest of the sentence, "...*since I died and came back.*"

Killian nods. "If you feel that's what's best for you. But can I ask you something?"

I nod and swallow because I know that he's going deep. I wouldn't expect anything less from Kill lately.

"Why are you so vehemently opposed to seeing a therapist? You've flipped out and shut down each time someone's mentioned it. Are you worried about what people will think, what we'll think of you?"

Tears burn behind my eyes as I contemplate his question. "Maybe partially. But it's more than that. I don't want to be medicated. My mom was medicated. It's what made her an addict. I don't want to go down that path. I promised Sev I wouldn't go there."

He nods and settles on the floor near me. "You know therapists can't prescribe medication, right? They can suggest you talk to a psychiatrist who can do the medication thing, but a therapist is just someone you talk with. It's not a slippery slope where people will be pushing medication on you at every turn. I promise."

He throws an arm over my shoulders. "You really should talk to one. Hell, you can talk to mine if you want." I had a feeling he'd been seeing someone. I'm pretty sure Callum insisted after he told me Cal lit into him for not wanting to see the psychiatrist from the hospital. "Or I'll help you find someone else if you want your own. We're all worried about you. You may not even realize it, but you aren't yourself. We're not complaining because at least we have you. But see someone. Please." He squeezes my shoulders. "I'll back off the 'you and Mel' shit if you'll see someone."

"I'll go. If you promise not to tell anyone." I take a deep breath. I'm so tired of people telling me I'm not myself. How could I be? I died and came back to life, and when I did, the solace brought to me by water was replaced by panic.

"Yeah?" A smile grows across his face. "I promise. We can say we are going out to do something and you can go, and I'll chill in the parking lot or whatever. Or you can go alone. Whatever works for you."

"Yours is good?"

"This new one. She is. You want to see her?" When I nod, he doesn't hesitate to pull out his phone. "Then let's do it." He makes an appointment for me with his therapist.

"First appointment is tomorrow, 4:00 pm. Okay?" I nod. "I'll go with you. But not into the office or anything. The guys won't think anything of it. We always go off together."

# Chapter 20

## *Melody*

Sampson: *I need to explain. For reals, Mel. Please. Give me a chance.*

I reread his text and contemplate how to answer. I haven't heard from him since I shunned his calls when he walked out on me. Again. It sent me into a depressive spiral and if it weren't for Sof and Clance, I probably wouldn't have left my apartment for weeks. I snuggle into my bunk at the firehouse and contemplate it. Do I give him yet another chance to break my heart or ignore him?

This thing with Sampson was nothing but a childhood crush revisited. It's probably better to just let it go. Except for that amazing night we shared before he pushed me away again. It ran its course. I should have known that before I let him in my bed. I sigh and the station alarm has me jumping up and heading to the bus without thinking.

After the grueling multi-vehicle accident on the freeway, we are heading back towards the station house.

"I'm dying for some coffee. You want some?" Stephen nods at one of the few all-night diners open.

"So much yes." I laugh.

"Cool, I'll just run in. Your usual?" He parks our ambulance in a well-lit area of the parking lot.

"Please. Strawberry if they have one. If not, I'll eat whatever." He nods and heads into the diner. He knows I'm talking about Carla's turnovers. They are so good. And she gives them to any first responders for free, along with the coffee. She's such a sweetheart. I unhook my seatbelt and move into the back of the ambulance to replace some of the supplies we carry in our go-bag that goes onto each scene with us, refilling all the empty pockets.

The driver's side door opens, and the engine starts.

"That was fast. Did she have strawberry?" I straighten from my crouch.

The next several things happen all at once. The ambulance shifts into gear before I'm even seated, something Stephen would never do. At the same time, I glance out the rear window and watch as Stephen steps out of the diner, balancing two coffees and two pastry bags. Our eyes connect through the back window and my stomach drops with the knowledge that he's not the one that has started our bus and put it into gear. We lurch forward into the street and Stephen drops what he's carrying and runs towards me in the ambulance just as it pulls out into traffic.

My heart drops into my stomach as I slowly turn towards the front of the bus. Flat, dark eyes stare at me in the rearview mirror.

"Sit down." His rough voice is as dead as his eyes. I move towards the jump seat to sit down. "You'll sit in that chair if you know what's good for ya."

My heart pounds. What do I do? He's driving this ambulance away from Santa Monica, taking surface streets to keep it on the down low. It's late at night. My eyes search the back of the bus, looking for something. Anything I could use as a weapon.

"Medic fourteen Santa Monica, please respond. Repeat, medic fourteen, please respond with your location."

It's Libby, tonight's fire dispatcher. Her voice waivers slightly, something it never does. She's got the coolest head in the dispatch center, and she's nervous. He probably didn't pick it up in her voice, but knowing her the way I do, I hear it. She's been told something's amiss. She repeats her call.

"They are calling for us. We are Medic fourteen." My voice is shakier than Livvie's, but I don't care. He knows I'm scared. He's carjacked my ambulance and taken me hostage. Of course, I am scared. "If you don't respond, they will come looking for us. The ambulance has a transponder, so they know where we are."

He pulls the radio towards his mouth. "If you want to see your little EMT nurse alive, you won't follow us. Come close and she's a goner. Medic fourteen is out of service." He turns off the radio. I don't know if turning off the radio turns off the transponder. I don't even know if he keyed the radio hard enough that they heard him.

My ambulance is one of the newer ones and most of the monitors and equipment are bolted into built-in cubbies to make transporting patients safer, so if there is an accident, equipment doesn't fly around. There's not a lot of loose stuff I can use as a weapon. I quietly slide open one of the drawers closest to me and slip out a scalpel. It's the closest thing to a weapon I have. The scissors are in the other drawer. They may be bigger, but the scalpel will be sharper. Plus, he'd see me get up to get the scissors.

I quietly reach for the IV tubing and roll out as much as I can, using the small scalpel to slice it free. The scalpel and the tubing are all I have to defend myself. Maybe I can use it as a rope and tie him up.

The ambulance stops, and he gets up and comes into the back.

"You're too quiet. What are you up to?" He has a large bowie type knife pulled out.

He sees the tubing at my feet and his eyes narrow at me. "Sit back in the seat. Now!"

I let the scalpel that I shoved up my sleeve fall into my hand. The dull lighting in the ambulance glints off the shiny knife blade in his hand and I swallow. His knife is huge, but I have the element of surprise.

"Sit back now!" he yells. I take the opportunity and lunge at him with the scalpel pointed towards his gut, where I can do the most damage with the least amount of effort. It makes it past his thick shirt and into his belly. I push it in as hard as I can until he grabs my wrist, squeezing it until I feel my bones grinding and let go. I didn't have time to make the ripping motion I was planning.

He shoves me back into the seat and makes quick work of the belts. He straddles me on the seat and runs the blade down my face lightly.

"Please don't hurt me. I'll give you anything you need. You want the drugs? I'll tell you which key opens which bin. Please," I beg him.

He presses the blade into my cheek harder. He smells like body odor and piss and his hair is dull and matted. My stomach acid burns the back of my throat. "Already bargaining. Pathetic. Just like this pathetic stick." He pulls the scalpel out of his stomach and tosses it aside.

"Ow." I feel the tip of the knife penetrate my cheek skin slightly as he presses it harder.

"Shut the fuck up. I don't want to hear you. I don't want your suggestions. I don't want you to beg for your life. Just shut the fuck up."

"Okay," I whisper.

My head instantly rings and pain blasts through my cheek

and head and all I see are bright little squiggles in my vision from the slap he gives at my response.

"I said shut the fuck up and I meant it. Got it?"

I nod slowly, tasting blood inside my mouth from where I bit my cheek when he hit me. He gathers the plastic tubing at my feet and fashions a rope out of it.

"Open." He presses it against my lips. "Open your fucking mouth if you know what's good for ya." I open and he shoves a wad of the tubing in my mouth and uses the rest of it to secure my head to the seat. "That'll shut you the fuck up."

He grins a sickening smile at me and then looks me up and down. "Let's just see what's going on here." He grabs the collar of my shirt and pulls. The buttons ping off the interior of the ambulance, leaving my shirt open to just my tank top. He starts pulling open drawers until he finds the scissors and cuts my tank top and bra open, much like we would do with a patient. I close my eyes as he runs the blade down my chest. He circles each of my breasts, then stops right in between them and presses against my skin, smiling as he slices through my skin slowly.

I can feel the coolness of the blade as it enters my skin. I'm bleeding and all I can focus on are his filthy, dirt-caked fingers and how that filth is going to give me an infection. It's almost like I'm watching myself be accosted on a television show.

"I just wanted the ride. But you're a nice diversion. It's been a while, if you know what I mean." He licks the side of my face, down my neck all the way down to the center of my chest where I'm bleeding, his hands gripping my breasts like they're doorknobs.

I fight myself to keep from gagging. Forcing myself to swallow so the acid slides back down into my stomach. The plastic tubing he shoved in my mouth would make vomiting impossible and possibly cause me to breathe it into my lungs. It's hard enough to breathe with the plastic in my mouth anyway. I unfocus my eyes, trying to numb myself away from what he's doing to me.

He removes the soft restraints from the gurney and uses them to cuff my hands behind me and then returns to straddling my lap.

All I can see are his dead eyes. All I smell is his acrid, vile breath and the coppery smell of my own blood. The bile rises again, and I can't hide the dry heave.

"Don't think getting sick would be pleasant with that in your mouth," he growls, motioning to my mouth stuffed with wadded up tubing. Something catches his attention, and he turns to look out the rear windows of the ambulance.

"Time to get going. More of this later." He moves back up to the front of the ambulance and we take off. While removing the restraints from the gurney, he must have accidentally unlocked the wheels because it crashes into the side of the ambulance when he takes a curve in the road with too much speed.

I'm tied to the jump seat with the gurney knocking into me with every sharp turn the ambulance takes. But I can still see out the rear window.

He weaves us through a neighborhood just on the outskirts of Santa Monica. He pulls into the parking lot of a huge apartment complex, pulling around the backside into a remote alley that houses the huge garbage dumpsters for the whole complex.

"Now, where were we?" He returns to straddling me. "What's the matter? Cat got your tongue?" His dark, humorless chuckle brings goose bumps to my arms, and I shiver uncontrollably.

"Puh, pease don." My words are slurred because of the tubing still stuck in my mouth. I squeeze my eyes shut and turn my head to the side. My lip trembles and behind closed eyes I see Sof and Clance and wish I could be with them and not here. Anywhere but here.

His tongue drags across my cheek all the way to my ear. "What did I tell you about making noise?" His whisper is hot on my ear. My head is still ringing from the last time he slapped me, so I say nothing.

"So you can learn," he whispers. "Good girl." He licks down my neck to my breast and tugs on it with his lips. I keep my eyes shut tight. I just want to be anywhere but here. Anywhere. He stops and pushes back slightly on my lap.

"Open your eyes, nurse," he commands. "Open your eyes or I'll slice your little breasts right off."

I open them in time to watch him remove himself from his pants. He strokes himself while he sits on my lap. I'm watching him from across the ambulance, like it's happening to someone else. His grunts and hip thrusts as he tugs on himself while sitting on my lap brings up the acid again, but I can't hold it back this time despite the tubing in my mouth. The acidy bile comes up all around the tubing in my mouth, some leaking out onto him.

"You fuckin' bitch." He slaps me again as he softens in his other hand. My vision flickers a bit more as I cough and fight not to breathe in the vomit still in my mouth, blocked by the tubing. "I hope you drown in your own vomit, bitch." He lifts his arm back with the knife and I close my eyes again. This time, I'm at peace, knowing that it will soon be over.

A siren sounds, and I open my eyes and can see the shadows of the flickering blue and red lights.

"Fuck!" He buttons his pants as he stands. "You're lucky for now. But I'll be taking my time with you later." He snarls as he moves past me towards the driver's seat. He pulls through the alley, crashes through a flimsy gate, and goes back through to the road.

Police cars follow us with their lights on. I can't hear their sirens. All I can hear is the blood rushing in my ears as I sit restrained in the back of my bus, tubing soaked with my vomit, making it hard to breathe. For a moment, I lock eyes with the officer in the car behind us, pleading silently for his help. I don't even care that he can probably see my breasts as my hands are still tied behind me, so I can't cover myself.

The faster the ambulance goes, the more the gurney rolls around and the harder my legs get knocked into.

We've finally merged onto the freeway and he's taking the ambulance, lights and sirens now activated, along the shoulder at an unsafe speed. Unsuspecting cars rush to clear a path for us, unaware of what is actually happening.

The gurney slides and jumps all over the back area. He's half on the shoulder, half in the emergency lane, going like a bat out of hell. The crashing of the gurney against my legs makes me nauseous again. Another turn and he is again taking it too fast. So fast. I'm tossed back and forth slightly, tethered by my belts as the restraints holding my hands pull my shoulders and wrists at awkward angles and the slice in the middle of my chest pulls.

Through the back window I can tell we've left the highway and are climbing a hilly area, probably somewhere in Malibu canyon, but it's hard to tell exactly where because it's dark outside. All the while I'm being jarred side to side in my seat and being followed by the blue and red lights on the back of the cop cars keeping their distance.

Tires screech and I'm momentarily weightless, and then the earth outside turns upside down and around like the inside of an agitating washing machine until the world goes dark.

# Chapter 21

## *Sammy*

"You aren't welcome here." Clance stands in front of the hospital room that my Mel is in, chest puffed out and thick arms crossed over his chest. All I know is what's been on the news, that she's in stable condition. It took me a while to ferret out where she was in this hospital, but now that I'm finally here, he won't fucking budge.

"I just want to see her for a minute. Is she okay? Is she going to be okay?" I beg him for information.

Clance stares down his nose at me, his jaw flickering with the muscles tightly clenched.

"Please, man. I love her. I just need to see her, see that she's okay." I keep my voice soft, trying to make sure he knows I need this. I haven't slept since I heard the news report of a carjacked ambulance. I texted Sof, but I knew before the reply that it was my Mel. I could feel it in my gut.

He shakes his head ever so slightly. "Not gonna happen, Denton."

"Can you just tell me how she is?"

He shakes his head again. "Leave before I call the police to escort your ass out of here."

I drop my head. I'm not getting in. I turn and start back towards the downstairs private waiting area Kill stayed in while I came up here. He looks up at me, hopeful, but then deflates when he sees me.

"Clance won't let me in. Told me he'd call the police on me. I just want to know how she is." Kill pats my back a few times.

"Let's go home, man."

# ℞

*Seven weeks later*

Kill and I walk on the boardwalk near the ocean. It's part of my therapy homework. Cheryl has me slowly getting used to bodies of water, working to reassure my fucked-up brain that the ocean isn't out to murder me. We started with the pool at Callum's. I can now get into the pool like I used to, much to Gibson's glee. I'm not as comfortable as I was pre-drowning, but I'm no longer bolting at the mere mention of pool time with my little buddy.

The ocean has been harder to conquer, though. And more important to me that I do conquer my fear of it. It used to be my happy place and I'm determined that it will be again. So at least three times a week, sometimes more, someone walks with me. We've worked up to the boardwalk. Walking with someone helps keep me accountable because my fucked-up brain still thinks it's in danger and throws up the alarm. That makes me want to stay away. Avoid it. But I can't do that if I'm going to get over it.

Usually Kill walks with me. Sometimes it's Kady or Ari, sometimes both. Mav wants to come, but the one time he did, it drew a crowd around us and that set off my freak-out alarm hard. Ironically, Cal, who was all pro-therapy, keeps a distance from me working through my shit. Maybe he feels I need to do it on my own.

Kill was right about therapy and my medication fears, though. Not once has Cheryl indicated that she thought I should be medicated. We've even talked about my fears of being a medicated zombie. Of my mom's addictions. Sometimes all we talk about is the ocean, the drowning, and the panic attacks. Other times we talk about the band and my relationships with each of the guys. Lately, we've talked a lot about Sev. Probably since the anniversary of her overdose is coming up on Thursday and she's been in my heart and head a lot lately.

Kill kicks at a bottle cap on the boardwalk as we go. When we get to it again, I stop to pick it up.

"I think I'm ready to try walking on the sand next time," I blow out, while looking at the expanse of sand and the water beyond.

"Did Cheryl tell you that?" Kill asks.

I shake my head. "No. I know it's time to try. This walk has gotten almost easy. Like it's nothing."

He reaches over and squeezes my shoulder. "That's great. If you think you're ready for the next step, we'll try the sand. Whatever you need, we're here. Every step, man."

"I know you are. Maybe next time instead of the boardwalk, we can walk on the beach at Mav's." Kill nods in agreement and we start walking again. At least at Mav's the beach is usually less populated, so when I freak out, because I will at first, there will be less of an audience.

"Speaking of steps," I blow out a breath because this one is almost as scary as walking on the sand. "It's time I start seriously thinking about selling the condo."

Kill stops our progress on the boardwalk, and a noise that's not quite a gasp escapes his lips. He clears his throat. "That's a big step, man. You sure?"

"No. Yes. No. I dunno. But it's ridiculous to keep a condo I can't sleep in. A home that isn't a home because Sev is in every damn room." I bite the inside of my cheek, so I don't cry right here out on the boardwalk. "I mean, I'll have to find someplace else first and—"

"Why? You've been staying with one of us since she died six years ago. Why rush to find some place just so you can get out of your condo? You always have a room at my place. Not that I've been staying there since the drowning, but we are adults and can go back to my place at any time. You'll always have your own bedroom at Cals. And at Mav's. You have keys to all three places. Why rush into getting your own place?"

I shrug. "I feel bad. Like I'm using you guys. Like I'm mooching or in the way."

"Stop. Sam. You are never in the way. Ever. I'd bet my ass. No, I'd bet my Harley that Cal and Mav would each say the same thing."

I shrug and move to start back down the boardwalk. Kill puts a hand on my shoulder. "Promise me you'll talk with Cheryl about it before doing anything with the condo."

I nod.

"If, uh, when, you know, it's time. To, you know, go through her stuff. Will you, uh," fuck why is it so hard for me just to ask for help? It's something that's even been coming up with Cheryl more and more.

"You know I will. We all will. We'll do it together. But when it's time. Okay?" He throws an arm over my shoulder and squeezes me to him. "But not before you talk to Cheryl. Maybe take on one thing at a time, Sam. Ocean. Then condo."

Kill turns us back towards the way we came. We walk in silence. I watch the joggers on the sand.

"I know we walk here because you hope to see her," Kill says. "You look for her each time a jogger goes by."

I shrug. I do look for her. I haven't seen or heard from Mel since I walked out of her apartment after having the panic attack on the beach with her. I worry about her since her ambulance was hijacked. But I've gotten radio silence from Mel, Clance, and Sof.

I've texted her, but I stopped when she stopped reading them, which was the day of the hijacking. I've called her. Her phone goes straight to voicemail. I've left messages, apologizing both before and after, asking to see her, if she needs anything. She hasn't responded. Clance won't let me near her. Sof stopped returning texts after the ambulance-jacking. I hate not knowing what is going on with her.

I sent her flowers a couple of times. Now, instead of sending *her* flowers, I send a bouquet weekly to Mrs. Chamske. She likes them more than Mel did anyway.

I've even driven past her place a few times and the gym she goes to. I don't go into either place. Just drive by, hoping to catch a glimpse of the girl I love.

I'm trying to accept that Mel and I don't work. That she's done with me, given up on us. It's a damn bitter pill to swallow because I know it's my fault. Again.

"I can't deny it. I miss her. But I messed that up." It's done with.

"I think she'd understand if you told her about the panic attacks. About therapy." Kill looks at me.

"She's ignored me for almost two months now. I think it's abundantly clear she wants nothing to do with me. I can't really blame her. Every time we get close, I end up shoving her away."

"You want me to talk to her? I could go try to see her, maybe talk her into seeing you? Explain?" Kill offers quietly.

"That's a generous offer, but I'm trying to accept that the Melody ship has sailed."

By the time we're almost back to the Jeep, I realize I'm hungry, ravenously hungry. Since walking out of Mel's like I did, food just hasn't had an appeal. I know it worries the guys since I was always eating and now have to basically force myself to eat. But right now I crave pizza. Not just any pizza, but Gianni's in Venice.

When I head towards Venice, Kill doesn't say anything. We go to Gianni's and share a pie in the back room. Cal and Mav and their wives join us. It's the first time we've all sat around having dinner out in a long time. It's nice.

"It's good to see you eat like you aren't forcing it down," Cal mentions quietly as Ari takes Gibson to the bathroom.

"When we got in the Jeep after the walk today, I actually felt hungry. It was weird since I haven't felt that at all lately. I had to indulge the craving. Thanks for joining us. Actually, thanks for everything. For worrying and letting me stay when I need to. Not just since the drowning, but since Sev."

"Dude. Not here. But also, not necessary. We're a family." His voice is thick, and he grabs his beer to wash the emotion down with. He smacks me hard on the back. "Seriously. Family. It's what we do." He nods and grins as Gibson comes running around the table at us.

"Coins?" he asks, his hand out. "Pease."

"Pah-lease." Cal sounds out to emphasize his 'L' sound.

Gibson nods. "I saided that. Pease." His little hand is out. Cal gives him some quarters and I dig out the few I have in my pocket too.

"Skeebaw!" Gibson grabs my arm and drags me to the small arcade in the very back. He likes to play skee-ball with me because he knows I'll hold him up so he can get the ball closer to the center.

By the end of the evening, we are all crammed into the small arcade at the back of Gianni's trying to best each other's skee-ball score. It reminds me of cornhole with Mel and Clance and that makes me sad. Turns out Mav is the king of skee-ball this time, with Kill coming in a close second. Ari and her sister Vi watch from a nearby table.

We break up into our own vehicles as we leave. Kill goes with Cal and Ari since he's holding a sleepy Gibs.

"See ya back at the house. I might be a few." I nod at Cal and head over to my Jeep. The night's perfect for a drive, especially one with the top off. I head the opposite way as Cal.

At the red light, I'm fiddling with my phone, trying to connect it to the Bluetooth so I can play some tunes when I hear a familiar voice.

*"Dammit, I can do it myself, Clance."* Mel! I know that voice anywhere. I turn towards her exacerbated voice and see her for the first time in nearly two months and almost don't recognize her.

Her hair's a lot shorter and has caramel highlights. But it's not the hair that has me shocked. She's got crutches under both arms, one leg in a hard cast to just under her knee. The other leg in some sort of hard black boot going midway up her calf. There's a hard set to her jaw and a scowl across her face that is half-pissed off and half-pain. She's thinner, bonier than I've ever seen her.

She eyes Clance hard as he backs off from assisting her into the car sitting at the curb. She expertly lowers herself into the car and Sof hands her the crutches that she pulls in with her.

The car behind me honks because I'm still staring after Mel. At the noise, Sof looks up and makes eye contact with me and shakes her head slightly before I gas it.

I fight myself not to chase them down. I didn't realize she was injured so badly.

I pull up to Cal's place and jump out of my Jeep. As I come in, Kill's coming downstairs.

"Oh, hey, I thought you were going for a drive."

"I saw Mel. She apparently got all busted up." It comes rushing out.

"She's hurt?" His forehead wrinkles.

"She was in casts. Two different kinds, one on each leg. She had crutches and was yelling at Clance on the sidewalk. Then they left. Well, I left actually. I had to. My light was green, and people were honking at me to go." I still feel like I should go back and see her.

"Casts? You sure it was Melody?" Kill looks skeptically at me.

"Yeah, it was definitely her. Plus, right after the cars behind me started honking, I locked eyes with Sofie. It was Mel. Sofie shook her head at me right before I left. It was so quick. I don't know if she was shaking her head at me, trying to warn me away from Mel, or if she was upset with me and that's why. I don't know. I should drive over to Mel's and see what happened to her. If she's okay. If she needs anything. I mean, don't you think I should?"

Kill puts a hand on my chest. "Slow up there. If she wanted you to know, don't you think she would have called or texted?"

The wind from my sails leaves immediately. Because he's right. She would have told me if she wanted me to know or if she needed me.

Kill's texting someone before I realize what he's doing. "I asked Sofie. I just said that you saw Mel and are concerned. That you wanted to know if there is anything you can do. That you've texted Mel, but she seems to have blocked you or is ignoring you or something." He shows me the text. "I'll let you know when she replies."

"Shammy, wet's get wet!" Gibson launches himself at me in a flying leap, dressed in nothing but swim trunks. He's lucky I caught him.

I change into my boardshorts and hit the pool just as Cal's throwing in Gibson's favorite floatie.

"You can say no to him, you know." Cal settles into one of the chairs poolside.

"I know. I could use the swim." I hold my hands out as Gibson takes a flying run towards me to jump into the pool.

"You want in the floatie?" He nods and I wrangle him into his ship floatie.

"You know, I'm okay in the pool now. I'm not going to freak out with Gibs here, Cal."

Gibson nods. "Shammy not feaking out wif Gibshon, Cal," he parrots, and I can't help the hearty laugh when he not only copies what I said but calls his dad Cal. This kid.

Gibson has me drag him around the pool in his floatie, then he jumps into the pool several times into my waiting arms. He's fearless in the water, this kid. To be like him again.

He knows I'll catch him. He practices kicking and putting his face in the water, just not both at the same time, yet. It'll come. He's gotten better since the accident. I'm glad I'm doing well enough that I can get into the pool with him again. I know he's missed it as much as I have.

Gibson's starting to tire out as we play, plus it's starting to get late. I know Cal will want him soon anyway for bedtime things.

"You done, bud?" He nods and I carry him out of the pool. Cal tosses me his Froggie pool towel, and I start drying him off before he climbs into his dad's lap. I'm just about to jump back into his pool to do some laps when Kill shows up, phone in hand.

"You heard from Sofie?"

He nods and jerks his head, indicating I should come look at something on his phone.

*Sofie: Clance will kill me if he finds me giving you information. She's got two broken leg bones (tib-fib) in one leg and a broken ankle in the other. They are healing well, and she should be out of casts within the next couple of weeks, according to the orthopedist.*

*Sofie: Her shoulder was dislocated but has been reset. She's been doing PT for the shoulder and wrist already. That will become more intense when the casts come off and they start on legs too.*

*Sofie: She's hurting physically and mentally. She's angry this happened, at the loss of independence (she's moved back in with us), at the possible consequences this will have on her career, since there's talk she might be medically retired depending on the outcomes of PT.*

The more I read, the further my gut drops. Mel lives for her job, despite the long shifts. I've never heard her complain about it. She was always on time for her shifts.

*Sofie: She could probably use a friend or two right now, but I can't force her to contact Sam. Or you. Clance has her convinced that Sam isn't good for her.*

I figured he did something like that. Dammit. Not that I don't deserve it. But still.

*Sofie: I'm starting to really worry. She never leaves, except for PT or doctor's appointments. She even avoids the guys from the station house. They drop by fairly regularly, but she refuses to see them. I can barely get her to eat dinner. Even when I make her favorite. I won't lie. It's tough. On all of us.*

*Sofie: Clance is devastated this happened to her. He beat the hell out of the paramedic that was on duty with her, even though it wasn't his fault. So now he's on administrative leave. She's depressed, he's moping. They bicker. Constantly.*

*Sofie: It's...a lot, Killian. Sorry to dump on you. I don't expect you to do anything. Guess I needed to vent to someone, and you happened to ask when I had half a bottle of wine with dinner.*

I need to help Mel, like she's helped me. And help Sofie and Clance too. I have just the idea.

# Chapter 22

## *Melody*

My physical therapist, David, critiques my form as I do more shoulder exercises with the resistance bands. "Pull that a little higher. Good. Good." He stops and really looks at me.

"You're even quieter than normal. Everything okay? How's the pain level?"

"Same as always," I reply, and he nods and makes a note in what I assume is my chart. I don't tell him that I had a really shitty morning.

*"You need to get out of the house a little, kid. You won't gain your strength back sitting on the couch feeling sorry for yourself, Mel."*

*"I don't want to get out of the house."* Because he's out there, lurking behind every fucking bush.

*"You need to move, Mel. You aren't doing yourself any favors."*

*"Fuck you Clance. Sofie can take me back to my apartment."* It's his biggest fear right now. Me alone. But he doesn't know that it's my biggest fear right now too.

"Another set." I should be glad that David is having me do another set. It means I am getting stronger, that he thinks I can handle more. But I'm not in the mood to be here today.

*"Please don't use me as a go-between."* Sof comes into the room, her voice strained. *"Seriously, you guys. I see both sides. Clance is pushing you out of your comfort zone, which you need. Mel, you're so pulled in on yourself, you're starting to worry us. You don't eat much, you hardly sleep, you never want to go anywhere."*

*"Will you stop mothering me? Just because you can't have your own kids doesn't mean you both can smother me."* I regret the words as soon as I say them. Sof winces and turns her head like I slapped her.

*"Woah,"* Clance steps up to me, so Sof is behind him. *"That was totally uncalled for, Mel."* His jaw ticks and his eyes are hard. *"What the fuck is wrong with you? We care for you, worry about you, fucking lose sleep over you because you're not eating or sleeping, and you throw that in her face. Our faces."* Clance's words aren't the patient and kind words he's been giving me. They are loud and hard to hear, so I can't even look at him. I look past him at Sof, who is full on crying now. She won't even make eye contact with me. She just turns and leaves the room.

*"That was a seriously low blow, Mel. I didn't think you were that person."* Clance's words pierce me. *"I'm so disappointed in you right now."* He turns and walks out on me too.

I didn't mean to hurt them. But I'm just so fucking angry and scared all the time. And that's on top of the pain. I look out the window because I don't want David to catch me crying. He'll think I'm in pain and fuck I am, but this is about this morning and not about my leg. I don't want him to stop pushing me. I must get better, stronger, so I can prove to the department that I am okay to be a fire paramedic.

"Good. I want you to add another set to all the home exercises except for the leg ones. We want to keep your strength up in the legs but not stress those healing fractures yet. Okay?"

"Yeah sure. Whatever you say." It's not his fault I am feeling less than enthusiastic. My head is still back at the house this morning.

*She didn't say a word to me the whole ride to therapy. Not her usual, "You got this." Not the "Fuck you, Mel" that I deserve. She wouldn't even look at me when I struggled to get out of the car or offer help like she usually does.*

"You sure you're doing okay? You don't seem to be as into it as usual. You're usually my most gung-ho patient." His lips pull down into a frown. Great. I've even disappointed my freaking physical therapist. It's an A-plus kind of day.

I've been coming to PT for weeks but have seen no real improvement because we can't work on my legs much yet. I just want to walk, to know if I'll be able to perform in a manner that will allow me to keep my job as a fire paramedic because my future is pretty bleak if that doesn't happen.

I shrug while we move slowly to the next exercise.

"Did you hear me when I said no extra sets on your home leg exercises? If you re-injure those healing bones, the casts will stay on even longer. You may even have to have more surgery." He's using his Mr. Serious Therapist voice and I hate that. I want to lash out at him too. Everyone. Everything. I am just over-all pissed off today and I want to make people hurt like I hurt, both inside and physically.

"Okay. Got it. Extra set on everything except for legs." I'm clipped and I don't look at him because it'll be too easy to lash out and as much as I want to, I know it's not right. He's here to help me, not be my verbal punching bag.

He nods and hands me my crutches. "Let's get to the massage therapy room and then you're done for today." At least they don't baby me here. They tell me where to go but make me get there on my own. Clance keeps coddling me, trying to do things for me. I get he's trying to help, and he feels bad for me, but I need to do things myself.

The massage therapist works my shoulders and my thighs and hips, then puts me on the electrotherapy machine for 20 minutes on my upper thighs to stimulate the muscles there.

She leaves the door open at my request, but the small dark room that's meant to be soothing actually reminds me of being in the back of the ambulance.

I can't wait to get the casts off. Even if I still have boots or supports of some sort, getting the stiff cast off will at least make everything a little easier.

I check out at the desk and slowly crutch myself outside. Sof's car is usually parked in one of the handicap spots in front of the building. But she's not there. Those spots are all taken so I scan beyond the handicap spots hoping to see her car, but the longer I look, the more I realize she's not here.

She finally gave up on me. Hot tears well up in my eyes. I deserve it. My heart drops to my stomach and I feel even worse about the things I said this morning and how I acted. I start towards the bench with my crutches. I'll give her a few and then text her an apology. I guess I could rideshare out to the house, but that will be a lot of money, and I have to skimp now, in case I am medically retired.

"Mel! Mel, wait." I turn. What the hell is Sampson doing at my physical therapy appointment? He's parked in the handicap spot out front. He opens the passenger door to a luxury sedan, a beautiful silver Porsche Panamera.

"Sampson?"

"I'm your ride this afternoon." He smiles a big Sampson grin at me. "Come on, or do you need help?" At least he's giving me the option of help without foisting it on me like I'm an invalid or a child.

I crutch myself up to his car. "I really pissed Sof off this morning, didn't I?" I mumble the words, thinking Sampson probably doesn't hear them.

He shrugs an arm at me, his smile faltering a bit. "I dunno. This has been in the works for a couple of days." Guess he heard me after all.

"She couldn't get Clance to come get me?"

Sampson grimaces at my suggestion. "I don't know that he knows. He's not my biggest fan. It's been worked out between me, Sof, and our chauffeur for the day, Killian. I didn't think getting into my beast of a Jeep would be good for you. And no one drives Kill's cars except Kill." Sampson grins at me again.

"I still don't understand why Clance couldn't come get me." I can't believe they dumped me on Sampson. How embarrassing. I know I've been a bear to deal with, but Sampson doesn't care about me.

"Because Kill and I are borrowing you." He smiles at me.

"Borrowing me? I'm not a cup of sugar or some printer paper, Sampson."

"I need to talk to you. Privately. Don't worry, Kill will give us some space for that part. But I also thought it might be fun for you to get away from Sof and Clance for a few hours."

"I think you mean for them to get away from me." His brows furrow at my interjection.

"Anyway, Kill was down for being the driver since my car would be impossible for you to get into with those." He points to my legs. One leg is in a plaster cast from ankle to mid-thigh. The dreaded tib-fib fracture, likely caused by the free-floating gurney when the ambulance rolled. The other leg is in a stiff walking boot up to my mid-calf.

Part of me wants to rage at Sampson. I have so much anger in my heart right now and most of it isn't even his fault this time. I'm pissed as hell at the world right now.

The psychologist for the fire department tells me it's because I'm holding on to my loss of independence and control, that I'm assigning and projecting blame on others and that it's pretty normal. Blah, blah, blah. I'm sick of having to talk about my injuries, and especially sick about talking about *him*. The one who took me, who touched me, who did things to me. Things that Clance and Sofie don't even know about because I can't sully their image of me. The *him*, who not only survived the crash but slipped into the weeds in the dark of night and disappeared completely. *He* did this to me and hasn't paid for it yet. So yeah, I'm fucking angry.

But there's another part that is glad for the possible outing. The change of scenery and people watching over me. Clance and Sof have been tiptoeing around me like I'm tied up with trip wires and just brushing one will cause me to detonate. Because maybe I will.

"Where did you get the handicapped parking permit?"

"It's yours. We got it from Sof, with the promise that we will give it back when we take you home. We didn't want you too uncomfortable or overdoing it since you had therapy today. Sof says sometimes it takes it out of you, so if you aren't up for anything that we have planned, just let us know and we'll do something else, okay?"

"I don't really have a choice, do I?" I mutter, getting into the front seat after handing off my crutches to Sampson, who puts them with him in the back seat.

"Of course you have a choice, Mel. Say the word, and we'll take you back to Sof's house," Killian says as he helps me buckle my seat belt.

"Let's see what Sampson has planned. Your car smells new."

"Good nose. It's a few months old." He fires it up and takes off.

Sampson pops his head between Kill's seat and mine. "Are you hungry? I thought maybe we could grab a quick bite and talk for a few minutes. I have some things I need to say."

"I could eat." I can feel Sampson's nervous energy rolling off him as he settles back in the back seat.

Killian drives us to a pizza place nearby. Sampson holds my crutches while I get out and get situated. He says something I can't hear to Killian before shutting the door. And Killian drives away.

"He's got some errands to do, then he'll be back for us.

What kind of pizza do you want?" He looks at me as he holds the door open.

"My taste in pizza hasn't changed," I snap, but he doesn't react in the slightest. I should apologize, but he just lets it roll off him like he's immune.

"You want to head to the back? I'll get the food ordered. We have the back room here." He nods to the door.

I crutch myself to the back room and select a table. Knowing Sampson, we'll have the run of the entire back room.

He comes in holding two cups.

"I got you a Diet Coke but let me know if you want something else." He sets my beverage in front of me and his orange soda in front of himself.

"This is good, thanks." I take a small sip. It's been a bit since I've had a Diet Coke and it tastes really good.

He sits across from me and looks at me, really looks at me. I squirm because it feels like he can see right through me. Like he knows I let *him* touch me.

"I need to talk to you, to apologize for that morning," he starts.

"I get it." I stop him. "No need to go back there. We just don't want the same things out of life, Sampson."

He winces a little at my statement. "That's not it," he says, releasing a long sigh. "Before you write me off completely, I need to tell you some things. And then if you decide that there's nothing I can do to change your mind, well then, I'll leave you be. But there are some things you need to know first."

He watches me for a few minutes, and when he's decided I'm listening, he continues. "You remember my mom?" he asks, watching me nod. She was an absentee parent even when she was there. "Her issues started when I was a kid. She was prescribed something that set her off on a long path of addiction. And I still think some of Seven's issues might have been hereditary."

Seven. I thought I was the only one who called Sevenya that.

"Anyway, as you clearly saw that morning, I had a panic attack. You recognized it right away. It had been happening anytime I got near water, at the ocean, in swimming pools. Hell, it even happened a few times in the shower." He stops and looks out the window. I hurt for him. I've never had a panic attack, but as a paramedic, I've treated a lot of them. They manifest differently with different people, and it can be pretty intense and devastating. I thought that was what was going on, but I couldn't be sure, because he wouldn't talk to me about it.

"When they happen in front of someone, or they call me out on them, I usually lash out with anger. You aren't the only one on the receiving end. I've lashed out at Kill more than once. Cal too. I even made Kady cry once. It was right before you came to the barbecue at Mav's house after the ceremony." He turns his head to avert his gaze. He's embarrassed. "It's probably why, no, *it is* why I acted like I did towards you that night." He still won't look at me.

"When I'm post-panic, my anxiety is high, and it comes out as anger. It makes me an asshole." He ties his straw wrapper in a knot. Then another one.

This is hitting a little close to home for me. Is anxiety part of what's fueling my anger at Clance, at Sof, at the world in general?

Sampson swallows hard, and he looks at me, wincing slightly again. "I'm not using this as an excuse. There is no excuse for the shit I do or say when this happens. I turn nasty and say things I don't mean. It's some sort of weird knee-jerk reaction that I can't control. Yet." He looks down at the table, refusing to meet my eyes. "But I, uh, wanted you to know that I'm working on it, with a therapist. I've been seeing her twice a week for two months now."

210

"Samp—" He raises his hand, indicating he's not quite done yet.

"It's helping. But it's also frustrating because there is no quick fix for any of this shit. It's all little steps. But I can swim with Gibson in Cal's pool now without 'feaking out' as Gibs likes to say. The ocean, well, that's another story. But, the point is, I'm working on it. And I'm really sorry that you got caught up in my bullshit. It still happens, but I'm quicker to realize what's happening, and take accountability for it. And hopefully, I'll get to a place where I recognize it before it happens so that I can stop lashing out at those I love. That's the idea anyway." He tosses his straw wrapper at the end of the table and takes a big sigh. *He said love, as in he still loves me.*

"So, that's what I wanted to say. Just in time too." He sits up as the waiter comes with our pizza. "Thanks, Marco. It smells great and I'm starving."

"When aren't you hungry?" I mumble.

He nods as he reaches for the stack of plates. "True, for the most part. Although after that last row with you, when you stopped talking to me, I lost my appetite. True story. It really freaked Cal out."

Sampson was a teenage boy who not only expended huge amounts of energy drumming and surfing but had a mother who was more concerned with feeding her habits than her children. Sampson was always hungry because he made sure Seven ate before he did. I always shared my food with them. I'd bring extra-large lunches, so they'd have something to eat. My mom didn't care most of the time anyway. She wasn't concerned with me, and when she was, it wasn't about food. It was about me looking or acting like my father. And I know others in Sampson's circle gave them food as well. I don't know that his metabolism ever recovered from always being hungry.

Sampson hands me a napkin, then grabs a slice and slides it into his mouth. He takes a bite, and his eyes roll back slightly.

211

"Mmm. They have the best pizza here," he murmurs before taking another bite.

"You should eat before Kill gets here. He'll probably grab some too." He nods at the pizza.

I grab a slice and pick the pepperoni off and eat it slice by slice while the cheesy part of my piece of pizza cools. When I look up, I catch him smiling at me with a soft, lazy smile.

"You used to eat pizza like that when we were in high school. I like that you still do it." He smiles when I take another piece and repeat the same process of pulling off the pepperoni and eat it piece by piece.

"Only sometimes. Depends on who I'm with, I guess."

"Well, I like it. Maybe it means you're comfortable with me. Are you? Comfortable with me?" He tips his head to the side while asking a totally loaded question.

"For the most part."

He nods. "Fair enough."

"What are we doing after we eat? Will it just be us again?"

He shakes his head. "My therapy, and no, Killian will come with us."

His therapy? He doesn't expect me to talk to his shrink too, I hope. It's bad enough that I have to go to the one through the department. The last thing I want to do is go over and over what happened and the aftermath. It's bad enough I'm still in casts and on crutches.

"Speak of the devil." Killian drops into the booth next to Sampson and grabs a piece of pizza.

"Told you." Sammy winks at me.

"Told her what?" Killian asks over another mouthful of pizza.

"That you'd eat our pizza."

He shrugs and takes another piece. He seems to be just as voracious an eater as Sampson.

"You guys ready?" He stands. Sampson throws some money

on the table and they both wait for me, but neither tries to hurry me nor do they assist me. They let me do it myself.

Killian drives us up to Mav's house.

"Your therapist comes to Mavrick Slater's house?"

They both chuckle. "It's more like therapy homework. We've been getting closer and closer to the ocean. This is only the third time I've been on sand. I have to warn you, the last two times I had freakouts, so it might happen again. I figure you've already seen me freak out, but Kill's there just in case I bolt and you need help getting back." He shrugs. "Because that's usually my first instinct, to bolt."

Killian nods. "He made it about fifty yards last time without taking off for Mav's house on a dead run." Killian locks eyes with me. "You'll be okay on the sand with crutches?"

I don't know. Clance would shit a brick if he knew we were doing this without him here to supervise. "Yes."

"Don't worry. We walk slow anyway. It's part of what his therapist wants him to do. Slow and purposeful. Right, Sam?" Sampson nods and bites his lip as we approach the gate to the beach off of Mav's rear patio.

And that's what we do. We slowly walk parallel to the shoreline, three abreast, me in the middle with Sam furthest from the water. I concentrate on my movement with the crutches on the soft surface. It doesn't take long for my legs and hips to start burning.

Killian quietly explains that they've been working up to this point steadily. I can hear the pride in Killian's voice that Sampson was the one who made the decision that he was ready to head onto the beach recently.

This is probably the longest outside of my physical therapy that I've been on my crutches in one go. It's kind of uncomfortable in my armpits, but it's also invigorating to have the salty air hitting my face, thick with that briny smell the ocean secretes, to be outside with the sunlight warming my arms, to be with people other than Sof and Clance and therapists or doctors.

Sampson stops, so we stop as well. Killian's attention shifts from me to his friend. Sampson turns towards the ocean, but not back towards Mav's.

"Can we sit?" Sampson asks. Then he looks at me. "Can you sit? On the sand? We'll help you back up."

"Um... sure. Why not?" By the raise of Killian's eyebrows, I assume that this might be some sort of breakthrough, and like hell do I want to impede that.

Killian strips off his hoodie and lays it on the sand. Sam takes my crutches and lays them next to the hoodie with one hand, while helping me balance with the other. Then Killian and he each take a side and help me lower myself onto the sweatshirt.

"You good?" Sampson's squatting next to me as I'm sitting on Kill's sweatshirt. When I nod, he settles next to me, and Killian drops down a few feet away on my other side.

The three of us sit there, facing the ocean in silence. This moment feels too big for words. Sampson reaches over and interlaces his fingers with mine. I don't know how long we sit this way, with nothing but the sounds of the ocean and the distant cries of a child from one of the houses behind us.

"I'm going to try something." Killian stands, breaking our silent meditation.

"Be back." He heads towards the water as we watch him. Sampson's fingers tighten around mine, but nothing else he does makes me think that it might be hard for him to watch his friend head towards the ocean alone.

Killian stops about halfway between us and the water to toe off his shoes and remove his socks and then continues his trek towards the water. He lets the very edge of the water lap over his feet. Sampson's grip on my hand tightens even more.

Killian bends over and rolls his pants up to his knees, something I wouldn't have thought possible considering how tight they look. And with each small progression Killian makes into the ocean, the tighter Sampson's fingers squeeze around mine.

Kill's up to about mid-calf, his back to us as he stands in the ocean. Technically, he's not that far out. But Sampson's grip on my hand is almost painful until he finally rips his hand from mine.

"That's far enough," Sampson barks, loud enough that it catches Killian's attention, so he starts back towards us, picking up his shoes and socks along the way. "Fuckin' asshole," Sam whispers when he realizes Kill's on his way back.

Killian drops down on the other side of Sam and knocks off the sand before he slowly puts on his socks and shoes.

Nothing is said between them, but Killian pats Sampson's back.

Sammy jumps up after a few minutes. "Shall we head back?"

The pair help me up just as they helped me down onto the sand, making sure that I am steady on my casted feet before Sampson bends over to pick up my crutches. Once I have them secure under my arms, we start back towards the house.

When we get inside, Sampson excuses himself to the restroom, while I take a load off on the couch. Killian brings me a bottle of water.

"Thanks." I take a few sips. "That was probably the longest I've been outside on my crutches. And the longest I've been away from Sof and Clance since what happened. It felt really good. But it's a little tiring too."

Killian nods. "I imagine it would be all of those things." He pauses. "Sammy had a huge day too. I think he just needs a few minutes to himself to process it. Yesterday he bolted. Today, not only did he walk, but he sat down and watched me get in the water. Those are two huge steps for him. I think having you here gave him the courage to do that. It took him six weeks to get to this point with the pool. Just watching someone he cares about in the water was big." He reaches over and squeezes my knee.

"He loves you. He tried to visit you in the hospital, but Clance threatened to call the police. I wasn't sure if you knew that." Killian sighs and looks down for a moment.

I can't believe Clance didn't tell me that Sampson came to see me. That he refused him without asking me. Now I begin to wonder about my phone, but I don't want Killian to know that I think Clance may have blocked Sam's number.

"Believe it or not, you gave him strength today. Thank you. I hope Sammy gives you the same strength you gave him." Kill smiles softly at me. He's so much different than what I've seen of him in the press. He always seems so closed off and hard. But that's not him at all.

# Chapter 23

## *Melody*

Sampson returns from upstairs and Killian stands. "Mav and Kady are out with Brio at some park or something. I'm going to go down to the studio to give you guys some space to hang. Text me if you need me." Killian heads down a hall, leaving Sampson and me alone.

"Are you hungry? Thirsty? Can I get you anything?" Sampson asks.

I shake my head and hold up my bottle of water. "Killian gave me some water. I'm good." He stands there fidgeting like he's not sure where he belongs. I pat the cushion on the couch next to me. "Sit with me?"

He does just that, leaving several inches between us, and turns to look at me. "Maybe Killian can take us somewhere. Is there anywhere you want or need to go? A store or something? Anywhere you want to go. We'll take you. I want this to be a good time for you." His talking gets more rapid as he goes. He's so nervous. This is what he does when he doesn't know what's expected of him, or when he's uncomfortable with a situation. It reminds of when I almost broke up with him our junior year. He got all flustered and just talked so fast.

217

"Sampson. Let's just sit. This has been a big outing for me already and my arms are a little tired."

"Of course. I should probably get you home." He jumps up again, like he's afraid of me. Like he's worried I'm tricking him.

"I don't want to go home yet. I want to spend time hanging out with you." I pat the seat again and he returns to sit next to me. He's stiff, but at least he's sitting with me.

I reach over and put my hand on his thigh. "You had a big day today too." I give him a pat and a gentle squeeze and he gives me a slow nod but says nothing.

I don't look directly at him because my heart couldn't take his rejection again, especially now. But I needed to put that out there for me more than him. Although I think he needs to hear it too. That it's okay to be vulnerable and face your demons. Maybe I can lead a little by example.

"It was scary. Being hijacked." I take in a shaky breath. "But in the brief times between trying to figure out how to protect and save myself, I thought of four people. I thought of Sof and Clance. I thought of Mrs. Chamske. And I thought of you." I take in another rattling breath and his hand joins mine on his thigh and his fingers interlace with mine again. Our eyes meet, and I feel the support as he holds my hand. Like he understands that this is hard to talk about. He has no fucking idea how hard it is. Or what the dreams are like.

"There was this time that he pulled the ambulance over to come back to see what I was doing. He restrained me to the jump seat in the back. He stuffed a wad of IV tubing in my mouth and tethered me to the seat. He, uh..." I gasp as my heart speeds up as I remember his words, my stomach. "Cut me here." I pull my hair back and show the pink scar on my cheek, mostly invisible because of the makeup and the delicate touch of the plastic surgeon stitching me back together.

"Then he cut me here." I motion to the middle of my chest. "He touched me, my, uh, my chest." I squeeze my eyes shut and shake my head. Then sit straighter. I won't let *him* win. "Sampson, I made promises to myself in the back of the ambulance. I promised if I lived to see the four of you again, I'd tell you all how much you mean to me." I watch him grimace out of the corner of my eye. "Today, while we were sitting at the beach, watching Killian push your limits, I realized that I haven't done that yet. I've been too wrapped up in my own pain, both physical and mental, to remember my own promises."

He doesn't say anything. Instead, he squeezes my fingers between his and then draws my hand up to his mouth for a kiss. His soft lips graze the back of my hand.

"Love's always been a hard concept for me. It came with a fist or a shove when I was a kid. You know this. You were there and saw it and me at my worst. But, Sof and Clance have shown me what love is supposed to look like both in how they treat me and each other. Mrs. Chamske shows me what family is supposed to feel like, act like. Give me a chance to experience love with you, Sampson." He stills his soft kisses of my hand at my last words and glances over at me from the side of his eyes.

"I don't know, Mel. I'm kind of a mess, if you haven't noticed," he says quietly.

"Aren't we all in some way?" I squeeze his hand and turn towards him on the couch.

"You know, one thing that this whole fiasco has taught me is that I need to tell the people I care about that I love them and not hold it in. Because it could all go away in an instant. Sampson, I love you. I always have." I say the words I regretted never saying to him when we were younger, back when love meant bruises the next day. But now I see what love should be, and I want that, with Sampson. I thought he wanted it with me too. But maybe I was wrong.

"After you left the first time, it was our talks that I missed the most. I missed sitting with you at the beach or in the quad at school or wherever we happened to be and just talking and listening and just being. Because with you, Sampson, I could always just be. I didn't have to fake it or project a false happiness. I'm always most comfortable and at my best with you. Even now, after more than a decade of being a part. That has to mean something." I heave out a sigh.

He's uncharacteristically quiet and just watches me. I can't tell if I am getting through to him or not. Because I realize now, I need Sampson in my life.

"Can't we try? Go into it knowing we are both messed up and giving each other the space that comes with that. Go in with the knowledge that we might mess up sometimes, but as long as we talk about it, know that we'll be okay?"

He's still quiet, but he stares back at me as he contemplates what I've asked. I pull his hand to my mouth and kiss his knuckles lightly, waiting for his reply.

"I want to try, Mel. I do." He breathes out a long breath. "But I don't want to hurt you in the process, again. Haven't I done that enough?" He looks at our interlocked hands. "I don't want you to get vested in an us and then I hurt you one too many times and have you back out. I don't want to lose you again, Mel. I don't think I could handle it again." His voice is quiet and wavering.

"I don't want to lose you again either, so, let's work hard at not doing that. We can make us work, Sampson." Who'd have ever thought that I'd be the one begging Sampson to give us a chance again. "You told Clance that you just wanted me in your orbit. I want to be in your orbit too. Let's give us a try. A full-on, whole-hearted, all-in kind of try. Just you and me."

He seems to be contemplating my request. There was a time not so long ago that I wanted to hate Sampson for leaving, like he did after high school. But we've both grown up and changed.

"I'm in." His words are quiet. "I'm all in, in a full-on, whole-hearted kind of way." He repeats my words back to me with a soft grin.

When the words leave his lips, a weight I didn't know was there lifts off my chest and it's as if I not only can now breathe but breathe deeply and my whole body relaxes against the couch. But I want to relax against him. I scoot my butt towards him on the couch, and when he figures out my motives, he wraps his arm around me and pulls me right up against him, so I am engulfed in the comfort that only Sampson provides me.

I lay my head on his shoulder, and he lays his head against the top of mine and sighs. But it's a content sigh and not one of frustration. A few minutes later, I feel his lips on my hair as he gives me a kiss and whispers, "I love you so much, Mel."

I must doze off because the next thing I hear is Sampson's sleepy voice saying, "Shit."

"Her phone's got like a zillion messages on it. Sofie finally texted me, worried when she didn't get an answer. Mentioned that they'd had a big fight before she dropped her off at therapy. You guys were out like lights. But someone needs to contact Sofie before she calls the cops or something."

Sampson shifts, pulling his arm from around me, and I open my eyes. It's now dark in Mav's house.

"Sorry, I must have been more tired than I thought." I yawn and pull my phone off the table. Killian's right. I have 18 messages from Sofie and three from Clance.

Sof's messages start out simple. *Having fun? What do you want for dinner?* And grow increasingly worried as they continue. *Are you okay? Please, just let me know you're okay.* And Clance's are downright rude. *You're being childish. Running away with a rockstar. You need to concentrate on your recovery, on getting your strength back. Not on someone who doesn't treat you right.*

The tone of Clance's texts upsets me, and I can't help my lip that begins to quiver slightly as tears prick my eyes. Then I get angry. He has no right to treat me like a child. I am an adult. I can hang out with whomever I want for as long as I want.

"Hey, it's okay. We'll blame it on me. He doesn't like me

anyway." Sampson pulls me back to him for a hug and a kiss on the top of my head. But it's too late. I'm already upset.

"He's being a dick. I'm an adult who has every right to hang out with whomever I want for as long as I want." The vicious, hateful remarks are out of my mouth before I think about it. Why am I so fucking hateful lately? It's not me and I don't like it.

Killian's eyebrows shoot up at my comment and Sammy's arms wrap around me and he squeezes me tight. "Hey. They care about you. They're just a little worried. It's my fault. I've been sleeping poorly. When we snuggled up on the couch, I fell asleep too. I'll explain."

I like being in his arms like this. A lot. I relax and a lot of the anger seeps out of me. But not all of it. "That's just it. You shouldn't have to explain. I won't be made to feel bad about my relationship with you or anyone else. I think it's time I went home, to my apartment. I can mostly get around. It's not like there isn't an elevator and delivery."

Sampson's whole body stiffens. "I love you, Mel, but I don't like the idea of you by yourself. What if you fall?" He squeezes me tighter. "Stay with them until you're a little more mobile. Either that or I'm moving in with you. Because I'd just worry about you all alone in that apartment."

# Chapter 24

## *Sammy*

She pulls back and looks at me, her eyes round but her grin wide. "Did you really mean that?"

"Yes, I'd worry about you. I have enough trouble sleeping knowing you were alone and not as mobile as normal would just add to the stuff I ruminate about at night." *Ruminate. That's a therapy word if I've ever heard one.* But I do. I toss and turn. When I do sleep, it's usually filled with dreams of someone drowning. Someone I love. This is a side effect of the therapy. But I talk to Cheryl about them, too.

Her head shakes, but her grin is still wide. "No. Not that. About moving in with me. It's the perfect idea. I can get out from under Clance and Sof's overly watchful eyes and be in my own home. And with you. It'd be win-win-win." Her eyes actually dance with the idea I put in her head.

I didn't mean for her to take it as a serious option. I meant it as a threat. But she sees it as an opportunity, and I could get away from Cal's watchful eye too. It might be the most brilliant unintentional thing I've ever said.

I look over her head at Killian. He's watching us, an amused expression on his face.

"I think you just agreed to live with her, Sammy." Killian slaps me on the back and chuckles. "Good luck getting out of that one."

I shake my head. "I don't want to get out of it."

Killian's eyes widen at my admission. I may not have meant it like she originally took it, but I don't see an issue moving in with her. I'll be there to make sure she's safe. I could get away from Cal, but still be close enough to him and Mav's to work on our music or whatever. Hell, Mel could even come and hang out with Ari and Gibson when we were doing studio work. It's a perfect idea.

"Seriously?" Mel squeals. "You'll do it?" If she weren't casted, I bet she'd be jumping up and down with her excitement.

I nod. "Yeah. But we should talk to Clance and Sof about it, so they don't worry even more."

She nods, but her lips pull down in a frown. "They won't like it. Especially Clance." She sighs. She's probably right about that. I've given them no reason to trust me with her heart, let alone her physical well-being.

"I know. But be firm that it's what you want." I grip her hands. "We'll talk to them together, okay?" She nods.

# R

"Abso-fucking-lutely not! Are you off your gourd, Melody?" The purple-green veins at the sides of Clance's neck stick out as he shouts at my Mel, and it's hard for me not to jump between them.

She cringes and takes a small step back from him. This alarms me because she's not normally so easily spooked. I'm not sure if this is some left over trauma from being hijacked or if it's reminiscent of her mom, so I subtly step between them, taking her out of his direct line of fire. "No way is that guy moving in with you."

"Melody wants to be in her own space. She wants to sleep in her own bed. It's nothing against you or Sofie." I put my hands up between myself and Clance. I'm trying my best to remember I'm the peacemaker here. It's a familiar role, the one I play in the band more oft than not. The way he's treating Melody is really pissing me off though, so it's getting kind of hard to keep *my* cool. She doesn't deserve his ire just for wanting to go home.

"We'll move your bed here if it's that big of a deal to sleep in your own fucking bed, Melody." Clance folds his arms across his chest and glares over my shoulder at her. Without turning my head, I can't be sure what she looks like, but the vibes running off her and into me are ones of hurt mixed with fear. I'd stepped in between her and her mother a time or two and I can't imagine he's not feeding into that fear. Either he has no clue about her past or he's a bigger asshole than I thought and using her past against her.

"That's not what I meant, and you know it." Melody's voice is shaky and quiet. She loves Clance and Sof. They are the closest thing to family she's had besides Mrs. Chamske. Even though she didn't expect our idea to be well received, I'm positive his anger is slowly killing her on the inside. I know that look and stance on Mel; it's the same one she'd have after a particularly rough night with her mom.

"Look, man, can you and I talk? Just us? Maybe in another room or outside?" I'm trying to get him away from Mel, so he'll stop staring her down like an alpha dog trying to make his subordinate piss her submission.

"Are you seriously asking me to take this outside, Denton?" He snarls my name. He's trying to make me back down. Won't happen. I'm not a fighter and don't do confrontation much, but I'm also not going to let this guy beat Melody down. I've wrestled my fair share with Kill and Cal and even Mav. It was mostly in fun but I'm not weak, and they made sure of it.

"I'm asking you, politely, to talk with me in another area away from Melody and Sofie. Please." I repeat myself, working hard to keep my voice level.

He blasts past me, knocking into me with his shoulder, and stalks out of the room. I reach out and grab Mel's hand and give her a reassuring squeeze and a smile. "Be right back."

I follow him as he stomps through the kitchen and out the back door beyond the patio and onto the lawn. At least I know that if it goes fisticuffs we have a soft place to land.

He turns and stares me down as approach him.

"I don't know what you're trying to do here, turning Melody against us." Again, he crosses his arms across his puffed-out chest.

"I'm not turning Melody against anyone. She wants the comfort of her own home. Would you rather she go home without someone? I don't know about you, but I'd never rest. I'd worry about her falling and not being able to get upright with those casts. Or what if she knocked herself out when she fell? This is the shit that's running through *my brain* when she said she was going back to her apartment."

His eyes widen for a minute and then narrow at me again.

"I suggested she stay with you and Sof until she got her casts off. But she was adamant, so I offered to stay with her. Because I know I'd never rest if she was up there by herself for any length of time alone."

He shakes his head. "You're using this as an excuse to get into her pants."

"Yeah, because casted chicks are so my fetish." My eyes roll. I thought I said it under my breath, but he must have heard me because he charges towards me.

Instead of backing up, I lower my center of gravity and stand my ground, hunching forward to take his hit.

We end up on the ground, him on top of me. I just hope Mel's not watching this through the window.

He tries to punch me in the face, but I move too quick for him. Remembering a maneuver that Kill uses against me, I use my leg to flip us so he's now under me. I press my weight onto his chest, just below his throat. He's probably stronger than me, but I have the element of surprise going for me. That and love for Melody.

"I'm not going to go fight you, man, but I sure as fuck will defend myself." I stare at him and push my weight down on him again.

"She loves you like a brother and Sof like a sister. I don't know what you know about Melody's past, but using anger towards her is going to turn her away from you."

My words seem to be doing something because he relaxes a little, so I sit back and un-straddle his ass. He sits up.

"I don't like you around her." His words are clipped.

"It's not your choice. It's hers. Maybe you should try talking to her about it rather than *intimidating* her until she bends to your will. Her mom would do that shit, make her feel small for choices she made. She'd also beat her. I can't tell you how many bruises I saw on her over the three years we dated. She never fought back. I guess because it was her mom. But I could see it killing her slowly. Every time new bruises would show up, she'd disappear into herself for a longer period of time." Just thinking about her haunted eyes back then makes me mad.

"I shouldn't be telling you this because she's obviously kept it from you for a reason. Probably because she didn't want you to look at her any different, to view her as a victim. But that look returned to her eyes tonight, the one that tells me she's disappearing into herself. While you were yelling at her. It's why I wanted to talk out here and away from Mel." I push myself off him and up to a stand.

"I'm going to help her pack up any stuff that she wants to

take home. But to be clear, I didn't offer to stay with her until she told me she wouldn't stay with you anymore." I leave him on his back lawn.

# R

"You don't have to do this." Sofie's voice is quiet as Mel watches me tuck her clothes into her duffle bag.

"I want to be at my place. This has nothing to do with living with Sampson and everything to do with me getting back to being independent. Sampson didn't offer to stay with me until I was adamant about moving back into my apartment."

There is a deep rift, a hurt that runs between Sofie and Melody. I don't know where it came from, but it's evident in Sofie's posture and the quiet way she speaks to Mel. The friendly, sassy banter I've heard between them is replaced with tentative, carefully thought-out words. And I don't think it has anything to do with her leaving, although that might be making the rift between them wider.

Mel lifts herself from her seat on the bed with the assistance of her crutches. She pivots, so she's facing Sofie. "I'm sorry for this morning. I'll call you in a few days or something." She turns towards the door and leaves without looking back.

I give Sofie a hug. "She'll be okay. I'll make damn sure. You have my number. Text me if you need anything, even if it's just reassurance that she's doing okay." She gives me a weak nod, her eyes turning shiny with unshed tears.

"Look, Sofie, Melody's always been the strongest person I know. She'll be okay."

I give Sofie an extra tight squeeze before turning to catch up to Mel. The front door is open and Clance is on the porch with her. She's balancing on her crutches, but maintaining a good three to four feet between them. His voice is a low rumble, so I stay back in the foyer, out of sight. I don't know what he's saying, but I give them a few minutes of privacy. I don't go out there until I hear the sound of Mel's crutches fading towards the car.

I sling her bag over my shoulder and move out the door, but Clance catches my arm before I make the stairs. "Watch out for her, for me, for us."

"I'll tell you the same thing I just told Sofie. Mel's the strongest person I know, and she'll be okay. I'll make damn sure of it. You have my number. Feel free to text if you need anything, even if it's reassurance on her."

I hold her crutches while she slides herself into the passenger seat of Kill's Panamera. I put the crutches in the back and shut the door. I get in and help her buckle in before I buckle myself.

"It was nice of Kill to trade cars with you for me."

"We share things, but this is a stretch for him to loan out his car. That tells me he really likes you." I wink at her.

"Killian's not my type. He's a little too, I dunno, emo or something."

I can't help my laughter. Kill is kind of emo, but he'd hate that Mel called him that because he doesn't see himself that way.

# Chapter 25

## *Melody*

"You need anything before we head out to therapy, Mel?" Sampson asks as he puts our dishes in the dishwasher.

"I'm good." I pull myself up with my crutches and watch him finish loading the dishwasher. He's been so helpful these last two weeks and living in my own space has been better for my mental health than living with Clance and Sofie. I feel more independent, more like the old Melody. And Sampson lets me do things for myself unless I ask him for help.

He worries about me, though. I can see it in the way he looks at me when he doesn't think I notice him watching me. He tries to get me out of the apartment much like Clance, but I don't like going out. Not knowing *he's* still out there.

We head downstairs and he walks with me to the car he's still borrowing from Killian. I don't think it was something either of them would have done unless it was to help someone else, but it is something that is so much easier for me to get in and out of.

"Are you nervous about therapy today?" he asks as he buckles his seatbelt.

"A little. It's like now the real work will begin." The casts came off on Friday. My legs look disgusting. They are all pale and spindly. You can see the lack of muscle tone. The doctor said it's to be expected after being casted and booted for 9 weeks. He warned me that he believes there is some nerve damage in the leg with the tib/fib fracture and it may or may not affect me. It's all about how I respond to the therapy.

"Do you want me to stay this time?" Sampson usually walks me into therapy and then leaves and comes back towards the end. There's no need for him to be bored. He usually hangs out down at the drum shop, which isn't too far away from my PT. He almost always has something for me when I get done. Flowers usually. Sometimes a treat from my favorite bakery.

"Nah. I'm good."

"Okay." He reaches over and holds my hand as he drives. He walks me into therapy and makes sure I get checked in, then he kisses me on the top of my head.

"Do your best." He whispers words of encouragement and gives me a hug before leaving. I'm not waiting in the lobby long before my therapist comes to get me.

We do some basic stretches, and he helps me balance without the crutches and helps me walk down a hall to evaluate my gait. Then he has me sit on a low table as he manipulates my injured ankle. The longer he manipulates it, the deeper his frown lines get.

"I'm concerned about the nerve damage. Some of the moves I made should have been painful, but you didn't even flinch. Do me a favor and lay back. I'm going to touch your foot and ankle with this, and I want you to tell me when you feel the pressure." I do this as he touches areas on both legs. Sometimes I think I feel things but can't be sure.

"Do you have any tingling or burning?"

"Sometimes in the foot with the broken ankle." I wonder if that is a good thing or a bad thing.

"But not in this other foot, the one that had the hard cast?"

I shake my head. He makes notes on his iPad. He turns to me.

"Well, the good news is that you've got a strong core, which helps a lot with mobility. I see some foot droppage on one side that is a little concerning. It's not an uncommon issue with tibial fractures. But the numbness that you're experiencing tells me the nerve damage on the side with the tib/fib break is fairly deep and extensive. This is not to say that PT won't help. At the very least, it will help you learn to compensate for any mobility issues. But with nerve damage comes an extended recovery. Usually six months to a year. But I'm willing to push you as hard as I can if you're willing to work hard."

My stomach burns. Six months to a year of rehab? Compensate for mobility issues? These aren't tangible recovery goals. They won't let me back in the ambulance if I have mobility issues. This job is the only one that pays decently and lets me do what I love. I don't make enough teaching First Aid and CPR to live off of. I'll have to find some other job. Do some other job. One I don't love. Because being in the ambulance is what I loved.

"You're saying that I'm still going to have issues even after a year of rehab?" My voice cracks because this is not what I wanted to hear. Any ideas I had about returning to the fire-house seem to be getting more and more dim. "So work is probably done?"

David takes a deep breath. "I don't make those kinds of decisions. But I've done this a long time and I don't want to give you false hope. The chances of you being able to continue work as a fire paramedic are probably not great, but like I said, I don't make those calls." He looks me in the eyes. "If you're willing to work hard with me and do your home exercises religiously, you'll get as good as we can get you, you'll get stronger. You might even be able to run again eventually. Maybe things will be different for you when it comes to work."

"Okay. I'm in."

"I had a feeling you would be. We'll be keeping the same twice a week in-person therapy schedule. I'm changing up your home exercises and we'll be building on them as we continue to build your strength back up. I'm going to get you the printouts for the exercises I want you to do starting tonight while you are with Dawn for deep tissue massage. Remember, it's important to drink a lot of water after therapy, especially today since we worked the legs harder."

He squeezes my shoulder. "I know it's a lot and some of it's disappointing. But let's prove the averages wrong, okay?"

"Yeah. Okay." He escorts me over to Dawn in the massage therapy area and then David goes over my home exercises with me. I take my sheets and hit the checkout desk.

Sampson is waiting for me, leaning against the car as I come out with my print outs.

"How did it go?" He takes the sheets and the crutches and puts them in the back as I settle into the front seat.

"Okay." I buckle up and take a long drink of the sports drink Sampson brought for me. He says nothing as he drives us back to my apartment.

We get upstairs and I get a big glass of water and suck it down too.

"You want to talk about it yet?" he asks as he returns to the table.

"About what?"

"You've been quiet since therapy, Mel. Let's talk about it. You'll feel better. Besides, you know that Sof and Clance will be here tomorrow morning, if not this afternoon, wanting to know how it went."

"Speaking of, I've got to do my exercises." I move onto the

floor and start some of the stretching. "Can you bring me over a chair so I can start?"

Sampson does as I ask and helps me maneuver into position as I go through my new exercises. He says nothing but helps me when I need it. I know he wants me to talk about therapy, but I don't. I just want to work and show everyone I can get better. Maybe David's wrong. Maybe I can do better than he thinks. People have always underestimated me.

"Want to go for a walk around the block, or are you too tired from therapy?" Sampson tries to make sure I go outside every day. On the days I don't have therapy, we go to the beach and walk slowly together on the sand. He's gotten to the point where he's comfortable about halfway between the parking lot and the ocean. But panic attacks still happen sometimes. He's also getting better at recognizing them and realizing what they are and knowing what he needs to do.

On therapy days, we just walk slowly around the block. "Sure."

While we walk around the block, Sampson sticks his head in the pastry shop and buys us each an éclair. "Our treat for therapy." He winks and carries our treats while we continue our walk.

Just as we're about half a block from the apartment, I see a group of guys from the firehouse come out of the front door to my apartment. I'm not ready to talk to them, especially after today.

"Shit." I stop.

"What?" Sampson stops and looks at me. "Are you okay?"

I nod. "I, uh, need to go to the grocery store."

He gives me a funny look. "I just went this morning. What did I forget that you need right now? It's not like we have to worry about dinner tonight since we're going to Mav's. Plus, we have eclairs." He motions with the box.

I don't know what to say, so I turn back towards the grocery store. "Come on."

But I'm too late.

"There she is. Hey, Tanner, wait up!" My head hangs momentarily before I put my firehouse game face on, even though I'm so not in the mood to see everything I've lost.

A few of the guys come jogging up to me, while the others saunter up behind. This group is most of the guys who worked my shift, including Stephen, who's hanging back from the rest.

"Oh, hey, guys." I shift on my crutches because my leg started throbbing about halfway through our walk. "What are you doing here?"

"Clance told us you were probably home, and we wanted to come see you. We miss you." Jason Becker reaches out to hug me. "We thought you'd have been to see us by now."

"I'm doing a lot of PT, trying to get it into shape." So they don't fire me. Tears burn the back of my eyes, but I refuse to let them fall. I will not have these guys feeling sorry for poor little Mel.

"We never even heard what kind of injuries you had. Privacy and all that." He rolls his eyes and scans down my legs. "Tib/Fib fracture?"

I nod. "Tib/fib on my left and ankle fracture in my right. I don't remember, but they tell me they think the gurney broke loose and got me. Just got my cast off on Monday. At least my shoulder's doing better." I make an exaggerated circle with my shoulder to show it off.

Becker grimaces. "Painful. The PT for tib/fibs is brutal too. My brother-in-law broke his skiing." I shrug it off, but at the mention of pain, Sampson stiffens beside me.

"This is my longtime friend, Sampson. Sampson, this is Jason Becker. He drives the ladder truck on the shift I worked. That's Greg Maloney, Marty Michaelson, and Sanderson Jones.

Firefighters. And the guy in the back is Stephen, the other paramedic I worked with."

Sampson shakes hands with everyone, making nice. But Stephen still hangs back behind everyone, despite being with me in that ambulance for hours together. Even now, while everyone rallies around me.

Clance blames him for what happened to me, but I don't. It was just as much my fault as his. We should have locked up the bus and gone into the diner together. I should have stayed up front and not made myself vulnerable to being hijacked by trying to refill our go bags. He hasn't said anything to me, or even looked in my direction. I assume that he knew they were coming to see me.

"We were hoping you'd swing by the firehouse. We miss your face and your cooking." Greg steps to the side so he can see me better, giving Stephen the perfect opportunity to step forward. But still, he remains outside the group.

"Clance said you were staying with him, and you weren't up to it. Then he said you'd moved back to your apartment. We thought you might come by and see us. We miss you."

"You know how it is. It's hard. I want nothing more than to be there going on calls. But I can't with this stupid leg." I try to make light of it, but the truth is, I might not be able to work at all anymore and that very thought both scares and disappoints the hell out of me. How can I keep Dee's memory alive if I can't do what I love and make sure I'm there to help people? And being around my firehouse family just makes me remember that this might be yet another family I won't be a part of anymore, especially in light of what the therapist said just a few hours ago. Just considering that my career is over makes me nauseous.

"Well, we better go. We have reservations for dinner."

"Enjoy, kiddo. Don't be a stranger." Jason leans out to hug

me and I pat his back. Sampson and I head back towards the apartment.

"They seem nice." Sampson sounds tentative.

"They are." I'll really miss working with them. I sigh.

"Want to talk about what happened at therapy now?" he asks as we settle into my studio apartment.

"You're not going to let it go, are you?"

He shakes his head as he settles back on the couch. He pats the cushion next to him. "Come. Put your leg up. I can tell it's bothering you. Tell Sampson all about it."

"How can you possibly tell my leg is bothering me? I haven't made a peep about it." I settle into the couch next to him and he immediately helps me prop it up and loosens the braced one.

"Your limp is more pronounced when you're hurting. Also, you get grumpy. You want some Advil?" He gently rubs lotion on the lower part of my leg, the skin still looking sickly from being casted up.

I tear up when I realize I can't feel him rubbing the lower part of my leg on the side with the nerve damage. My eyes well up. I'm never going to be able to work again, not as a fire paramedic anyway.

"Fuck, I'm sorry Mel." Sampson yanks his hands from my leg. "I didn't mean to hurt you."

"You're not hurting me, Sampson." His brow is furled, but his hands don't go back to my leg.

"Then why are you crying?" His forehead crinkles in worry.

I reach up and touch my cheek. He's right, I am crying. *Shit.* "I, uh..." I take a deep breath, gathering my nerve to say it out loud, the bad news that David gave me today.

"It's numb. I couldn't even feel half of what you were doing. The therapist believes I have extensive and likely permanent nerve damage in my leg. Damage that'll affect my gait and possibly the strength in that leg." I take a breath. "It's not uncommon for tib/fib fractures. If that is the case, I'll probably be medically retired from being a fire paramedic."

I hate the words "medically retired." Helping people was my life, my career and now it's been stolen from me by some jerk who hasn't even been caught or punished for what he did to me. Who could be lurking around every corner to do it again, to me or someone else. We don't even know why or how he picked me.

"We'll find you another job. One you love just as much, but one that's less physically demanding." Sampson pulls me in for a hug.

"It won't be the same. Being a fire paramedic was what I wanted to do with my life. You don't understand. *It was my life*, Sampson."

He hugs me, and I cry on his shoulder. And he lets me. He doesn't try to fix the problem or give me false hope. He lets me cry it out. Because he knows this is exactly what I need. I have to mourn for my losses before I can move on, and if anyone knows about mourning their loss, it's my Sampson.

After a while, he tightens his hug and then pulls back. "You be sad, but only for today. Tomorrow, we do your exercises and my therapy and work hard to figure out what to do *if* you end up being retired from the fire department." He leans back in and gives me a tight squeeze. "We'll do it together. We won't let *him* win."

# Chapter 26

## *Sammy*

### Six months later

**M**elody stands tall at the retirement ceremony in her honor. Her face doesn't show one bit of the devastation that I know she feels inside. She worked so hard over the last six months to get to the point where she can now walk without aid, but it wasn't enough for the medical evaluator with the fire department. It's been almost 9 months since the accident, but the real damage to her now is on the inside. She's devastated and angry.

David says that she's probably gotten back all the mobility she'll get, but he's willing to keep working with her if she wants. She might get to the point where she can run. But that doesn't seem to interest her and hasn't been to see him since the fire department made its decision.

Even from way back here, I see the shine in her eyes. She's fighting tears. She's proud of the work she'd done in the time she had. But she's also pissed as hell that it was taken away from her. She's disappointed in herself, especially in her body, which didn't respond quite the way she'd hoped to physical therapy.

And that's just the physical stuff she's been dealing with.

She tries not to go there, but the things that *he* did to her in the ambulance did a number on her too. She has dreams, well, nightmares really. But she doesn't want to talk about it. Not with me, anyway. It doesn't help that he hasn't been caught. I've held her many nights as she cried, asking why they haven't caught him yet. Sadly, I don't have any answers for that. But I can hold her while she cries.

She doesn't know I'm here. I've been on the east coast doing a few shows with the band. She insisted I go. That she'd be fine at the ceremony alone. But it felt wrong not to be here. I Face-Timed with her yesterday from my hotel room in Connecticut. The longer I've been away, the more tired she's looked.

I flew out early this morning with the blessings of the guys. They're coming back tomorrow as we have a few more interviews to do, but they were fine with me ducking out for this. We're releasing an album in a few weeks and will be announcing our Blind Rebels Rock the World tour will start in a few months.

Clance, Sofie, and some of the guys I recognize from her firehouse are in the audience. I slip into a seat in the back. I want my being here to be a surprise. But I also need to stay away from Clance. There's still bad blood between us. He still believes I tricked Melody into us living together. He couldn't be more wrong. We've just meshed so well together as a household that it's comfortable for both of us. Mel doesn't need someone to look after her anymore, but I stay because we want this.

All of the people on the stage retiring from their public service are probably at least twice her age. She doesn't belong up there and she feels it in her heart. And truth be told, I'm angry about it for her. Angry that this happened to her and that that asshole took away her happy, her purpose.

The spring in her step and the light in her eyes haven't been there in the last nine months, and that's what kills me most of all. She's not my Mel. She tries hard to project my Mel, but she's not. And that makes me want to wrap my hand around that fucker's throat and punch him until... no. My therapist says I can't go there, and she's right.

Mel's been looking for a job where she can use her para-medic training that doesn't have a physical fitness requirement, but that's not easy. She still teaches First Aid and CPR at the community center and adult school, and she loves it, but it's not full-time work. Not that she needs full-time work, but she won't let me just take care of her. It's a matter of pride for her, but a bone of contention with me. She wants to stay busy and love what she does.

When the ceremony is over, she joins Clance, Sof, and some of the firehouse guys near the stage. It looks like they are trying to get her to go somewhere, and she doesn't want to go. She goes out only when she needs to, for doctor's appointments, our beach walks, or to teach her class, but that's pretty much it.

I walk up behind Sofie, and Melody's eyes catch me standing there. They widen enough that the rest of the group turns to look at what's caught her attention.

"Sampson! You're here." She lunges at me in a flying hug. Clance stiffens and grumbles at my presence, but Sofie quickly elbows him in the side, and he stops his bellyaching.

"Hey, Sam, we're trying to convince Mel to come back to the firehouse for a little celebration in her honor. Can you convince her to come?" one of the firefighters from her shift asks me. "She's giving us gruff. You're invited too, of course."

I put my hand on Mel's lower back. "I say we go, Mel."

"I don't want to go, at all," she mumbles, so only I can hear. I rub the small of her back. She straightens and paints on a totally plastic smile. "Sure, we'll come for a little bit."

We all break apart, making plans to meet at the firehouse in a few minutes. She brought Kill's Porsche, which makes me smile because she's comfortable driving it. Kill would probably flip out if he knew she was driving *his Porsche* as an everyday driver. But then again, maybe he wouldn't.

"I'm glad you brought the car. If you hadn't, we'd be waiting for a ride share."

"I wanted to come alone, or I'd have been stuck riding with Clance and Sof. I didn't want to be obligated to go to the firehouse." She looks up at me with her lip pouted out.

"They put something together in your honor, Mel. They miss you as much as you miss them."

Her pouted lip turns down. "It's hard to be there. I'd rather go home and watch TV with you or do something else." She pulls me to her firmly, trying to distract me with ideas of sex. Not that sex with Mel isn't off the charts, but I can tell she's trying to use it as a distraction.

I hug her to me because I can't make her feel better about going. She loved her job, but that's just not possible for her anymore. I've watched her slowly lose her sense of purpose and self as the realization hit her that life is changing for her.

"Let's head to the firehouse, let them celebrate you, and then we'll go home as early as possible, okay?" She nods, but I can tell she's disheartened that her attempt to distract me wasn't successful by the curve of her shoulders.

"By the way, Mel, I missed you." I pull her back to me tight. "A lot." I kiss her neck, then move up to just behind her ear.

"I missed you too," she mumbles into my ear softly as her hands go around my back to hold me to her.

Clance honks at us from his red truck, causing us to jump apart.

"Asshole," I mutter.

"We'll see you there. Don't even think about skipping out. These guys planned this for you, Melody." He eyes me coolly as he calls out his window as he creeps by our parking spot.

Mel presses her forehead into my shoulder as I hold her. I don't know if she's mad at Clance, at me, or just resigned to the fact that she's stuck going somewhere she doesn't want to go.

I kiss the top of her head. "It probably means a lot for them to say goodbye. We'll do it together and then we'll leave. Okay?"

"'Kay," she whispers quietly into my shoulder and stays in that position for a few long beats before she straightens up, nods, and makes her way to the passenger seat of the car, tossing me the keys to the Panamera.

At the firehouse a few minutes later, she gets out of the car slowly. She waits for me to come open her door and give her my hand to help her out. This is not something Mel used to do.

She used to jump out of the car like her ass was on fire. She didn't want to be helped out. She doesn't want people to think she's in any way handicapped by her injury. She only started waiting after she got the news from the fire department that she'd been labeled as disabled in the line of duty and retired. It's like she's given up on herself and that's killing me the most.

One of the bays in the garage has been cleared of the ambulance that sat there. I saw it parked along the side when we pulled in. The door is open and music drifts out of the opened door. Tables have been set up in two long rows, lined with tablecloths that have little fire engines on them. Various snacks are on the tables and a barbecue pit on wheels is sitting in the driveway, where Clance and Jason are starting to grill some chickens and steak. On duty firemen mill about in their uniforms along with off-duty, who are in regular clothes, with wives, girlfriends, and a handful of children complete the group. Mel's grip on my hand tightens the closer we get, but then we are enveloped by the entire group.

Mel introduces me to so many people, I'll never be able to remember them all. A few ask for my autograph, which feels weird since this party is for Mel, not me. But most people seem cool with me being there as Mel's boyfriend, not Sammy the drummer.

There is laughter, and then we sit and eat. The food's incredible. Mel barely eats half of what's on her plate. Clance keeps glancing at her plate and then up at her.

"Mel, did you taste Gloria's potato salad?" Clance holds up a spoonful. "I swear it keeps getting better each time she makes it." He makes a show of eating the bite. "Mmm, so good."

"It really is good, Gloria. You know how much I love it." Mel smiles the fake plastic smile she's been wearing since we got here as she takes a bite, ignoring Clance.

"I know how much you've always loved it. I have a tub in the fridge for you to take home." The small brunette woman smiles as she nods to the door leading into the station house.

"That's so sweet. You didn't have to do that. Thanks," she replies as she shovels another spoonful into her mouth and swallows without chewing.

We get through the rest of the meal, with Mel covering her plate with her napkin and stealing away to throw the rest out without anyone noticing, or so she thinks. She barely ate, and I saw that Clance's eyes were still locked onto her plate all the way to the trash. Thankfully, he keeps his mouth shut. I know if he had said something, she would have used it as an excuse to leave early. It's been another bone of contention between us. Her lack of appetite. I try to get her to eat, and she uses my attempts to try to pick fights.

The captain stands at the head of the table and starts making a speech when an alarm goes off, followed by a dispatcher giving codes over a loudspeaker that obviously mean something. More than half the uniformed firemen jump up and head to the fire truck, throwing on equipment in something of a coordinated dance. They all take their places, and the truck rolls out of the bay. Stephen and another person run to the displaced ambulance and follow.

"Car accident, with extrication needed," Mel says to me quietly. "Out on the freeway. They'll be out there awhile."

The captain waits until they've pulled away before starting back up by giving his accolades to Mel. A few others stand and tell stories that have her eyes filling up with water. I squeeze her hand under the table, and she squeezes mine back.

An amazing cake in the shape of her ambulance is brought out as well as a present. She opens the present and finds a model of her ambulance along with a figurine made to look like her standing next to it, with a tiny placard with the name of the firehouse.

"Thank you. Everyone. I love it." We get to hear the story of how it was made by a couple of the guys in the firehouse, using a model as a base. It's amazingly detailed, including a gurney with a patient tucked into the back.

We have cake even though it's almost too cool to cut. By then Mel's ready to go home. Her fake happy façade is starting to crack as she stabs at the last piece of cake on her plate with a little too much pressure. Her little plastic fork breaks, so she picks up the piece and shoves it in her mouth with her fingers.

"That was delicious," she announces, her mouth still partially full of cake. "It was so accurate, I almost didn't want to see it cut, but I am so glad it was because that was amazing." Jason's wife, whose name I've since forgotten, beams at Melody's words.

I stand, willing to help Melody make the quick exit she wants without her taking the blame. "Thank you all. I hate to eat and run, but I'm running on fumes. I had a show last night in Connecticut and had to be at the airport early to fly out to make it for the ceremony." Various people boo and hiss but the goodbyes that I know Melody wanted, but felt bad initiating, begin.

The ambulance and firetruck roll in just in time for everyone to say goodbye. Mel carries her model ambulance close to her body as she stops with the last few people saying goodbye. I offer to take it from her, but she insists on carrying it.

She won't even let me hold it when she's trying to snap her seatbelt and hold the model. I end up being the one to snap her seatbelt for the drive back to Santa Monica.

When we walk into the apartment, Melody walks directly to the shelf on the wall across from the couch and moves the plant to the breakfast bar, putting the ambulance in its place. Wrapping my arms around her from behind, I hug her to me, then spin her so she's facing me. Her lip quivers as she pulls her gaze from her ambulance back to me. I attempt to kiss the quiver right off her lips.

It doesn't work. Sobs rack through her, and I hold her while she cries, an all too regular scene these days. When she starts sputtering, I loosen my grip, thinking she's all cried out. I'm right. Her eyes flash with anger as her fists ball up at her sides. She's moved solidly back into the anger phase.

"I fucking hate *him!*" Melody spits, her face turning from the crumpled devastation mapping it to the hard lines of a vicious, vengeful wrath. It twists her face until I almost don't recognize her.

"I hope he rots in hell for ruining me. That they tell him it's because of what he's done to me specifically." She pounds her hand into the middle of her chest. "That he's remorseful, but no one cares because he doesn't deserve care or concern. He doesn't."

These are not the kind of words I'd ever expect to come from my Mel. Her face is so red, and her body so tense, that I can feel the anger rippling through her. Anger that's eating away at my Mel, changing her, and not for the better.

I stumble backwards a few steps, caught off-guard by the pounding of her fist against my chest. The other hand joins in and she raps out a frantic, furious beat against my chest.

I grab her wrists to stop her pummeling, mostly because I don't want her to damage her hands as the punches get harder. "Whoa, Mel. Either we need to get you back into the gym to work off some of this aggression on a heavy bag or you take up drumming."

My weak attempt at humor has her face wrinkling with sadness as the waterworks start back up. She's trying to say something, but it doesn't come out as anything more than a harder sob. She fists her hand in my shirt as I hold her, her sobs so hard that her breathing stutters every couple of minutes. I gently rub her back with one hand while holding her to me with the other.

I don't give her false platitudes, nor do I tell her it's okay. It's not. It sucks that this happened. And I know more than anyone that she needs to work through it.

"Let's take a shower, change into our comfy clothes, and binge something on TV." She nods, so I steer her into the bathroom and turn on the shower. We disrobe and I pull her into the shower stall with me before she's even done undressing.

"Sampson, I'm still half dressed." She tries to peel her now plastered on underwear off.

"Let me." I gently peel the wet fabric from her and slide it down her legs, and toss it over the shower door. Standing, I unhook her soggy bra, leaning in to kiss her neck as I work the straps down her arms to remove it.

She clenches my biceps with her hands after I toss her bra over the shower door like I did her underwear. Her eyes dilate, and she squeezes my arms as her tongue peeks out and dampens her lips.

Mel backs herself against the shower wall and then pulls me to her, our lips crashing together frantically. She hitches one leg over my hip, pulling me even closer.

"I need this. I need you." She swivels her hips into me.

I press her to the wall, and she leverages herself between me and the wall, helping me enter her as she wraps both legs around me, her fingers digging into my shoulders as she seats herself slowly.

I let her control the pace, knowing she needs to piece out her anger and disappointment and work them into something good. Real fucking good, which is exactly how she feels, slick and warm around me.

The water rains down on us as we slide against each other, with her moving up the wall slightly with each of my thrusts. As our tempo increases, so does her grip on my shoulders and the pressure of the heels of her feet against the cheeks of my ass.

I should probably be offended that she's using me to feel better, but when she lets out the soft breathy moans on each thrust, I can't think of anything but holding off until she's ready. Because I'm so close. I try to run drum drills in my head so I can work my hand between us to help her along.

All it takes is a few well-timed rubs against her nub and she's tightening all around me, head thrown back in pleasure. That's all it takes for me to join her.

# Chapter 27

## *Sammy*

After showering again and drying off, we spend time just cuddling on her bed with the TV on. It doesn't take long before she's drifted off, and I'm not far behind when there's a knock at the door.

It's probably Mrs. Chamske. I know she saw us return from the party at the firehouse, because her door was ajar when we got back. Untangling myself from a sleeping Mel, I throw on my sweatpants and don't bother looking before flinging open the door.

Instead of little Mrs. Chamske, I'm standing face to face with Clance. He's holding a couple of food containers.

"Um, hi?" I look at him, unsure how he'll actually react to me opening the door shirtless. He hasn't come over to the apartment since I moved in with Mel. Instead, he invites her out for lunch or coffee.

"Mel, um, forgot the potato salad and the rest of the cake." He holds out the two containers. I take them. "Is she, um, here?"

Nodding, I open the door a little bit farther, unsure whether I should invite him in when she's sleeping. "She fell asleep

about twenty minutes ago while we were watching TV in bed."
I open the door even wider and nod towards the sectioned off
bedroom area behind the dressing screens.

He nods. "Oh, good. She looked a little tired at the
firehouse."

"Probably my fault. I FaceTimed late yesterday when I was
still on the east coast. I probably shouldn't have, but we'd been
doing it every night, and I wanted to surprise her by coming
back early."

"Can I come in?" He shifts from one foot to another. "I'd like
to talk."

"Sure." Leaving the door open, I head towards the fridge
with the containers of food. He closes the door quietly and
joins me in the kitchen area of the studio apartment, sitting on
one of the stools at the breakfast bar.

"So, Sam, Sampson—"

"You can call me Sam or Sammy. Mel's the only one besides
my sister who's ever called me Sampson."

He nods. "Sam. Is she okay with all this? How's she
handling it, the retirement thing?" He folds a napkin into tiny
squares. "I mean, it's got to be hard for her. But she doesn't
really talk to me much. Not about what's in her heart." I *knew*
the fit he threw when Mel left had damaged their relationship.

"She seems a little lost, honestly. She's back to teaching CPR
and First Aid, but she wants something full-time. Preferably
something that'll allow her to still teach for the community
center and adult school. But she hasn't found anything yet."
Clance nods. He probably won't like what I'm about to tell him.

"I've been trying to convince her to come out on tour with
us when we leave. I think it'd be good for her to get out of here
for a while."

Clance nods with me, which surprises me. "She doesn't
want to go?"

"She's more focused on getting a job. She's worried about

money. I wish she'd let me just take care of her, go on tour with me, and get away from the memories of what happened here. It's not like I can't take care of her."

"You want me to talk to her? I think traveling a little might be good for her." Clance might as well push me over with a feather. He's actually agreeing with me?

"I don't know if it'd help or make her more insistent about not going. She's been pretty surly lately."

Clance nods vigorously, like he expected to hear that. "How's her pain level? Is she hurting from therapy? Pain can make anyone surly."

"She'd been pushing it right up until she got her FD evaluation results. She hasn't been back to therapy since. I don't think she's in pain because usually the more pain she has, the worse her limp gets. I think she's frustrated more than anything."

He nods, his lips a thin line. "I was afraid of that. Make sure she's ready at 8:00 am sharp tomorrow morning. The three of us are hitting the gym." His jaw is set in determination. "We'll exhaust her tomorrow in the gym and then she won't be able to say no about the tour."

I'm not sure about this idea of his. Sure, I run and workout some with Mel, but I don't hit the gym like she and Clance did. They'll kick my ass all over that place, but if it helps Mel, I'm all for it.

Mel stirs in the cordoned off bedroom and it catches Clance's attention. "I'm going to go. Remember, 8:00 am. See you both tomorrow." He heads to the door, slipping out before Melody gets up.

# Chapter 28

## *Melody*

Sammy's kissing me awake at some ungodly hour. While I love the kisses, I don't like the hour. We went to bed kind of late since we took a nap in the evening last night.

"Why are you even awake? Go back to sleep, Sampson." I groan and roll away from his onslaught.

"Wakey, wakey, Mel." He plants a kiss on my shoulder. "We have plans. Get up and shower. I'll get your outfit together while you're in there."

"You're dressing me now, Sampson?" I'm not sure who he thinks he is, waking me up early and telling me what to wear.

"Just trust me, Mel. You'll want to be showered and dressed before 8:00." A knowing smile ghosts his lips.

"Why?" Sampson's up to something. I can tell by the glint in his eye and the lift of his one eyebrow.

"I told you to trust me. Now get up, woman. Or I'll carry you to the shower."

I grumble the whole way to the bathroom, while Sampson chuckles and heads into the walk-in. True to his word, he's laid out an outfit by the time I'm out. It's one of my workout outfits. Oh joy. I don't really want to go for a walk today.

Sampson comes out of the closet wearing basketball shorts and a t-shirt, a towel over his wet curly mop of hair. He towel dries his hair and heads to the kitchen to make us some scrambled eggs and toast.

"What are we doing, Sampson?" I am not in the mood for scrambled eggs or for a walk.

"Sit, have some juice and eggs." He slides a plate towards the spot I favor at the breakfast bar. "Fuel up. We don't have a lot of time."

He puts the pan in the sink and stands over it, eating his eggs. Or inhaling his eggs would be a more accurate description of what he's doing. As soon as he's done with the eggs and toast, he swills his orange juice before starting the dishes. At least I have him well trained.

"Done." As I slide my plate towards him, there's a sharp knock at the door that makes me jump.

Then the door opens and Clance, dressed in his workout gear, waltzes in with a smug look on his face. "You two ready?"

"What are you doing here?" I squint at him. I thought Sampson and I were going on one of our beach walks. But why would Clance come with us for that? And Clance hasn't stepped foot inside the apartment since Sampson moved in with me.

"It's Monday, right?" Clance cocks his head at me.

"Uh, yeah."

"We're heading to the gym. Every Monday, Wednesday, and Friday, you two will go. I will join you when I'm not on shift. Grab a water and let's move it." He stands by the door.

Clance means total business and doesn't even drive us. Nope, he has us walk to the gym.

"Maybe next time, we try jogging it," he suggests and

Sampson nods. "Rule one is you can't drive it. Not even if it's raining."

"Clance, I—"

"Rule number two is no excuses, no complaining. You know this, Mel. You've got to get back to it. No more of this moping around and feeling sorry shit. We don't want you to lose any more muscle mass."

"But I don't need it anymore. I only did it so I wasn't the weakest link in the firehouse."

"You need it even more now than ever. You need the discipline back. You need the confidence, hon. We'll get you back, Mel. One step at a time." He claps my back.

Clance spends the next forty minutes walking us through a circuit routine at the old gym. He leaves a copy in the locker there so we can refer to it. It's similar to the circuit he and I used to do, only more emphasis on legs. By the time we're done, I'm a jelly-legged, sweaty mess. One leg is tight, the other just throbs.

He even has me bench press. I'm not as strong as I used to be. "See, Mel. If you don't use it, you lose it. We'll work you back up slowly." I nod.

"You can do this, kiddo." He hugs me, even in all my sweatiness.

"It won't get me back on the crew."

"Do it for the discipline, and for the self-confidence. For the routine. Do it for you because you're worth it." He pokes me in the chest. Am I worth it, though? I'm ruined. *He* took away my career, my confidence. I feel my chin wanting to quiver, so I look away quickly before it does. The relationship between Clance and I hasn't been an easy one since I moved back into my place, so it surprises me he's here trying to get me out of my permafunk. My chin wants to quiver again, but I take a deep breath and tamp it back down deep.

We walk back to the apartment. Well, they walk. I limp. A

lot harder than when we were leaving, but they don't baby me. I wonder if Sof knows where Clance is. She's kept her distance from me lately and I can't say that I blame her, really. I was a bitch to her. She was just trying to help me. My heart aches at that.

"Ice, then heat," Clance offers as we part at the apartment. "See ya Wednesday, guys."

"So when did you and Clance plot against me?" Sampson's eyes bulge at my question as he continues to gulp down his orange sports drink while standing in front of the fridge.

He slowly wipes his mouth and looks up at me. "We didn't plot against you. This was Clance's idea, but I am behind it one hundred percent. You've given up on yourself. It kills me to see you so drawn inside yourself. That's not my Mel, and it's obviously not Clance's Mel either because he brought his concerns to me."

He relaxes against the counter. "Clance and Sofie love you and want you to be the best you. I want that too. What happened to you sucks. It's taken more than just your job, Mel. It's stolen your confidence, bravado, and the fire from your eyes." He opens his arms, beckoning me to hug him. I walk into him, wrapping my arms tightly around his waist as he envelops me. His strong arms circled around me make me feel like home. His beeswax and wood scent comforts me and I lay my head on his chest.

"I want you to seriously consider touring with us. I know I have asked before, but I really think the change of scenery would do you good. Clance thinks it's a good idea too. Just saying."

I pull my head back so I can see his face. "You told Clance that I said no? And he thinks I should go?" It might be nice to get away from here for a while. Away from the possibility *of him* at every turn.

Sampson nods, his curls bouncing on his shoulders.

"Weird, huh? I expected him to throw another fit like he did when you left them, but he was all for you traveling around the country with me. Who'd of thought?" Sampson smiles.

"I'll think about it, okay?" I press my lips together tightly. I don't really want to tour with Sampson and the band. It's not my scene. I definitely don't want to watch women throw themselves at him. And what would I do? He'd be busy all day, and I'd be stuck inside a hotel or a bus or whatever.

"Deal. Thinking about it is better than an outright no." He winks at me. "You're still coming to Mav's with me this afternoon, right? Kady, Ari, and Vi are looking forward to getting to know you better."

I roll my head on my shoulders, trying to loosen the tension building in my shoulders. I agreed to this, but I shouldn't have. I really am not in the mood to socialize, especially after getting my ass kicked all over the gym this morning.

I'm not much of a social butterfly and the idea of sitting around making small talk makes me itchy.

Sampson moves behind me and rests his strong hands on my shoulders and squeezes and kneads my shoulders with his thumbs. That feels so good. The tension I was holding releases under his wonderful hands.

"We'll be working in Mav's studio, but the girls are looking forward to hanging out with you. They are good people, Mel. Kady's been through a lot. She's so much different now than when I first met her. And Ari, she's such a sweetheart. I don't know Vi that well, but she's Ari's older sister. She seems nice, but really quiet." I nod, hoping he'll keep rubbing, but he stops and turns me around, so I face him.

He sticks his bottom lip out. "The band, the women that come with them, these are my people, Mel. We are more of a family than just a band. And that includes the ladies. That includes you too, if you'll let them get to know you."

"Sampson, I won't have anything in common with them.

They won't like me. And I don't do well with the pressure of small talk." I can hear the whine in my voice.

Sampson's lips upturn slightly because he knows. He freaking knows I'll end up going.

"For me?" His bottom lip juts out again, and he looks down at me through his thick dark lashes that have always made me jealous. "Please."

"I don't know how you do that." I reach up and yank on one of his curls.

"Do what?" His face is almost cherub-like, with his curly hair and that bow-shaped lip sticking out.

"Get me to agree to things I don't want to do."

# Chapter 29

## *Melody*

Sampson comes out of doorway leading to the lower-level studio, shooting me a soft smile and a wink as he heads to the fridge and pulls out a sports drink, and several bottles of water. He rifles through the Slater's kitchen like he lives here, pulling out family sized bags of both pretzels and beef jerky. He gathers his bounty and starts to head back towards the doorway leading to the studio.

"Sam, we're about to order food. You can forgo the snacks," Kady says, holding her phone up. He shrugs at her. "For later," he mumbles, and disappears back through the doorway.

"I don't know where he puts it." Kady shakes her head.

"He was always hungry as a teen. They didn't get a lot of food at home. I used to bring two lunches back when we were dating in high school. A normal one for me. And an extra-large one for him. He'd eat part of it and keep the rest for his sister. My theory is the lack of food screwed up his metabolism. Between that and being so active, he never gains weight. Like ever. Seven was the same way. She could eat an entire cake in a sitting and not gain an ounce." I roll my eyes to emphasize the ridiculousness of it all.

I become very aware of three sets of eyes staring me down. I tug at the collar of my shirt, suddenly hot. "What?"

Ari is the first to speak. "No one really talks about her."

"Who? Seven?" I look at them and the three nod, in near unison. Why wouldn't Sampson talk about his sister?

"Seven was Sam's little sister. She was two years younger, but she spent a lot of time with Sampson and I when we'd hang out, he'd bring her along a lot of the time. I didn't know the subject was taboo." I hope what I've said doesn't piss him off. But if it does, then maybe he should have either warned me not to mention her or not have forced me to come when I didn't want to.

"What happened to her?" Ari looks over her shoulder towards the door that leads to the studio, then turns back and scoots towards me.

"She overdosed. I wasn't with Sampson anymore by that point. I went to the funeral. She was my friend too. Or she was until they moved to Hollywood. They both kind of ghosted me when they moved." I shrug.

"They didn't have the best home life. Seven had issues back when I was dating Sampson. She confided in me once that one of her mom's dealers had been touching her, um, inappropriately." I can still see her. That stick-straight hair I was so jealous of and the way she'd hitch her hip when she was mad and trying to be so grown up. "I should have said something, but I was just a kid and she made me swear I wouldn't tell Sampson."

Sampson and Seven couldn't have looked more opposite if they tried. His hair is curly, and hers was straight. He was tall, and she was petite for her age. He was quiet and laid back. She always seemed eager for attention, for the love she didn't get as a child.

"That must have been tough," Kady says. "For both of you."

I nod and there's that awkward silence I hate when hanging

out with people I don't know. I want to fill it, but I don't know what to say. Why am I like this?

"How are you feeling?" Kady asks Ari.

"I'm still a little nauseated," she answers her friend and then turns to me. "I don't think you know this, Mel, but I'm pregnant." Ari smiles at me.

"Congratulations." I hug her.

"Thank you. Cal's so excited."

"Shit. Who's getting the food?" Kady asks.

"We'll go." Ari indicates to her sister, who nods.

"Thanks. Brio should be getting up any minute from his nap. I am surprised Gibs isn't already up. He'll be so excited to see you, Mel," Kady gushes. "That little boy loves you. He's been asking about you."

Ari and Vi leave to get the food, and as if he heard his name, Gibson is soon letting us know both he and Brio are awake.

"You want to get them with me?" Kady flicks her head towards the staircase.

I have to admit, Gibson's absolutely adorable, with his bouncy curly blonde hair and big dark blue eyes. He's sitting up, clutching his favorite little stuffed dog that he puts in his backpack as soon as he's set on the floor.

Kady picks up Brio, who's also just woken up and changes him as he keeps his weary little eyes on me.

"Pay outside? Pease. Thank you." Gibson asks me.

"Let's ask."

"KayKay. I pay outside?"

"Sure." The four of us go outside and Gibson starts climbing and playing on a recently installed play set.

"Ari didn't mention this, but this is her second pregnancy. She got pregnant right after their honeymoon, but she lost the baby. They were devastated." Kady looks over at me. "Cal's worried about the tour and the stress of all the traveling on her and the baby."

Brio starts fussing. "Do you mind running in and getting one of his sippy cups out and filling it with half water, half apple juice? There should be a couple of clean cups on the counter next to the fridge."

"Not at all. Be right back." Even with Kady's permission, it feels weird to me to just open the refrigerator in someone else's house and rummaging around for their apple juice. The complete opposite of Sampson, who just opened the door like he lived here. But then again, according to him, he did kind of live here on and off.

I'm just snapping the lid on the sippy cup when I hear a scream that has the paramedic in me snapping to attention. It's the pained scream of a hurt child.

Abandoning the juice and sippy cup on the counter, I rush back out to the backyard play area. Gibson is lying on the grass next to the play structure, screaming, and Kady is kneeling next to him, holding Brio to her.

"Oh God. Gibson, don't move, baby. Mel, help. He fell off. He whacked his head, but I also think his arm might be broken." She looks up at me, her face turning white.

Gibson's stopped screaming and now only whimpers. I rush over and lower myself to him. "Hey, buddy. It's okay. I'm going to take a look, okay?" He's pale and his arm is definitely bent at an unnatural angle between the wrist and the elbow. "Yeah, that's definitely broken. Get Cal. We can transport him ourselves or call an ambulance. But he needs to go to an ER, preferably Children's, because they'll have a pediatric ortho on staff."

She nods and gets up with Brio. "I'll get him."

"Bring back a pillowcase or a towel and a magazine." She nods and rushes into the house.

Soon, the entirety of the Blind Rebels come rushing out of the house, followed by Kady. Cal reaches me first.

"What happened? Where the hell is Ari? Who was

261

watching him?" Cal fires at me. As soon as Gibson sees his dad angry, he starts to cry again.

"I was watching him, Cal." Kady hands me the pillowcase and magazine. "I turned my back for a second and he fell off the play structure.

"Obviously not well." He sneers at Kady, who takes a step back.

Mav's chest puffs up and he steps between Kady and Cal.

"Cal." I'm trying to get him to focus on his son and not on Kady or Mav. "I'm going to splint his arm. Then we should either take him to the children's ER or call an ambulance to do it for us. He definitely needs it set and casted."

Cal's face goes ashen when he sees his son's arm deformity and starts to sway, his eyes rolling back.

"I got him." Killian grabs his brother under the arms from behind and starts to lower him to the ground. "Do your thing, Mel."

I carefully wrap the magazine around Gib's lower arm, trying not to move it, but he cries because I am sure it hurts like hell. Cal lets loose a quiet string of curse words and turns even whiter as he looks over at us from his new position seated on the grass a few feet away from his son.

"Get his head between his knees." I nod at Cal as I create a makeshift sling out of the gray pillowcase Kady handed me while Killian pushes Cal's head down between his legs.

I tie the toddler's arm to his chest to keep it as immobile as I can. Looking back over at Cal, I notice he's got some of his color back now that he can't see the arm deformity.

"You doing okay? Do you want me to drive?" I ask him. He can't drive us if he's woozy. Cal shakes his head at me.

"Jax will drive," Mav announces, looking up from his phone. "He's waiting at the door in Cal's SUV."

Gibson cries out for his stuffed dog as I pick him up.

"On it." Killian jogs back inside.

"Come on, you wuss, get up and let's get your kid to the hospital." Mav chuckles as he helps Cal off the ground.

"Get his blanket too, Kill," Cal hollers after his twin. "Someone text Ari."

"Already did." Kady's voice is quiet as she holds Brio to her closely. Her chin trembles and her eyes get shinier with moisture. "I'll wait here for her and Vi, and we'll meet you there."

Sammy's eyes are wide as I pass him, carrying Gibson, and he falls in behind me as we file towards the front door. Killian joins us with the well-loved stuffed dog and a green blanket and falls into line as we leave the house and all get into the large SUV.

Cal watches as I carefully strap his son into his car seat, careful of his arm. We head off to the hospital as a group. Thankfully, Ari and Vi came separately, so Cal still had his SUV and car seat when they left to pick up food. Getting a text from Ari, Cal reroutes her into coming directly to the hospital. I feel bad about Kady back at home alone with her son. Cal was harsh with her when it was an accident. Kady probably couldn't have prevented his fall, even if she'd been looking directly at him.

I don't think Cal meant to be so unforgiving, but he was, and she took it to heart. This little boy has so many people who love him. The SUV is chucked full of them.

Cal carries a whimpering Gibson into the ER when we arrive and Ari's already at the desk filling out forms. Seeing his mom, Gibson immediately starts whimpering. The family is soon whisked to a room and the rest of us are shown to a private waiting room, as to not cause a scene in the ER waiting room at Children's.

Sampson drops into the seat next to mine and hands me a diet Coke.

"Thanks."

"You were amazing. The way you just took charge of everything at Mav's. I mean, I know it was your job, but I've never actually seen you do that kind of thing before. Was it like that when you were saving me? That's what I kept thinking back there." He stares at me much like he was in the yard at the Slaters.

"Actually, with you, I kept having to push Killian out of my way to give you rescue breaths. But yeah, I told a jogger to call for help while I helped Killian get you out of the water and to the shore where I could start CPR. Obviously, with your case, the situation was much more dire. I was trying to get you to start breathing again."

Sampson pales a little and nods. "Well, luckily for me, it worked." His mouth pulls up in a faint grin. "Real lucky, according to my doctor."

"With Gibs, it was just a matter of trying to keep him still and get him splinted and hoping Cal and Mav didn't go to blows." I remember both men's chests puffed out in the back-yard. "Or that Cal didn't pass out again."

Killian interrupts, "That's a Cal thing. He looks all tough on the outside, but when it comes to medical emergencies, he cannot be relied on. I impaled my arm when I was eight and he was the one that passed out. Oh, and what about the time Gibs split his chin open? He passed out at the hospital, just catching a glimpse at the gash. It's like his party trick. Show him some blood or something and down he goes."

Sammy chuckles. "It wouldn't be the first time Mav and Cal had gone to blows either. But usually, they'll work things out before it gets to that. Once Cal knows Gibs is good, he'll feel bad about being a dick to Kady. He didn't mean to do it. It was like dad brain took over or something. Eventually, he'll apologize to Mav and Kady, and everything will be forgotten."

"Still, I feel bad for Kady. He was hard on her."

"Kady understands," Mav says from across the small room we are in. He holds up his phone as he lounges across two chairs in the small, stark waiting room we've been shown to. "I was just giving her an update. She offered to come with Brio. I told her to stay home. There's nothing she could do for Gibs anyway, and honestly, why expose Brio to hospital germs?"

We settle in for a wait. My head is on Sampson's shoulder, our hands interlocked.

"You were so good today, Mel. Thank goodness you were there," Mav says. "You really know how to take charge when there's an emergency."

"It's my training." I shrug it off. "Paramedics are trained to command a scene."

"Well, I was impressed as hell. We should hire you to be our tour medic or something. You could take care of all our scrapes, scratches, and stuffy noses. Be there should something major happen. Like you heard, on our last big tour, Gibson took quite a spill and needed to be taken to the hospital for stitches. We were lucky because that venue had a paramedic on duty, but they don't normally. There was this one time that Sammy's drum riser collapsed. He got scraped up pretty good. I mean, it would be good to travel with someone who knows when we need to get to a hospital and when they can just patch us up."

Sammy straightens in his seat. "Can we hire her for something like that?"

Mav shrugs. "I'll take it to Darren who can take it to Monumentus, but I don't see why not. She can take care of roadies too. I mean, it makes sense, right? If that would be something Mel'd be interested in, of course."

Sammy looks at me with his brown eyes. "Would that be something you'd consider? Technically, you'd be an employee of the record company and not us. But it would be nice to have someone there who cares about us and already knows us."

I've never been out of southern California. This would be a chance to travel while working as a paramedic that didn't have a restrictive mobility requirement. I've been working hard in the gym with Clance and Sampson, but I'll never be up to fire department fitness requirements. At least this will have me working in my preferred occupation. But is it just because I know Sampson? What if things go south between us? What if he gets tired of me and leaves me high and dry again?

"I don't know," I sigh.

Sampson squeezes me to him. "Just think about it for now. We'll talk about it later."

I nod, but my head continues to spin with the possibilities. This would be a great boost for me, to be working as a paramedic privately. I'll be working in my field despite my injury. Plus, I'll be able to travel and be with Sampson.

What seems like seconds later, but I know was a lot longer, Cal comes strolling into the waiting room. Gibson is in his arms, head on his father's shoulder, his little eyelids at half-mast. His broken arm now sports a bright green cast from hand to elbow, and the fingers of his other hand are woven into his dad's long hair. Parts of his well-loved stuffed animal are visible between his body and Cal's as it seems sandwiched in between them. Ari trails behind the father and son, holding the green blanket Killian retrieved from upstairs.

"Boken," Gibson says softly and wiggles his fingers in the casted arm, then sticks his bottom lip out and a couple of big tears come down his face.

"Yep, Mel was right. It was broken. The doctor said that was a heck of a splint job, by the way. He already has an appointment in three weeks with the children's orthopedist. They'll check the break and decide if the cast can come off then. He says young bones tend to mend quickly. It will likely come off then."

Everyone gathers around Cal and Gibson, and Gibson seems to eat up the attention. Mav promised to be the first one to sign his cast after Gibson's nap.

Crammed back in the SUV, Cal watches as his son starts to doze off, clutching his stuffed dog with his good arm.

"I don't know if it's the stress of being hurt, that it's naptime, or the pain medication that's making him so sleepy." Cal looks at me.

"Probably all three, honestly." Cal nods at my answer and then looks at me intensely.

"Thank you for all that you did for him. I know we took that class from you, and we would have probably eventually remembered what to do, but I am so thankful you were there to take care of him." His eyes are glossy with unshed emotion.

I lean forward and give his arm a quick squeeze. "You're welcome."

Cal turns to Mav in the back seat with me. "I need to apologize to Kady and you for going off."

Mav leans up and flicks his ear in a playful gesture. "Just say you're sorry to Kady. I'm a dad now, so I get it, man. I'm sure she'll understand."

Sampson was right about them being good again, just like that.

# Chapter 30

## *Sammy*

Mel is lounging on the couch in Cal's living room, her bare feet peeking out from under Gibson's green security blanket that covers her and Gibson's lower halves. Instead of returning to Mav's, we went to Cal's house. Kady meeting us there with Brio. Gibson is stationed between her legs, laying against her with his broken arm resting on a short stack of pillows off to the side, his eyes half-closed as he watches another episode of Paw Patrol and munches on a baggie of fish-shaped crackers. Brio is laying on her torso, head on her shoulder. His lips apart, soft breathy snores emanating from them. Mel gazes at the TV, but I don't think she's as vested in Chase and Marshall's latest adventure as Gibson is.

She didn't even notice me come in from the music room. She's a natural with these kids. I doubt she gets that from her paramedic training. A vision of her holding a curly headed baby, our baby, comes to mind. She's a natural mom and suddenly I want that life. The one with a beautiful wife and kids in my own house, no, our own house. Not in a one-room studio apartment, but a house with a yard and everything.

"You look comfortable," I say quietly, so as to not rouse Brio or distract Gibson.

She smiles. "I'm nice and warm." She looks down at Brio. "Guess I'm their preferred nap spot."

"Where'd Kady, Ari, and Vi get off to?" I look around and see no sign of the other women.

"Ari and Vi went to the store to get something or other. And I think Kady's in the kitchen starting dinner for all of us, even me."

"Of course, even you. You're part of us. Part of our family." I lift Brio off her chest and carry him into the kitchen.

"Can I put him upstairs in his crib? He fell asleep on Mel."

"Oh, shoot. I told her to tell me if he fell asleep. I'll do it, Sammy." Kady washes her hands quickly and takes him and heads upstairs.

I sit back next to Mel and pull her free hand into my lap. "Got any room to snuggle with me?" She leans her upper body against me, and I kiss her temple. "I have to tell you, Mel, this looks good on you." I nod down, looking at Gibson who's steadily losing his battle to stay awake.

Her eyes stop on mine for a second and then move on to gaze outside. "It's nothing I ever imagined for myself." Her words are quiet and tinged with a heavy sadness that I feel in my chest.

"Because of your mom, or because of me?" I don't want to know if it was because of me, but I have to. It's important to know where her head is at here.

Her eyes move back to mine. "Because of all of it? My whole life." She sighs. "My mom wasn't the best of role models, Sampson. What if I'm like her?" She's quiet for a minute. I know with every part of my being that Mel would never hurt a child. Ever.

"My life just never works out. I mean, look at what happened. I loved being a fire paramedic and now I can't do that anymore." She glares at her legs, but I know it's not them she's mad at. She's angry with the guy, still on the loose, who's responsible for her injuries.

She takes a breath and looks up at me, pain and sadness pulling at the corners of her mouth and eyes. "And then there's you. You're the only one I'd probably even consider going there with. But I worry. That you'll..." Her voice trails off.

"Leave again." I finish her thought and she nods, her face suddenly ridden with the hard lines of solemness. I hit bingo with that. She doesn't say it, she doesn't have to. It's in her downcast eyes and slumped shoulders.

I grab her hand and pull her to me. "Mel, what I did after high school... I was barely 18, and I had Sevenya to worry about. I didn't leave you for any reason other than I didn't have a choice. As much as I wanted to, I couldn't have provided you with what you needed. As it was, we were four guys and a girl living in a two-bedroom apartment. You do the math there."

"I know." She still won't look at me. "It's not something I envisioned ever happening since I was a teenager. Because it was only something I wanted with you." She looks up at me. "But you were gone, so..." Her voice trails off as she locks eyes with me, and I can see the fear of abandonment in her eyes.

"It's definitely something I want with you, Mel." Trying not to disturb Gibson, I pull her into a hug and kiss the side of her head. "I'll do it right this time."

Before we leave that night, Gibson demands Mel read to him instead of Ari or Cal. And she does. I watch her snuggled up with him and RuffRuff, reading a story about trains and courage.

# R

AS WE WALK into her apartment, that's now become my apartment as well, we sit in the darkened room and snuggle on the couch.

"After the tour, I'm going to clean out my condo and put it on the market," I tell her, finally releasing the breath I've been holding.

"Are you sure? Sampson, if you're not—"

"I'm sure. It's time for me to let Seven rest. It doesn't make financial sense to hold on to a property that I can't spend any time in. I've talked about this with my therapist and with Kill. He promised to help me go through her stuff. It's time." I squeeze her, even though my eyes well with tears.

She squeezes my waist and tucks into my side harder. "I'll help too. However you want me to."

"Do you want to go to her grave with me next week?" I don't think she even knows where it is. "We picked the best spot we could afford for her. But I think she'd like it."

Mel nods. "I think she'd like it too. It's peaceful and shady under the tree. And she'd love her marker, Sampson. It's perfect. And yes, I'll go next week. Or any time you want me to."

Mel lays her head against my chest and rubs her hand in small circles over my snare drum tattoo.

"You know where she's buried?" How could she? We weren't together then. God, I remember wishing she were there, that I had her to hold me. By the time Sev was gone though, she and I were no longer talking. Hadn't been for years. But she was there?

She nods against me. "I was at her service," she says into my t-shirt. "I go a couple of times a year. Ironically, she's close to Dee."

"Wait." There is so much going on in that sentence that I need to unpack it because I don't comprehend most of it. "You were there?" I gasp. "Seriously?" I wrack my mind, trying to remember. There were so many people. It seemed like everyone came to talk to me. But I was completely wrecked the whole week and so drunk by the time the service rolled around that

271

Killian and Mav had to stand close enough they could prop me up graveside. Without them, I have no doubt I would have stumbled into her grave and begged them to bury me with her. By the wake, I was completely blitzed, but even in that state, I would have remembered Mel being there.

She nods again, not looking up. "I was there. I could have sworn you looked right at me. I thought you were purposely ignoring me. I admit that hurt me. At least I know now that you didn't see me. I stayed through the graveside service, paid my respects to Seven quietly, then left. I didn't come up to you or go to the wake or anything. I didn't think I'd be welcome."

"I wish I'd known you were there." My words come out as a half sob and I take a deep breath to try to hold the emotions of that day, even though Cheryl says I need to experience the emotions and stop bottling them up. "The one thing I wanted that morning, more than anything, was you. You were always my anchor, and I was so lost that day, Mel, so lost."

She squeezes me tighter. "I wish I'd have come up to you now. So you'd have known I was there for you."

"Who's Dee?"

She takes in a hitched breath. "She was my best friend after you left. I met her at the beach, actually. We went to community college together and then to the university. We were room-mates. It was awesome. Until one night, we had both been drinking. We walked back to our apartment on campus, and I went right to bed. At some point during the night," she stops and takes a few breaths. "She apparently got up and fell in the bathroom. She cracked her head on the toilet and had thrown up and, and I found her the next morning. She was already gone by the time I found her. I remember shaking her and screaming. I was so upset that the paramedics who were called ended up sedating me once they realized she was gone. That was the day I met Clance. He was the paramedic who sedated me. Then I guess he went to her funeral. I ran out. It was too much to hear her mom so devastated. I ran out and fell on the lawn of the church. He came out and sat with me. He told me I had two choices. Let her death be in vain or to find my purpose and live it for her. That's what I was trying to do."

I didn't realize she'd known Clance for so long. I squeeze her to me.

"I honestly don't know if he even remembers that. A few years later, I was assigned to his bus, uh, his ambulance, by coincidence. He never mentioned it if he remembered."

I don't know how long we sit on her sofa snuggled together. The TV's not even on. Just us in the dark. Mel grounding me like she always has and hopefully I'm some sort of peace to her too.

"I'd like you to come help if you want. To pack up the condo. It's going to be hard. Not just for me, but for Killian too." I tell her, leaving a kiss in her hair.

"I'll help. Whatever you need."

She's quiet, even though I can feel the question she wants to ask in her grip around my middle.

"Killian?" is all she says.

I nod. "I'm pretty sure they were in love. He tried just as hard as I did to save her from herself."

"I had no idea." Her hand makes small circles on my pec above my heart.

"No one does, Mel. Not even Cal. You can't say anything, not even to Killian. He has no idea I know."

"I won't say anything. Were they together long?"

"About two years, maybe a little longer. I think they thought they were hiding their relationship, especially Killian. I don't know why they didn't tell me. Kill's my best friend. I thought he was good for her and that she was good for him. I don't know why they kept it a secret." It's never made any sense to me. But I guess it did to them for whatever reason.

"He was just as devastated as I was when she overdosed. But

I almost think it was worse for him because he felt he had to grieve silently. I don't know how he did it without Cal figuring it out, the way they have that weird twin connection thing they have."

We're quiet again in a kind of comfortable silence I've only ever felt with Mel.

She breaks the silence again. "Do you think it's real? That twin connection thing?"

I nod against her. "I've seen it in action more times than you can count. They just know things that they can't have known any other way. It's like they know what each other's thinking sometimes. Not all the time, but sometimes it's like they can have a whole conversation without saying a damn word. If you come on tour with us, you're bound to see it too. It'll freak you out the first couple of times. Then you just accept that it's their deal."

She doesn't reply, and I think she's fallen asleep on me. I'm just about to try to pick her up and carry her over to the bed when she lifts her head up. Since it's dark, I can only make out the outlines of her eyes as she looks up at me.

"You want me to tour with you." It's a statement, not a question.

I nod, even though she can't really see me. "I do. Whether you do it as a medic or my girlfriend. I think it'd be good for you to get out of here for a few months, Mel. See some things you probably haven't seen before. You already hang out with us. Although, I do have to warn you, it's probably not as glamorous as you think. It can get tiring. The privacy is limited, and we get on each other's nerves sometimes. But there's also nothing like it. And I get to do it with my best friends."

# Chapter 31

## *Melody*

### Four months later, one month into tour

"Ahhh! No catchin' me," Gibson screeches as he blasts stark naked down the hall that houses the bunks towards the main living area on the bus. He's escaped the clutches of a frustrated Cal who's standing just inside the big bedroom's open door, glaring at his naked son during his freedom run. We're on a bus, so it's not like he'll get far.

"That little shit," he mumbles, then looks over at me in the doorway of the bathroom. "You didn't hear that."

I just shrug my shoulders and carry on to the bunk that's been mine for nearly a month. We've been on tour for about three weeks now, maybe almost four. Most of the time, I don't even know what city we're in, or between, like now.

"Woah, little dude." Sampson captures the naked runaway. "Why are you naked again?"

"No pants!" He giggles and clutches Sammy around the neck. "Pease. No, thank you."

"Sorry, man, we've got to wear pants to keep our private parts, well, private."

"No pie-vet parts, Shammy!"

"Yes, you've got private parts. They are the parts that go in your pants. You should really be talking to your dad about them." Sammy's brow furrows.

"Cal, man, I'm not a dad, but shouldn't you talk to him about his private parts? So he knows it's not okay for strangers to touch them and all that stuff?" Sammy hands the naked child over to Cal, who just eyes Sammy hard.

"Just a thought, man. Just a thought." Sammy puts up his hands in surrender as he retreats back to the common area of the bus.

Sammy probably didn't hear Ari's quiet voice saying, "He's probably right, Cal." Oh, to be a fly on the wall for that conversation. I can already tell by Cal's glare at Sammy that he's not looking forward to that talk. I chuckle and head back to the common area after stowing my toiletries.

I grab a yogurt and sit on the floor next to Sampson, who's up on the couch with a game controller in his hand already. The weird over-politeness that hung over the bus during the first week is long gone now. Everyone just helps themselves and is totally comfortable around each other. Sometimes too comfortable.

The Slaters have their own smaller bus, and Killian goes back and forth between our bus and the Slater's depending on his mood. I think he feels our bus is too crowded with me and Sam coupled, and Ari and Cal coupled.

Either that or he's putting the moves on the Slater's pretty blonde nanny, Elsie. Although, right before we left on tour, I thought I saw him staring at Ari's sister Vi. She's not on tour with us yet. She put in her notice from the practice she's a nurse at. She'll be joining the tour next week, where she'll be helping Ari with Gibs.

He's been an active little booger, and Ari's expecting, so I think she'll need all the help she can get. She's been nauseous and tired the whole tour so far. Cal's really trying to take the pressure off her by doing what he can, hence the reason we've seen a bus streaker in the mornings lately.

Sampson slips down onto the floor and lays his head on my shoulder, abandoning the game controller to weave his fingers with mine. He's been affectionate lately and doesn't hold back, not even in front of the other band members or if we're in public.

During the stop for the driver's break, we find a diner, and instead of sitting with our partners, we sit with the guys in one booth, and girls in the other.

Inevitably, the conversation turns to children. Mav has Brio on his lap and Cal is taking care of Gibson, who keeps turning towards our table and yelling "Hi, Mail! I gots shicken!" at me and waving his chicken strip, much to the chagrin of his father. I can't help but giggle.

"Are you thinking of having kids with Sammy?" Ari pats my arm. I look back and she and Kady are staring at me. It's hard for me to accept sometimes, but they've opened up their arms to me and incorporated me into their circle of friends. Vi too, even though she isn't here.

"It's complicated. I didn't have the best home life, and neither did Sampson. When I was dating Sampson in high school, I used to fantasize about that. Him and I bucking the odds and being these kick ass parents. But after he left, I kind of left that dream behind." I glance over at him at the adjacent table just in time to catch him staring at me. I throw him a quick wink. "Sampson wants kids. He's mentioned it a couple of times before we left. I might want one or two, but not for several years. If Sampson and I even work out." I shrug.

"Oh, you'll work out. I just know it." Kady bounces in her seat. After lunch, the guys cab up in the Slater's bus to work on music and the girls in our bus to just hang out.

Elsie comes in with Gibson and Brio after playing with

them at an indoor playground at the mall whose parking lot we're parked in. She has both Jax and Aiden in tow as well.

"Hi, Mail! Hi!" Gibson climbs into my lap.

"Hey, buddy, did you have fun with Elsie and Brio?" He nods and launches into a list of things he did at the play area.

When it's finally time to get going, Ari takes Gibson to the big bedroom with Cal for some family time.

Sammy turns on a movie, and I pop some popcorn. I settle in between his legs on the couch, and we watch the movie. But I keep thinking about my discussion with Kady and Ari. I'm a few days late. I'm on the pill, but my breasts have been tender, to the point of pain, which isn't normal for me.

I casually slip out my phone and launch the app I use to track my period. I'm later than I thought. Fifteen days late. I'm almost never more than a day or so late. I haven't been nauseated or exhausted like poor Ari's been since the beginning of her pregnancy.

"You okay?" Sampson squeezes me to him. "You tensed up all of the sudden."

"I'm good." I try to keep my voice level when I am freaking out on the inside. He's been using a condom. This can't be happening.

Sampson's hands start kneading my shoulders. "Jeez, Mel, your muscles are super tight." He digs his thumbs into my shoulders and works them with just the right amount of pressure. He's so good at this. The tightness relaxes in my shoulders as he works his magic, and the next thing I know, he's rousing me.

"Hey, Mel, we're at the venue." He leans in and kisses me. "Good nap?"

I nod and get up and grab my medic bag to head into the venue with the guys. After ditching my supply bag, I station myself on an empty road case to keep an eye on everything.

Jeff, their road manager, stops when he sees me. "Did Domino come see you?"

I shake my head. "I just got here."

"He's cut open his hand during set-up. Can you take a look?"

"Of course. Green room would probably be best because the lighting back here is terrible."

"I'll send him your way as soon as I see him."

I'm only in the green room long enough to get my bag open and a few things set out when the lanky roadie comes in. "You're with Sam, right?"

"I'm his girlfriend, but I'm also the tour medic. How'd you hurt your hand?"

He rolls his eyes at me. "Stripping a wire with a pocketknife instead of wire strippers. I know, bonehead mistake." He sighs at himself.

"We all do things like that." I unwrap his hand. "How long ago did you do it?"

"Maybe an hour, if that." He shrugs.

"Let's wash it with this antiseptic in the sink and then I'll put some antibacterial ointment and a sterile dressing on it. Try not to get it wet. I'll want to check it tomorrow."

I get him doctored up. It's not really that bad, and he did cover it over right away. He should be fine, but I make a note to check his wound tomorrow. We'll be here for a second show. He leaves and heads back out to do his job. I pack the stuff back in my medical kit and see the pregnancy test at the bottom of my bag. I know that Sampson is doing soundcheck, because I can hear The Rebels setlist even way back here in the green room.

After peeing on the stick, I set it on the counter and go get another bottle of water from the cooler between the hospitality tables. Then I hear Gibson sobbing and head towards the door where Kady and Aiden meet me. "He scraped his knee again. I think he's fine, but he wanted to see you."

Gibson's had a few scrapes and bumps on the tour, and he knows that if he comes to see me, I'll give him extra love and a cartoon bandage whether or not he needs one. And he always gets a sticker which seems to make everything better for him.

"Let's see, buddy." He sits on the arm of the couch so I can see his scraped knee. "Let me guess. You and Aiden were racing to the door across the parking lot again?" He nods and sniffles.

"Well, this doesn't look bad at all. It's just a little, teeny tiny scratch. But let's get it cleaned up. Remember, this is the part that doesn't feel too good. But I'll let you pick your bandage and sticker after, okay?" He nods again, trying to look into my bag. I get an antiseptic wipe and rip it open and gently clean his scrape. It's a small surface scrape, not deep at all. He whimpers a little at the burn and I blow on it slightly.

"So, for bandages I have a car, a dinosaur, and a guitar. What would you like?"

He thinks for a few minutes, and I show him his options. He points at the guitar. "Gee-tar, like daddy."

"You got it, buddy." I carefully bandage his scraped knee, then pull out my sticker sheet. Again, he carefully peruses his choices, picking a dog with a tennis ball. "Do you want it on your shirt?"

He nods, and I put it on his shirt. He points at it. "Brave."

"Yes, you were very brave." I give him a hug.

Ari comes out of the bathroom, her mouth open. It takes me a second to notice that she has my test in her hand. "Uh, Mel. Did you take a test? Or is this Kady's?"

"It's mine. What's it say?"

"You're pregnant."

"I am?" My voice sounds small, and Ari nods. I snap the test out of her hands and look at it. Shit. There's not even a question; it's positive alright. There's a commotion at the door and I realize that the band's done with soundcheck. I shove the test in my bag and move it under the table.

The band files in with Jax stationing himself outside the door.

"What did you do to your leg, Gibs?" Cal drops down and examines his guitar bandage.

"I falled. It's a gee-tar. Like you." He holds his knee out so Cal can see it. "I okay."

"Looks like Mel fixed you up good." Cal leans in and kisses his knee near his scrape.

He agrees. "Fixed good."

Sampson gives me a hug before heading for the drinks.

"Mail pegnet." His words are unmistakable and very casual, like he was talking about his cars or that stuffed dog he loves.

Sampson spews out orange sports drink all over Killian. The blood drains from my face. I can't believe Gibson just outed me in front of the entire band. My stomach tenses and I can't tell if I'm nauseated because of the pregnancy or because everyone now knows thanks to an almost four-year-old who can't keep his trap shut.

"I'm pregnant. Remember?" Ari says, trying to cover for me. She rubs her tummy. "Brother or sister's in here."

"No. Mail pegnent." He's adamant. And Sampson starts choking again, orange sports drink flying out of his mouth again. Killian ducks and grabs a towel to wipe down with.

"Dammit, Sammy. Now I've got to change." Killian stalks out of the green room, back to his dressing room down the hall.

"I asked her if she wanted to have a baby. He must be confused." Ari glances at me and grabs Gibs's hand.

This seems to settle the debate.

By the time the guys go onstage, I feel bad for not telling Sammy that Gibson was telling the truth. I'm not ready for that discussion. Maybe when we hit Fort Lauderdale, we'll have some alone time. I know he'd make a great father. I see him with Gibson and Brio, and he loves them. But being the fun uncle figure is a lot different than being a father. We've been doing so well together. Sampson was talking about looking for a bigger place together and kids someday. But this is now, not someday. This is real. This is now. I thought maybe we'd start slower, like with a dog or something.

"Are you going to tell Sampson?" Kady asks as we wait in the green room. Ari must have spilled my beans.

"Sheesh, did Ari tell everyone? I thought I'd wait until Fort Lauderdale. This wasn't planned. Sam's mentioned kids but, like, in the faraway future. We were talking about maybe getting a bigger place. I thought we'd start with a freaking puppy or something, not a kid." The reality that I am carrying a child is becoming more real the longer I think about it. Even back in high school when I dreamed of Sampson and I together, we were married before we started with kids.

As we sit backstage waiting, I suddenly stiffen. I swear I smell *him*. I look around us. We are surrounded by roadies and security. Everyone here has a backstage pass and has been vetted by someone. How could he get back here? My stomach clenches and I look around anyway. I don't see anyone out of place.

"Are you okay, Mel?" Ari asks. I nod.

"We were careful. I never miss my pill. Sammy always wears a condom. I'm not sure how this even happened." I gasp.

"I think you know how babies are made, Mel," Ari jokes.

A strangled gasp escapes my lips, and my eyes fill with tears. Sampson and I made a baby, while actively trying not to. What if he leaves me? I can't raise a baby alone. And then I smell that acrid body odor/piss combination that reminds me of *him*, and I can't hold it in any longer. I bolt to the bathroom and throw up. I don't want the girls to think I'm crazy. But he's here. I feel him watching me.

"Woah, Mel, breathe. You'll be okay. And I know Sampson. He'll be a great dad. I've always thought so." Kady rubs my back. "It'll all work out. You'll see."

# Chapter 32

## *Sammy*

Something's up with Mel. She's super distracted lately. Clingy when we're backstage. I don't think anyone's been harassing her. Luke has been watching her when we aren't together, and he hasn't mentioned anything. We've just gotten to Fort Lauderdale.

After tonight's show, we're all breaking off to do our own things for a couple of days here in Florida. I have a side trip to Key West with Mel all planned out. Early tomorrow morning, we'll take a chartered helicopter to the island. We'll be there all day and most of the next day. She's been dropping hints all tour that she wants to visit the Hemingway House, so I have a private tour booked, along with an ocean view bungalow at the Southernmost House. She has no idea though, that the biggest surprise of our little trip will be the sunrise walk we'll be taking on the beach.

After I finish packing Mel a bag, I get to packing an overnight bag for myself for our little getaway. Killian comes breezing in through the big bus, throwing his duffle onto a bunk.

"You all set?" He pats my back as I stash our getaway bags

into the big bedroom of the bus. "Make sure you have *everything*."

"Yep. I've got it. It's in the inside pocket." I nod to the duffle before straightening. "I'm kind of nervous, though."

His lips turn up. "Don't be nervous. You got this. It'll all work out exactly how it's supposed to." He claps me on the back.

The bus door flies open with a bang, causing Killian and I to jump. Jeff appears at the top of the stairs. "Mel?!" His eyes are wide, and he's panting like he's been running.

"Other bus, with the girls. What's going on?" He doesn't answer, instead he turns on his heels and takes off running for the smaller bus. Kill and I follow, but by the time we get to their bus, Mel and Jeff are both running towards the venue, Mel with her medical bag. Her slight limp becomes more pronounced the harder she runs.

"Shit, that can't be good." Kill looks at me right before we give chase. We fly into the back door and follow them down the corridor and into a storage room, where Killian's bass tech Giz is out cold on the floor, turning bluer by the second.

Mel drops to her knees and puts her ear to his mouth. Locking eyes with Jeff, she says, "Call 911." He nods with his phone already to his ear.

Mel starts assessing him. "What did he take?" She fists a hand and rubs her knuckles firmly over the center of his chest. "Giz? Wake up, Giz."

She glances up from her assessment at the small group of roadies gathered around, then leans in and gives him two rescue breaths like we learned about in class. "I need to know what the fuck he took." She leans in and gives him two more breaths.

One of the roadies coughs out, "I think it's probably heroin."

"What the fuck? Since when is Giz taking heroin?" Killian grabs the guy.

"I don't know. He's been doing it all tour." He shrugs. "I'm clean. Piss test me if you don't believe me."

"Why didn't someone say something?" Kill seethes and the guy just shrugs.

Using scissors from her bag, Mel cuts from his pocket down to his knee and then tears his fucking pant leg wide open with her bare hands, exposing his thigh. She grabs a cartridge from her bag and tears open the packaging. She pulls some tab thing off the end and presses the whole cartridge into the side of his thigh. It clicks and starts counting down and then beeps and says the injection is complete. She starts back with the rescue breathing, stops and rubs her knuckles down the center of his chest again.

His eyelids start to flutter.

"Giz? Wake up. Come on, Giz!" She leans over him, looking into his eyes.

He takes a deep breath and then sits up suddenly and pushes Mel hard in the center of her chest, moving her a good three feet back.

"Leave me the fuck alone, bitch." His words are slurred like he's drunk, and he kicks at her, connecting with her shin on the leg with the nerve damage. Mel grimaces and reaches down to rub the spot. I grab him by the shoulders, hard. Giz struggles against my hold.

"You just overdosed. I gave you Narcan." Her voice is calm and level as she holds up the used cartridge. She moves her hands between them. "I'm just here to help. You weren't breathing. Narcan brought you out of it, but you'll need to be monitored at a hospital. If that heroin was laced with Fentanyl, there's a good chance you'll lapse back into the OD in an hour or two."

"Fuck that, I ain't going anywhere." He tries to stand, but

I'm still pushing down on his shoulders. He twists, trying to get me to release him.

"If Mel says you have to go to the hospital, you're going to the hospital, Giz," Jeff states. "End of story." He glares at the roadie. "Speak of the devil."

Jeff steps aside as paramedics hauling a gurney come into the room behind him.

Mel takes charge, standing. "Probably a heroin overdose. I administered a Narcan auto-injector about ten minutes ago. He came out of it agitated like they do." She shows the paramedic her cartridge and they take it from her.

The paramedics talk Giz onto the gurney, and as they buckle him in, he notices the rip in his pant leg. "Bitch, you cut my favorite jeans."

"That rip in your pants allowed her to administer the Narcan that probably saved your damn life." Jeff slaps the side of his head. "Don't be disrespectful to the person who saved your fucking life. Moron."

One of the paramedics tells Jeff to move so he can get the gurney into the hall.

"Are you okay? Did he hurt you?" I hug her to me.

"I'm okay." She relaxes against me, but I can feel her heart pounding through her shirt and into my side. I wonder if she'd get this way when she worked at the firehouse.

"Let's go chill in my dressing room." I grab her bag and escort her to my dressing room, where she drops onto the small loveseat that sits against one of the walls.

I pack some ice from the cooler under the snack table, wrap it in a towel, and roll up her pant leg. A darkened outline of Giz's boot is already starting to appear. My jaw clenches as I lightly press the ice to it, knowing that's the leg with the nerve damage. "That had to hurt."

She nods and lays her head back, looking at the ceiling. I swear I see tears in her eyes. "It's a weird tingling pain."

The door to my dressing room swings open, hitting the wall with a thud. Mav steps through, followed by Cal and Kill. The three take me in, kneeling in front of Mel with the ice pack.

"Shit, is she okay? Her leg?" Mav steps closer and I pull the ice pack away so he can see the bruise that's already darker than when I placed the ice on it.

He looks to Mel. "Do you need to get that x-rayed or anything?"

She shakes her head. "It's okay. I'm fine. Really." She pulls her leg away from me and rolls her pant leg back down.

"Jeff is raving about how you saved Giz's life, and Killian agrees. Good job. But are you sure you're okay? Kill said you got shoved around a bit."

"I'm fine. It's part of the job." She sits up and Killian hands her a bottle of water that she sips out of. "I might suggest some random drug testing of the crew to your management team. Heroin's no joke."

"Jeff's already on it." Mav nods towards the door. "I didn't think our guys were into anything hard like that. I hate to mess with the relationship we have with them. Most have been with us forever. But like you said, heroin's nothing to mess around with. All we need is for Gibson or Brio to accidentally get into someone's stash."

"That's the second time I've seen you save someone's life, Mel," Killian says as he sits gently next to her, shaking his head. He picks up her hand and pats it between his. "It's fucking intense."

She nods. "It is for me too. Look." She removes her hand from his and holds it out in front of her. It shakes. "It's the adrenaline."

Jeff pops his head in. "On in 15, guys. Kill, we've moved Domino over to tech for you tonight." He nods and leaves with Jeff, likely to talk to Dom about his basses. He's very particular about which one he uses when. Cal and Mav follow a few minutes later to give us a minute before we hit the stage.

Mel bolts for the bathroom in my dressing room and I swear it sounds like she's vomiting. "Mel? You okay?"

I push the door open, and she's hunched over the toilet on her knees.

"Shit." I hold her hair as she heaves again. "Maybe you should go to the hospital and have your leg x-rayed after all."

She shakes her head. When she's stopped, she sits back on her heels and looks up at me. "I'm okay. It's the adrenaline dump. It happens to me sometimes after calls. I get nervous but after instead of before. I've always been this way. Ask Clance. He'd laugh and say he'd never seen someone get nervous after a call, when it was already done with."

I hand her the water bottle and help her up. She swishes and spits in the sink. "I'm okay Sampson, really. I promise. I'm looking forward to our mystery trip tomorrow."

Jeff pops his head in. "Let's go, Sam, you're up."

I take Mel's hand. "Watch tonight?"

She grins and nods. "I'd love to." She lets me drag her to the side of the stage and watches as we go through our pre-show rituals.

Throughout the show, Mel never leaves the side of the stage. I shoot her a couple of winks and smiles when I can, and each time her grin grows toothy. It's somewhere during the chorus of "Burn It Down" that I settle into the realization that Mel just calms me. Like no one has ever done in my life. I hope that I'm that person for her. Because it's a good place to be. No, it's the only place to be.

After a sweaty kiss with Mel and a few hours of signing autographs for fans, I'm still on a high from being onstage and from knowing what's coming tomorrow and the next morning. As the last few fans straggle through from band member to band member, I look around for Mel and notice she's nowhere in sight. My chest tightens with worry. I catch Jeff's attention.

"Where's Mel?"

"The green room. I just got back from making sure everything was set up for you guys, and she's sound asleep. She never even moved a muscle." Jeff stops over at my table. "I got this if you want to cut out before everyone gets done and ends up waking her up."

"Good idea." I cap my sharpie and toss it back on the table. I'm pretty much done here anyway.

Mel's sprawled on the couch on her back, head facing the back of the couch. Her gorgeous lips gape slightly. I slip an arm under her neck and another under her knees and roll her into me, so I can carry her back to the bus. She snuggles into my shoulder, not fully waking until the cold hits us when I step outside with Jax and Aiden flanking us for the short walk to the bus.

"Sampson?" Her voice is heavy with sleep. "What are you doing? I can walk." Despite her claim, she snuggles into me harder.

"Putting you to bed. We have an early morning, beautiful."

"Okay," she mutters, softly nuzzling into my shoulder and smacks her lips.

Jax opens the door of the bus, and I wait for Aiden to sweep it quickly before carrying her in. He's pulled her bunk curtain open for me and I gently roll her in. I slip her shoes off and unbutton her pants, but there's no way I can wiggle her out of them while she's in the bunk. Instead, I reach up her shirt and unbuckle her bra and carefully shimmy it off her arms before returning her arms through their respective arm holes.

Pulling her blanket over her, I lean in. "Night, beautiful. See you in the morning."

"See ya in the mornin', Sampson." She doesn't even open her eyes back up, just rolls up onto her side, her back to the bunk opening. I slide her privacy curtain shut and go take a quick shower in the small bus bathroom before crawling into my bunk, wishing there was room to spoon her in one of these bunks. She doesn't sleep well in the bunks alone. The small area bothers her and it's not uncommon for me to find her out on the couch in the middle of the night on long hauls across the country.

The alarm on my phone wakes me, and I can hear both Mel and Killian moan in protest. I shut it off and slip out of my bunk. Pulling back the privacy curtain just enough, I peek in at Mel. She's rolled onto her back, her arm slung over her eyes.

"Mel, time to get up. We have to be somewhere in an hour." I kiss her elbow since I can't get to her face.

"Since when do you get up at the crack of dawn, Sampson? Stop it. That feels weird." She slaps a hand towards me.

"Since we're in Lauderdale and have plans. Come on. Get up, take a shower. I'll set your clothes out for you. Unless you want me to shower and use all the hot water first."

"No!" Her squeak makes me chuckle. She feels her waistband. "I'm moving. Why am I sleeping with my pants on?" She looks over at me and blinks the sleep from her eyes.

"I couldn't shimmy them off you after I put you in the bunk last night. You were *out* last night in the green room." I lean in and kiss her, really kiss her. She licks her lips when I pull back, a small smile pulling up the corner of her lips.

"Come on. We have to be somewhere in an hour. We don't have much time."

She slips out and heads into the bathroom. I grab the sundress that I bought her and hang it on the back of the door and leave her unmentionables I picked out on the counter. She peeks out of the small shower stall.

"So you're dressing me again, Sampson?" Her eyes squint shut.

"Humor me. And hurry up. I need to get ready too."

She pulls the door to the shower stall open a little wider so I can see her breasts, and the small bruise on her shoulder. Fuckin' Giz. That makes my blood hot. "You could always join me." Oh, she doesn't play fair.

She notices me zero in on her shoulder and looks over at it, then rolls her eyes. "Sampson, it doesn't even hurt. Join me." She wiggles her shoulders so her breasts jiggle. God, she's torturing me.

But I didn't even notice he hit her there. Fuckin' Giz.

"I can't. We're in a hurry and if I join you, we'll definitely be late." As much as I don't want to, I back out of the bathroom, shutting the door behind me.

A shirtless Killian pulls his curtain back and leans out of his bunk, just enough. "Hey, man. Have a good time. See ya in a few days. Be quiet until you leave, though. I'm trying to sleep." He smiles and then returns to his bunk, pulling his curtain with him.

By the time I'm done with my turn in the bathroom, Killian and Mel are sitting in the living room area. Mel's pulling on sandals and Killian's sipping coffee.

"I thought you were sleeping in." I lift my chin at Killian, who returns the gesture with a spark in his eye that has me wondering if he spilled my secret to her.

"Between the talking and the hair dryer, I gave up." He smiles at me over his steaming cup of coffee, but Mel's nose crinkles.

"Ugh, just the smell of that stuff is making me nauseous, Kill." She steps a few steps away. I pull her to me.

"You want to grab a muffin or something? We have enough time." I triple check the time. We do. Just enough.

Mel shakes her head. "I'm good with just my water. She holds up a brand-new water bottle.

"Okay, then. See ya in few days, man." I nod to Killian as I escort her to the car Aiden has waiting for us.

I grab Mel's free hand and pull it to my lap. Her eyes narrow on me. "Why do you seem nervous?"

I shrug. "I'm not. Just excited. I've been planning this for a while, and I hope you like it. I'm not used to doing this kind of planning and stuff." I shrug and give her the eyes that I know she loves.

We pull up into the small airport near the waiting helicopter. Mel yanks her hand from mine.

"Oh, hell no, Sampson. I'm not getting into that thing." Her eyes grow big, and she pushes herself into the seat of the car with her feet as if to brace herself. I don't think I've ever seen Mel scared like this. It almost makes me chuckle because she's usually so brave, but it also has my heart beating faster. What if she seriously won't get on the helicopter? It's too long of a trip to drive down to Key West from here; it'd waste most of the day and we have things to do.

"It's just a helicopter. It's a short flight, I promise. I've been on them plenty of times. It's not a big deal, Mel." I rub her arm, trying to calm her.

"I don't care. I'm *not* getting in. What if the top part flies off and we plunge to our death into the ocean?" She's thinking that using the ocean to appeal to my anxiety about the water will get her out of this, but she's so wrong.

"Then at least I'll die with the woman I love. Seriously, Mel. It's safe. I'd never purposely put you in danger. You know that. This is the same company that the label uses. They have a spotless safety record." Her head is still swinging side to side in her denial, but I grab it and pull her to me for a kiss. I just keep kissing until she relaxes into it. "I love you, Mel. We'll be fine. I'll hold your hand the whole time."

Aiden gets out and grabs the bags I packed up to the helicopter, then comes back and opens our door.

"Please don't make me get in," she says softly, and I stop. Well, this is fucked.

I sigh. "If you seriously won't do it, then we'll go back to the bus. I won't force you, Mel. You know better than that." I've planned this getaway for weeks. Paid for everything, everybody in advance.

The breath I didn't know I was holding releases when she finally steps out of the car. I take her hand and lead her to the helicopter. We get in the back while Aiden sits in the front with the pilot. I lean over and slip her headphones on, and she looks over at me. She is truly frightened. I take her hand and pull it up to my face.

"We'll be fine. It's an adventure." She nods and turns her head from me, looking out the window. The pilot tells us we'll be taking off shortly and I swear I see her swipe at her face. Shit. She's crying. The first week we were on the bus she had trouble moving around freely, especially when we were underway. She didn't like not feeling in control. I know it had everything to do with being carjacked, about being stuck in a small space with someone else in control of the drive. Maybe this is part of that too.

I kiss her hand, trying to get her attention. She finally looks back at me, her face plastered with a huge fake smile. This is not an okay Mel. This is the 'I'm minutes away from freaking out' Mel.

"Aiden's here with us. Everything will be okay," I reiterate. She nods a slow nod, like she's trying to accept it but is having a hard time. The pilot starts the rotors, and she looks up at me, startled by the noise. I point up to let her know it's the blades. Her fingers tighten around mine and she squeezes her eyes shut. Soon we are gently lifting off the tarmac, and Mel's missing it because her eyes are still screwed shut.

I run my hand along her jaw. "Look out the window, babe. You're missing it." When she slowly opens her eyes, Mel startles, noticing that we've left the ground already.

Over our headsets, the pilot tells us the weather is clear and mild. He emphasizes that it's the perfect day for an island hop. About five minutes into the flight, Mel's fingers finally start to loosen from the clenched death grip since before we took off.

"Look, there's a pod of dolphins swimming." The pilot points them out and Mel actually leans away from me and towards the window so she can see them. Eventually, she even lets my hand go so she can try to take a picture of them with her cell phone.

In no time, we are setting down on Key West. Aiden takes over driving the waiting town car and pilots us towards Southernmost House as if he's lived in Key West all his life.

"Are we really in Key West?" Mel looks up at me from where she's snuggled into my side in the back of the car.

"We really are. It was worth the helicopter, right?" She nods into my side, her hand curled into mine.

Aiden pulls us right into the Southernmost House and we check into our ocean view bungalow room. Aiden's room is directly next door.

Aiden puts our bags in the closet while Mel heads right to the view. "Sampson, come look at this. It's amazing." She steps out onto our balcony and enjoys the fresh air. "It's stunning, Sampson." She looks up at me, her eyes spark, and this time not with fear, but instead with warmth. I pull her to me and wrap my arms around her, kissing the side of her head.

"We have a private tour of the Hemingway House in an hour. We can walk there from here if you'd like. It's only about 10 minutes or so away."

"Did you bring my chucks?" She looks down at her sandaled feet.

"I brought your white ones and your black ones." I nod at her bag. "And a couple of changes of clothes, just in case."

She lifts up on her toes and kisses me. "Thank you."

"For remembering to bring you clothes?" I kiss the end of her nose.

"No. For listening and bringing me here. I seriously thought you were going to take me to Disney World. Killian had me all but convinced." She rests her head on my chest. "This is going to be way better than Disney World."

"Way better." I agree. Although we will be going to Disney World too. We have a show in a couple of days, minutes from there. We'll be having some Disney fun together, the whole group of us.

We walk to the Hemingway House hand-in-hand, Aiden following behind us. I know Hemingway is a writer, but I can't say I've ever read anything by him. Cal probably has. He's the reader of the group. But if going here makes my Mel happy, then we are going. Because that's what makes me happy now, making her happy and making her smile like she did when we were kids. Maybe, someday, we'll even surf together again. I'm not quite there yet. But maybe. Someday.

All I think about is her as she oohs and ahhs through our private tour, which also includes time for Mel and me to sit on the floor and play with some of the freaky-toed cats on the premises. And let me tell you, there are a ton of cats here. And I haven't seen Mel smile the way she has been smiling since we got to Key West since I was a teenager. It's as if she's lighting the world with that smile. And she is. She's lighting my world.

When we're done, we wander around until we find a restaurant for a quick lunch. And then we wander Key West, stopping at a Shipwreck Museum, an aquarium, and every kitschy store in between. Always hand-in-hand, until we have too many bags and have to hold them instead. And when we run out of hands to carry the bags from the souvenirs Mel has bought, we end up piling some on poor Aiden too.

By late afternoon, I direct us back towards the Inn. Mel's limp is growing more pronounced the more we walk. She'd never say anything because she's having fun, but she's obviously hurting. And I need her to be able to walk with me on the beach tomorrow morning. Yesterday's episode with Giz probably didn't help matters, as glimpses of the purplish-blue bruise he left her with have been peeking out from the end of her sundress all day and they make me mad every time I catch sight of them.

When Aiden takes his leave from us, Mel shucks off her shoes and sits on the small couch in our bungalow, tucking her legs underneath her.

"Dinner should be here in about an hour. I thought we'd just relax until then." I join her. "We can eat on the balcony if you'd like?"

She shifts so she's lying on the couch with her head in my lap. "That sounds perfect." She smiles and lets out a contented sigh. Brushing the hair from her face with my hand, she captures it and kisses it. "Thank you for today. It was even more perfect than I thought. And so much fun. I still can't believe no one recognized you."

"They weren't expecting me to be here, so they weren't looking for me. It's all about the vibe. If I project a laid back, touristy vibe, people are less likely to look than if I'm all Sammy-the-drumming-machine-rock-star vibe, which is completely different."

She giggles at my explanation. "What about Sampson, the awesome kisser, smoldering lover persona? I'd like to see him right about now." She runs her hand along my face.

"Oh, is that so?" She smiles up at me as I lean down to try to kiss her, but from this angle it's almost impossible to meet her lips, so she giggles and sits up. When she swings her legs back to the ground, her dress catches, and I catch sight of the bruise that's been taunting me all day. I pull her feet into my lap and carefully pull her dress back to examine it. It's dark and has the definite shape of a boot toe.

"It's not that bad." She reaches to pull her dress back down, but I push her hand away. "Sampson, it's okay. I'm okay." I caress her leg above it, while I drop to my knees so I can kiss her leg. I'm careful to steer clear of the bruise itself, and to not press too firmly on her leg. I work up to her knee and pull her dress up further, trailing more light kisses up her smooth thighs.

"Sit up for a sec." She does and I work the dress over her head and toss it behind me, moving up to sit on the edge of the couch, then lean in to kiss her. She fists the hair at the nape of my neck and pulls me down with her onto the couch.

I kiss my way over to her ear and then down her neck and silky-smooth shoulder, slipping her bra strap off as I go. Reaching behind her, I unclasp her bra and bring it down her arms and toss it by the dress.

There's a three and a half inch, deep pink scar between her breasts. The new skin is shiny and smooth. I know she's self-conscious, and it brings up memories she doesn't like to talk about. But I lay a soft kiss at the top of it anyway, feeling her chest expand with the breath she sucks in and holds as I work my way down it, leaving a trail of soft kisses over it as she keeps a steady pressure on my arms, nails digging in slightly, not exhaling until I move over to her breast.

She sighs my name as I release one breast, only to shower the other with my affection. Her arms move to my back as she pulls me to her, trying to get as much skin-to-skin contact as she can. Mel loves, no needs, to feel I'm totally with her. I'll happily give her what she wants. I pull back to pull my shirt up and over my head. As soon as it clears my head, her hands are at my fly, her trembling fingers working quickly. I stand up and push them down.

"Those too." She nods at my boxer briefs as she lifts her hips from the couch to pull her underwear down her legs and then kicks them off.

"Sampson." She reaches to pull me down to her.

"What's the hurry?" I take a step back. I don't want this to be all wham, bam, thank you, ma'am. I want to enjoy Melody, all of her.

"Sampson." She almost whines my name, drawing it out like I'm drawing out her frustration. "Before dinner gets here. Please."

She sits down on the couch and pulls me to her, kissing my abdomen. And when she grabs the base of my shaft firmly, I can't help the moan as my hips tip upward, begging for more.

"Melody," I growl, a warning, as she leans down and gives him a soft kiss before she takes my head in her mouth, swirling her tongue around it. My hips jerk uncontrollably as she increases the suction and depth. My eyes roll back as I fight to keep from grabbing her and just letting loose.

"Mel!" I pull up on her shoulders, but she resists, sucking me into her mouth again. I yank up on her shoulders just a little more firmly and she finally releases me with a pop, her dilated eyes clouding over.

"Hey, I was enjoying that." Her lips curl lasciviously at the ends.

"So was I, too much."

She lies back, and I position myself between her legs. She throws her legs over my hips and tightens them around my waist. I hold myself off her with my forearms. I don't want to crush her. I'd much rather continue teasing her opening until she lifts her hips in an attempt to complete our connection.

"Dammit. Sampson." The last part of my name leaves her lips on a moan as I finally enter her, fully intending to just give her a little, but she pulls me deeper, squeezing her heels against my ass.

"Yesss," she hisses, her hands roaming my back as I pull back, only to re-enter her over and over.

There's nothing but her, Mel. Her soft sighs when I press into her, the desperate scratches of her nails as I slide back out.

I press my chin into her shoulder as the familiar pressure builds between us.

Gripping her hips, I pull her up just a little, and she tightens around me unexpectedly as she gasps.

"Damn, Mel," I groan as everything tightens until I burst inside her, joining her in our mutual release. I drop down onto her, spent, resting my head on her soft shoulder as we heave in unison.

# Chapter 33

## *Melody*

"Shit," Sampson pants in my ear, pausing for a moment to catch his breath. But then he sits up on his knees. "Shit, shit, shit. We didn't use a condom. I'm sorry. I wasn't thinking."

"It's okay." I pull him back down on me. Now would be the perfect time to tell him about the baby, but my tongue is tied. I just need to feel him against me. For him to pull me into him and hold me. Just for a few minutes. "We'll be okay."

He nods against me as he settles back in and holds me. "Okay."

Still, my words fail me. Because I'm a coward. I don't want to lose this, what we have. Today was such a perfect day. If he were to walk away from me now, it would break me. And there's always the chance that he will.

Sampson shifts so he's not crushing me, but still holds me tight to him.

"Mel, I love you. I—"

There's a knock. Room service. He stands and pulls me up to him, depositing me in the bedroom where he throws on some sweatpants, stopping to give me the smile he always gave me back when we were kids, before he closes the door to the bedroom to afford me some privacy.

Going through the bag Sampson packed for me, I pull out a pair of pajamas. They don't match. He's packed my bacon pants with my unicorn cami. I shake my head. I slip on the dark blue PJ pants with the slices of bacon on them. I usually only wear them on the bus, because even though I'm completely comfortable with Cal, Ari, and Killian, I don't like parading around them in my short sleep shorts. I can't believe he grabbed my pastel cami with a unicorn in the middle when I have a bacon one that matches the pants.

"Come on, Mel, dinner's here," he calls through the door. "It's all clear."

I open the door and he's standing by the slider to our private ocean view balcony. His chest is still bare, and his sweats are low slung on his waist. His curly hair is messy, but it looks good on Sampson. I haven't seen him this relaxed in a long time.

We eat as the sun disappears, talking about everything, and anything, and still, I don't bring up the baby. There's been every opportunity to. But I cannot bring myself to break this calm, relaxed happiness. Something I previously only felt in our spot on the California coast.

We fall asleep wrapped in each other, listening to sounds of the ocean.

"Mel," Sampson whispers in my ear. "Mel, it's time to get up." He kisses my neck, working his way up to the ticklish spot behind my ear. I open my eyes and it's still dark outside.

"Sampson, it's still nighttime. Why are you always trying to wake me at ungodly hours?" I try to roll away, but Sampson wraps his arms around me and pulls me to him.

"Mel," he mumbles into my neck. "I need to show you something. Come on." He gets up and gently tugs the blankets from around me, then helps me up. He rushes me through showering together, too harried for the fun stuff showering together usually entails. We dress quickly and then Sampson slides our cardkey in his pocket as we hurry down to the car, Aiden dressed and waiting behind the wheel.

"Are we leaving already?" I try to stifle my yawn. I knew it was a short trip, but I didn't think we'd meet up with the others until late tonight, when we joined them back up the coast to wherever they are playing for the next two days.

"No." He pulls me to him. "We aren't leaving yet. I want to walk on the beach. Will you hold my hand and walk with me?" He drops his head to my shoulder and leaves a soft kiss.

"Of course. But why so early?" He rubs his scruff on my neck.

"Less people to see me if I freak out." His words are soft as Aiden pulls through a gate to a parking area. He was doing better before the tour, but still couldn't make it all the way to the water. He'll get there, I know he will. The ocean is too big of a part of Sampson's soul not to know he'll get back to it one day. And I'll hold his hand the whole way.

Our car is the only one here as Aiden parks it. Sampson and I walk down a path to the beach. It's still pretty darn dark out. We kick off our shoes once we hit the soft, silty sand and leave them by the walkway.

Hand-in-hand, we walk, the sound of the surf gently lapping at the sand the only sound. He says nothing but squeezes my fingers occasionally. I can't tell if he's reassuring himself or me that he's okay.

We stop, and he turns towards the surf. It's starting to get light; the impending sunrise should be happening any minute. I scan Sampson for early signs of a panic attack, but there's nothing. While he seems a little off, his breathing isn't erratic. There is no constant scanning, looking for the quickest way back to the car.

He pulls me to him and holds me in front of him with his

arms wrapped around me. "Any minute now," he whispers. I look up and he nods to the sea. "The sunrise. I want to watch it with you. I hear they are spectacular here."

We stand, his arms firmly wrapped around me as day breaks in Key West. He was right. It's breathtaking as the colors move from dark purple to pink and orange as the sun finally peeks over the horizon, bathing everything in its white-yellow warmth.

"Wow, that was beautiful, Sampson," I whisper, not wanting to break the serenity and beauty around us.

Sampson spins me so I'm facing him and slowly kisses me. He smiles and looks at me. "Not as beautiful as you." He touches his forehead to mine and kisses the tip of my nose, whispering, "I love you so much, Mel. So fucking much."

His knee suddenly buckles, and he's on one knee in front of me in the sand.

"Oh my God, Sampson, are you okay?" I look him over. He doesn't appear to be in pain.

He looks back up at me and smiles. "I will be in a few minutes."

"Do you need help with deep breathing?" He doesn't look like he's having a panic attack, though. He fumbles with something and then looks back up at me. His eyes are shiny and it's then that I see a small box in his hand.

"Mel." His voice breaks, and he clears it. "Melody." He takes my hand with his free one. "I've known you since we were kids. You saved me and Sevenya then. More than you could ever realize. Little did I know that you would save me again, quite literally, when our paths crossed on the beach that day in Venice. I like to think that Sev brought us back together because she knew I needed you. And I do. Not just because you saved my life that day, but because you are by far the best thing, my light in the world, and I will not lose you again. Please, Melody, keep lighting my life and be my wife. Will you marry me, Mel?" He looks up at me, his face a mixture of adoration and honest to goodness fear. Does he really think I'd say no to him? He's offering me all of him. Forever.

"For reals?" I drop down on my knees in front of Sampson so I can look him in the eyes.

"For reals, Mel. So much for reals." His face is tight with anticipation, his eyes the same color as the ocean beside us.

"Then yes, Sampson Denton. I will marry you. For reals." His face relaxes and he smiles.

He slips the ring on my finger with a slight tremor in his hands. Then he pulls me to him and kisses me. It starts off sweet but gets increasingly urgent. He finally pulls back and touches our foreheads together. "I love you so much, Mel. So much. It's always been you for me."

I look at the ring he slipped on my finger. I've never seen a ring like this one. The band is silver with swirly ridges and the stone isn't a diamond, but a beautiful milky blue, almost iridescent, stone.

"It's called a black opal, even though it's really blue. They actually come in different colors. But when I saw this stone, I thought of you." He rubs his thumb over the ring.

"It's beautiful. The whole ring is. I love it." And I do.

Sampson smiles. "I'm glad. I made it. The swirls all around the band? They're my fingerprint ridges. So I'm always holding your hand."

"You made this? Like my bracelet, like the guys' pendants?" I look back down at the ring and the detail of the ridges.

He nods. "I like working with my hands and metal. I've got a little workbench set up in Cal's garage. When we find a house, I'll move it to *our* garage." He shrugs like he didn't just make the most impressive, intimate, and truly Sampson-esque ring.

He stands and offers me his hand, pulling me up with him. "Come on. We have brunch by the pool waiting for us back at the hotel."

I stay curled into Sampson on the ride back to the hotel, and he holds me to him, my head tucked under his chin as I continue to gaze at my ring. We're engaged. Sampson and I are committed to spending our lives with each other.

Aiden drives us back to the hotel and we walk through the lobby hand-in-hand, out to the pool area. There's a large table set up in the corner we head towards, and Killian stands up and announces, "They're here."

Gibson stands in his chair as everyone else stands up. "Hi Mail! Hi!" He waves at me. "We havin' a bekfast pawty!" All of Sampson's bandmates, their wives, and Vi are here. Jeff is here too. Good, I'm hoping to get an update on Giz since he's here.

"Well?" Killian asks. "Are we celebrating an engagement or consoling Sammy because you turned him away?" He stares at me and his eyes trail down my left arm to my hand. But my fingers are tightly entangled in Sampson's.

I defer to Sampson, who grins and holds my hand up. "She said yes."

They whoop it up and Sampson and I are parted. The girls fawn over my ring. "It's so pretty. Did Sammy really make it?" Ari looks it over.

"He did. Isn't it beautiful? Picked out the stone and everything." I don't tell them about his fingerprints on my band. That's my little secret and I love it.

Kady takes a turn examining the ring. "If the Rebels ever broke up, Sammy could make a good living making jewelry." She squeezes my hand and leans in. "Did you tell him?"

I shake my head.

"Oh, Mel. You have to tell him. Soon." Kady pulls me in for a hug. "It'll be okay."

"I will. Before we leave Key West."

Before we return to sitting down, I grab Jeff's attention. "How's Giz doing?"

"He's doing okay, thanks to you. As soon as he's detoxed, he's on his way to Big Sur to an inpatient rehab."

"Good. I hope he takes it seriously," I say. Jeff nods his agreement.

We settle back down at the table and start to partake in the beautiful and delicious brunch that the Inn had catered in our honor. There's everything you could want, and Gibson's bouncing around, but he keeps eyeing the pool.

"Mail? You going swimming?" He wiggles up onto my lap and reaches onto my plate and grabs a piece of pineapple and starts chewing it.

"No, I'm not going swimming, buddy. Maybe we can swim at the next hotel, okay?"

"Okay. Next time." He settles into my lap and grazes from my plate, which is fine by me. I'm not really that hungry.

"Don't eat off of Mel's plate without asking, Gibson." His dad notices him sneaking another piece of fruit from my plate, this time a strawberry.

"He's fine, Cal. We're sharing." Sampson looks over at me and gets this goofy look on his face as I hold Gibs. It's something between a grin and deep thought.

"We sharing, Cal," Gibson says matter-of-factly, as he grabs my toast and starts munching. I *was* going to eat that. It humors everyone when Gibson uses his dad's name instead of calling him daddy. And Gibson lives for the chuckles he gets.

"Hey," I turn to Ari. "How did your appointment go?"

She pales a little. "Um, Cal. Mel wants to know how our appointment went. Might as well tell everyone."

All heads turn towards Cal. "Everything was perfect." He shrugs. "All good. We even got to hear the hearts, which was super cool." He takes a big mouthful of scrambled eggs and chews slowly.

"Hearts? Are you having a baby octopus?" Mavrick's head cocks to the side as he looks at Ari and Cal.

"Nope. No octopi, just twin humans."

"Twins! No way." Mav stares at Cal.

He nods. "Yep." Cal looks at Killian and shrugs like it's no big deal. But something tells me it's a big freaking deal for Killian. But I don't know why.

Congratulations go around the table for Ari and Cal. "But everyone is healthy?" I can't help but ask, thinking about how tired and nauseated Ari's been.

Cal nods again. "He said that it actually could explain her being so tired and nauseated. But everything is looking really good." He leans over and kisses Ari's temple. "They appear to be identical, if anyone is wondering."

After brunch, we make plans to meet downtown before we all head to the airport together. Sampson and I walk hand-in-hand back to our bungalow to pack up so we can check out.

"You seem quiet. Everything okay?" Sampson turns and looks at me before slipping our keycard into the door.

I nod. "I could say the same about you. You didn't say much for most of the brunch. You just gave me this weird look that I couldn't decipher when I was holding Gibson. What was that look about anyway?"

Sampson tilts his head. "I was thinking that..." he hesitates. "That you'd be a great mom, Mel. I can't wait until we get pregnant."

"Good. You won't have to."

"I mean, I know you want to wait. But seeing you with Gibson gave me all kinds of ideas of what it would be like if *we* had a baby. I don't want to wait too long, Mel. All our kids could be friends, which would be awesome. Expanding our band family and our family—"

Sampson stops listing all the reasons he thinks we should start having a baby, and his eyebrows shoot up when he realizes what I said. "Wait, what? What did you say?"

"I'm pretty sure I'm pregnant, Sampson. I took a pee test a

few days ago. It was positive. I haven't had a blood test or anything, but I'm late and I'm almost never late. Not since I've been on the pill. My breasts have been tender as hell lately and don't even get me going about the smell of coffee. Ugh, just thinking about it absolutely turns my stomach lately. Prob—"

He grabs my face between his hands and kisses me without a word, only passion. He kisses me so I feel the zing of our connection all the way to my toes. He pulls back and looks me in the eyes. His are still wide, and his mouth has a soft reverent smile on it.

"We made a baby? For reals?" The awe in his voice makes my eyes well with tears and all I can do is nod.

"I think so. We'll have to get married sooner rather than later because I don't want to have to wear a tent. Oh, and—"

He kisses me again, this time pulling me against him.

# Chapter 34

## *Sammy*

Mel grabs my hand and squeezes tight as her body stiffens when we enter the backstage area in Orlando. Her eyes are screwed shut.

"What is it, baby?" I whisper into her ear. She's been nauseated a lot lately, ironically, usually in the evenings. So much for morning sickness.

She flips towards me. Her eyes are wide open, and her face is pale. "*He's* here."

"Who's here?" I look down at her and she's burrowed into me so closely. "That fucker that hurt you?" She nods and buries her face into my shirt. "Where is he?"

"I can smell *him*. He's here." Her voice is small, so I hold her to me protectively. I motion to Luke, my security guy, and he comes over.

"Mel says the guy who hurt her is here. I need you to make sure Jax knows and sticks close with Mel at all times." He nods and steps two steps to the right of us and pulls out his phone, his eyes constantly scanning the area. The whole security team's been briefed about him. They've all seen the composite sketch that she made in the hospital.

We walk to my dressing room as a unit and Luke sweeps it before we go in and stations himself right outside the door.

This dressing room is smallish, but there is a nice settee in it, and she sits on it, her face kind of dazed.

"Did you see him?"

She shakes her head. "I smell him. It's so—" she gags a few times and then runs into the bathroom connected to my dressing room. I follow her in and rub her back. I don't know if this is due to the shock or due to morning sickness she has every evening or some weird combination. When she's done, I hand her my water bottle, and she takes a mouthful and spits it out.

"I think he's following me." My heart falls to my feet at her words.

"What do you mean, he's following you?" My voice is louder than I mean it, but what the actual fuck? How can he be following her, and this is the first I've heard of it?

"I keep smelling him. The first time was before Lauderdale. But I thought I was crazy. Then again, at the Lauderdale show and now this one." She shakes her head. "It's got to be him. That smell." She gags again and I hold her to me.

"Shhh. We'll find him." I don't know that we will, but we better.

She curls up on the settee and it's not long before my small dressing room is filled with the band and the girls and security. Kady's got her arm wrapped supportively around Mel, who's balled up and small against Kady.

"Do you think he's actually here?" Cal nudges my foot with his to get my attention.

"She says she smelled him. She really freaked out. I don't doubt that he's here," I reply. "She's also just told me she's pregnant. So I'm worried about her and the baby, obviously. Maybe I should send her home to be with Clance and Sofie."

"I wouldn't," Mav interjects. "You'll still worry from afar.

And we have plenty of security here. Keep her where you have eyes on her as much as possible."

"Did you say she's pregnant?" Cal asks and I nod. "Ari's sense of smell has been crazy sensitive. I had to stop wearing my aftershave."

"I say we have all the girls and kids stay in my dressing room with security in and outside the room. Just in case. I don't want some sicko roaming around backstage with them." Mav steps up as he talks. "I'm serious. My dressing room is bigger than this one. We can all fit into it easily."

Soon we are on the move as a unit flanked by our security. Jax insists that there be no visitors to the dressing rooms. None. I admit that I'm edgy on stage and really just want the show to be over and done with. I think we all do. Once we are done with the show, we meet back in the dressing room, and no one has heard or seen anything that could result in the person that carjacked Melody being apprehended. The mood in the dressing room is subdued after the show and our VIP appearance has been canceled for security reasons. I'd like to say I feel bad about the fans, but I really don't. I'm more worried about my Mel. Ari told me she didn't really eat anything.

"Can I have your attention?" Jax's booming voice has us all turning our heads.

"In light of the security issue, we have changed your travel plans. Instead of getting on the busses and driving to our next stop, you'll be flying to the next show and staying at a hotel until the show tomorrow night. Because of the possible danger, I do not want anybody, and I mean anybody, Killian, leaving that hotel. You need something, you let me know and I'll procure it for you. Is that understood?" Everyone nods somberly and even from here I can see Mel's bottom lip quiver and Kady pulls her to her tighter.

"This is just a precaution."

We don't even bother showering. We all change into sweats

or whatever was gathered from the bus for us, and we are taken to a chartered plane that hops us up to South Carolina. We are checked into the hotel under aliases and escorted to our rooms and only let in after our security does a thorough sweep of each room. I know I'm practically dead on my feet and I think Mel is too.

"I'm going to take a quick shower." She holds her bacon PJ pants over her arm like a maître de.

"Okay. I'll be out here." She nods and goes into the bathroom. She sobs through her shower. I don't know whether she wants me to know or not, so I stay out here to give her privacy.

When she finally comes out, I am messing around on my phone, which I set down the minute I see her. I open my arms and she crawls up the bed and curls up in my lap and I gladly hold her to me.

"Your fans hate me."

"You don't know that."

"Actually, I do. I saw the comments online. They blame me for the cancellation of the VIP event. How did they even find that out, Sampson? How?"

"I dunno." I squeeze her to me. "But it's not your fault."

"But it kind of is."

"No buts about it. This is *his* fault. No one else's."

"Why is he following me? Why? What did I ever do to him? I mean, beside stuff a scalpel into his gut."

"I don't know, baby." I hold her to me tight and eventually transition us from sitting on the bed to lying in it, but I remain holding her to me tightly.

I awake to Melody tossing in my arms and muttering something I can't hear. "Mel. It's okay, baby."

She wakes up when I squeeze her. "You okay?" I kiss her temple and hug her to me.

She nods and nuzzles her face into my neck. She's quiet for

so long I think she's fallen back asleep until I hear. "I can't sleep." Her words come out as hot breaths on my neck.

I squeeze her to me tighter. "Me neither, baby, me neither."

"Do you think my brain just made it up? That he's not really following me?" Her words are quiet, something I can barely hear.

"I think if he's not following you, there is someone out there that smells just like him. Either way... I want you safe. Would you feel safer going home to stay with Clance and Sof for a while? I could even send Luke home with you." I know what Mav thinks, but I want Melody to feel safe.

"No! I feel safe with you, Sampson. Please don't send me away." She snuggles into me as tight as she can, and I pull her to me.

"Okay. I just wanted to make sure you feel safe."

"I just want this over. I want him caught. I thought traveling would leave him behind."

"I know, baby, me too." I plant my lips in her hair and keep a steady pressure in my hug until she falls back to sleep. We sleep late into the next day. As a band, we decide to eat together and gather in Cal's room since it's the biggest.

"Hey, you," Ari greets Mel with a hug as we stroll in, the last two to arrive. She holds on to Mel a little tighter and longer than usual, and I realize that Mel's crying. Ari pulls her into one of the bedrooms of their suite while I walk into the main room where all the guys are situated.

"Hi, Shammy." Gibson offers me a truck to play with.

"Thanks, bud." I take the truck and set it on the table, and he looks at me like he's confused. I'm usually the first to play with him, but right now I just can't. No one is saying anything, so I just look at the guys. Judging by the faces of my brothers, no one slept well last night.

"It was a rough night," I mumble and they all mumble something back and nod. Kill claps me on the back and tells me to sit and that the food will be there soon. Even Mav's usually animated face looks stark as he holds Kady on his lap, Brio napping in a playpen next to the couch.

The food comes, and the server is watched like a hawk by security as she sets it all out. Mav hands her a hundred-dollar bill, and she leaves.

"Ar? Mel? Food's here." Cal raps on the bedroom door.

When they come out, we all make ourselves a plate and sit wherever we can. Mel chooses to sit on my lap, which is fine with me, even if it does make my eating hard. I'd rather she eat anyway. She's got the baby, and he needs nutrition. I wrap my arm around her and pull her into my lap further and nuzzle her neck as she picks at the food on her plate.

"You need to eat, Mel. It's not just you anymore," I whisper in her ear. She sets her plate on the table and turns so she's facing me on my lap and hugs me, nuzzling into my neck. Her hot tears make my neck wet.

"I love you, Sampson," she gasps in my neck as I rock her.

"I love you too, Mel. So much." It doesn't even bother me that my brothers are witnessing such an intimate moment between us. They know it's been a lot, quickly, for us. We got engaged. She told me we are having a baby. And now the asshole who hurt her, who fucking *touched her*, is stalking her? I'll hold her and comfort her anytime.

Usually there'd be light-hearted ribbing. Someone would tell us to get a room, or to quit sucking face. But there is none of that. Instead, they eat their breakfasts sitting around the room. Everyone in their own head.

We spend the day together as a family. Circled wagons and all. We all take a collective nap. Melody falls asleep in my arms on the couch, and I doze off not long after her. Ari, Cal, and Gibson take one of the bedrooms in the suite, Mav Brio and Kady the other. Killian drops off where he is on the floor. Seems none of us slept well last night.

After we wake up, it's worked out that Ari and Elsie will stay at the hotel with the children in Mav's suite. The rest of us will head to the venue as expected. Even Mel. I was adamant she stay with Ari, but she refused. Aiden and one of the other newer security guys stay at the hotel. Luke is to not let Melody out of his sight and Jax is to be floating around backstage.

Mel grips my hand as we walk into the new arena, Luke behind us. Jax greets us.

"I've swept the whole backstage area. It's clear." I nod, but Jax looks over at Mel. "You catch his scent, you let Luke know as soon as you smell it. Okay?" Mel nods.

We follow Jax through the backstage area when Mel stops and grips my hand hard. When I look over at her, she twitches her nose.

"He's here." Her eyes go to me, her words quiet yet shaking. "He's here."

Both Jax and Luke coordinate without a word and move us into the nearest dressing room, which happens to be Killian's.

"Hey, what's—" His words die on his lips when he takes in Melody, who's quaking beneath my hand on the small of her back as I escort her into the room. Luke remains stationed at Killian's door and Jax searches.

Forty minutes later, Jax returns with a small shake of his head and Melody crumples in on herself. She spends the entire show in my dressing room. After the show, we board the buses and head to the next show.

The next several shows, everyone's on high alert. Mel comes to each show and spends most of it in the dressing room. If she catches sight or smell of him, she keeps it to herself. I ask her every night and she shakes her head.

At a show in New Hampshire, one of the crew guys sticks his head into our collective green room. "One of the crew guys for Raspberry Whine is hurt. Mel, can you come take a look? We think he needs to go to the ER, but he doesn't want to."

Mel tentatively grabs her bag and Luke goes with her. I want to go with her too, but I stay behind because we have a media session any minute. The girl from a music magazine and then a guy with some sort of music blog come and go one at a time. When we're done, it's been a while and Mel and Luke aren't back yet.

# Chapter 35

## *Melody*

Luke and I follow Domino through the back of the arena to an area next to the stage. All I can see of him is his hand being held down by a fellow crew guy. There's something sticking out of the back of it. I set my bag down next to him. "Hi. I'm Mel, I'm a paramedic and I'm just going to give your hand a look, okay."

"Go ahead, nurse me up so I can get back to work." His voice rumbles with a familiar grit and he sticks his hand out towards me. His hands are filthy and the smell. *Oh, God, the smell.* I have to hold in the gag. I look him in the face. Those same dead, vacant eyes stare back at me, the ones from the rearview mirror in the ambulance. He doesn't make any indication that he recognizes me, but I certainly recognize him.

I'm in a small room filled with people and *him*. And what's worse is, *he's* my patient. My heart pounds in my ears as I look at his hand and concentrate on the injury only right now. I gently pick it up to see if the metal rod goes all the way through his hand. It doesn't. It also doesn't appear to hurt him as much as it should. Either he's got one hell of a pain tolerance or he's on something.

*Sampson.* I wish more than anything Sampson was here. He'd understand because Luke doesn't understand my subtle differences, but Sampson's in tune with me. He'd understand that this is *him* without me having to say a word.

"Have you taken anything today?" I ask as I continue my assessment.

He shrugs one shoulder.

"I'm not trying to get you in trouble, but it's important that I know, so we know how to treat this."

He mumbles something about meth. I'm trying to figure out how to get Luke's attention without causing this guy to realize I know exactly who he is and what he did to me. But if I make a commotion, this guy could grab me and take me hostage again.

"When was the last time you used?" I ask, trying my hardest to keep my voice level, yet commanding. I don't want anyone to know I fear for my life in this second because the second I give that away, *he's* got the advantage. I work not to stare or treat him any differently than I would any other patient.

I repeat my question, and he doesn't answer.

"What's your name?" I need it. I have to give *him* a name. It's stupid, but in this moment, I need to know it. It won't seem odd; it will seem like I'm trying to connect with my patient. But I am not trying to connect with him. I'm trying to keep him distracted before he catches the fear I know is playing out in my eyes and over my face. A fear that only he's seen in me.

"Why the hell do you need to know my name? You sure do talk a lot."

"I'm just trying to get to know you. Develop a rapport. It's part of what we do. So, name? I'm Mel."

"You ask a lot of questions for a nurse." He narrows his eyes at me when I take a minute to look over at Luke and I feel the guy tense.

"We have to take your medical history to make sure we get the whole picture."

He's probably seen the scar that runs faintly down my one cheek. It's faded and make up helps me cover it, but you can still see it if you look hard enough. It's the scar that *he* gave me.

"You remind me of a bitch I knew. She wouldn't shut up either."

Domino speaks up. "Dude, she's trying to help you. Shut the fuck up and treat Mel with respect."

This draws *his* attention away from me. I quickly wrap his hand up in gauze, the metal piece still in it, then stand.

"This needs to be seen at the hospital. They'll safely remove it there and clean the wound. Then he needs to be taken to the police, because he's the guy, Luke. This is the guy. It's him." I hear the waiver in my own voice. It doesn't even sound like me.

It takes a full second for Luke to understand what I'm saying. When he does, he jumps between me and the guy sitting there with his hand wrapped up. He says something into his walkie-talkie and within minutes we are surrounded by Blind Rebels security, venue security, and a couple of sheriffs.

I realize I still don't know *his* name. But that doesn't matter anymore. What matters is that there are handcuffs and police and that he is going to finally get *his just desserts*. He struggles with the police, and I can't look away. I don't care about his hand injury. I just want to make sure that he doesn't somehow get away. Again.

My breathing speeds up as I continue to watch. The small room becomes even fuller and smaller as more people try to push in. It's cool in here, and I feel like I'm in the back of the ambulance again, but this time, this time, there are people here to help me. I'm not alone this time.

*Sampson. I just want Sampson.*

Jax puts an arm on my shoulder, and I jump as I watch the commotion from the corner I've been pushed into by the descending forces.

"Mel? Melody? Come on hon. Let's get you to the green

room." He pulls me gently by my arm towards the door and walks briskly, his hand on the small of my back.

The reality of what just happened hits me and I slow down, unable to keep up. I shake uncontrollably. It was *him*. *He's* been here the whole time we've been on tour. Did he follow me? The shock of the situation is getting to me and the paramedic in me knows I need to sit somewhere, take a few quiet minutes to calm down before I freaking faint.

"You're safe, Mel." Jax slows down but keeps us moving towards the green room. But it's suddenly hard to take in a breath. "You're okay. Keep moving. Sam's in the green room. Let's keep moving, hon."

*Sampson.* That's just who I need.

Aiden steps aside from the green room door and Jax opens it and ushers me through into the room.

"Hey Me—" Sampson's words die on his lips the second he takes me in. I have no idea what I look like, but something about my appearance causes him to jump up. "What happened? Fuck. Mel." He has me in his arms and that's all I need. My Sampson. My safety. My home. I breathe in his smell as he pulls me to him tight. "Fuck, are you okay, baby?" I shake my head, my face buried in his chest. He rocks us slightly.

"The suspect has been captured," Jax announces and a collective and very audible sigh of relief echoes through the room. I can hear it, even though I'm ensconced in all that is my Sampson.

"The show is going to be delayed at least 30 minutes. Take care of her. I'll send Jeff back with an update about stage time." Jax turns and leaves the room.

As soon as the door shuts, what just happened catches up to me and my knees start to give out. Sampson grabs me around the middle tight. "Woah, baby, I've got you. Come on." He walks me to the couch and pulls me down as he sits, situating me across his lap and tucking me into him, arms around me tightly, lips in my hair. "It's over baby. It's all over," he murmurs, rocking me back and forth gently.

I don't know how much time goes by, or what's going on in the room. I'm only aware of Sampson. He keeps me close, cocooned to his chest in a safe bubble, and it's the only place I want to be right now. I hate that he'll eventually have to go play onstage. I just want to stay here in my Sampson bubble for as long as possible.

Someone, Killian, I think, offers me a bottle of water. I take it but I don't drink it. I just hold it to me in my little protected bubble. I can feel the vibration of Sampson talking sometimes, but I'm not listening to anything being said by him or anyone else.

# Chapter 36

## *Sammy*

The second I see Mel walk into the green room escorted by Jax, I know something's really wrong. She's pale and quaking. I don't know what happened, but I jump up and hold her.

"The suspect has been captured," Jax announces. He mentions that the show will likely be delayed by at least half an hour, but the show is the furthest thing from my mind. The asshole has been captured. That must mean he's here. I want a few minutes alone with him. Jax breezes out before I can mention it. As he leaves, Melody's legs buckle beneath her. Thank God I had her wrapped up in a hug because she nearly goes down. Killian helps me guide her to the couch where I pull her onto my lap and hug her to me. She burrows into me tight and seems to like my arms wrapped around her. She tucks her hands in and draws her knees up into a little ball. My Melody ball. I hold her and rock her and kiss her hair.

Nobody's talking, not really. We're all more relaxed knowing that the threat has been found, but also somewhat worried because Mel doesn't say a word. Killian tries giving her a bottle of water. She takes it from him and draws it into her little ball, but she doesn't drink it. She nuzzles into me.

I rock her. Jeff comes back in. "It's going to be at least an hour, guys." He slips back out.

This is one of the very few times I really don't want to play. I honestly don't know that I'll be able to let Mel go so that I can.

"I don't think I can do it tonight." I glance up at Cal and Mav over Mel's head tucked tightly under my chin. "I'm sorry, guys. I just can't." I squeeze Mel to me. "Maybe Kev can sit in?" Kevin's my drum tech this tour. He's a pretty good drummer in his own right. I think he'd do it.

Cal comes over and pats my shoulder. "Take Mel back to the hotel and take care of her. We'll check in as soon as we can." He goes into the hall and talks to Aiden and comes right back in.

"Aiden will drive you." He pats my back. "I'll get the door for you."

I stand up and she moans at being jostled when I stand, but I keep her balled up the best I can as I carry her out into the waiting car. The drive to the hotel is short. Aiden parks in the front and leaves the car and walks with us to the elevator and gets the door to our room.

"Thanks, man, I owe ya," I whisper as I carry her past him as he holds the hotel room door open.

"Nah, it's part of the job. I'll be outside if you need anything." He closes the door for me. I settle onto the little couch in my room and just hold her like I did in the green room for a while, rocking her slightly.

"Baby?" I stop rocking her and try to look at her. "Mel? You're starting to worry me, sweetheart." She sighs into my chest and unlocks her legs and stretches out a little bit.

"It was *him*. The Raspberry Whine roadie *is him*." She says it quietly to my chest. "As soon as he spoke, I knew it was *him*."

I squeeze her. "I treated *him* like he was any other patient." Her emphasis on him guts me with every sentence she speaks.

"I didn't know what else to do. He didn't seem to recognize me at first. But then he saw my scar." She reaches up and runs her finger over the barely-there scar.

"Domino, he didn't like how he was talking to me and distracted the guy. I wrapped up his hand and jumped back and told Luke it was *him*. That he needed to go to the police because it was him. Then they all came to get *him*. They got *him*." She lets out a sigh and her stomach growls.

And then my heart lightens when she lets out a small giggle at the sound of her stomach growling again.

"What do you want? I'll get you anything. Anything you want, baby."

She uncaps her water bottle from Killian that she's still clutching and downs three fourths of it in one go and then wipes her mouth on her sleeve. "Eggs and bacon. And maybe a pancake or three."

This is *my Mel*, and she's hungry. I call room service and warn Aiden they'll be up with the food in about forty minutes. As I turn from the door back into the room, I look at Mel. She looks exhausted.

"I want to take a shower. Will you wash my hair like you do sometimes?" Her cheeks pink a little, asking me for something. I love that it comforts her. I'll wash her hair every day if she wants me to.

"I'd love to." I strip my shirt off and head into the shower to heat up the water. "Come on in, Mel."

I wash her hair and as I massage her scalp and her eyes roll back as she purrs her appreciation. This is *my Mel*, and I'm fucking grateful she's back. We eat our late, or early, breakfasts and snuggle together while watching stupid reality TV. She falls asleep on my chest.

There's a little bit of guilt. Just a little, for not playing. But being here with Mel was worth it. I hate disappointing the fans and the guys, sure, but Mel's my forever.

My phone alerts a text.

*Cal: I'm at the hotel, can I come in?*

*Me: Mel's asleep, so keep it down, but yeah.*

Minutes later, Aiden opens the door and Cal slips in. He brings a chair close to the bed.

"She's exhausted and a fairly sound sleeper, so we're good to talk," I say in a whisper. "How'd the show go?"

"We did an abbreviated acoustic set. Domino recorded some of it. We'll get it to you. I think, overall, everyone was understanding. Mav just announced at the beginning that you had a family emergency to attend to. The fans liked the different set, I think." I sigh out a breath I didn't even realize I was holding.

"I'm sorry, man, I just couldn't leave her. Not like she was. She needed me."

He nods and pats my shoulder lightly. "I would have been pissed at you if you had. Some things are more important than the show, Sam. Family is one of them. I learned that the hard way. Trust me." We sit in a comfortable silence.

"You think she's okay?" Cal asks, his brow creased as he looks over at a sleeping Mel.

I nod. "She had a shower and ate the best I've seen her eat in weeks. I think she's more than good. She just needed some time to process, I think."

"Good. I'm glad. We pushed the bus call back a little, but we'll need to be at the busses by 1:00 pm." He pats my arm and stands. "I just wanted to make sure she was good. That you are good."

I nod. "We'll see you at the busses. Thanks, man."

Cal nods and slips back out of the room. I grab my phone and pull up a new message, this one to Clance.

*Me: I wanted to tell you before this hits the news. The hijacker has been apprehended here on tour. He was working on the crew of one of our support bands. The police think it was a coincidence, but we aren't sure about that yet.*

He texts me back almost immediately despite the late hour.

***Clance:*** *Mel?*

***Me:*** *She's okay. Better than okay. She's asleep right now. Best sleep in weeks so far. In months, really.*

***Clance:*** *Thanks.*

***Clance:*** *Seriously, not just for the news, but for being there for her.*

***Me:*** *Of course. I love her. I'll have her call you or Sof tomorrow, but it might be in the afternoon.*

I don't want to spoil our engagement news. I know Mel wants to tell them in person when we see them after the tour.

***Clance:*** *Okay. Thanks again.*

# Chapter 37

## *Melody*

Sampson and I join the group at the busses at 1:00 pm. We were hoping to sleep in, but I had to be interviewed by the local police and speak with the LA police on the phone. Sammy and I have to fly back to LA on our next off day for the tour to meet with the detective and the district attorney, both of whom are chomping at the bit to prosecute Burt Milshnick. That's *his* name. Well, technically Sammy doesn't have to come with me, but he insists, and honestly, I want him there.

As soon as we get out of the car where the busses are staged, Kady and Ari run over to us and tackle me in a hug.

"Oh, Mel, I'm so glad you're okay and that he's finally been caught," Kady cries into my ear. Ari is a little quieter but squeezes me just as tight.

"Me too. I feel like I can breathe again. Finally."

"We all can," Ari confirms.

As we get underway, I settle between Sampson's legs on one of the black leather couches that spans the side of the bus. He's put something on the TV that is Gibson approved because he's playing on the floor with his truck while his dad and mom take a nap in the back bedroom. But I don't care about the TV. I'm just enjoying being close with my Sampson.

He plays with a lock of my hair with one hand while the other is firmly planted on my stomach.

"How are you feeling? Really." He kisses my neck.

"A little nauseous. A little tired. A lot relieved." I hum at the contact of his chin rubbing against my neck.

"I'll go wake Cal and we can take naps." He rubs my stomach.

"Don't. They need the nap and alone time. We'll nap later. I love you, Sampson."

"I love you too. And you too, baby." He gives my stomach a rub.

Gibson looks up at us. "Baby?"

Sampson nods. "Mel's got a baby in her belly."

Gibson rushes over. "Aww a baby for Mail! Kisses?!" He plants a few kisses on my shirt over my stomach, then goes back to playing on the floor with his trucks.

"So, when Gibson announced you were pregnant that day in the green room?" Sammy tilts his head to look at me.

I nod, confirming his suspicion. "Ari found my test in the bathroom. I had just taken it, then Gibson had fallen and scraped up his knee. I was freaked out, so I chatted with her about it, and you know who was listening."

"Well, she did an excellent job covering for you." He kisses my neck some more. "You little sneak."

"I wasn't trying to be a sneak. I just didn't want to announce it like that in front of everybody when we hadn't talked about it first."

"But I've been telling you I wanted to have some kids. Even before the tour, remember?" He pulls me to him.

"That seemed like you were talking about future Sampson and Mel, not right now Sampson and Mel." I shrug and rub my engagement ring. "We need to get married. As soon as the tour's over. I don't want to have to wear a tent."

"I'd get married to you tomorrow if you'd let me." He peppers me with kisses on my neck. "Anything I can do to make it easier on you, I'll do it. We can hire one of those fancy wedding planners. Buy a shit ton of books or magazines—"

I cut him off by turning around and giving him a big kiss that makes him moan. "Let's do the planner thing. They can work on it while we are out here."

"You got it, beautiful."

# Epilogue Sammy

Mel squeezes my hand as we walk back to the Jeep. We started today with an early morning visit with Sevenya and Dee. I had to tell my sister that we're clearing out the condo today. I've put it off long enough.

Mel and I got back from our honeymoon in Fiji a few days ago and immediately started looking at houses. She doesn't want to renew the lease on the studio apartment, and there really isn't much room there anyway. We found the perfect house near the ocean up in the Palisades and close on it in a few weeks. We'll be closest to Killian and farthest from Cal, with Mav right smack between, but we are all still within a forty-minute drive from each other at the farthest.

There's a pending trial for Burt. From what the detective told me, Mel wasn't being stalked. It was a weird coincidence that he was on our tour. Management for Raspberry Whine told us that he was hired via a typical cattle call road crew announcement.

"Everyone's waiting for us." Mel slides her phone back in her pocket with her free hand, then squeezes my hand again. "She'd want you to move on, Sampson."

"I know." I sigh. Today is not going to be easy. I didn't even go in when I unlocked my condo for the listing agent yesterday. I stood outside while he walked around and made a list of things we could do to make sure that we get the maximum value for the place. The biggest thing on his list was clearing out most of the stuff in there, leaving basic furnishings so that prospective buyers can envision their own stuff in there.

I pull into my parking spot and Mel slides out and makes her way over to the group assembled to help. Mav wraps his arms around her in a greeting while Kady starts talking and gesticulating towards the condo, all while Killian stands off to the side, his expression blank. But I know he's struggling today just as much as I am. I can feel the heaviness of his distress weighing him down from here.

Cal starts towards my Jeep, so I hop out. When I turn, he's right here in my space. His eyes work me over, concern pulling his brows together, but he says nothing. Instead, he slings an arm across my shoulders and squeezes.

"We're all here for *you*." His gruff voice is low, so only I can hear.

Emotions I can't even process clog my throat, so I just nod.

"We already have a game plan. The girls will do a majority of the sorting and boxing of the small stuff. Kitchen cabinets, living room, that kind of thing. Mav's doing the moving of the larger stuff in those rooms. You concentrate on your bedroom. Kill's got the hall closets and bathrooms. I'll work on Sev's room."

It means a lot that he'd go through her stuff for me. Leave it to Cal to organize it so that we're in and out of the condo as quickly as we can be, and so that I don't have to go into Sev's room.

"Cal, I, uh..." My words stick to the emotion clogging my throat.

He shakes his head abruptly before squeezing my shoulder

tight again. I don't have the words right now. How can I thank any of them for helping then, helping now? They're all here, making this as easy as possible on me.

"We're family and this is what family does." He gives my shoulder one more squeeze and then withdraws his arm, giving me a slap on the back. "Ari and Vi stayed home because someone had to watch Gibs and Brio. We'll all go there after to eat some food and relax."

"Sounds like a plan."

"Oh, and, Sam, Kill's already moody as fuck today, just a warning." He nods towards his twin, who's carrying a stack of flattened boxes towards my door. I don't tell Cal that I'm not the only one trying to let go of a loved one today.

# R

I glance around my bedroom one more time. Almost anything personal I had in this bedroom is either packed in one of the three brown boxes stacked by already in my storage unit. I even double-checked under the bed. The house is mostly quiet, except for the sounds of stuff being boxed and quiet conversation between Mel, Kady and Vi in the kitchen. Vi showed up about an hour ago with some snacks and extra boxes at Ari's insistence. Thank goodness we're almost done. I don't think Cal likes the idea of Ari alone in her condition.

I sit on the bed for a few minutes and just close my eyes. This place seemed so big when we moved in. I had so much hope that this place would become not just where we lived, but our home. That Sev could finally find a place she felt comfortable, happy, and loved.

"Hey, you okay?" Mel's soft voice has me opening my eyes. She's leaning against the doorjamb of my room, accessing me with those beautiful eyes of hers. She knows me best.

"Um, yeah."

"The living room is done. We're almost done in the kitchen. Do you want to keep the plates and stuff, or do you want to donate them?" She sits next to me and takes my hand.

"Donate them. Donate everything in the kitchen unless it's something you think we'll need."

She nods and lays her head on my shoulder. "You're done in here?"

"Yeah. I haven't lived here since she died. If it was important to me, it's in one of those boxes or already at your place. I don't know why I was so scared to get this over with before."

My hand goes to her stomach. She's just starting to show. If you didn't know her, you probably wouldn't be able to even tell yet. But I can. *Our baby.*

She squeezes my fingers between hers. "Because it wasn't the stuff you were concerned with, Sampson. It's the memor—"

Cal walks into my room, ashen, holding a large manila envelope in his hand.

"Did you know?" His voice is shaky as he wiggles the envelope in his hand.

*Shit. What did you hide, Sevenya?*

"Know what, Cal?"

"I found these in her room, in a shoe box in her closet." He pulls a sonogram out of the envelope and then another. "The dates on these, it was from before rehab and then while in rehab in Montana."

*Shit Sev. You were pregnant? My chest hurts for my sister.*

"Wha, why?" Callum's voice goes up a couple octaves, and soon, Killian, Mav, and Kady are sandwiched in the doorway behind him. "Sammy, why do these say Baby Donogue?"

Cal turns to his twin, who looks like he's about to pass out, and then back around the room at each of us. "Someone please explain this to me because it's not making any sense. Why do these sonograms have Sevenya's name but say Baby Donogue?"

Killian turns even whiter and a terrible gasping sob tears from him right before he turns around and barrels down the hall.

# The Playlist

I've made playlists for each of the Blind Rebel books. The playlist for *Reviving the Rhythm* can be found on my Spotify.

This is a small sampling of the songs found on the Spotify playlist for *Reviving the Rhythm*:

1. We All Die Young- Steelheart
2. Somebody Save Me- Cinderella
3. Close My Eyes Forever- Lita Ford, Ozzy Osbourne
4. Don't Close Your Eyes- Six
5. Kickstart my Heart- Mötley Crüe
6. Poisonous- Jet Black Romance
7. Silent Lucidity- Queensrÿche
8. You're Crazy- Guns N' Roses
9. Born Again- Black Veil Brides
10. I Remember You- Skid Row

The full Spotify playlist for Reviving the Rhythm is 58 songs and is a little over four hours long. I listened to it while writing, while editing and while procrastinating both writing and editing (and formatting).

You can find me on Spotify: Amy Kaybach

# Acknowledgments

I refer to my books as my "book babies." They truly are pieces of myself that I painstakingly pour over and nurture before sending them into the world. Most people have heard it takes a village to raise a child. Similarly it takes a village to create a book.

This is my village. My go-to peeps. My ride-or-dies. And I couldn't do it without you.

**Misty:** Thank you for shamelessly plugging my book wherever you go and for being so excited about my Blind Rebel boys. I love our conversations about the complexity of the characters and especially love it when you point things out about the books that I didn't do consciously or even pick up on.

**My ARC readers & Bookstagrammers who help me get the word out:** Thank you for reading and loving the Rebels like I do! I appreciate your work sharing my teasers and making your own content around my books! I love reading your reviews and watching your videos- nothing makes my day better than stumbling across your content. Your support means the world to me!

**The Blind Rebels first groupie:** You know who you are. Thank you for all the love you spread about the Blind Rebels and my books. I see you and I love and appreciate what you're doing for my books (and me)!

**Jamie:** Thank you for always being a sounding board for my writing ideas. And for planting the little seed that maybe I should consider publishing them! But mostly thank you for being my friend!

**Tricia:** For your undying and enthusiastic support and reads in the rough form. For your willingness to give me feedback in all things! I am grateful for you!

**Shayna Astor and Sherry Bessette:** I mean it when I say these books would not be the same without either of you. You provide endless feedback about characters and plot...and non-book yet still "authory" things. (Yes I made that work up. I can do that. I'm a writer after all).

**Caelan Fine:** Thank you for being my go-to graphics guy and enabling my love of swag by making the ideas in my head come to life. You always seem to just know how to fit the vibe of my story and are an amazing person to work with! Thank you! I hope you have a spot on your calendar for book 4!

**Emily Wittig:** For these amazing covers that all look so great and for being so kind and patient with all my new author questions. I'm so looking forward to having all the books together on my shelf so I can see your art all in one place!

**Hayleigh of Editing Fox:** Thank you for helping me make this story flow and for helping me suss out Melody a little more. I don't think I truly understood her until we talked about her and worked through what kind of character I wanted her to be!

**Mackenzie of Nice Girl, Naughty Edits:** One day I will master commas. Maybe. But probably not.

**Charli of Charli's Book Box:** Thank you for your continued help with my web page and your awesome support for my books and my Rebel boys!

**Pat Vassar:** After these books, my next book cover will have flowers on it. You're welcome.

**My parents:** Are you ready for round three?

# Finding Harmony

By now you think you know Killian Donogue, the quieter, darker of the Donogue twins and bass player for the Blind Rebels.

In Finding Harmony, you'll learn you don't know as much about Killian as you think you do. And so will the rest of the Rebel family.

**Viola**

I should have seen it. I should have realized what my despicable ex was doing. But I was so busy trying to be a mother, father, and provider to my little sister that I missed all the signs.

She's grown into a beautiful, loving woman I couldn't be prouder of. Yet now I realize I've put *my* entire life on hold out of guilt over my former husband's monstrous ways. Can I find a way to let go of the past or will I continue to deny myself any sort of future?

343

## Killian

I guess I fit the stereotypical brooding rocker role. But all I've endured since the launch of the Blind Rebels has molded me into the person I am. Love. Loss. Success. Soul-crushing truths. It's all led me to indulging in an endless stream of one-night stands to avoid ever developing feelings for a woman again.

Then Viola walked into my life, just as tragic revelations threatened to destroy me. For her, I suddenly need to right my wrongs and repair the relationships I left in ruins. Can the two of us forgive ourselves enough to have a loving future together?

# About the Author

Amy Kaybach has been writing since she learned to hold a pencil at three. When she's not daydreaming about sexy rock stars and how to put them into print, she's working in IT or planning her next great adventure with her best friend since junior high. She lives on the central coast of California with her two obnoxious, but well-loved beagles.

As a motorsports fan she loves her cars loud and fast and as a music fan she loves her music hard and loud.

She loves to connect with her readers: